MAIN LIBRARY

REA BRARY

AC S0-BKZ-831

DISCARDED

B D27
EDMOND, MARY.
RARE SIR WILLIAM DAVENANT

7141909

B D27E
EDMOND, MARY.
RARE SIR WILLIAM DAVENANT

7141909

ALLEN COUNTY PUBLIC LIBRARY

FORT WAYNE, INDIANA 46802

You may return this book to any agency, branch,
or bookmobile of the Allen County Public Library.

The Revels Plays
COMPANION LIBRARY
E. A. J. HONIGMANN, J. R. MULRYNE
and R. L. SMALLWOOD
general editors

For almost thirty years *The Revels Plays* have offered the most authoritative editions of Elizabethan and Jacobean plays by authors other than Shakespeare.

The Revels Plays Companion Library

provides a fuller background to the main series by publishing worthwhile dramatic and non-dramatic material that will be essential for the serious student of the period.

The books in the series fall into main groups:

(1) Editions of plays not included in the main series and less exhaustively annotated. Usually several plays to a volume either by the same author or on a similar theme.

(2) Editions of significant non-dramatic works: masques, pageants, and the like.

(3) Theatre documents and similar source material.

(4) Criticism: collections of essays or monographs.

(5) Stage histories and eye-witness accounts.

Documents of the Rose Playhouse ed. RUTTER

The court masque ed. LINDLEY

Shakespeare and his contemporaries ed. HONIGMANN

Three Jacobean witchcraft plays ed. CORBIN, SEDGE

John Weever HONIGMANN*

Rare Sir William Davenant EDMOND*

Further titles in active preparation

including THOMAS HEYWOOD *Three marriage plays* ed. MERCHANT

*these titles published in the USA by St. Martin's Press

Rare Sir William Davenant

Sir William Davenant crowned with the bays as poet laureate: engraving by William
Faithorne, from a lost portrait by John Greenhill. From the frontispiece of the 1673 folio edition
of the *Works*, reproduced by permission of the Bodleian Library, Oxford, A.2.18.Art.

THE REVELS PLAYS COMPANION LIBRARY

Rare
Sir William
Davenant

POET LAUREATE · PLAYWRIGHT
· CIVIL WAR GENERAL ·
RESTORATION THEATRE MANAGER

MARY EDMOND

'A man of quick and piercing imagination'
JOHN DRYDEN

St. Martin's Press, New York

COPYRIGHT © MARY EDMOND 1987

All rights reserved. For information, write:
Scholarly & Reference Division,
St. Martin's Press, Inc., 175 Fifth Avenue, New York, NY 10010

First published in the United States of America in 1987

Printed in Great Britain

ISBN 0–312–00919–4

© MANCHESTER UNIVERSITY PRESS 1987

All rights reserved. For information, write:
St. Martin's Press, Inc., 175 Fifth Avenue, New York, NY 10010

First published in the United States of America in 1987

Printed in Great Britain

ISBN 0–312–00783–3

LIBRARY OF CONGRESS CATALOGING IN PUBLICATION DATA
Edmond, Mary
Rare Sir William Davenant (The Revels plays companion library)
Bibliography: p. 251.
Includes index.
1. Davenant, William, Sir, 1606–1668 – Biography.
2. Authors, English – Early modern, 1500–1700 – Biography.
3. Theatrical managers – Great Britain – Biography.
4. Generals – Great Britain – Biography. 5. Great Britain – History –
Civil War, 1642–1649. 6. Theater – England – History – 17th century.
I. Title. II. Series.
PR2476.E35   1987   821'.4 (B)   86–33913
ISBN 0–312–00783–3

Allen County Public Library
Ft. Wayne, Indiana

CONTENTS

LIST OF ILLUSTRATIONS

GENERAL EDITORS' PREFACE

Since the late 1950s the series known as the Revels Plays has provided for students of the English Renaissance drama carefully edited texts of the major Elizabethan and Jacobean plays. The series now includes some of the best known drama of the period and has continued to expand, both within its original field and, to a lesser extent, beyond it, to include some important plays from the earlier Tudor and from the Restoration periods. The Revels Plays Companion Library is intended to further this expansion and to allow for new developments.

The aim of the Companion Library is to provide students of the Elizabethan and Jacobean drama with a fuller sense of its background and context. The series includes volumes of a variety of kinds. Small collections of plays, by a single author or concerned with a single theme and edited in accordance with the principles of textual modernisation of the Revels Plays, offer a wider range of drama than the main series can include. Together with editions of masques, pageants, and the non-dramatic work of Elizabethan and Jacobean playwrights, these volumes make it possible, within the overall Revels enterprise, to examine the achievement of the major dramatists from a broader perspective. Other volumes provide a fuller context for the plays of the period by offering new collections of documentary evidence on Elizabethan theatrical conditions and on the performance of plays during that period and later. A third aim of the series is to offer modern critical interpretation, in the form of collections of essays or of monographs, of the dramatic achievement of the English Renaissance.

So wide a range of material necessarily precludes the standard format and uniform general editorial control which is possible in the original series of Revels Plays. To a considerable extent, therefore, treatment and approach is determined by the needs and intentions of individual volume editors. Within this rather ampler area, however, we hope that the Companion Library maintains the standards of scholarship which have for so long characterised the Revels Plays, and that it offers a useful enlargement of the work of the series in preserving, illuminating, and celebrating the drama of Elizabethan and Jacobean England.

E. A. J. HONIGMANN
J. R. MULRYNE
R. L. SMALLWOOD

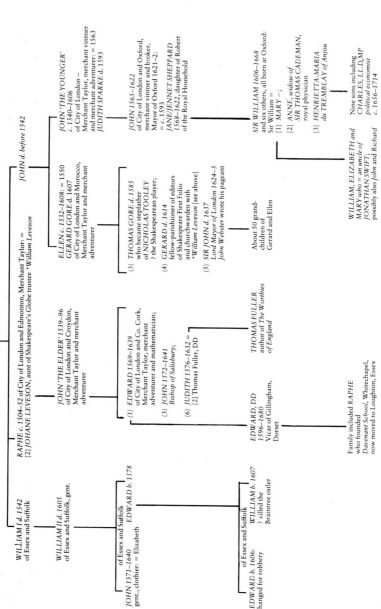

The Davenant pedigree

CHAPTER ONE

Origins

◦⟨⟩◦⟨⟩◦

In the village of Sible Hedingham in north Essex, close to the Suffolk border, stands a large old house, much restored, called 'Davenants'. This was long the home of the Davenants of 'Davenants Lands', described in an eighteenth-century manuscript by William Holman, now in the Essex Record Office,[1] as one of 'three families of great Antiquity' in the parish. These were the forebears of Sir William. Another long pedigree, set down in 1725 by Richard Mawson, Portcullis Pursuivant, and still at the College of Arms,[2] roundly asserts, in a sonorous Latin preamble, that this 'most ancient and illustrious family de Avenant . . . came into England with William the Conqueror', and starts off with a Sir John said to have lived in the reigns of Henry III and Edward I. The late date of the manuscript, and demonstrable inaccuracies in it, mean that it must be taken with pinches of salt, but by the beginning of the sixteenth century there is further documentary evidence. A manor court roll[3] shows that Sir William's great-great-grandfather, Edward of Sible Hedingham, died in 1507, and mentions his property called 'Russells' at Halstead which can be traced in subsequent Davenant wills through five more generations. Edward's heir, William, gentleman of Sible Hedingham and Halstead (died 1542)[4] became head of the family in his turn, and his son William II (died 1605) rebuilt 'Davenants' in 1571, secured a coat of arms in 1588, and presumably compiled the earlier part of the pedigree at the College of Arms. The Essex branch of the family will be shown to have some bearing on the life of Sir William Davenant.

William I left three young children at his death in 1542. He had also had to care for two brothers, Raphe and John; when Raphe, who was born in about 1504,[5] was old enough, he sent him to London to be apprenticed, thus initiating the Davenant family's long and important connexion with the Merchant Taylors', one of the Great Twelve livery companies. Raphe established his home and business in a house just south of Cheapside which was to remain a Davenant stronghold for many years; it stood behind the church of St Mary-le-Bow and close to St Paul's, having 'egresse and Regresse . . . by the wayes leadinge from Bowe Lane, as also from Wattlinge street'. Part of it is described in his son and heir's will of 1596:[6]

> the Kitchin, and the Larder, the Chamber over the same wherein I vsually doe lye, with the privy to itt, the Chamber and a Privye over the same, a roome leadinge to my great garrett, and the great garrett, my best Chamber called the Great Chamber with y[e] Comptinge howse and the Pryvie to the same now vsed, my greate parlor with a Little Buttorie nere to ye, my great Celler vnder my great parlor . . .

Obviously a handsome house, and surprisingly well supplied with privies.

Raphe Davenant was a parishioner of Allhallows Bread Street (the next little street west from Bow Lane out of Cheapside). His numerous children – of whom not many survived – were baptised there,[7] and in addition he assumed responsibility for the young children of his brother John, who had presumably died. The eldest, Ellen, lived with him – he calls her 'my dawghter' in his will[8] – until on a spring day two years before his death she was married at Allhallows to one of his close friends and colleagues, another very wealthy and distinguished freeman of the Merchant Taylors' and merchant adventurer called Gerard Gore. There will be more to be said later about the Gore family.

Ellen had two brothers, James and John, and John – Sir William's grandfather – continued to live with his uncle until Raphe's death in 1552. Thereafter he and James were apprenticed to their sister's husband Gerard Gore, and in the customary manner they would have lived with him. He presented James for freedom of the Company on 20 October 1559 and John on 5 October 1562.[9]

Raphe Davenant's funeral on 18 December 1552, which the two boys no doubt attended, was an impressive occasion. Henry Machyn, the contemporary diarist and fellow-freeman of the Merchant Taylors', was in business as a furnisher of funeral trappings, and probably made the arrangements, for he writes at some length of the funeral of 'good master Deyffenett'.[10] The dead man left tenements, gardens and tentergrounds – where cloth was stretched on frames after passing through the fulling-mill – in the City parishes of St Giles Cripplegate and St Michael Paternoster Royal, as well as the big house off Cheapside; there was also a country place at Edmonton, with gardens, orchards, a dovehouse and 'two great closes of Lande'.

At the time of Raphe's death his heir John was thirteen years old, and his nephew John about a year younger. Both Johns became freemen of the Merchant Taylors'; both pursued notable careers in the City; and each was bequeathed the freedom of one of the new overseas trading organisations, the Muscovy Company. In many contemporary manuscripts they are referred to as 'the Elder' and 'the Younger' John Davenant – which has never prevented complete confusion between the cousins. John 'the Elder' (1539–96) was to have a large and distinguished family which included Edward (1569–1639), Merchant Talyor, merchant adventurer, Greek and Latin scholar and mathematician, described by John Aubrey as 'an incomparable man in his time';[11] John (1572–1641), President of Queens' College, Cambridge, and Bishop of Salisbury from 1621 until his death; Judith (born 1576), mother by her second husband of Dr Thomas Fuller, author of *The Worthies of England*; and Margaret (born 1585) whose second husband, Dr Robert Tounson, as Dean of Westminster attended Ralegh at his execution, and who preceded Dr Davenant as Bishop of Salisbury.

John Davenant 'the Elder' did not marry until 1567, but his cousin John 'the Younger' (*c*. 1540–1606) married at Allhallows Bread Street on 15 February 1562/3, four months after becoming a freeman of the Merchant Taylors'. Machyn the diarist evidently regarded this as one of the principal pre-Lent social engagements in the City that year. After the marriage, he wrote, there was a 'a grett dener, and at nyghte a maske'.[12] It is very fitting that the grandparents of Sir William Davenant, the future writer of Court masques, should themselves have had a masque on their wedding night.

The bride was Judith Sparke, daughter of yet another distinguished Merchant Taylor and merchant adventurer. Many brethren of the Company were engaged in promoting the export of good English cloth, and it was that, no doubt, that had prompted John Sparke to become a founder-member of the Muscovy Company in 1555. He bequeathed his freedom of the Company to his son-in-law Davenant at his death in 1581. Davenant had provided a home for him towards the end of his life; and not only for him, but also for a younger man of the same name (the relationship between the two Sparkes is not clear), again a freeman of the Merchant Taylors', who was a paid (or, more often than not, unpaid) employee of the Muscovy Company. It was probably the younger man who took part in the journeys to Russia and Persia on the Company's behalf in 1566, 1568 and 1571 – journeys so celebrated that they are described at length in Hakluyt's *Voyages*. One or other Sparke also travelled extensively in Spain: in 1565 he was exporting cloth there, and twelve years later he was a member of the Spanish Company, and was said to 'have the Spanish tounge'.[13]

On the journey of 1566, a 'way by water' was discovered from Kholmogory in northern Russia to the city of Novgorod by two of the Company's employees, Thomas Southam and Sparke.[14] The 'fourth voyage into Persia' in 1568 resulted from the Tsar's grant to Queen Elizabeth of new privileges for the English merchants to trade with Russia, and through Russia with Persia; this journey was undertaken by a small group of Company servants headed by Arthur Edwardes as agent. (It was Edwardes – who died in Astrakhan while promoting trade with Persia – who bequeathed his freedom of the Muscovy Company to John Davenant 'the Elder'.)[15] The objective of the journey of 1571 was Moscow: while the Englishmen were there, Tartars set fire to the city, and some twenty-five to thirty men who had taken refuge in one of the cellars of the Muscovy Company's headquarters, Thomas Southam among them, were burnt to death; three others, including Sparke, survived.[16]

No children were born to John and Judith Davenant between their first, John – Sir William's father – in 1565 and Katherine in 1574: I think it very probable that John senior was abroad in the interim, taking part in the great journeys to Russia and Persia of 1566, 1568 and 1571. The wills of John Sparke the elder, his father-in-law, and John Sparke the younger (1581 and 1596) survive, and each is beautifully written in the testator's hand.[17] The will of the younger man is of quite unusual warmth, charm and informality. One intriguing bequest to Davenant ('your good self') hints at possible shared travels by the two men even more extensive than those that can now be traced (I modernise his exotic spelling):

> a ring of gold you made for me and to be refreshed, and your own mark to be put thereinto, with the same date it beareth, as 'Africa' and 'America' also refreshed, as more plainly to know from whence the same metal came that may be counted very rare for so long time past . . .

The younger children (Sir William Davenant's aunts and uncle) were then aged between twenty-one and twelve: bequests for Katherine include ' a Persia golden girdle', for Judith a silk Persia girdle and 'a shirt of Muskovia for the strangeness of the fashion', for Mary 'a Muskovia candlestick to light her to work', and for twelve-year-old Edward, 'a ship chest in the warehouse' containing two books bound up together (Elyot's *Boke named the Governour* and Erasmus), and 'certain Spanish books to sell'.

The eldest of the family, John – Sir William Davenant's father – was now nearly thirty-one, married and living in his own separate household: he is referred to indirectly, his apprentices Thomas Smithe and

Robert Land being bequeathed two French books.

This will provides information about the extensive household of Sir William's grandfather. In addition to the three daughters and younger son, bequests are made to his apprentice William Rix; Joan and Blanche the maids; Goodwife Wood; the cooper's man; Goodman Graye the waterbearer; and Davenant's sister Mary Keeling, who had been keeping house for him since her husband's death (Davenant's wife Judith had died in 1593), and her daughter.

The only tenuous clue to the identity of Sir William Davenant's mother was in the unreliable Davenant pedigree at the College of Arms: it describes her simply as 'Jana filia. . . . Shepherd de Durham'. Intensive research now establishes that her surname was indeed Sheppard; that her family did indeed come from the north of England, and almost certainly from County Durham; and that they had a tradition of service in the Royal Household, although they could not be said to equal the Davenants in social standing – which probably explains why Henry Molins Davenant Esquire, 'late his Majesty's Envoy Extraordinary to the Italian Princes', and the poet laureate's grandson, was not able (or anxious) to supply full details about his great-grandmother to the College of Arms for Mawson's eighteenth-century pedigree.

In fact, Jane was baptised at St Margaret's Westminster – appropriately for the child of a family employed at Court – on 1 November 1568;[18] her parents' names were Robert and Elizabeth, names which she and her husband John Davenant would give to their first surviving son and daughter. Jane's father died intestate when she was not quite six years old, and was buried at St Margaret's on 19 August 1574.

Jane's uncle William Sheppard, who died five years later, was also 'of Westminster', and so also probably employed at Court: but he actually died at Fulford outside York,[19] and had married a Newark of Acomb nearby. One of his in-laws, to whom he made a bequest, had also served a Tudor sovereign – *olim armiger pro corpore Reginae Mariae*.[20] It emerges from his will that his niece Jane was known in the family by the charming diminutive 'Jennet': no doubt her future husband John Davenant addressed her in the same way.

She also had a great-uncle called John Binks, who was one of the Queen's Messengers in the Court of Receipts (part of the Exchequer Court at Westminster), and a fellow-parishioner of St Margaret's – he died in 1583.[21]

It seems that the Sheppards, like so many English families in Tudor days, had begun their social ascent at the time of the dissolution of the monasteries. A Robert and William then acquired tithes and lands in the village of Startforth in County Durham, formerly the property of Eggleston Abbey nearby; and Jane's uncle William speaks of his lease of the tithe of Forcett. Startforth is on the Tees, and opposite Barnard Castle, Forcett in the green rolling country a few miles away,[22] and north of the historic town of Richmond. The little church of Forcett is dedicated to St Cuthbert (after whom one of Jane Sheppard's uncles was named), and was one of the chapels raised to commemorate the resting-places of the bones of the saint in his wanderings. It has been remarked that Jane had a great-uncle Binks, who died some four hundred years ago: on the twentieth-century lychgate leading to the churchyard are inscribed the names of the nine men of Forcett who were killed in the First World War – and the second name is that of Private *William Binks*.

Jane Sheppard had three brothers, Thomas, Richard and William, and one sister, Phyllis – Sir William Davenant's uncles and aunt. Thomas and Richard were Court embroiderers, glovers and perfumers, while William worked in the Catery, the office which procured provisions in bulk for the Royal Household.[23]

The quack doctor and astrologer, Simon Forman, now enters the story. By the 1590s Forman, a self-taught man from Wiltshire, had built up a thriving, although officially unauthorised, practice in the City near Billingsgate. Six of his casebooks, leather-bound volumes covering the period from March 1596 to November 1601, survive, and are now in the Bodleian Library at Oxford. A methodical man, Forman divided each page into two columns, and made entries about the hundreds of patients and clients of all classes who sought his help and advice on their health, finances and prospects of advancement, their travels, lost or stolen property, their love affairs and marriage prospects.

In 1582 Thomas Sheppard, who was a parishioner of St Bride Fleet Street, had married a girl called Ursula Mallorye.[24] In July and September 1597 she called on Forman to consult him about her husband's health, and on the second occasion he helpfully noted that the couple lived 'at the sign of the Pomegranate'. The Sheppards had no children, and when Ursula returned to the consulting-room in October on her own account, being then thirty-five years old, Forman considered that if she were with child, it would 'hardly prosper'; and in the following February, he noted: 'She hath not bin well A good whill . . . She supposeth her self wth child & is very big but I think yt is a false conception.' He was right: and she was buried at St Bride's in November 1601.[25]

A letter at Penshurst provides evidence that her husband had been employed in Court circles at least as early as 1595, when Sir Robert Sidney's agent wrote to his master reporting the dispatch of fourteen pairs of gloves (two trimmed with gold and silver lace and two lined throughout with velvet). 'The prices I hope are reasonable', he added. 'Shepheard did them.'[26] Thomas's younger brother Richard doubtless worked with him.

Thomas's house at the sign of the Pomegranate was at Fleet Bridge – the Fleet now runs underground, and the bridge has given way to Ludgate Circus. By the last years of the century Thomas was a Groom of Her Majesty's Chamber ('groom' in the special usage denoting an officer of the English Royal Household), and as such he had a proper sense of his own importance, well exemplified in a petition addressed by him to Robert Cecil. He had stepped along to the Strand to call on the great man on a Sunday night 'wth a Iewell and a Ringe', and on his way back had been arrested, by an officious potter acting as provost-marshal, for being out and about overlate. In spite of his indignant protestations that he had been with Cecil 'about speciall affayres' and that he was 'the Queenes man', he had been taken to one of the City prisons (the Counter in Wood Street), and forced to spend the rest of the night 'amongst a sorte of lothsome persons . . . to his great discreditte'.

The unsigned petition, still at Hatfield, is endorsed with a note that the matter had been taken up with the Lord Mayor.[27] No doubt the ruffled Queen's man was speedily released.

Sheppard duly appears in the Lord Chamberlain's accounts for the Queen's funeral in April 1603, among the 'Groomes extraordinary but dailie Attendaunts' allotted lengths of black cloth for mourning livery.[28] And in the first warrants of the new reign, 'Thomas Sheppard o^r perfumer' is provided with the customary red livery trimmed with black velvet; he is in a list of twenty-two 'Artificers', specialists serving their sovereign by appointment, having reached the top of their respective callings.[29]

On 15 March 1604 King James, with Queen Anne and Prince Henry, made his progress through the City – postponed because of the serious outbreak of plague in the year of his accession. In the Lord Chamberlain's Book detailing expenses incurred,[30] Sheppard is again among 'The Artificers', forty-five of them this time. Perhaps for the same occasion, the Royal Wardrobe accounts for the year show that he perfumed robes of crimson velvet, trimmed with ermine and other furs, for the King and the nine-year-old heir to the throne.[31]

In addition to being officially designated perfumer to the King, Thomas Sheppard was separately commissioned by Queen Anne to make her gloves. On 12 September of that year, 1604, Robert Sidney wrote to his wife:

Sweetheart, I came to Windsor with the Qu on Saturday . . . I feare it will be Monday at the soonest before I come to Penshurst. . . . I am wel I thank God and long to see you. I know not what order you have taken for the Queens gloves. Shepharde is the man that makes them for her . . .[32]

Although Simon Forman had predicted in July 1597 that Sheppard would die within three months, he survived for nearly ten more years: Thomas Sheppard 'perfumer of gloves' was buried at St Bride's on 27 February 1606/7[33] (a year to the month, if not the day, after the birth at Oxford of his nephew William Davenant, the future poet and playwright).

His brother then assumed the formal title *Suffitor Domini Regis*, The King's Perfumer: and by warrant dated Westminster 20 January 1607/8,[34] 'o^r wellbeloved servaunt Richard Sheppard o^r perfumer' was to receive his red-and-black royal livery yearly, for life, at the Feast of All Saints:

3 yards of red cloth for a coat..12 shillings a yard
2 yards of black velvet to gard (trim)...............................18 shillings a yard
6 yards of cotton to line ....12 pence a yard
For embroidering (with the royal arms and monogram) .... 4 shillings
For making... 3s. 4d.

The cost of living being what it always is, the charge for the velvet doubled in the next three or four years, the cost of the red cloth trebled, and the cotton went up sixfold.[35] Thereafter Sheppard appears regularly in the Household accounts.

In the autumn of 1612 an elaborate programme of festivities began, to celebrate the marriage – solemnised on St Valentine's Day in the following February – of Princess Elizabeth and Frederick Elector Palatine. And the Wardrobe accounts include an entry authorising payment to Richard Sheppard for 45 pairs of gloves of stag's leather and 63 pairs of long gloves, all perfumed, £105 16s 0d. 1614 was a particularly busy year: entries dated 15 May relate to 48 pairs of gloves of stag's leather faced and fringed with silk and silver, charge £43 4s 0d; four pairs of Spanish and four of kid's leather furred with sables (£24); 78 pairs of long plain gloves perfumed with musk, civet and ambergris (£23 8s 0d); a pair for Sir Thomas Morrison made of stag's leather faced and fringed with silk and gold (25s 0d); and the perfuming of outer garments and a waistcoat for the King (£69). The next warrant, dated 28 September, lists more than two hundred pairs of gloves (£106 10s 0d). And there are three entries about the perfuming of Garter and other robes for the King and thirteen-year-old Prince Charles (now the heir to the throne) for the opening of the short-lived

'Addled' Parliament.[36] Poignant entries indeed, in the light of the later history of Charles and his Parliaments.

Richard Sheppard (like so many other members of the Household) in fact received very little payment for these and other lavish commissions: for he declared in his will[37] that there was owing to him, 'out of the office of the Roabes and greate warderobe', the enormous sum of £600 'and upwards', plus £125 or thereabouts from the Master of the Wardrobes, Lord Hay. And when his son Robert, who was also employed (and resident) at Court – as a King's Messenger – died in 1626, the royal debts to his father were still unpaid.[38] (Young William Davenant had arrived in London from Oxford in 1622, and probably called upon his cousin Robert at Court.)

Richard Sheppard was buried at his parish church of St Martin-in-the-Fields on 6 November 1617, and obviously in appropriate style, since the funeral cost forty-six shillings, making it one of the most expensive in that large and important parish for the whole year.[39] He had been in no position to make many bequests, but he left a piece of gold worth twenty-two shillings (a 'Jacobus') to each of the seven children of his sister Davenant, and made his brother-in-law – Sir William's father – one of the three overseers of the will.

CHAPTER TWO

The parents;
London and Oxford

John and Judith Davenant made their first home in the little City parish of St Thomas the Apostle, in the Ward of Vintry; and there their first child, John, was baptised on 6 August 1565. He was to become the father of Sir William.

I have suggested that John senior was travelling in Russia and Persia in 1566, 1568 and 1571; by the time the second child, Katherine, was born in 1574, the family had moved down the hill to the riverside parish of St James Garlickhithe – and the reason, no doubt, why they have not been traced there hitherto is that the registers of the parish have never been printed.[1] When John was nearly ten years old, his father sent him to the Merchant Taylors' excellent school, then in Suffolk Street a short walk from home; he and eleven other boys entered on 6 March 1574/5.[2] The school had been founded only fourteen years before (with Edmund Spenser among the original pupils), and was still under its first and great headmaster, Richard Mulcaster, who promoted music, drawing and the drama, and had already attracted attention as a constructor of pageants before being appointed by the Company at the age of twenty-nine. In 1573–6 inclusive and 1583, some of his boys – young Davenant probably among them – performed at Court.[3]

John became free of the Merchant Taylors' Company by patrimony – by virtue of his father's freedom – on 22 June 1590, the same day as his first cousin (Sir) John Gore, the future Lord Mayor of London.[4]

The Davenants' parish church stood, and Wren's replacement still stands, on the north side of Upper Thames Street (Thames Street in their day), almost opposite Vintners' Hall. This part of the City had by the late sixteenth century been connected with the wine trade for a very long time indeed, and there were 'many faire and large houses with vaults and cellers for stowage of wines and lodging of the Burdeaux merchants'. Next to a large building called The Vintry was Three Cranes Lane, 'so called not onely of a signe of three Cranes at a Tauerne door, but rather of three strong Cranes of Timber placed on the Vintrie wharfe by the Thames side, to crane vp wines there'.[5]

Since the John Davenants lived in this part of the City, it was no surprise to find that both were active in the wine trade. John junior – Sir William's father – is specifically described as 'Marchant Vintner' in the parish register, and the Vintners' account books show that his father rented a house from them. To begin with, he was paying £14 13s 4d every two years; from 1591–2 he paid eight pounds a year; and by 1594–5 he had two houses, at the very substantial sum of twelve pounds – the second no doubt being for his son who was now married. From the order of the entries, it can be deduced that the home of Davenant senior was on the south or river side of Thames Street, and exactly opposite the church. The churchwardens' accounts[6] show that both father and son were generous parishioners; and in 1579–81 Davenant senior was himself a churchwarden. At the end of most years from 1584 to 1597 he signed – in an elegant hand – as one of the 'Maisters of the parishe beinge Auditors'. (Another was the founder of Aldenham School, Richard Platt.)

In value, wine was probably the most important commodity imported into Elizabethan England.[7] Every Londoner was accustomed to the sight of ships berthing with wines – as Doll Tearsheet says of Falstaff, 'there's a whole merchant's venture of Bordeaux stuff in him, you have not seen a hulk better stuffed in the hold'. Among those merchant venturers were the John Davenants. From Easter 1565, customs officers had been required to enter their transactions in special parchment books, and entries for the port of London in the 1590s include several about 'John Davenant', senior or junior.[8] Under 28 November 1594 he is entered as paying duty on 15 tuns of Gascon wine from 'le Barke *Rowe* de newcastell', and on 25 November 1596, on 30 tuns from the *Leopard,* inward bound from Bordeaux; during the first three months of 1597 he bought 153 tuns and one hogshead from the *Swan,* the *Barnard and Michaell* and the *Peter* of London, and from the *Elizabeth Constant,* the *Primrose* of Sandwich, the *James*, the *Tryall* and the *Gift of God.* The casks would have been ferried upstream by lighter and landed at Three Cranes Wharf.

The John Davenants were more than wine merchants, they were also brokers – general agents or middlemen operating between merchants of all kinds; Davenant senior had been licensed by the City authorities to practise as such in 1579.[9] And they could probably manage some French when the boats came in from Bordeaux – they may even have gone over to France themselves, as it seems that Englishmen sometimes went to Bordeaux to select wines for the Royal cellars.[10] It will be remembered that the younger John Sparke bequeathed two French books to the apprentices of Davenant junior.

Documents surviving from three lawsuits provide some specific evidence about the scale of the Davenants' business dealings. In a complaint to the Court of Requests, Davenant senior is described as a 'Marchant Venturer' who in March 1589 had sold to a certain vintner wines valued at the very large sum of £550, and a Chancery deposition by him in the same year relates to three sums of £100 each which he had borrowed on behalf of Lord Windsor. The evidence that Davenant junior, Sir William's father, also became a broker is in a Chancery document of 1615 which states that about sixteen years before – that is, at the time when he left London for Oxford – he had been 'in great tradinge of Brokage for divers marchants w^{th}in the Citie of London'.[11]

The place and date of his marriage to Jennet Sheppard have not come to light, but the year was probably 1593. The registers and churchwardens' accounts of St James Garlickhithe tell a melancholy tale of the first years of their married life; the first five children were all buried, stillborn or very young, between Christmas 1593 and Christmas 1597. Due payment is recorded of 3s 4d or 3s 8d 'for the ground and hours knell' for each little body, the entries seeming to echo the sullen tolling of the passing bell. The fifth baby did achieve a name: he was christened John after his father on 24 October 1597, but was buried on 11 December. By then, Jennet was in her thirtieth year, and in the following month she turned in desperation to Simon Forman[12] – as her sister-in-law Ursula Sheppard had done in the previous October and was to do again in February. 'She supposeth herself with child', the doctor wrote in his casebook, 'but yt is not soe.' He added the information that the Davenants were living in Maiden Lane – the one which, as John Stow tells us, had 'diuers faire houses for Marchants', and ran along the north side of the Davenants' parish church of St James Garlickhithe (it is now called Skinners Lane). If John Davenant was keeping a wine-tavern in London, as he was to do at Oxford, it would have been the one on the corner which had been owned by a member of the Chaucer family in the fourteenth century.[13]

A sixth child was born to the Davenants at the beginning of 1599, and christened John on 14 January; he too must have died young, for a third John was born at Oxford in 1607, entered Merchant Taylors' School in London in 1619, and figured in his father's will in 1622. He was probably the John Davenant who was buried from the Counter (predominantly a debtors' prison) in Wood Street off Cheapside in 1634.[14]

In the autumn of 1599 Davenant senior, Sir William's grandfather, was busy as one of the two collectors for the Ward of Vintry; and in the resulting subsidy roll dated 1 October, he and his son are entered among only twenty-six parishioners of St James Garlickhithe liable to pay tax.[15] On 19 December there was a family wedding at the church – between Jennet's younger sister Phyllis, who had no doubt been living with the Davenants, and John Doughty. All the Davenants and Sheppards would have assembled at the church – including the bride's brothers from the Royal Household, snatching a little time from the hectic preparations for the Christmas season at Court. This constitutes the last appearance in London of Sir William Davenant's parents.

The evidence now assembled conclusively disposes of the long-standing belief that Sir William Davenant's father John 'disappeared from London' after becoming a freeman of the Merchant Taylors' in 1590.[16] He did not leave the City until 1600 at the earliest: the first Oxford reference so far discovered is of the baptism of his second daughter, Jane, at St Martin Carfax on 11 February 1601/2.[17]

John Aubrey (1626–97) was acquainted with a number of London and Oxford Davenants, including Sir William and his elder brother Parson Robert (who once told him that Shakespeare had 'given him a hundred kisses' when he was a young child);[18] Aubrey was often at Oxford, as an undergraduate and later, and lies buried there. His *Brief Life* of Sir William which he prepared for Anthony Wood[19] is unusually long and (for him) notably neat, and it is here that he writes the crucial passage about Sir William's parents:

> His father John Devenant was a Vintner there [at the celebrated wine-tavern in Cornmarket subsequently called the Crown], a very grave and discreet Citizen: his mother was a very beautifull woman, & of a very good witt [intelligence] and of conversation extremely agreable. ... Mr William Shakespeare was wont to goe into Warwickshire once a yeare, & did comõnly in his journey lye at this house in Oxõn: where he was exceedingly respected. . . . . Now S^r W^m would sometimes when he was pleasant over a glasse of wine with his most intimate friends . . . say that it seemed to him that he writt with the very spirit that [did] Shakespeare, and was ['seemd' above] contendended [*sic*] enough to be thought his Son . . .

(Not surprisingly, stories circulated later in the century about young William running to see his godfather whenever he came to Oxford, and being told 'not to take the name of *God* in vain'.)[20]

The splenetic and melancholy Anthony Wood (1632–95) lived in Oxford all his life, and although he once irritably dismissed Aubrey as 'magotie-headed', he used his friend's testimony about the Davenants almost word-for-word,[21] endorsing the description of Jennet as 'very beautifull', and hardly altering Aubrey's 'of a very good witt and of conversation extremely agreable'. This from Wood is praise indeed, since he was ever more inclined to criticise than to commend. The tribute carries the greater weight because he had every opportunity to consult Mrs Davenant's family. The wine-tavern in Cornmarket, which was one of his favourite drinking-places, was run by Sir William's sister Jane (1602–67) until Restoration days, first with her husband Thomas Hallam (her father's former apprentice) and then, after his death in 1636, on her own. Her elder sister Elizabeth (?1601–72) returned to Oxford after the death of her second husband who had been rector of Didcot in Berkshire, so that Wood must have known her too. Jane made a home for Sir William's first two children, William and Mary, for a time, and his son Charles was at Balliol in Wood's lifetime.[22] There was also a professional connexion between the Wood and Davenant families, since in 1616 Wood's father had acquired from Merton College the lease of the Flower-de-Luce at Carfax, a few steps from the Davenant tavern. We can accept that the beauty and intelligence of the poet laureate's mother were exceptional.

As for his father: Wood makes the all-important addition to Aubrey's notes – his *only* factual one, apart from adding the word 'sufficient' (able) to Aubrey's description of him as a vintner. He says that although Davenant was, in Aubrey's words, 'a very grave and discreet Citizen', he was '*yet an admirer and lover of plays and play-makers, especially Shakespeare* [my italics]'.

There is no reason to dismiss the long-standing Oxford tradition that Sir William Davenant was Shakespeare's godson: if the playwright was staying at the wine-tavern early in 1606, he went across to the parish church of St Martin Carfax with the Davenants on 3 March, and held the new baby in his arms at the font. (William, says Aubrey, was born 'about the end of February'; his grandfather Davenant was buried at St James Garlickhithe in London on the 21st.) St Martin Carfax was pulled down at the end of the nineteenth century – all but the familiar clock-tower; the font is now in the church of St Michael-at-the-North-Gate, with its great Saxon tower which, in the days of Shakespeare and the Davenants, guarded the entry to the walled city from the north. St Michael's is on the east side of Cornmarket, as was the Davenants' wine-tavern.

Although in later life Sir William would not be averse to giving his intimate friends the impression that he was Shakespeare's son, it could mean no more than that he liked to regard himself as Shakespeare's literary heir (what poet and playwright would not). Whatever it means, it has inevitably stimulated the keenest interest in and speculation about his clever and beautiful mother (the more so because he was the only poet and playwright among her seven children); and many people have felt an urgent desire to cast her as the Dark Lady of the Sonnets. George Vertue, writing only about a hundred years after her death, made the extraordinary statement that she was a daughter of John Florio – writer, translator and Italian tutor of Shakespeare's patron the Earl of Southampton. Sir Walter Scott, in *Woodstock,* chose to present her not as the hostess of an Oxford wine-tavern, but as the 'good-looking, laughing, buxom hostess of an inn between Stratford and London'; while in the early years of our own century, an American, Arthur Acheson, in his *Mistress Davenant* – which purported to be a work not of fiction but of fact – described her as the 'fascinating, black-eyed hostess' of an inn (not tavern) in Cornmarket whom Shakespeare introduced to the Earl of Southampton at the time of the Queen's visit to Oxford in 1592, thus supposedly precipitating the relationship between his two loves of 'comfort and despair'. The Acheson theory had a good run. Bernard Shaw, in the *Preface* to his own *Dark Lady of the Sonnets,* observed that she might have been Maria Tomkins for all he cared: but at the time of writing he felt that, had he wished to be up-to-date, he should have backed the Acheson runner, Jane Davenant, rather than another strongly fancied candidate, Mary Fitton.[23]

So long as it was believed that Sir William's parents were already at Oxford in the 1590s, no one could adequately explain – and no one seriously attempted to do so – how his father actually became a 'lover of plays and play-makers, especially Shakespeare'. Now, at last, we know that he was then living in London, the headquarters of the Elizabethan stage – and not only that, but in a parish which lay exactly opposite the Bankside theatres. He could look across the water to see the flags fluttering to announce performances, and could hear the brassy summons of the trumpets. The great Globe joined the Rose and the Swan in 1599, shortly before he left London, so that he probably attended early productions there – including, perhaps, the one of *Julius Caesar* on 21 September described by a Swiss visitor to London. For professional theatre people and playgoers coming down to the north bank to take boat across for rehearsals and performances, Three Cranes Wharf and Queenhithe – where a little inlet still recalls the ancient dock – were the landing-stages from which to make the shortest crossing. Three Cranes Tavern was one of the most popular theatre pubs, roaring with talk, song and laughter before and after the show: we have Ben Jonson's word for it, for in *Bartholomew Fair* (I.i.32–4) Littlewit couples the name with those of two other famous houses: 'A pox o' these pretenders to wit, your Three Cranes, Mitre and Mermaid men!'

A number of plausible suggestions can now be made on how Sir

William Davenant's parents actually made the acquaintance of Shakespeare. The actor and playwright, and Mrs Davenant's brothers Thomas and Richard the glovers and perfumers, were all employed at Court from the mid-nineties. Shakespeare the glover's son had an easy familiarity with the Sheppards' craft, and could take an informed interest in their work. Mistress Quickly finds it natural to ask Slender's servant: 'Does he not wear a great round beard, like a glover's paring-knife?'; and both Feste and Mercutio speak knowledgeably of cheveril, the soft leather used for fine glove-making: 'A sentence is but a cheveril glove to a good wit – how quickly the wrong side may be turned outward', says Feste to Viola, and Mercutio, at a sally from Romeo, exclaims: 'O, here's a wit of cheveril, that stretches from an inch narrow to an ell broad!'

Shakespeare and Thomas Sheppard both appear in the Lord Chamberlain's Book about the royal progress through the City in 1604, the one heading the list of 'The Players' and the other among 'The Artificers'. And the accounts of Queen Anne's Household for the following year record – in successive folios – payments to Sheppard her glover and Marie Mountjoy her tirewoman or maker of headdresses;[24] so Jennet Davenant's brothers were close professional colleagues of the Huguenot couple who provided Shakespeare with lodgings in Cripplegate at this period. Marie Mountjoy had something else in common with Thomas Sheppard and his wife, and with Thomas's sister Davenant: they were all seeking the help of Simon Forman in 1597–8 (Mrs Mountjoy's trouble was a lost purse). And although the Mountjoys' famous lodger does not appear in the Forman casebooks, several other theatre people do – among them Winifred, the wife of his leading actor Richard Burbage, and the rival theatre manager Mr Philip Henslowe, who was afflicted with 'tincling & ytching in his hed' and 'moch melancholy' in February 1597.[25]

Of particular interest is the seventeen-year-old 'Nicolas Tooly' who sought Forman's help in July 1599,[26] complaining of 'moch gnawing in his stomak & stuffing in his Lungs'. I think it very probable that this was the Nicholas Tooley who was apprenticed to Burbage and became one of the twenty-six 'Principall Actors' named in the First Folio. This brings us back to the Gore family. It will be remembered that Sir William Davenant's grandfather was apprenticed to his uncle Gerard Gore, and presumably lived in his household. Gore helped to found Merchant Taylors' School in 1561, and was Master of the Company in 1567–8; he traded extensively with Spain, Portugal and Morocco; he was a founder-member of the Barbary Company, and in the 1590s at least four of his eight sons – first cousins of Sir William's father – were also trading with Morocco, and the family owned houses in Marrakesh and Agadir.[27] Two of the younger sons, Robert and Raphe, who became founder-members of the East India Company, were at school with their cousin Davenant. In 1584, at the church of St Stephen Walbrook, another brother, Thomas, married a widow called Susan Tooley, and thereby acquired a young stepson, *Nicholas Tooley*. Thomas Gore died a year after his marriage, having bequeathed[28] gold memorial rings to his uncle and aunt Davenant, Sir William's grandparents – evidence that they were on affectionate terms. The name of his stepson is entered several times in City records: for, as usual in the case of an orphan of a citizen of London, four sureties – in young Tooley's case, it was usually four of the Gore brothers – appeared from time to time before the Lord Mayor and Aldermen sitting as a Court of Orphans, to give assurances about their charge's progress and about the administration of any property. On the attainment of majority, the orphan Tooley was duly brought before the Court in October 1604, to be 'adjudged by inspection' to be 'of full age and above'.[29] Since all the Gores were freemen of the Merchant Taylors', one would have expected them to apprentice young Nicholas to a freeman of the Company; but his name is not to be found in their manuscript records. So he could well be the player Tooley. At the time of his death in 1623, this Tooley was lodging in the house in Shoreditch of Burbage's brother Cuthbert (Richard having died in 1619), and in his will[30] he expresses his gratitude to Cuthbert's wife for her 'motherlie care'.

Susan Gore married twice more after Thomas's death, and was probably glad enough that the son of her first marriage should be in somebody else's motherly care; but Nicholas is not mentioned in the wills of any of the Gores who died before him, which suggests that although the family discharged its obligations to him while he was under age, there was otherwise no close bond. This, too, supports the proposition that his adult life was spent not in the world of the merchant adventurers but in the theatre.

I discover that his mother Susan was Flemish – daughter of Hans Lanquart of Antwerp, where Nicholas was born. His father, William Tooley, was a freeman of the Leathersellers' Company and merchant adventurer; he died at Antwerp, in the large house of his father-in-law, in 1583, having expressed a last wish that his wife take their little boy to England to be brought up.[31] William Tooley came from the village of Burmington in Warwickshire, which is but a dozen miles from Stratford on the road to Oxford and London. Shakespeare most probably knew the family before ever he went to London; so if the orphaned Tooley showed talent, what more likely than that the playwright should encourage him to train as an actor under his friend and fellow, Burbage. The dates fit, for Chambers believed that Tooley the player joined the King's Men as an adult actor in 1605,[32] and the Anglo-Flemish Tooley had been adjudged to be of age in the previous autumn. The dates also fit the 'Nicolas Tooly' who sought Simon Forman's help in the summer of 1599; and it is significant that the wife of young Tooley's master Burbage also consulted the doctor. All in all, it seems that the Anglo-Flemish stepson of Thomas Gore, first cousin of Sir William Davenant's father, achieved a measure of immortality by becoming a member of Shakespeare's company, learning his profession from its leading actor and being the first to play some Shakespearean roles.

Yet another Gore brother, Gerard junior, was a fellow-parishioner at St Mary Aldermanbury of Heminges and Condell, the editors of the First Folio; and in 1599 he was churchwarden with William Leveson – who was one of two trustees whom Shakespeare and his fellows had recently called in to help with the business arrangements preceding the building of the Globe on Bankside.[33] This man (1560–1621) was a freeman of the premier livery Company, the Mercers', and a merchant adventurer – like so many of the men in the story of the Davenants. And he was a nephew of Johane Leveson, the second wife of Raphe Davenant (c. 1504–52) and the mother of his children – and the woman who helped to bring up Sir William Davenant's grandfather.

It is clear now that the life of Sir William's father – who would have begun to acquire his love of the drama through the influence of his headmaster at Merchant Taylors' School – touched the world of the Elizabethan theatre at many points.

In 1389, William of Wykeham secured some important tenements on the east side of Cornmarket at Oxford for his New College. One (now No. 5) was a handsome inn subsequently called the Cross: it is now the Golden Cross, and has been serving the public without a break for some eight hundred years.[34] To the south of the Cross was the Bull, the major part of which (now No. 3) subsequently became a wine-tavern, known by the later years of the seventeenth century as the Salutation and then as the Crown, but before that simply as 'the tavern' – not, as has often been stated, because it was 'unpretentious',[35] but for exactly the opposite reason. A Wine Act of 1553[36] had set down the maximum number of wine-cellars or taverns allowed in named places in England – the City of London was allowed forty; York, eight; Bristol, six; Gloucester, Canterbury, Cambridge and others, four; and Westminster, Salisbury, Southampton, Winchester, Oxford and others, three; others again could have only two. There was a clear distinction (often not now appreciated) between inns and taverns: the former retailed beers and ales, and offered sleeping accommodation to the travelling public, the latter – like our wine-bars – retailed wines but did not have public bedrooms. Thus a visitor staying at the tavern in Cornmarket, as did Shakespeare with the Davenants, was staying not as an ordinary member of the public, but as a friend.

The Cross inn and the tavern stood on the main route through Oxford, and the point has been well made that before the development of college common rooms in the eighteenth century, the wine-taverns were the common rooms of the University, 'where the Master, Bachelors and undergraduates, each in a special room, drank their wine in the evening'.[37] The tavern which Sir William Davenant's father took over some five years before the poet's birth was very large – returned in 1665 as having twelve hearths, and in 1696 as having twenty windows, the same number in each case as the Cross inn; and the college inventories show that it was just as richly furnished as that handsome establishment. The rear of the gabled, timber-framed tavern – not then a two-storey house,[38] but a four-storey building – was pulled down in 1934; but in the Davenants' day the tavern ran back from Cornmarket for about 120 feet, and had more than twenty rooms. There were a parlour, and a shop parlour, on the street, with a room known as 'the Sheriff's Chamber' probably behind the parlour. On the first floor was a large wainscotted dining chamber; and a gallery connected the front part of the building with a block at the back, where the kitchens and larder were on the ground floor. Above the gallery was an attic or cockloft; and among the upstairs rooms were probably the one described by John Davenant in his will as 'my Study', and certainly 'the Elm Chamber', 'the Great Chamber by the Court', 'the White Chamber' and the handsome surviving Painted Room. Early in the present century, the brick benches in the cellars were still intact,[39] which three hundred years before had supported Davenant's barrels of 'Gascoyne Wyne' and 'Butts and pipes of sweet wynes'. At the back of the tavern was a garden, separated from it by a narrow passage-way owned by Christ Church: it adjoined the larger garden of the Cross. On chill, dank Oxford days the Davenants' patrons, sometimes joined by their distinguished guest from London, sat round fires of logs from the woodyard mentioned in Davenant's will; in summertime they could be out in the courtyard and garden.

The manuscript New College leasebooks show that by the 1580s, all three Cornmarket properties – inn, tavern and a small tenement between them – were in the hands of a family called Underhill (distant

relations of the man who sold New Place at Stratford to Shakespeare).
Thomas Underhill had run the inn until his death in the 1560s, and his
children Pierce, John and Joan were born there. In 1567 Joan was
married at All Saints in the High Street[40] to a furrier called William
Hough, and by 1574 if not earlier, Hough held the lease of the inn; at
some stage Pierce moved into the small tenement; and the other brother,
John, Doctor of Divinity, sometime scholar of New College and since
1577 Rector of Lincoln, held the lease of the tavern.[41] In 1592 the
Houghs' lease of the Cross was renewed, and their eldest son William –
who had come of age – became lessee of the tavern, his father remaining
as tenant and occupier.[42] John Underhill – who had become Bishop of
Oxford in 1589 – died in 1592, William Hough senior in 1593, and
William Hough junior – the lessee of the tavern – in 1595;[43] shortly
after that, Joan Hough *née* Underhill, the experienced hostess of inn and
tavern, went off to London and married a freeman of the Girdlers'
Company called John Staunton, and her brother Pierce took over the
inn. Staunton lived in Bishopsgate, at a house called The Vine – which
suggests that he too was in the wine trade. And after the marriage, he
and Joan acquired a large and celebrated Bishopsgate inn called the
Angel; Joan later stated that they had spent the very large sum of £200
on rebuilding and repairing the inn and adjoining tenements.[44]

Joan's brother Pierce Underhill was a considerable figure at Oxford.
He had been a highly skilled craftsman in his younger days – a saddler;
he served for a number of years as one of the city bailiffs, with his
brother-in-law William Hough; and for a time he was Manciple of
Merton, the most highly paid college servant and the officer responsible
for buying provisions for the college. Thus he ranked as one of the
'privileged persons' exempted from taxation by virtue of service to the
University.[45] He was an active parishioner of St Martin Carfax, which
was then the official city church, and served twice as churchwarden.

In 1587, at Uxbridge, Pierce had married Anne Waters as his second
wife, and when he took over the Cross inn at Oxford he had the
decorations modernised: over a fireplace in an upstairs restaurant can
be seen a cartouche incorporating the letters 'P^{V}A', for Pierce and Anne
Underhill.[46] But by the end of the century things were not going well in
Cornmarket: Pierce was getting on in age, and he was running the large
and busy inn hampered by a difficult wife who was leading him an
'unquiett life'.[47] Entries in the New College leasebooks were made only
at irregular and sometimes fairly long intervals, and they do not show
who was running the adjoining tavern just before the Davenants'
arrival; but in an Oxford subsidy roll of October 1600, 'William Grice
vintner' is entered as the tenant, no doubt a stopgap appointment.[48]

Pierce was clearly in need of professional help, since his sister Joan had signified her intention not to return to Oxford by marrying another London man as her third and last husband, and going to live in the parish of St Giles-in-the-Fields.[49]

Since the Davenants did not arrive in Oxford until 1600 or 1601, Shakespeare must have stayed with someone else during the 1590s on the annual trips to Stratford – assuming that he always broke his journey at Oxford, as would have been customary – and thus would already know the Hough and Underhill families well. Joan Hough *née* Underhill married Staunton and moved to Bishopsgate in about 1596[50] – just when the playwright was lodging there; it would be natural for him to lodge in Bishopsgate with the woman with whom he had already lodged at Oxford. Furthermore, the Bishopsgate regime ended in 1599 with the death of Staunton, and that was the year in which the playwright presumably moved south of the river, to be near the newly erected Globe. The year also marked the sixth and last unsuccessful attempt by John and Jennet Davenant to found a family in the plague-haunted City, and their presumed conclusion that they might do better elsewhere (as they did: all seven children born at Oxford survived). It seems possible that Joan *née* Underhill and Shakespeare advised Davenant the experienced merchant vintner to take on the tavern at Oxford, thus helping Joan's brother professionally and assuring the playwright of a continued welcome.

The roads were atrocious, and the Davenants would have moved from London to Oxford by water, embarking at Three Cranes Wharf across the road from their home. They could hire a wherry with two oarsmen, or a tilt-boat (a large boat with an awning) with four oarsmen and a steersman, and worldly goods would go in barges. Davenant's sister Katherine had recently married a London merchant called Nicholas Smith living in the adjoining parish of St Martin-in-the-Vintry, who could act as his London agent and ship consignments of wine upriver for the Oxford tavern.[51] The 'William Grice' who in 1600 was in charge of the tavern proves to have been a friend and colleague of Davenant in both London and Oxford, and had presumably gone ahead to hold the fort at the tavern in Cornmarket – he subsequently took over the Three Tuns in the High Street. When Davenant made his will in 1622, he appointed no fewer than five overseers, including three mayors of the city – but it was 'my frend Mr Grice' whom he put in overall charge of his business affairs.[52].

Advice to Davenant about the move to Oxford may also have come from an unexpected source: John Donne. The poet's father was a freeman of the Ironmongers' Company, and the family lived in Bread

Street, just round the corner from the big Davenant household where Sir William's grandfather spent part of his youth. John Davenant the future Bishop of Salisbury, and the future poet and Dean of St Paul's, were born within yards of each other in the same year, 1572. It is inconceivable that the Donne and Davenant families – both the Davenants near St Paul's and their relations engaged in the wine-trade down by the river – did not know each other well.[53] The young John Donne and the young John Davenant, father of Sir William, shared a passion for the theatre in the 1590s – Donne 'a great frequenter of Playes'[54] and Davenant a 'lover of plays and play-makers, especially Shakespeare'. Also significant is that there was a Donne aunt at Oxford[55] – and in the same line of business as John Davenant, since her husband Robert Dawson kept the Blue Boar, a large inn at St Aldate's. Mrs Dawson died in 1585 (shortly after her nephews John and Henry had matriculated·from Hart Hall), but Dawson remarried and remained at the inn until his death in 1605, four or five years after the Davenants' arrival. John Donne's cousins Edward and Grace Dawson, with whom he always kept in touch, carried on at the Blue Boar – professional colleagues and near neighbours of the Davenants, and fellow-tenants of New College.[56]

There is no record of the baptism of the Davenants' first surviving child, Elizabeth (?1601–72) at St Martin Carfax – which does not prove that she was not baptised there, since the first register-book is far from perfect. For their three daughters and four sons, the parents chose the names Elizabeth, after Mrs Davenant's mother; Jane (1602–67), after herself; Robert (1603–74), after her father; Alice (1604–60), probably after Pierce Underhill's elder daughter Alice Brise, whose husband Thomas became lessee of the Cross in the Davenants' time;[57] William (1606–68), after his presumed godfather Shakespeare;[58] John (1607–?34), after his father; and Nicholas (1611–after 1672), probably after the Davenants' brother-in-law and agent Nicholas Smith in London.[59]

Chambers chose for the frontispiece of the second volume of his *William Shakespeare* (1930) a photograph of the Painted Room at No. 3 Cornmarket, the former tavern, and gave it the caption 'John Davenant's Painted Chamber'; Nethercot (1938) assumed that this had been the 'best bedroom', and indulged a fancy about the Davenant children studying its wall-paintings; while Schoenbaum (*Shakespeare's Lives*, 1970) revived Nethercot's notion that if Jane Davenant and William Shakespeare ever shared a bed, it was within these painted walls. John Tattleton, the Underhills' stepfather, had had the paintings done during his tenancy of the tavern; but a New College inventory of 1594, taken after the death of William Hough senior – and, as we now know, about six years before the arrival of the Davenants – shows that the walls of this and other rooms had been covered with wainscotting by then.

John Davenant took out his freedom of the city of Oxford by purchase, a not uncommon practice, on 4 June 1604, paying £8 to 'have a lycence of this Cytie to sell Wyne & a Bayliffs place'.[60] It has been asked how he could have been operating as a vintner by 1603 – as the parish register says he was – before he had become a freeman; the answer no doubt lies with Pierce Underhill, who in 1596 as a 'privileged person' had been granted a University licence (now in the Bodleian) to sell wine. He no doubt passed it on to Davenant, as he was entitled to do, at some time before his death early in 1604.[61]

Although Davenant had had to leave the world of the London theatres, Oxford was a good place for the playgoer. He would have been in one of the very early audiences for *Hamlet* (written 1600–1) – for according to the first quarto of 1603, it had by then already been performed 'in the two Vniuersities of Cambridge and Oxford'. At this time, companies of players lodged at the galleried King's Head inn in Cornmarket almost opposite Davenant's tavern (it survived until the nineteenth century); plays would be put on in the inn yard, and when Shakespeare was at Oxford he could stay with his friends at the tavern and cross the road to supervise rehearsals and take part in performances.

In August 1605 the new King, with Queen Anne and Prince Henry, visited Oxford, and the dignitaries of town and gown, John Davenant among them, rode out in their finery to greet them.[62] The royal party advanced through the North Gate into Cornmarket, and past the Cross inn and the tavern to Carfax, where they were greeted with a Greek oration. Dr Matthew Gwyn, first Lecturer in Physic at Gresham College in Bishopsgate, had helped to supervise the plays put on during the Queen's visit to Oxford in 1592, and he supervised again this time (the King dropped off to sleep during a performance of his Latin play *Vertumnus* at Christ Church). No doubt he foregathered with John Davenant at the tavern: both had been at Merchant Taylors' School, and Gwyn's brother Roger became the fourth and last husband of the Anglo-Flemish woman who has figured earlier – both as the wife of Davenant's cousin Thomas Gore, and as the mother of Nicholas Tooley the presumed member of Shakespeare's company.

The churchwardens' accounts of St Martin Carfax for 1614–15 list nearly fifty parishioners who had lent money 'towards the payment of the last yeares surcharge'; twelfth in the list is Mr John Davenant – and, in a later hand, someone has pencilled in the margin: 'J^{no} Davenant Shakespears Vncle'! Davenant does not figure in a list of 1619–20, of

men who had contributed 'toward the Clocke & chimes', but among
those who did is 'Mr Iohn Hemmings of London . . .x^s'; this perhaps
was the man then preparing the First Folio, and staying with the 'lover
of plays and play-makers' as Shakespeare had done so often before. Will
Davenant, then fourteen, could talk to him about his recently deceased
godfather.

In the summer of 1615, John Davenant had sent his eldest son Robert
up to London to his old school: the then headmaster was William
Hayne, who in 1622 was renting a house at Deptford at the sign of the
White Bear owned by Davenant. In 1618, Robert entered St John's
College, Oxford, as a Merchant Taylor scholar, and father and son later
made presentations to the college library.[63] Robert's younger brothers
John and Nicholas went to Merchant Taylors' School in 1619; William
was the only one not to do so. Aubrey reports that he studied first, at
Oxford, under 'Mr Sylvester . . . ,[64] but I fear he was drawne from
Schoole before he was ripe enough'. He then studied for a year or two,
as Anthony Wood notes, under Daniel Hough, the eldest surviving son
of William Hough senior and Joan née Underhill, who was a fellow of
Lincoln College (where he died in 1644); he obtained from him a small
smattering of logic, 'but his geny which was always opposite to it, lead
him in the pleasant paths of poetry'.

His father had been moving steadily up the municipal ladder, and in
the autumn of 1621 he was elected Mayor of Oxford, gave his banquet
in the handsome wainscotted dining-chamber of the tavern, and rode to
London to take the oath and present gloves to the officers of the
Exchequer in accordance with ancient practice. According to another
custom, long and hotly disputed by the City of Oxford, Mayors also
had to proceed to St Mary's and swear to observe the privileges of the
University: Davenant did so on 4 October.

Six months later his wife Jennet died, and was buried at St Martin
Carfax on 5 April. John at once composed a long and meticulous will[65]
to provide for the future of 'the many Children I have and the mother
dead wch would guide them'. He had himself been ailing for some
months, but he fulfilled his mayoral duties to the last. The full Council
met at his bedside on 17 April,[66] and he died two days later. A contemporary poem 'on Mr Davenantt', once in the Earl of Warwick's library,
asks:

> What meritts hee whom greate and good doth praise?
> What meritts hee? Why, a contented life,
> A happy yssue of a vertuous wife,
> The choyce of freinds, a quiet honour'd grave,
> All these hee had; what more could Dav'nant have? . . .

And another poem in the same 'curious manuscript volume of miscell-anies' asks:

> Why should hee dye?
> And yett why should he live, his mate being gone,
> And turtle-like sigh out an endlesse moone?
> No, no, he loved her better, and would not
> So easely lose what hee so hardly gott.
> He liv'd to pay the last rites to his bride;
> That done, hee pin'd out fourteene dayes and died . . .[67]

One would like to know the significance of that 'so hardly gott'.

Davenant was buried in considerable state at St Martin Carfax on 23 April – six years to the day after the death of William Shakespeare, who had stayed so often with the family. The City Council agreed elaborate arrangements for the funeral. They would attend in their best apparel, followed by the constables with their staves and the serjeants with their maces, 'And all the Aldermen & rest of the Thirtene and Bayliffs here present do think yt fittest & soe agree to goe to the Church in Skarlett if the Vicechauncello[r] & other the Docto[rs] that bear them Company to the Church goe in like Manner, And the great Mace to be carryed next before the Hearse . . .'.[68]

The late Mayor bequeathed the very substantial sum of twelve hundred pounds to his young family – £200 to each of the three daughters and £150 to each of the four sons, to be paid within a year. A good neighbour who lived next door was asked to move into the tavern with her youngest son 'for the better comfort and countenancing of my 3 daughters' until Davenant's senior apprentice Thomas Hallam completed his term of service, receiving free board and lodging and five pounds a year: she had 'bin alwaies to me and my Wife loving iust and kind'.[69] As for the running of the tavern, the two younger daughters would 'keepe the barre by turnes' under Hallam's eye, and the rent would continue to be paid to 'M[r] Huffe'.[70] Davenant hoped that Hallam might marry one of the daughters – 'if he and shee can fancy one an other', as he pleasingly put it: Thomas and twenty-year-old Jane evidently did, for by the time the will was proved on 21 October they were already married, and running the tavern together.[71]

Sixteen-year-old William had by then departed for London. His father had expressed the wish that he be 'put to Prentice to some good marchant of London or other tradesman' within three months of his own death, with £40 for his future master and 'double apparrell', over and above his forthcoming portion of £150; this was to be done 'For avoyding of Inconvenience in my house for mast[er]shippe when I am gone' – a remark interpreted by Nethercot as indicating that William, as a potential troublemaker, was being 'expelled' from Oxford. A similar view is taken by Harbage. I believe this is mistaken: Davenant's will represents a thoroughly sensible and well-considered plan to provide for the future of his young, large and motherless family. His senior apprentice Thomas Hallam was the only person equipped by age and experience to continue running the tavern – with the help and advice of the five overseers of the will, all influential citizens of Oxford, and four of them experienced in the running of inns and taverns. The eldest son, undergraduate Robert, is explicitly instructed not to 'meddle' with the business; and after a further six months at school, the younger brother John is, like William, to be 'put to prentice' (I have not discovered whether this was done, but his brother Nicholas *was* apprenticed, to a Merchant Taylor in London, in 1626, with Hallam as a guarantor).[72] Nevertheless, it is reasonable to deduce that the poetically inclined William was lively, mercurial and unconventional, and not suited to the orderly life of an important university wine-tavern – a deduction fully supported by the nature of his forty-six years of life to come.

CHAPTER THREE

1622–9
The early years
in London

❖⊂⊃◦⊂⊃❖

It was an attractive youth of substantial family who arrived in London in the summer of 1622. Anthony Wood noted that he had inherited his mother's 'very good wit and conversation', and it seems that he also inherited her striking good looks, for Aubrey speaks of his 'beauty & ['spirit' crossed out] phancy'. His twentieth-century biographer Professor Nethercot is well off the mark in presenting him as the son of a 'mere vintner' who within seven years had completed 'what education he had' (a gross slur on the excellent Merchant Taylors' School), and who was himself a 'small swan . . . hatched out among the ordinary barnyard ducks and chickens' constituting a family living in an 'eccentric' and cramped old Oxford tavern.

As soon as he reached London, William approached a tailor called John Urswick, who would have been recommended to him by his Davenant and/or Gore Merchant Taylor relations in the capital: but the 'apparel' which he ordered was nothing like the sober garb of an apprentice which his father had envisaged. Some years later a protracted lawsuit involving Davenant and his tailor began in the Court of Chancery:[1] in the opening Bill of Complaint, dated 30 November 1632, Davenant says that he had ordered 'certain stuffe cloth lace and other necessaries' which Urswick obtained and made up, subsequently putting in 'vnreasonable' bills. It is easy to understand why he wanted handsome apparel, for, as Aubrey tells us, he had secured employment as a page in the household of the Duchess of Richmond at a famous place, Ely House in Holborn.

She was Frances *née* Howard, daughter of Viscount Howard of Bindon and granddaughter of the Dukes of Norfolk and Buckingham. Shortly before young Davenant joined her household, she had become the wife (for both parties it was the third marriage) of a kinsman of King James, Ludovic Stuart, second Earl of Lennox and in 1623 created Duke of Richmond.[2] The Duke died early in 1624, but Davenant's mistress remained at Ely House for a little while, and a characteristically lively and sardonic report from John Chamberlain the letter-writer to his friend Sir Dudley Carleton, dated 8 January 1624/5, shows what state she maintained there:[3]

> we haue much talke of this Diana of the Ephesians, and her magnificence in going to her chappell at ely house on Sunday last to a sermon preached by D[r] Belcanquell, where she had her closet or trauerse, her fowre principall officers steward chamberlain Treasurer controller, marching before her in velvet gownes wth their white staves, three gentlemen vshers, two Ladies that bare vp her traine, the countesses of Bedford and mungumerie following wth the other Ladies two and two, wth a great deale of other apish imitation . . .

Frances's second husband had been the elderly Edward Seymour, first Earl of Hertford, a man 'of very small stature, and of timid and feeble character' who had secured a licence on 27 May 1601 to marry her at his house in Cannon Row, Westminster:[4] he was in his eighties at his death, which took place only two months before his widow's marriage to the King's cousin.

Nethercot refers to Frances as 'an elderly but stately ruin' at the time of the third marriage, and then oddly suggests that Richmond's death two years later was 'hastened by the friskings of his elderly Duchess'. However, once again the invaluable Simon Forman comes to the rescue. For between May 1597 and November 1601 (when his last surviving casebook ends), Frances consulted him more than a dozen times, about health, possible pregnancy, suitors and husbands, and the doctor twice records that she was born between nine and ten o'clock at night on 27 July 1578,[5] so that she was nineteen when she first consulted him. (He needed such precise details for the casting of horoscopes.) Thus she was only in her early forties when she married Ludovic Stuart, hardly a 'stately ruin' even by seventeenth-century standards.

The most important marriage of Frances Howard, in the story of William Davenant, is her first. It was to a man called Henry Prannell, who up to now has been totally misrepresented. A tale is sometimes told[6] that when she got above herself, her second husband the old Earl would tap her on the cheek and ask: 'Frank, Frank, how long is it since thou wert married to Pranel?' – or 'to the vintner?'; Harbage writes of her 'perpetual urge to live down this old disgrace', and Nethercot dismisses the husband as 'a fellow called Prannel'. In fact it was the father, Henry Prannell senior, who was the vintner (as Nethercot realised), and their family story is a classic example of the upward mobility of Elizabethan society. Prannell senior, who died in 1589, had served a normal apprenticeship within the Vintners', prospered exceedingly, taken a number of apprentices of his own, been Warden and Master of his Company, acquired landed property in Hertfordshire and become an alderman; his friends Sir Roger Townsend and Mr William Fleetwood, Recorder of London, consented to oversee his will.[7] His son Henry was born in about 1566, entered the new Shrewsbury School some years after Fulke Greville and Philip Sidney, went up briefly to Cambridge (Caius) in 1581 and was admitted to the Middle Temple on 1 July 1584.[8] This was the young gentleman – described at his death at the end of 1599 as 'of the Middle Temple Esquire' – to whom nineteen-year-old Frances Howard was already married in 1597. At his death Henry bequeathed much property in Hertfordshire and the City of London, as well as suits of armour, books of music and musical instruments, 'books of histories' and a portrait of himself by the Serjeant-Painter, John de Critz.[9]

William Davenant's grandfather John the merchant vintner and broker, who had so many dealings with the Vintners' Company, would have been well-acquainted with Henry Prannell senior, Frances Howard's father-in-law; and it is significant that Frances's early consultations with Simon Forman in 1597 and 1598 were at exactly the same period as those of Davenant's mother and his aunt Ursula Sheppard. The three women all asked, among other things, whether they were pregnant (none was), and it is very probable that they knew one another. Presumably the good-looking young William Davenant exploited these connexions in securing employment at Ely House later on. The fact that his uncles Thomas and Richard Sheppard and cousin Robert had served the Jacobean Court may also have weighed with Frances, whose husband at the time was King James's cousin.

Davenant's troubles with his tailor were continuing, and he later maintained that Urswick had had him arrested four times over the years. Urswick in his Answer to the original Complaint agreed that he had had Davenant arrested in about 1623, but said that in all he had had him detained 'but twice'. William had added to his difficulties by getting married, to someone called Mary, very soon after arriving in London, for on 27 October 1624 – when he was still only eighteen – the first of his numerous sons, also William, was baptised at St James Clerkenwell.[10] Once again Nethercot and Harbage are tempted towards downgrading. Of the wife, Nethercot asks: 'Was she a citizen's homely daughter, or some noblewoman's modish lady-in-waiting?'; and Harbage suggests that she was 'some gentle attendant upon the Duchess of Richmond' but more likely 'an apple-cheeked barmaid in one of the numerous Holborn taverns'. In fact, we have no idea who she was: Aubrey believed her to have been the daughter of 'a Physitian . . . by whom he had a very beautiful and ingeniose son, y^t dyed above 20 yeares since' (William junior died at the Oxford tavern in 1651). But Aubrey may have been muddling the first wife with the second, who was the *widow* of a physician: he was not aware that Davenant had had three wives in all. A second child of Davenant and his first wife, called Elizabeth, was buried at St Benet Paul's Wharf on 9 October 1631, and I discover that their daughter Mary was baptised at St Martin-in-the-Fields on 11 January 1641/2.[11] A Bill of Complaint by Davenant's widow in 1684[12] confirms that in 1653 the laureate had had but one child living, a daughter by Mary 'his first wife'.[13] (This daughter married an uncle of Jonathan Swift who was a fellow of Balliol, and whom she presumably met while she was living with her aunt Jane Hallam at the Oxford wine tavern.)

Davenant told Aubrey just one anecdote about his service with the Duchess of Richmond – or, at any rate, he records only one: that she once 'sent him to a famous Apothecary for some Vnicornes-horne, wch he was resolved to try with a Spider wch he empaled ['incircled' above] in it, but without the expected successe: the Spider would goe over & thorough & thorough unconcerned' (the young man showed praiseworthy scepticism). Isabella, in Webster's *The White Devil* (II.i), also speaks of how men, 'to try the precious unicorns horn / Make of the powder a preservative circle / And in it put a spider' to charm a poison; while in Davenant's *The Cruel Brother,* Lothario asks (Act III, p. 159): 'Know ye not, rogues, that I can muzzle up / The testy Unicorn in a spinners thread?'

From Ely House William Davenant moved to the household, also in Holborn, of Fulke Greville, Lord Brooke (1554–1628), the statesman and patron of poets who was to describe himself, in the epitaph for his tomb at St Mary's, Warwick, as *Servant to Queen Elizabeth, Councillor to King James, and Friend to Sir Philip Sidney* (the two had been friends since they entered the new Shrewsbury School on the same day in 1564). According to Anthony Wood,[14] Davenant's new master 'being poetically given . . . was much delighted in him'. 'As I remember', says John Aubrey, Davenant was a page in this household as he had been at Ely House, but his memory was probably at fault – Davenant by now was likely to have attained to somewhat higher rank. No wonder that in 1625 the tailor Urswick was required to procure and make up further 'cloth lace and other necessaries' for apparel for the young man. Mary Davenant and her baby son presumably had to lodge elsewhere, and a later reference by the tailor to some £9 owing to him by Davenant 'for meate & drincke & apparell makinge' for his wife suggests that she may have lodged with him.

It was probably about now that Davenant met Endymion Porter, the leading courtier and patron of the arts who was to become his greatest friend and benefactor.[15] Aubrey calls Porter one of his two 'Macenasses' (the other being Henry Jermyn, favourite of Queen Henrietta Maria and later Earl of St Albans), and says: 'He writt a Playe, or Playes, and verses, wch he did with so much sweetenesse and grace, that he got the[ir] love and friendship.' He may have met Porter before he left Ely House, since the Richmonds and Buckinghams were friendly, and Porter had married Buckingham's niece Olivia Boteler, and was his Master of the Horse.

One of Davenant's earliest poems, 'To the Lord B. [presumably Brooke] in performance of a vow, that night to write to him', was composed at this period. (All the shorter poems and songs have recently been edited and published for the first time, by A. M. Gibbs.)[16] To the question, why he had not chosen to write first to his new master of the few he had 'singled out for Fame', his bland reply is:

> There are degrees that to the Altar lead,
> Where ev'ry rude, dull Sinner must not tread:
> 'Tis not to bring a swift thankes-giving Tongue,
> Or prayers made as vehement as long,
> Can privilege a zealous Votarie,
> To come where the High Priest should only be . . .   (ll. 6–12)

He had waited 'till I could prove / My Numbers smooth, and mighty as my love' (ll. 17–18). An adroit tribute by the young poet.

His first 'Playe, or Playes' referred to by Aubrey were *The Cruel Brother: A Tragedy* and *The Tragedy of Albovine, King of the Lombards*.[17] *Albovine* went unperformed, but *The Cruel Brother* was licensed on 12 January 1626/7[18] – when the author was still not quite twenty-one – and performed at the Blackfriars Theatre by the King's Servants. Both plays are, as one would expect of so young a man, old-fashioned Jacobean-style dramas of blood and revenge, with bodies heaped on the stage at the end. One is set in 'Italy', the other in Verona.

It was obviously of the greatest importance for the budding playwright that the Shakespeare First Folio and Webster's *The Duchess of Malfi* should have been published in 1623, a matter of months after his arrival in London. Webster lived all his life in Holborn, where the young man spent his first years in the capital; and the Webster family, like the Davenants, had the strongest of links with the Merchant Taylors' Company.[19] In 1624 it was Webster who was commissioned to write the pageant for the new Lord Mayor, Sir John Gore – a relative

of William Davenant who had become a freeman of the Merchant
Taylors' on the same day as his first cousin, Davenant's father. It is
improbable that Davenant did not see the pageant, and meet its author.

The Cruel Brother[20] owes obvious debts to Webster, Shakespeare
and other eminent contemporary or near-contemporary playwrights;
its theme (like its title) resembles that of Fletcher's The Bloody Brother
– a ruler's lust after the wife of his favourite. In Davenant's piece the
ruler is the Duke of Sienna, and the favourite, Count Lucio. Nethercot
remarks cautiously upon the 'furtive suggestion of abnormal male
passion' between the two, commenting on the young author's audacity
in view of the 'sexual proclivities' of the late King, while Harbage
prefers to ignore the subject altogether. In fact the suggestion is a good
deal more than furtive. In the opening scene, Foreste (the 'Cruel
Brother') greets Lucio with the words:

> You are the Duke's Creature! Who dotes by art,
> Who in his love and kindness, method keeps:
> He holdeth thus his arms, in fearful care
> Not to bruise you with his dear embracements . . .   (Act I, pp. 119–20)

and the Duke's first words to him are: 'My glorious boy . . . / The Sun
and you do visit me at once'; 'Royal dotard!' exclaims Castruchio, 'a
satirical Courtier', as they depart.

Lucio is in love with Foreste's sister Corsa – later, when he is about to
marry her secretly, he declares: 'Excellent wretch! I am undone with
joy' (Act II, p. 139) – the young author had been reading Othello:
'Excellent wretch! Perdition catch my soul / But I do love thee'
(III.iii.91–2). But the Duke, as yet unaware of the situation, is still
pressing his attentions on the young man: 'I study how to make thee less
/ That I may make thee more and more my own . . . / Could'st thou
resign thy titles and thy cares / To make me yet more capable of still /
Enjoying thee?' (Act I, pp. 128–9).

As the horrors accumulate, Foreste first accuses his wife Luinna of
having betrayed him with the Duke, and on the entry of two men in
vizards, furiously cries:

> Hear, my she goat! These men are full and free!
> But, if they cannot tire ye out, I will procure ye
> Some of larger thighs . . .
> Or bring the riotous horse, and the town bull
> To drownd ye in the act. Take her aside,
> And agree who shall begin.   (Act IV, p. 176)

It recalls the dark violence of The Duchess of Malfi, and especially

Ferdinand's imagining of his sister with 'some strong-thigh'd barge-man' (II.v); and once again the scene is reminiscent of *Othello*.

The Duke, to whom Lucio has now confessed his marriage, pretends to acquiesce, but explains to the audience: 'The credulous Count, her husband, I have sent / To Lucca. And tomorrow he returns', so that he must assail the bride in the interim: 'What I did mean / Adultery at first, will now, I fear, / Become a rape' (Act III, pp. 161–2). When Corsa assures her brother that it was indeed a rape, he deploys – in a powerfully written speech – an argument still not unheard today:

> If compulsion doth insist until
> Enforcement breed delight, we cannot say
> The female suffers. Acceptance at the last
> Disparageth the not consenting at the first:
> Calls her denial, her unskilfulness;
> And not a virtuous frost i'th' blood . . .   (Act V, p. 181)

He ties her to a chair on stage and slits her wrists:

> . . . Thy wrist-veins are cut. Here
> In this bason bleed; till dryness make them curl
> Like lutestrings in the fire.   (Act V, p. 182)

Corsa bleeds to death, to the music of recorders 'sadly'.

The scene had begun with a song, sung by a boy at Corsa's bidding (Act V, pp. 179–80):

> Weepe no more for what is past
>   For *Time* in motion makes such hast
> He hath no leasure to discry
>   Those errors which he passeth by . . .[21]

at which her brother entered with the words 'This is your dirge.'

Harbage argues that although Foreste is convinced of his sister's moral innocence, he is expunging the stain upon his blood and Lucio's honour – it recalls the tone of the exchanges between the brothers of Webster's Duchess about her 'infected blood' and the threat to 'the royal blood of Arragon and Castile' (II.v.), further underlined by the fact that Foreste and Corsa, like Ferdinand and the Duchess, are twins. The horrors of Corsa's death, Harbage charitably maintains, 'are somewhat alleviated by the elevated, almost sacramental, atmosphere which the dramatist strove for'; the play 'pleads strongly, almost oppressively, for moral rectitude'. And Nethercot suggests that the young playwright really felt 'something of the disgust and hatred toward the court life he had witnessed which he infused into his pages', while lacking 'the strength or integrity to renounce the life which he presumably abhorred and condemned'. The twenty-year-old dramatist would probably have been surprised at such comments.

At the beginning of September his employer Lord Brooke was stabbed by a long-standing employee who had been passed over in his will – and who then immediately committed suicide; Brooke died on the last day of the month. His murder would normally have caused a stir, but as Davenant later told Aubrey, 'the great noise & report' caused by Felton's stabbing of the Duke of Buckingham at Portsmouth on 23 August 'quite drowned' the news about Brooke, 'that was scarce taken notice of'. Two poems addressed by Davenant to the widowed Duchess,[22] the first ending with reference to 'the Peoples wound; . . . / His Nation feels the rancour, and the smart' (ll. 42, 44), and the second,

> gone is now the Pilot of the State,
> The Courts bright Star, the Clergies Advocate,
> The Poets highest Theame, the Lovers flame,
> And Souldiers Glory, mighty *Buckingham*,   (ll. 13–16)

in no way reflected the general rejoicing over the removal of the detested royal favourite.

Nethercot, Harbage and Gibbs all believe that during his period of service at Brooke House, young Davenant broke away to go abroad on military service – probably joining Buckingham's first disastrous expedition to the Ile de Rhé in the summer of 1627, and perhaps also the second expedition a year later which went ahead under the Earl of Lindsey after Buckingham's murder. They base their case largely on a letter from Dr John Davenant the Bishop of Salisbury to Secretary Edward Nicholas which is now in the Public Record Office.[23] The letter is dated 8 April 1628, and commends to the Secretary a 'young gentleman, Mr William Davenant', who is 'serviceable, & of good abilities', and 'has heertofore been imployed in ye warrs abroad in forrain countries. Hee is my near kinsman, & one whome I wish well . . . As hee tells mee, hee hath ye place of an Ancient, or lieftenant already and is in some hope when any new Regiments shall bee raised, of further advancement . . .'.

I believe that the young William commended by the Bishop was one of the Essex Davenants. He was a grandson of the William II mentioned in Chapter 1, and was a year younger than William the poet, having been baptised on 23 March 1606/7 at St Mary's, Bury St Edmunds, where his widowed grandmother Davenant was living with one of her married daughters from an earlier marriage;[24] there was, too, some inclination towards military service abroad in the Essex family – as there was not among the Oxford Davenants – for William's brother

Edward was later licensed to 'passe to Dort to serve as a souldier'.[25] Edward was the heir of his childless uncle John, gentleman and clothier of Halstead (1571–1640), and John's will[26] stipulated that in the event of Edward's death, the Davenant family's mansion house 'Russells' at Halstead in which he lived, plus the Sible Hedingham property, was to pass to his 'very Loveinge Kinsman' the Bishop, 'and to his heires for ever' (similarly, the will of the Bishop's father John, already referred to,[27] includes references to Essex relations and to Sible Hedingham). Thus it is clear that there were close ties between the Bishop and the Essex branch of the Davenant family. Harbage – who was not aware of this – argued that the Bishop was 'well-disposed towards his distant cousins from Oxford', but in the Bishop's own very long will[28] there is only the briefest of references (and that near the end) to any one of them – the poet's elder brother Robert, whom the Bishop mentions fifth and last among a group of clergy 'friends' (he had presented Robert to the tiny living of West Kington in Wiltshire where he spent most of his life).

By arguing that the poet went abroad in 1627, Nethercot is forced to say that it must be 'a moot question' whether he saw *The Cruel Brother* performed. The young man would surely not have deliberately absented himself from the staging of the first heir of his invention: the tailor Urswick states that in 1627 Davenant called on him again, this time with his brother Robert, and that the latter ordered apparel, and one may surmise that Robert had come up from the country for the great occasion at Blackfriars Theatre. (Characteristically, the brothers subsequently told Urswick that they could not yet pay the bill of £14 16s 0d, 'in respect that they were disapoynted of the Receipt of some monyes'.)

The other piece of evidence adduced by Harbage is a letter (also in the PRO),[29] unsigned and undated but endorsed in pencil in a later hand 'abt 1628', in which an offer is made to blow up 'the Storehowse, or Magazin of Dunkerck, and is to be effected, by a secrett illumination of Powder'. The writer explains: 'The meanes to this performance I arrive at, by the easinesse of a friend; who is now Officiall in the Magazin; and his assistance hath given me power to receave imploymentes there. I have knowledge of a small Engine, that will inforce a usefull fire. . . . If ought in this certificate, give hope of advantage to his Matie, I shall performe the service, though with the losse of my life.' This *is* the poet – but needless to say, his madcap offer, made at a time of war fever, was not followed up: and of course the letter provides no evidence that he went abroad. There is no reason to think that Lord Brooke would have allowed his young employee to do so – and we have Aubrey's word for it that Davenant stayed with him 'to his death'. Sir William would hardly have failed to tell Aubrey about exciting military adventures in his youth, or Aubrey to mention them in the *Brief Life*: Nethercot can do no more than suggest that there was 'obviously an oversight'.

The letter about the 'small Engine' is endorsed by Secretary Dorchester as being from 'Mr Dauenant Lodging in ye middle temple wth Mr Hide'. So after Lord Brooke's death Davenant, who seems never to have lacked generous friends, moved into the select world of the Inns of Court. The only surprise is that the lively and gregarious young poet and playwright should have been offered hospitality by the studious and delicate future Lord Clarendon, who was later to write disparagingly of this time:[30] 'There was never an Age in which . . . so many young Gentlemen . . . were insensibly and suddenly overwhelmed in that Sea of Wine, and Women, and Quarrels, and Gaming, which almost overspread the whole Kingdom, and the Nobility, and Gentry thereof . . .'. Edward Hyde had entered the Middle Temple at the beginning of February 1626, and two of Davenant's Gore relations, William and Gerard, were admitted later in the same year, on 2 November: perhaps it was through them that he met Hyde. These Gores were grandsons of the man to whom Davenant's grandfather had been apprenticed, and sons of the Gerard mentioned earlier who had been a fellow-parishioner of the editors of the Shakespeare First Folio.[31]

Muriel Bradbrook has recently written[32] of the Inns of Court as literary centres at this period, and the move to the Middle Temple was obviously of immense importance to William Davenant professionally. The dramatists Marston and Ford had been Templarians, Webster may have been so, and Ford contributed commendatory verses on the publication in 1623 of *The Duchess of Malfi*. With the increase of litigation, the Inns had become the third, and the most sophisticated, university in England, where everyone aspired to some connexion with the Court. This was the privileged society which young Davenant now entered, without being formally admitted, and with no intention of studying law.

His unacted play *Albovine* – which may or may not have been written before *The Cruel Brother* – was published in quarto in 1629, and he promptly adopted what Nethercot describes as the 'aristocratic apostrophe' in his surname which he was to use for the rest of his life, although he continued to write 'Davenant' in private papers. He linked the 'D'Avenant' with fanciful claims that the family had come originally from Lombardy – setting *Albovine* and later his epic poem *Gondibert* there, and introducing Heildebrand, King of the Lombards, in *The Unfortunate Lovers*. This was naturally a subject for continuing mirth: to quote a single example,

As severall Cities made their claim
Of *Homers* birth to have the fame;
So, after ages will not want
Towns claiming to be *Avenant*:
Great doubt there is where now it lies,
Whether in *Lombard* or the *Skies*.

Some say by *Avenant* no place is meant,
And that this *Lombard* is without descent;
And as by *Bilke* men mean ther's nothing there,
So come from *Avenant*, means from *No-where*.[33]

For the *Albovine* quarto the playwright prevailed upon eight of his friends to contribute commendatory verses – and four of them obligingly addressed them to 'D'avenant' (the rest to 'the Author'). The verses are in the customary highflown style, even Hyde asking: 'Can aught of mine / Enrich thy Volume? Th'ast rear'd thyself a Shrine / Will out-live Pyramids . . .'. Apart from 'H. Howard', the other contributors can be identified. Roger Lort the poet had been admitted to the Middle Temple on 23 May 1627, having graduated from Wadham College, Oxford; Richard Clerke of Lincoln's Inn, admitted on 25 April 1627, was a cousin of the poet Abraham Cowley, and possibly related to the John Clerke of the same Inn, brother-in-law of Henry Prannell who married Davenant's first employer; Henry Blount was also an Oxford graduate (Trinity), and had been admitted to Gray's Inn on 22 June 1620; another Gray's Inn contributor was the poet William Habington[34] – who also wrote verses for Shirley, commending his *Wedding*, published in the same year as Davenant's *Albovine*. (James Shirley, like so many of the Davenants and Gores, went to Merchant Taylors' School; he took up residence at Gray's Inn in about 1625, and became a servant of Henrietta Maria at about the same time as Davenant.)

The remaining two contributors were brothers, Robert and Thomas Ellice, whose father Griffith was a near neighbour and professional colleague of the London Davenants near St Paul's, being a freeman of the Merchant Taylors' and merchant of Bow Lane. The sons were exact contemporaries of the playwright, baptised at St Mary-le-Bow in 1605 and 1607. The elder, Robert, graduated from Oxford (Merton) in 1625 and entered Gray's Inn on 10 August 1627; the younger, Thomas, had been admitted on the previous 23 February. Thomas Ellice was admitted to the Inn on the same day as the poet John Suckling, who was to become Davenant's 'great & intimate friend', to quote Aubrey: he, too, would no doubt have contributed verses for *Albovine* had he not been abroad.[35]

All these literary contemporaries at the various Inns were a closely knit group: Ford dedicated his play *The Lover's Melancholy* to 'Master Henry Blount, Master Robert Ellice and all the rest of the Noble Society of Gray's Inn'. Three of the young men were subsequently knighted – Suckling in 1630, Blount in 1640 and Davenant at the siege of Gloucester in 1643; Lort was created a baronet in 1662.[36]

Albovine[37] is even more blood-boltered than *The Cruel Brother*, and has an even more complicated plot. There is perhaps something of Tamburlaine in Albovine himself, the first Lombardian King of Italy; and it is again apparent that the young author has been reading Shakespeare (and *Othello* in particular) and Webster. The scene in which Paradine, a captive soldier who is now the King's favourite, stabs his supposedly unfaithful wife Valdaura, reads as in part a paraphrase of the final scene of Shakespeare's tragedy: Valdaura cries (Act IV, p. 86) 'Hold, hold! leave me a little breath / To use in prayer', to which Paradine responds 'I would / Not hurt thy soul' (compare *Othello*, V.ii.31–3, when the Moor urges Desdemona to 'be brief' in her prayers – 'I would not kill thy unprepared spirit; / No – heaven forfend! – I would not kill thy soul.'). 'Dare you trust my last words?' Valdaura asks her husband, to which he replies: 'O speak, ere thou dost catch an everlasting cold, / And shalt be heard no more' (Act IV, p. 86), echoing Webster's 'I have caught an everlasting cold; I have lost my voice / Most irrecoverably!' (*The White Devil*, V.vi.270).

Rhodolinda, daughter of the former King and now Albovine's Queen, lusts after Paradine, and just before he stabs her she cries:

> *Rhod.* Dear Paradine, I sure shall ravish thee,
>   My appetite is grown so fierce. Let me
>   Begin with thy moist lip –
> *Para.* Let's to't like monkeys, or the reeking goat [again, compare *Othello*].
>   (*Paradine pulls her to kiss him in the chair.*)
> *Rhod.* Oh! Oh! Oh! help! help!
>   (*Both are bloody about their mouths.*)
> *Para.* Cease your loud clamour, Royal whore!
> *Rhod.* Thou didst eat my lips.   (Act V, p. 102)

Even Harbage, who considers the first half of the play 'admirable', and the writing 'strong, vivid and marvellously ingenious in hyperbole' throughout, admits that the language revealing the lust of the King and the evil Hermegild ('a man created in the dark') after Rhodolinda, and of Rhodolinda after Paradine, is 'too rich to be digestible'.

The piece ends with Paradine drawing aside an arras to reveal Albovine, Rhodolinda and Valdaura 'dead in chairs' (Davenant was partial to placing his victims upon the stage in chairs: compare the slitting of Corsa's wrists in *The Cruel Brother*) before stabbing Hermegild and finally being wounded and disarmed by the guard. Davenant and Ford would have become acquainted at the Middle Temple, and similarities between the younger man's first two plays and Ford's *The Broken Heart* suggest that in the late 1620s and early 1630s they discussed each other's work in progress. In *The Broken Heart* Penthea, too, is discovered dead in a chair (IV.iv) – after which her twin brother Ithocles, who had driven her to despair, meets an even more horrible death than Corsa's in *The Cruel Brother*: Penthea's former betrothed, Orgilus, persuades him to sit in a chair to which a mechanical device has been fixed, he is 'catcht in the Engine', and Orgilus stabs him.[38]

As in *The Cruel Brother,* there is much in *Albovine* about the ruler's passion for his young favourite, and at the beginning of the play the repellent image of eating lips is employed again, when Grimold, 'a rough old Captain', remarks of Paradine that 'the royal fool greets him with such / Ravenous kisses, that you would think he meant / To eat his lips' (Act I, p. 21) (it recurs a few years later in *The Wits,* where the Elder Pallatine says to his brother: 'I've a great mind to kiss thee . . . and eat up thy lips so far / Till th'ast nothing left to cover thy teeth' (V.iii, p. 217). Harbage guardedly remarks that the King's affection for Paradine is 'too demonstrative after the fashion of King James'; and when Hermegild says later of the King 'He hath of late hung thus – / Upon my neck; until his amorous weight / Became my burden: and then lay slabbering o'er / My lips, like some rheumatic babe' (Act V, p. 90), the nineteenth-century editors of the plays comment that this 'evidently refers to the practice of James I, who was accustomed to use his favourites after a similar fashion'. Even more pointed is a passage (Act III, p. 52) – almost unremarked upon by previous commentators – in which Cunymond, a courtier, says to Grimond:

> *Cun.* The king is now in love.
> *Grim.* With whom?
> *Cun.* With the queen.
> *Grim.* In love with his own wife! that's held incest
> In Court; variety is more luscious.

With such a seemingly obvious reference to King Charles – whose love for his Queen did not begin to develop until after the murder of Buckingham – and to his late father, it is surely not surprising that *Albovine,* unlike *The Cruel Brother,* did not achieve performance by the King's Men at Blackfriars. And perhaps the author did not expect it, for he dedicates the play to the late King's favourite Robert Carr, Earl of Somerset, who had been disgraced on conviction thirteen years before of the murder of Sir Thomas Overbury. 'You read this Tragedie', the

playwright says, 'and smil'd upon't, that it might live. . . . My Numbers
I do not shew unto the public Eye, with an ambition to be quickly
known (for so I covet *noise*, not *fame*)'; he signs himself 'Your
humblest Creature, D'avenant'. Surprisingly, Edward Hyde in his
commendatory verse praises the choice of patron.

Although the play is in blank verse, a prose version appears in the
folio edition of Davenant's dramatic works published in 1673, five
years after his death. There was then, say the nineteenth-century
editors, 'an attempt, but a clumsy one, to render the play more suitable
for what is now termed family reading'; but there is no evidence that
this version, either, was ever performed. It must have been a rather
lonely contemporary admirer who wrote:

> *Shakespeares Othello, Johnsons Cataline,*
> Would lose their luster, were thy *Albovine*
> Placed betwixt them . . .[39]

However, the play has achieved performance in modern times – by the
Davenant Society of Lincoln College, Oxford, in February 1931, when
the then Poet Laureate, John Masefield, was present.[40]

Two more plays were licensed in 1629 – *The Colonel* on 22 July and
The Just Italian on 2 October. The fate of the former is not known, but
it is presumed to have been the piece included in revised form under the
title *The Siege* in the 1673 folio.[41] *The Just Italian,*[42] like *The Cruel
Brother,* achieved performance by the King's Men, and print in 1630.
But again it seems to have met with no success, and in his dedication to
Edward Sackville, fourth Earl of Dorset, the author declares that 'the
uncivil ignorance of the People had depriv'd this humble Work of life;
but that your Lordship's approbation stept in to succour it. Those
many that came with resolution to dispraise, knowing your Lordship's
judgment to be powerful above their malice, were either corrected to an
understanding, or modesty . . .'. A poem 'To Edward Earle of Dorcet,
after his Sicknesse, and happy recovery', was published in 1638.[43] In a
later poem to the Earl, possibly written in the 1640s,[44] Davenant says
'you adorn'd my Muse and made her known'; and he speaks of the
poet's self-absorption and longing for praise:

> Ah, what are Poets? Why is that great Law
> Conceal'd, by which their numbers seek to awe
> The Soules of Men? Poets! whom love of Praise,
> A Mistress smile, or a small Twigg of Bayes,
> Can lift to such a pride as strait they dreame
> The Worlds chiefe care is to consider them.
> Of this fond race (my Lord) am I . . .   (ll. 1–7)

Davenant's reference to 'malice' in the dedication of *The Just Italian* was to be followed in later years by many similar complaints about the opposition of a hostile 'faction', a hostility not perhaps surprising, for from the start of his professional career he had chosen to align himself decisively with the royalists – in a London that was predominantly puritan. *Albovine,* it will be recalled, had been dedicated to the Earl of Somerset, and the choice for *The Cruel Brother* was Richard Weston, who – through Buckingham's influence – had been appointed Lord Treasurer in July 1628 and would be created Earl of Portland in 1633.[45]

For *The Just Italian,* two poets contributed commendatory verses, William Hopkins, and Thomas Carew – who was to become one of Davenant's close friends. (Davenant's poem 'To Tho: Carew' gives us the information that at the time of writing, Carew was living in King Street, Westminster.)[46] Hopkins writes of the 'giddy fools' who rush off to Paris Garden or the puppet plays, and 'extol the Jew's trump, or the morris bells', leaving only 'the wiser few' to savour Davenant's work; while Carew declares that now only 'noise prevails'; 'the rabble' have no taste for Davenant's 'strong fancies, raptures of the brain', or for anything above what is on offer at the Red Bull or Cockpit playhouses – while 'the true brood of Actors, that alone / Keep natural unstrain'd action in her throne, / Behold their benches bare, though they rehearse / The terser Beaumont's or great Johnson's verse' (his complaint recalls Hamlet's sentiments of thirty years before).

This time Davenant's play is a 'Tragi-Comedy', set in Florence and written with a lighter touch than its predecessors. The 'Just Italian' is Altamont, who in the first scene declares that he might as easily 'collect the scatter'd winds into a bag, / Or from the wat'ry surface scrape the gilt / Reflections of the sun' as bring the heart of his wife Alteza 'Within the quiet list of wives, that will / Obey and love' (there is a touch of Petruchio here, as later in the Act (pp. 214–15) when he threatens to starve Alteza into submission). As part of his plan to tame his wife, Altamont pretends that his sister Scoperta is his mistress, at which Alteza counters by inviting a young Florentine, Sciolto, to be her lover: he jauntily tells Altamont (Act II, p. 223): 'I am come to get your children for you' and Alteza adds: 'D'ye want a clearer paraphrase? He is / My servant, Sir; my stallion, if I please. / A courtly implement, and much in use / Among ladies of my growth and title.' Sciolto boasts (p. 228) that 'some three and forty ladies or thereabout' will soon produce male twins begotten by him, but when he advances to kiss Alteza, she declares:

> Stay, my pregnant Signior! Our love is not
> Yet ripe . . .
> I am too proud to have my favours soon
> And easily conferr'd. Such smiles are cheap.
> I mean to procreate by prescription, Sir.
> Make my lust as physical as my meals.

'Death!', Sciolto exclaims, 'I'm suitor unto Galen's widow.'

As might be expected, Altamont and Alteza become convinced of each other's innocence, and all ends happily. There is an engaging subplot involving Altamont's brother Florello, a soldier home from the wars who resolves to win Alteza's sister Charintha: he poses as a Milanese Count, Dandolo, who has been wooing her by correspondence, and (on borrowed money) throws riches about with gay abandon – a ruby and a diamond for Alteza ('I have enow. Wear 'em!'), and for Charintha a sapphire chain ('tie thy monkey in't – / Take it! for by this hand I am in haste, / and cannot offer twice', adding 'I will give thee a bushel of seed-pearl / To embroider thy petticoat': Act II, pp. 230, 232). He pretends to have many servants:

> This is my parasite, and this is my pimp.
> I've a fool, a dwarf too at home. I made
> My jaunt too early by a month, or else
> My train had been enlarg'd . . .
> I've instruments distinct, that take a charge
> O'th' several quarters of my frame. My dwarf
> Doth dress me up unto the knees, and, when
> His stature leaves his reach, young Virgins then,
> Th'issue of decay'd barons, do begin
> And govern to the navel. Whilst upwards,
> Barbers, painters, and parasites are us'd.   (Act II, p. 231)

When the real Dandolo turns up, with his 'champions', Jonsonian characters called Stoccata and Punto, Florello is unabashed and accuses the Count of being a bastard (Act III, p. 239). He is finally shown up, but Charintha forgives him – ' 'Has got a sweet and powerful way in speech' (Act V, p. 270) – and accepts him as a husband.

At the beginning of Act V, when Alteza enters 'in her night-gown', a song, 'This lady, ripe, and calm, and fresh / As Eastern Summers are . . .', is sung by two boys (p. 265). This is an early version of one of Davenant's most familiar songs, 'The Philosopher and the Lover; to a Mistress dying',[47] of which the first two stanzas read:

> LOVER.
> Your Beauty, ripe, and calm, and fresh,
>   As Eastern Summers are,

Must now, forsaking Time and Flesh,
  Add light to some small Star.

PHILOSOPHER.
Whilst she yet lives, were Stars decay'd,
  Their light by hers, relief might find:
But Death will lead her to a shade
  Where Love is cold, and Beauty blinde.

Music and musicians were to become increasingly important to
William Davenant during his career, both as a writer of masques and
poems, and later in his experiments with opera production. A number
of seventeenth-century settings of his poems survive, and these are
printed by Gibbs.[48]

At the beginning of the year in which *The Cruel Brother* and *The Just
Italian* appeared in quarto, Davenant wrote an Ode 'To the King on
New-yeares day 1630';[49] it seems to be his only poem addressed to
Charles I, for his real royal patron was to be Henrietta Maria. Also in
1630 he wrote his mock-epic in two cantos, 'Jeffereidos, Or the Captivi-
tie of Jeffery', on the capture by Dunkirk pirates of the Queen's famous
dwarf Jeffrey Hudson, who had been dispatched to France with her
dancing-master to fetch her a French midwife.[50] In a spirited account of
the capture, which took place when the party from the royal household
were on the return journey, Davenant tells how Jeffrey was found
hiding 'beneath a spick / And almost span-new-pewter-Candlestick' (ll.
27–8), at which the indignant captive exclaimed: 'This, that appeares to
you a walking Thumbe, / May prove the gen'rall Spie of Christendome'
(ll. 35–6). After various adventures, including being mounted on a
poodle, falling off and being 'forc'd to wander on his Feet' (Canto the
second, l. 24), and doing battle with a 'halfe blinde' turkey which had
pecked at him 'with intent to eat / Him up, in stead of a large graine of
Wheat' (ll. 56–8), the dwarf and the rest of the party were released. The
two cantos of this early example of mock-heroic writing were composed very soon after the event, and the second ends with a promise of a
third 'if the Court-wits please' (l. 106), but this never appeared: if it had,
it would no doubt have celebrated the return of the party to London and
the successful delivery on 29 May of the future Charles II.

The poet's 'Ode To the King on New-yeares day' had begun by
wishing him 'The joyes of eager Youth, of Wine, and Wealth; / Of Faith
untroubled, and unphysick'd Health'. Davenant himself was now to
suffer ill-health and disastrous physic which together almost cost him
his life.

CHAPTER FOUR

1 6 3 0 – 6
Illness; plays and masques;
Servant of the Queen

❧⊸⊷❧

The sudden halt to Davenant's writings early in 1630[1] indicates that it was then that he contracted venereal disease, and nearly lost his nose and his life. *DNB* refers simply to 'an illness', and the nineteenth-century editors of the plays and masques to an 'unlucky accident'; the twentieth-century biographers inch up to the subject with caution, and although Nethercot eventually mentions syphilis, Harbage speaks only of 'a complaint . . . at that time sonorously known as the Grand Pox', and apologises for mentioning the nose 'with what may seem distasteful insistence': it was, he explains, a vital part of Davenant's career. But he hastens to assure us that the laureate was 'not a roué, and that in an age much given to literary indecencies, he was never indecent'.

Syphilis first appeared in Europe in the fifteenth century, and was called *morbus neapolitanus* by the French, *morbus gallicus* by the Italians and 'the French disease' by the English. Some authors have taken literally Suckling's remark that Davenant became ill through 'travelling in France', but this was probably a contemporary euphemism for the 'French' infection. Aubrey, whose informant was Davenant himself and whose information is specific, is almost certainly to be believed when he says that the poet 'gott a terrible clap of a Black [dark] handsome wench that lay in Axe-yard Westm[inster]'. (The yard was a cul-de-sac off the west side of King Street, close to the site of our Downing Street – and the place where Pepys and his young wife made their first home in 1658.)[2] In his light-hearted poem 'A Journey into Worcestershire',[3] the poet tells how a party of four – Endymion Porter, 'a Captaine', 'my Lord' and himself – took pleasure at leaving behind in London 'ill Playes, sowre Wine, / Fierce Serjeants and the plague', and adds that in his own case, he was also leaving something 'farr worse', an 'Ethnick ['heathen' or 'pagan'] Taylor' (ll. 5–8). This probably dates the trip and the poem to the late 1620s, just before he became ill, and when he was in the thick of his legal wrangle with the tailor Urswick.

The only known portrait of Davenant, by John Greenhill, which survives in an engraving by Faithorne, shows his afflicted nose as decayed rather than destroyed. John Aubrey writes that 'many witts were so cruelly bold' on the subject, and there was indeed a stream of ribald comment for the rest of his life – some wits combining the subject with his tampering with his surname: to quote one example:

Thus *Will*, intending *D'Avenant* to grace
Has made a Notch in's name like that in's face . . .[4]

The infection was popularly regarded as no more than a 'mischance' – the word used by Suckling and Aubrey – and when Davenant had recovered, he himself made Lucy, one of his characters in *The Wits,* speak cheerfully of 'lewd gallants / That have lost a nose' (Act III, p. 171). (His friend and fellow-poet Thomas Carew also contracted syphilis at an unknown date, for Suckling addressed to him a poem 'Upon T. C. having the P[ox]'.)[5]

When Davenant became ill he turned, as was customary, to quick-silver or mercury, then the only recommended treatment for syphilis. Finally he resorted in desperation to the Queen's physician Dr Thomas Cademan, to whom he later addressed a poem[6] which begins with the following lines of heartfelt gratitude to a clearly remarkable man:

For thy Victorious cares, thy ready heart;
Thy so small tyranny to so much Art;
   For visits made to my disease
   And me (Alas) not to my Fees;
For words so often comforting with scope
Of learned reason, not perswasive hope;
   For Med'cines so benigne as seeme
   Cordials for Eastern Queenes that teeme;
For setting now my condemn'd Body free,
From that no God, but Devill *Mercurie* . . .   (ll. 1–10)

However, after a catalogue of what he has endured, the poem ends not with explicit expressions of gratitude, but with characteristically cheerful insouciance:

May (thou safe Lord of Arts) each Spring
   Ripe plenty of Diseases bring
Upon the Rich; they still t'our Surgeons be
Experiments, Patients alone to thee;
   Health to the Poore, lest pitty shou'd
   (That gently stirs and rules thy blood)
Tempt thee from wealth, to such as pay like mee
A Verse, then thinke they give Eternity.   (ll. 35–42)

He would have been confident that Dr Cademan (whose widow he was later to marry) knew him well enough to smile at all this. The former afflictions he enumerates (surely not with 'macabre and cheerful vividness ... almost with gusto', as Nethercot puts it,[7] but with the fascinated horror of one snatched from the grave) are a grossly swollen face, loss of voice, rotting teeth, head sewed up in a hood, foaming at the mouth, sore throat and loss of appetite. No wonder he felt such gratitude to the doctor for 'My new returne of Senses, strength and blood' (l. 30).

A poem 'To I. C. Rob'd by his Man Andrew'[8] also refers to the young man's illness – 'my sick Joints cannot accompany / Thy Hue-on-Cry; ... Midnight parlies be / Silenc'd long since 'tween Constables and me' (ll. 16–18; a regretful memory of the 'chimes at midnight', although, unlike Falstaff's, his were not gone for ever). Davenant breaks off this poem with the words 'But Hark! who knocks? good troth my Muse is staid / By an Apothecaries Bill unpaid' (ll. 34–5) – an echo of Cademan's unpaid 'Fees'.

Grateful as he undoubtedly was to the royal physician, the poet constantly expresses even more fervent thanks to Endymion Porter – 'Lord of my Muse and heart', as he calls him in one of the poems addressed to him at this period.[9] He recalls how he had lain so long near to death that

> when my long forgotten Eies and Mind
> Awak'd, I thought to see the Sunne declin'd,
> Through age, to th'influence of a Starre, and Men
> So small that they might live in Wombes agen ...   (ll. 9–12)

– a striking description of how all sense of time is lost during serious illness. But now, he continues, writing as to Dr Cademan of his joy at recovery,

> my strength's so giantly, that were
> The great Hill-lifters once more toyling here,
> They'ld choose me out, for active *Back,* for *Bone,*
> To heave at *Pælion* first, and heave alone.
> Now by the softnesse of thy noble care,
> Reason and Light my lov'd Companions are ...   (ll. 13–18)

And as to Dr Cademan, he promises payment by 'Poesie'. His next play, *The Wits,* is dedicated to Endymion, who 'hath preserv'd life in the Author' (Act II, p. 119). (Not surprisingly, word went round that he had died, as is shown by a poem 'To the Lady Bridget Kingsmill; sent with Mellons after a report of my Death'.)[10] In another poem to Porter,[11] Davenant recalls having made his will, and begins: 'I gave, when last I

was about to die, / The Poets of this Isle a Legacie . . . I gave them thee.'
(ll. 1–2, 6). He now promises to 'Take care, that Plenty swell not into
vice: / Lest by a fiery surfet I be led / Once more to grow devout in a
strange bed:' (ll. 34–6); this, says Gibbs, is 'the most direct reference in
Davenant's poetry to his amorous misadventure'. Commenting on line
32, which refers to 'our Fleet-street Altars', he says this may mean that
Davenant was living in Fleet Street at the time, 'and, if so, it is the only
reference we have to his place of residence in the 1630s'. In fact, we
know that he was living in the Strand – a continuation of Fleet Street –
for in his Bill of Complaint against the tailor Urswick, dated 30 November 1632, he describes himself as being 'of the parishe of the Savoy in the
County of Midd[lesex] gent[leman]'.[12] (Endymion Porter's town house
was then a little further along the Strand going towards Charing Cross,
on the other – north – side.)[13] Urswick, in his Answer of 10 December
1632 to Davenant's Bill, says that in spite of his prolonged efforts to
extract payment from the poet, he failed to get him to court in the
previous August, but that he *did* appear at the end of the Michaelmas
law term, putting in a subpoena against the tailor on about 27 November (three days before entering the Complaint). Urswick also says that
Davenant 'did now of Late obscure himselfe and keepe in some private
places being hard to be mete w[th]all'. It seems therefore that although he
was back (even if temporarily) in London by the end of 1632, during the
summer he had been away – his saviour Porter had perhaps provided
some haven where he could convalesce. It is noticeable that one of the
characters in The Wits,[14] written in the following year, sums up the
capital succinctly as a place of 'smoke, *diseases, law,* and noise [my
italics]' (I.ii, p. 131). Enforced exile is perhaps recalled in some lively
exchanges in the play about the horrors of country life (II.i, pp. 146–7):

Lucy. Pray how do the ladies there? poor villagers,
    They churn still, keep their dairies, and lay up
    For embroidered mantles against the heir's birth . . .
Thwack. Poor country madams, th'are in subjection still;
    The beasts, their husbands, make 'em sit on three
    Legg'd stools, like homely daughters of an hospital,
    To knit socks for their cloven feet.
Elder Pallatine. And when these tyrant husbands, too, grow old,
    As they have still th'impudence to live long,
    Good ladies, they are fain to waste the sweet
    And pleasant seasons of the day in boiling
    Jellies for them, and rolling little pills
    Of cambric lint to stuff their hollow teeth.
Lucy. And then the evenings, warrant ye, they

> Spend with Mother Spectacle, the curate's wife,
> Who does inveigh 'gainst curling and dyed cheeks;
> Heaves her devout impatient nose at oil
> Of jessamine, and thinks powder of Paris more
> Prophane than th'ashes of a Romish martyr.
> *Lady Ample.* And in the days of joy and triumph, sir,
>   Which come as seldom to them as new gowns,
> Then, humble wretches! they do frisk and dance
> In narrow parlours to a single fiddle,
> That squeaks forth tunes like a departing pig . . .
> *Lucy.* And when a stranger comes, send seven
>   Miles post by moon-shine for another pint!

And later the Elder Pallatine speaks (V.iii, p. 223) of

>   dull country madams, that spend
>   Their time in studying receipts to make
>   March-pane and preserve plums; that talk
>   Of painful child-birth, servants' wages, and
>   Their husband's good complexion, and his leg . . .

The subject is partly determined by the theme of the play which strikingly anticipates Restoration comedies – but the lines are written with such conviction that they surely recall the reluctant exile of the young London playwright.

Nethercot deals with the subject of Davenant's illness in a chapter entitled 'Disease and Murder':[15] the 'murder' refers to the stabbing of an ostler called Thomas Warren at Braintree in Essex. In spite of a complete absence of evidence, Nethercot asserts that when the playwright became ill, he went down to stay at 'Davenants', the old family seat at Sible Hedingham, with his distant cousins John and Elizabeth. He was not aware that the couple were living at the other Davenant 'mansion house', 'Russells' at Halstead. In arguing that it was the poet who stabbed the ostler, Nethercot concedes[16] that his account is 'based in a few minor particulars on circumstantial and inferential reasoning', buh he insists that 'the main outlines . . . are clear'. It was J. P. Feil who first challenged Nethercot's proposition[17] – although his account of the Davenant tribe as a whole is incomplete and inaccurate. And it was he who suggested that the murderer was the William Davenant of Essex of whom I have written already. Nethercot does know of the existence of this William, 'not the poet', but he makes nothing of the knowledge.[18] A crucial point in the relevant documents at the PRO (all but one of them in Latin)[19] is that the accused is described as '*Will. Davenett alias Danett nuper de Halstead generosus*' – 'lately of Halstead gentleman' –

which is true not of the poet, but of the young man baptised at Bury St Edmunds in 1607, but later living, along with his brother Edward, at 'Russells' at Halstead, with the childless uncle and aunt John and Elizabeth. Through a misunderstanding of the system of regnal dating, Nethercot places Warren's murder in 1633 instead of 1632; he then dispatches William the poet, his supposed murderer, on an imaginary flight to Holland – although he has to admit that 'naturally the extant records of permissions to leave the country at this time do not reveal his name', and suggests that the poet was tried *in absentia* and sentenced to death. A sentence of transportation – not death – was passed on the murderer, who was eventually pardoned in 1638, after a petition by his wife in the same year:[20] here Nethercot is faced by the insuperable difficulty that she refers to her husband as being 'still absent' – although, as Nethercot concedes, Davenant the poet was 'back in England, perhaps under a suspended sentence' (in fact, of course, he had never left), and was 'moving freely in his old circles by the end of 1633, if not earlier'. Nethercot has to dismiss the words 'still absent' as being a sort of 'legal fiction'.[21]

As a footnote to the story of the stabbing of the ostler, it is interesting and probably relevant that the Essex Davenants at this period were a rackety lot. John of Halstead, the uncle of William the murderer, had himself stabbed a man in 1602.[22] Not only that: according to the Holman MSS in the Essex Record Office mentioned in Chapter One, Edward, William's elder brother, was 'eventually hang'd at Chelmsford for a Robbery committed some where in Suffolk'; Holman adds, in a marginal note, 'This Edward was famous for Robbing.' Feil also speaks of Edward's attempting to rape a woman at Sible Hedingham in her husband's presence, and of the brothers Edward and William attacking a clothmaker of Braintree.

As Feil cogently remarks, a major difficulty for Nethercot, in trying to pin Warren's murder on the poet, is 'the total absence of reference to the crime in an exceedingly scurrilous age, one in which such close friends as Suckling frequently and publicly reminded Davenant of his decayed nose and in which such legal and poetic adversaries as Urswick, Shirley and May would not have hesitated to blacken their antagonist's name by calling him a murderer'. To that I add the complete silence of John Aubrey, who would have found the story of the ostler of Braintree irresistible.

By 1633 Davenant was better – and how much better can be judged from *The Wits*, which by the end of the year had been not only completed, but read by Endymion Porter, by Sir Henry Herbert the

Master of the Revels who had to license it, and probably by King Charles. Davenant had written four full-length plays before his illness, no mean feat for a man in his early twenties, but the new one was the first comedy – and it marks a great advance from previous work, being assured, lively and now set firmly in an authentic seventeenth-century London. There are copious references to such places as the landing-stage at Billingsgate, archery at Finsbury, 'the decays of Fleet Ditch', Spring Garden, Hyde Park, Cheapside, the stalls of Lombard Street, the Dutch brewers of Ratcliffe, Temple Garden, Tower Wharf, Covent Garden and the silk-knitters of Cock Lane; and – in scenes with constable Snore (V.ii, pp. 210, 215, and iii, p. 217) – to such evidently topical offences as stealing a font-cover, the vicar's surplice, the brasses of an alderman and his two sons from his tomb, and all the pulpit-cushions, hearse-cloths and winding-sheets 'that have been stol'n about the town this year'. The editors of the plays boldly declare that in their opinion, The Wits is 'the most perfect comedy as regards plot, character, and language that appeared during the latter portion of the reign of Charles I, or the earlier part of that of his son'. When it was published in quarto in 1636, the playwright's friend Carew contributed verses saying that he had feasted his epicurean appetite 'With relishes so curious, as dispense / The utmost pleasure to the ravish'd sense'.

The Wits was to become Davenant's most long-lasting success: he revived it for the opening of his new theatre in Lincoln's Inn Fields after the Restoration, and the first performance on 15 August 1661 was attended by Charles II, and by his brother the Duke of York (after whom the theatre was named) and his Duchess – the daughter of Lord Clarendon with whom Davenant had lodged when they were young. Also present was Samuel Pepys, who adjudged it 'a most excellent play'. Indeed, so pleased with it was he that he went again two days later, with his friend Captain Ferrers; this time the King's widowed aunt the Queen of Bohemia was present, with her faithful admirer Lord Craven. A characteristically rueful Pepysian note follows: 'So the Captain and I and another to the Divell tavern and drank; and so by coach home – troubled in mind that I cannot bring myself to mind my business, but to be so much in love with plays.' The Wits had an unusually long run, of '8 days Acting Successively':[23] on the 23rd Pepys was back again, this time with Elizabeth, and again he was 'most highly pleased'.[24]

Sir Henry Herbert had been reluctant to license the play, and Endymion Porter had had to intervene on his friend's behalf. Herbert's entry in his records, dated 9 January 1633/4, sheds revealing light on the characters of the King, his Master of the Revels and the dramatist:

This morning . . . the kinge was pleased to call mee into his withdrawinge chamber to the windowe, wher he went over all that I had croste in Davenants play-booke, and allowing of *faith* and *slight* to bee asseverations only, and no oathes, markt them to stande, and some other few things, but in the greater part allowed of my reformations. This was done upon a complaint of Mr. Endymion Porters in December.

The kinge is pleased to take *faith, death, slight,* for asseverations, and no oaths, to which I doe humbly submit as my masters judgment; but, under favour, conceive them to be oaths, and enter them here, to declare my opinion and submission.

The 10 of January . . . I returned unto Mr. Davenant his play-booke of *The Witts,* corrected by the kinge.

The kinge would not take the booke at Mr. Porters hands; but commanded him to bring it unto mee, which he did, and likewise commanded Davenant to come to me for it, as I believe: otherwise he would not have byn so civill.[25]

As C. V. Wedgwood remarks,[26] King Charles showed 'surprising realism' in restoring Davenant's expletives; the incident is interesting, too, in showing how directly he was prepared to intervene in such matters. The play was finally licensed on 19 January, and performed by the King's Men at Blackfriars as *The Cruel Brother* and *The Just Italian* had been. (It was printed in 1636, and on the title-page the author is described as 'Servant to Her Majestie'.) In addition to being put on at Blackfriars, Herbert notes that there was a performance 'on tusday night the 28 January . . . at Court, before the King and Queene. Well likt.' Since there was obviously no love lost between him and the dramatist, he may be underplaying the King's approval when he continues: 'It had a various fate on the stage, and at court, though the kinge commended the language, but dislikt the plott and characters.'[27] He would surely have expressed his 'dislike' earlier if that had been so.

It will be remembered that when *The Just Italian* was printed in 1630, the playwright had expressed much concern about 'malice', and 'those many that came with resolution to dispraise'. Now, in his poem addressed 'To Endymion Porter, When my Comedy (Call'd *The Wits*) was presented at Black-Fryars',[28] he writes:

I that am told *conspiracies are laid,*
To have my Muse, her Arts, and life betray'd,
Hope for no easie Judge; though thou wert there,
T'appease, and make their *judgements lesse severe* . . .

adding defiantly:

But I am growne too tame! what need I feare
Whilst not to passion, but thy reason cleere?

> Should I perceive thy knowledge were subdu'd
> T'unkinde consent with *the harsh Multitude,*
> Then I had cause to weepe . . .   (ll. 9–12, 21–5)

In his dedication of the play to Porter, 'The Chiefly Belov'd Of All That Are Ingenious and Noble', he says that having saved his life, his patron 'then rescu'd his work from *a cruel faction*; which nothing but the forces of your reason, and your reputation, could subdue'; and the Prologue begins:

> Bless me you kinder Starrs! How are we throng'd?
> Alass! whom hath our harmless Poet wrong'd,
> That he should meet together in one day
> A Session, and *a Faction* at his Play,
> To judge, and to condemne? . . .[29]   (ll. 1–5)

All the italics are mine. Perhaps there was some continuing and organised puritan opposition to this royalist poet and playwright;[30] probably, too, there was resentment over his steady preferment at Court.

The theme of *The Wits* is not courtly wit, but people living on their wits – the phrase constantly recurs. The Elder Pallatine and his friend Sir Morglay Thwack have come up to London, a journey of eighty miles, to pursue women; as Thwack puts it to the Younger Pallatine, who lives in the capital:

> Your brother and myself have seal'd
> To covenants. The female youth o'th' town are his;
> But all from forty to fourscore mine own.
> A widow, you'll say, is a wise, solemn, wary
> Creature. Though she hath liv'd to th'cunning
> Of dispatch, clos'd up nine husbands' eyes,
> And have the wealth of all their testaments,
> In one month, sir,
> I will waste her to her first wedding-smock,
> Her single ring, bodkin, and velvet muff . . .   (I.ii, pp. 135–6)

Young Pallatine shrewdly observes: 'But, sirs, / The city, take't on my experiment, / Will not be gull'd' – and so, of course, it proves. The country gentlemen endure many embarrassing experiences, engineered by the charming Lucy and the 'Inheritrix' Lady Ample, including being locked up in a chest, relieved of money and a diamond hatband, lured to supposed assignations and surprised by Snore the constable, Mistress Snore his wife, her neighbour Mistress Queasy and the watch (more Shakespearean echoes here). In the end Lady Ample agrees to marry the chastened Elder Pallatine, provided it is understood that she has 'the better wit / And can subdue you still to quietness, / Meek sufferings, and patient awe' (V.iii, p. 220); and Thwack makes the Younger Pallatine his heir, enabling him to marry Lucy, rescuing her from the 'cruel aunt' about whom so much has been heard during the play, a 'rich old hen' who will now be expected to provide a celebratory dinner after the Elder Pallatine has gone to church with his bride to secure her 'skittish person'.

Lady Ample had herself been living on her wits, as she explained to Lucy earlier in the piece:

> My guardian's contribution gave us gowns:
> But cut from th'curtains of a carrier's bed:
> Jewels wee wore, but such as potters' wives
> Bake in the furnace for their daughters' wrists:
> My woman's smocks so coarse, as they were spun
> O'th' tackling of a ship . . .
> Our diet scarce so much as is prescrib'd
> To mortify: two eggs of emmets, poach'd,
> A single bird, no bigger than a bee,
> Made up a feast.   (II.i, p. 140)

This exemplifies one of the engaging stylistic features of Davenant's writing, his delight in things tiny. There are examples in *The Just Italian,* and of course in the mock-epic about the dwarf Jeffrey, but it is much more pronounced in *The Wits.* To the young mercenaries Pert and Meager, just returned from service abroad and off to Billingsgate to unship their trunks, the Younger Pallatine says:

> Why such haste? do not I know,
> That a mouse yok'd to a peascod may draw,
> With the frail cordage of one hair, your goods
> About the world?
> *Pert.* Why, we have linen, sir.
> *Y.P.* As much, sir, as will fill a tinder-box,
> Or make a frog a shirt . . .   (I.i, p. 122)

(The passage recalls Mercutio's Queen Mab speech in *Romeo and Juliet,* and the fairies in *A Midsummer Night's Dream.*)

To the two girls, the Elder Pallatine says:

> if you'll needs marry,
> Expect not a single turf for a jointure;
> Not so much land as will allow a grasshopper
> A salad.   (II.i, p. 148)

Sometimes the poet goes to the other extreme, as when he writes of an upper room hung with cobwebs,

> and those so large they may
> Catch and ensnare dragons instead of flies,
> Where sit a melancholy race of old
> Norman spiders, that came in with th'Conqueror.   (II.iii, p. 156)

And he has a talent for evoking a sharp image with great economy, as when Thwack speaks of

> the dexterity
> Of a spaniel, that with a yawn, a scratch
> On his left ear, and stretching his hind legs,
> Is ready for all day.   (III.iii, p. 174)

In the Epilogue to the play as printed in 1636, Davenant writes once again of his wish 'To guide *severer judgements* [my italics] (if we could / Be wise enough) until they thought all good, / Which they perhaps dislike . . .'.[31]

The next play, *Love and Honour* (not printed until 1649),[32] was put on only a matter of months after *The Wits* – it was licensed on 20 November 1634 and performed at Blackfriars in December. It might almost be by a different man, and shows how hard (and how success-fully) the versatile author sought to please his new royal mistress, for the Queen had it revived at Hampton Court on New Year's Day 1636/7. Presumably, like its predecessor, it was at first 'likt' at Court rather than by the public: but it did well on the commercial stage when Davenant brought it back after the Restoration, and once again it met with the full approval of Pepys: he attended the first performance on 21 October 1661, went again on the 23rd, and took Elizabeth on the 25th: 'a play so good that it hath been acted but three times and I have seen them all, and all in this week'.[33] John Evelyn, as usual half-ashamed, went to see it on 11 November: 'I was so idle as to go to see a play called *Love and Honour*.'

The plot of this romantic confection is set in Savoy, and based on the enmity between Italian states: the Duke of Savoy is determined to execute the captive Evandra, heiress of the Duke of Milan, but Savoy's son Prince Alvaro, Count Prospero and a third young man, Leonell, all fall chastely in love with her, and in a contest of chivalry and in the course of a most convoluted plot, they vie – along with Leonell's sister Melora – to sacrifice their lives to save Evandra's. Prospero, who had been expecting praise for capturing her ('I thought I had done well . . . she was the daughter of our greatest enemy'), is taken aback by Alvaro's anger:

> had I
> Encounter'd her in the mad heat of chace,

> In all the fury of the fight, I would
> Have taught my angry steed the easy and
> The peaceful motion of a lamb,
> She should have set his back, soft as the air,
> And in her girdle bridle[d] him, more curb'd
> Than in his foaming bit, whilst I, her slave,
> Walk'd by, marking what hasty flowers sprung up,
> Invited by her eyebeams from their cold roots . . .   (Act I, pp. 109–10)

– a quotation which conveys some idea of the sort of language in which the piece is couched. All ends happily, with Leonell conveniently revealing himself to be (Act V, p. 179) not a mere knight, 'But Leonell the duke of Parma's son, / Heir to his fortune and his fame'; Evandra accepting his hand, and Alvaro that of his sister Melora; and two 'Embassadors' whipping off false beards to reveal themselves as the Duke of Milan and the Duke of Savoy's brother, and joining in the general rejoicings. A much more earthy sub-plot, which may have come more readily to the author's quill, concerns Vasco, a colonel, who had been compelled to marry a rich but old and ugly widow whom he had captured in battle (to a soldier colleague who asked: 'Thou dost not mean / To court her at her window with rare music?' (Act II, p. 128) he had cheerfully replied: 'No! she's very deaf; so that cost is sav'd.') There is a happy ending for him too, for Milan declares: 'What the profits of her dowry / Would have been, I will myself bestow on you.' (Act V, p. 184).[34]

From now on, nearly all Davenant's work was for the Court.

There had been a fundamental difference of opinion between Inigo Jones and Ben Jonson ever since they first collaborated on a Court masque, *The Masque of Blackness* in 1605: Jonson sincerely believed that the dominant role was the writer's – as expressed succinctly in his comparison in *Discoveries* of the poet and the painter, 'the Pen is more noble than the Pencill [brush]'; Jones was equally convinced that the role of the designer was paramount – as Jonson puts it of him in *A Tale of a Tub,*

> Hee'll do't alone, Sir, He will joyne with no man,
> Though he be a Joyner: in designe he cals it,
> He must be sole Inventer . . .

There was increasing ill-feeling between the two men, and by 1618 Jonson was telling Drummond of Hawthornden that 'when he wanted words to express the greatest villaine in the world he would call him ane Inigo'. Matters came to a head in 1631, with the publication of their Christmas and Shrove-tide masques *Loves Triumph through Callipolis* (for the King) and *Chloridia* (for the Queen). Jones was now the acknowledged master of the Court masque, but although Jonson (generously, in his own eyes) put the designer's name on the title-page of *Callipolis,* he put his own first, thus:

> The Inuentors.
> Ben. Ionson.   Inigo Iones.

And on the title-page of *Chloridia,* he put no names at all. The two never collaborated again.[35]

This gave an opportunity for younger men. Next Christmas, the young poet Aurelian Townshend was commissioned. For the season of 1633/4, the King suggested that the Inns of Court present him with a masque, and Shirley wrote *The Triumph of Peace*; a fortnight later in February, the King danced in *Coelum Britannicum,* by Davenant's friend Thomas Carew.[36] Finally the choice fell upon William Davenant himself, and he wrote all the remaining Caroline masques. Needless to say, he made no attempt to challenge the supremacy of Inigo Jones – and through his appointment he was able to acquire experience which would be invaluable to him as a theatre manager at the Restoration.

In addition to the Queen's love of romantic comedy, which had led to his writing *Love and Honour,* he now had to contend with the fashionable Neo-Platonism which so appealed to her. Anne Barton has recently written[37] that this 'represented an attempt to reform the sexual licence of the court according to the model provided by the royal marriage. . . . On the evidence of James Howell's *Familiar Letters,* Neo-Platonism as a court game . . . did not manifest itself until 1634. . . . This would seem to be the point at which a serious idea became trivialized, so that Davenant in his masque *The Temple of Love* (1635), and in his comedy *The Platonic Lovers* (1636), could laugh at its fashionable excesses while retaining respect for, indeed glorifying, its embodiment in the union of the king and queen'. The novel conception of platonic love, and plans for a Court masque on the subject, had been arousing considerable interest and speculation for months, and in a letter to Philip Warwick in Paris on 3 June 1634, Howell reported that the only real Court news was of 'a Love call'd *Platonick Love,* which much sways there of late; it is a Love abstracted from all corporeal gross Impressions and sensual Appetites, but consists in Contemplations and Ideas of the Mind, not in any Carnal Fruition. This Love sets the Wits of the Town on work; and they say there will be a Mask shortly of it, whereof Her Majesty, and her Maids of Honour, will be part'.[38]

The Temple of Love,[39] 'By Inigo Jones, Surveyor of his Maties Workes, and William Davenant, her Maties Servant', was put on at

Whitehall on Shrove Tuesday, 10 February, with the Queen and fourteen of her ladies taking part, while nine 'Lords and others' played
'Noble Persian Youths'. It was the last Court masque ever staged in
Jones's great Banqueting House.[40] Divine Poesy descends 'in a great
cloud of a rosy colour' to inform Queen Indamora of Narsinga (Henrietta Maria) that the ordained time has come for the Temple of Chaste
Love to be re-established in Britain. Its enemies, three magicians, come
forth from underground caves, 'their persons deformed'; Magician No.
3 ruefully declares that the Queen and the beauties of her Court,

> Though they discover summer in their looks,
> Still carry frozen Winter in their blood.
> They raise strange doctrines, and new sects of Love:
> Which must not woo or court the person, but
> The mind; and practice generation not
> Of bodies but of souls . . .

> . . . Is there not [asks No. 2]

> One courtier will resent the cause, and give
> Some countenance to the affairs of the body?

to which No. 3 replies

> Certain young Lords at first disliked the philosophy
> As most uncomfortable, sad, and new;
> But soon inclin'd to a superior vote,
> And are grown as good Platonical lovers
> As are to be found in an hermitage, where he
> That was born last reckons above fourscore.

The masque ends on the familiar Caroline theme of the royal marriage as an ideal pattern, with Chaste Love flying down, 'clad all in
Carnation and White', to invoke 'the last and living Hero', Charles,
now seated beside his Queen.[41]

The Platonic Lovers[42] followed a few months later: it was licensed on
16 November, performed at Blackfriars by the King's Men, and printed
in 1636. This time Davenant dedicated his play to the Queen's favourite
Henry Jermyn, whom he invites to 'be pleas'd to become my first reader.
If it shall gain your liking, the severe rulers of the stage will be much
mended in opinion; and then it may be justly acknowledg'd you have
recover'd all the declining fame, belonging to Your Unfortunate
Servant, William D'avenant'.

In his Prologue, the poet speaks of his bafflement at 'the Title' – the
word 'platonick', which he had 'learned first' at Court and was at a loss
to write about as commanded: at first he had thought the play would
'take', because of the novelty of the subject, but then he feared that more

than half the city audience would be lost, 'That knew not how to spell it on the post' – the posts near the theatre on which playbills were exhibited. And it seems that his hopes of a popular success were indeed not realised, although the piece was reprinted in 1665 with *The Wits* under the title 'Two Excellent Plays'.

The play is set in Sicily, and Duke Theander and Eurithea – 'lovers of a pure Cœlestial kind, such as some style Platonical; / A new court epithet scarce understood' (Act I, p. 17) – are contrasted with Duke Phylomont and Theander's sister Ariola, who 'still affect / For natural ends . . . such a way as libertines call lust, / But peaceful politicks and cold divines / Name matrimony'. Buonateste, a physician and philosopher, provides an aphrodisiac to be administered to Theander, to make him less 'platonical' – although talk of another character's being 'very much platonically given' rouses Buonateste to indignation:

> My Lord, I still beseech you not to wrong
> My good old friend Plato, with this Court calumny;
> They father on him a fantastic love
> He never knew, poor gentleman. Upon
> My knowledge, sir, about two thousand years
> Ago, in the high street yonder
> At Athens, just by the corner as you pass
> To Diana's conduit, – a haberdasher's house,
> It was, I think, – he kept a wench!

When Phylomont asks Theander's permission to marry his sister, a lengthy debate ensues:

> *Theander.* How! marry her! your souls are wedded, sir,
> I'm sure you would not marry bodies too;
> That were a needless charge . . .
>   . . . To what purpose would you marry her?
> *Phylomont.* Why, sir? to lye with her, and get children.
> *Theander.* Lye with my sister, Phylomont? how vile
> And horridly that sounds! . . .
> *Phylomont.* This is strange, being married, is't not lawful, sir?
> *Theander.* I grant it may be law, but is it comely? . . .
> *Phylomont.* But who shall make men, sir; shall the world cease?
>
> (Act II, pp. 42–3)

Theander concedes that some people must produce those who are to 'fill up armies, villages, / And city shops; that killing, labour, and / That coz'ning still may last', but he himself wants no part of such 'coarse and homely drudgeries'. However, he eventually does agree to the marriage; and by the end of the play he is coming round to the idea of marriage for himself, with Eurithea (Phylomont's sister); 'I shall incline in time' (Act V, p. 104).

By now William Davenant was still only in his twenties: yet in addition to numerous poems, he had already written seven full-length plays – four (two apparently unperformed) before his illness, and *The Wits*, *Love and Honour* and *The Platonic Lovers* in 1634 and 1635. In addition he had written his first Court masque, *The Temple of Love*, in 1635, and had become the 'Servant of Her Majesty' – in the words of his widow, the Queen 'did graciously take him into her family', a nice description of Henrietta Maria's Household.[43] But none of this would have earned him much money: sales of such plays as had been printed would not be very profitable, and the plays themselves had been put on at the 'private theatre' at Blackfriars. Becoming the Queen's Servant would also not have been profitable in cash terms. So in the summer, Davenant also wrote a play for the commercial theatre, the Globe on Bankside – the only one of his early plays known to have been performed there, and certainly the only one expressly written for it. The piece is called *News from Plymouth*;[44] it was licensed on 1 August, and presumably staged soon afterwards. As the author acknowledges in the Prologue, there is not much plot: 'This house, and season, does more promise shows, / Dancing, and buckler fights, than art or wit' – but he hopes the play will 'please those that do not expect too much'. The fact that it did not appear in print until the 1673 folio suggests that it did not 'please', but it is nevertheless a lively piece, with sharply – drawn sketches of contemporary characters. These are headed by three captains of the fleet – Seawit, Cable and Topsail – 'wind-bound' in a dull port, and naturally all broke. In terms appropriate to such men in any age, one of them complains:

> This town is dearer than Jerusalem
> After a year's siege; they would make us pay
> For day-light, if they knew how to measure
> The sun-beams by the yard. Nay, sell the very
> Air too if they could serve it out in fine
> China-bottles. If you walk but three turns
> In the High-street, they will ask you money
> For wearing out the pebbles.   (Act I, pp. 111–12)

The place is also 'vilely destitute of women'. The trio try to win the affections of the wealthy Widow Carrack and her guests Lady Loveright and Mistress Jointure without becoming committed to matrimony – that 'fool's noose', as one of them calls it. In this they fail, and when the wind 'stands fair' and they are recalled to duty, Lady Loveright has remained faithful to her suitor Warwell. However, Mistress Jointure and Widow Carrack hold out hopes of matrimony to Seawit and Cable when they return, and Topsail says he may 'find a wife too' (Act V, pp. 198–9). Among the other characters are Bumble, a comic Dutch captain, and such Jonsonian figures as Lady Loveright's uncle Sir Solemn Trifle, 'a country knight' Sir Furious Inland, and Scarecrow, Zeal and Prattle, 'Intelligencers'.

The play includes two songs[45] – one a charming aubade sung by Topsail to Lady Loveright:

> O thou that sleep'st like *Pigg* in Straw,
>   Thou Lady dear, arise!
> Open (to keep the Sun in awe)
>   Thy pretty pinking [blinking] eyes:
> And, having stretcht each Leg and Arme,
>   Put on your cleane white Smock,
> And then I pray, to keep you warme,
>   A *Petticote* on *Dock*.
> Arise, Arise! Why should you sleep,
>   When you have slept enough? . . .
> The Shops were open'd long before,
>   And youngest Prentice goes
> To lay at's Mrs. Chamber-doore
>   His Master's shining Shooes.
> Arise, arise; your Breakfast stayes . . .

In the course of the play, Captain Cable speaks of its now being 'dead Vacation' time in London (Act V, p. 182), and Davenant's poem 'The Long Vacation in London, in Verse Burlesque, or Mock-Verse', almost certainly dates to the same year, 1635.[46] This is a splendid evocation of seventeenth-century London in late summer, when the law-courts were closed. The 'Town-wit' has departed for the country, and the prostitute laments that her earnings will be small until the new term 'brings up weak Countrey Heir';[47] the 'Gamster poor' sneaks away early in the morning (on a very slow mount) because he can no longer pay his rent; and four humble apprentices, jumping for joy that they have completed their seven year terms, 'Hire meagre Steeds, to ride and see / Their Parents old, who dwell as near / As Place call'd *Peake* in *Derby-shire*'. The out-of-work actor sits all day in a rowing-boat, fishing the river with worms for eels. Among the better-off, the Lord Mayor

> > on Sadle new,
> Rides into Fare of *Bartholemew*:
> He twirles his Chain, and looketh big,
> As if to fright the Head of Pig,
> That gaping lies on greasy Stall . . .   (ll. 91–5)

– a reminder of Jonson's great play. The Alderman, the 'wealthy Blade', the attorney and the 'aged Proctor' spend the day practising archery at Finsbury; others go off to Islington for syllabub, cream and duck-hunting on the ponds – as soon as the shopkeeper learns that his wife and daughter have departed in a hackney-coach, with a tasty picnic in 'Snow White Clout', he follows ('Fetch *Job* my son, and our dog *Ruffe!*') – ll. 97–110, 21–38. The village was one of the most popular places for a day's outing for Londoners – in later years, Samuel and Elizabeth Pepys were very often among them.

At intervals throughout the poem there are affecting references to the 'small poet . . . call'd *Will*' – obviously himself – lurking in his garret:

> From little lump triangular
> Poor Poets sighes are heard afar.
> Quoth he, do noble Numbers chuse
> To walk on feet that have no shoose? (ll. 61–4)

But he has to go out to the theatre, to placate the impatient company:

> Then forth he steales; to Globe does run;
> And smiles, and vowes Four Acts are done:
> *Finis* to bring he does protest,
> Tells ev'ry Play'r, his part is best.
> And all to get (as Poets use)
> Some Coyne in Pouche to solace Muse. (ll. 75–80)

Finally an importunate friend accosts him in the street – 'old Rogue! what living still?' – and tries to borrow money, although the poet protests that he has only got a crown:

> But stay my frighted Pen is fled;
> My self through fear creep under Bed;
> For just as Muse would scribble more,
> Fierce City *Dunne* did rap at Door. (ll. 169–72)

It recalls the earlier poem 'To I. C. . . .', halted when someone knocked at the door with an apothecary's bill. It must be a tribute to Davenant's talent and charm, and to the continuing generosity of his friends, that he ever kept his head above water.

The Palatine Princes – the King's nephews Charles and Rupert – came to London in the following winter of 1635–6; Van Dyck's fine portrait of them in armour, now in the Louvre, was painted before they left in midsummer 1637. Very soon after their arrival, Davenant was commissioned to write a masque for their entertainment.[48] It had been intended to put this on as part of the Christmas revels,[49] and the poet explains, in his note 'To Every Reader' in the printed edition of 1636, that the masque had been 'devis'd and written in three days'. It would have been a good thing 'if the presentation had been so suddenly perform'd as it was prepared'. But the Queen had given birth to Princess Elizabeth on 28 December, and performance had been delayed until 24 February. Davenant had had no opportunity to revise his work, and he feared that 'in a malignant time' this would give scope to his critics.

The masque was put on at the Middle Temple, with settings not by Inigo Jones but by 'Mr Corseilles'; the musical settings were by the King's Servants, the brothers Henry and William Lawes. Henry (1596–1662) was the leading English songwriter of the mid-seventeenth century, and set songs for many other poets also, including Carew, Suckling, Herrick, Lovelace – and Milton, whose sonnet 'To my Friend Mr Henry Lawes' begins: '*Harry,* whose tunefull and well-measur'd song / First taught our English music how to span / Words with just note and accent . . .'. William (1602–45) was an instrumental as well as vocal composer; he was killed at the siege of Chester.[50]

The masque for the young Princes was called *The Triumphs of the Prince D'Amour,* 'Prince d'Amour' being the title of the man chosen by fellow-members of the Middle Temple to preside over their revels. The theme – inevitably, as there had been so little time to prepare – is very slight: the main action, which is interspersed with comic antimasques, shows the Knights Templars being influenced in turn by Priests of Mars, Venus and Apollo. It ends with twelve of the performers, 'wildly habited', advancing towards the Princes and setting down a banquet of 'precious fruits', resting on leafy branches and 'covered with blossomed twigs and flowers'.

The Queen attended the performance, wearing 'a citizens habitt' – as did her four ladies – and sitting with the rest of the audience; her four male attendants included Henry Jermyn. 'The Masque was very well performed', Sir Henry Herbert reports,[51] 'in the dances, scenes, cloathinge, and musique, and the Queene was pleased to tell mee at her going away, that she liked it very well.'

At the end of the printed text, the author – still concerned about hostile criticism – expresses the hope that the piece 'may live . . . a while, if the envy of such as were absent do not rebuke the courteous memory of those who vouchsafed to enjoy it.'

CHAPTER FIVE

1637–40
Poet Laureate;
·rehearsal for war

❧⊙⊂❧

Between *The Temple of Love* on Shrove Tuesday 1635 and *Britannia Triumphans* in January 1638, there were no masques at Court (although the last of the Queen's pastorals, a French play called *Florimène*, was performed by her maids-of-honour in the Great Hall of Whitehall Palace on 21 December 1635).[1] In the interim, the ceiling of the Banqueting House was being 'richly adorn'd with pieces of painting of great value, figuring the acts of King James of happy memory, and other enrichments', as Davenant's introduction to *Britannia* explains.[2] Thus austerely does he phrase the first public reference to the great works by Rubens which are still in place. It had rightly been feared that they 'might suffer by the smoke of many lights' from the clusters of candles, and the King had instructed his Surveyor of the Works, Inigo Jones, to have 'a new temporary room of timber' built for masques.

In the summer of 1637, during the enforced 'intermission', as Davenant calls it, he and his friends Jack Young and Sir John Suckling (he had been knighted in 1630) made the trip to Bath described by John Aubrey. It was of course Davenant himself who supplied Aubrey with most of the information about his 'intimate friend' on which the *Life* of Suckling[3] is based. He had a 'readie Sparkling witt', and was 'the greatest gallant of his time; and the greatest Gamester, both for Bowling & Cards . . . of middle stature & slight strength . . . his hayre a kind of sand colour . . . a briske & graceful looke'. For the trip to Bath he 'came like a young Prince for all manner of Equipage & convenience', and with 'a Cart-load of Books'. There is a lyrical beauty (no doubt partly at least derived from Davenant) about Aubrey's account of those vanished days: ' 'Twas as pleasant a journey as ever men had; in the height of a long Peace & luxury, and in the Venison Season. The 2d night they lay at Marlborough, and walking on the delicate fine downes at ye Backside of the Towne, whilest supper was making ready, the maydes were drying of cloathes on the bushes . . .'. From Marlborough – where

Davenant and Suckling played an elaborate practical joke on Young, which made them 'ready to dye with laughter' – the three young men went on to Bronham House, '(then a noble seate, since burnt in the civill warres) . . . where they were nobly entertained severall dayes'; and thence to West Kington to stay with Parson Davenant, William's elder brother – 'where they stayed a weeke, mirth, witt, & good cheer flowing'. It will be remembered that John Davenant their father was described as 'a very grave and discreet Citizen', and Anthony Wood further declared that he was 'of a melancholic disposition, and was seldom or never seen to laugh, in which he was imitated by none of his children but by Robert his eldest son'. The description both of the father and of his eldest son would seem to be belied by the account of the entertainment at West Kington in 1637. But the visitors were not entirely frivolous young men: from time to time they evidently gave considerable thought to problems of religion. Robert Davenant told Aubrey that Suckling wrote his 'tract on Socinianism . . . at the Table in the parlour of the Parsonage' before the party left for Bath, 'six or 7 miles'. (This tract was his *An Account of Religion by Reason*.)[4] As for Davenant, Aubrey notes right at the end of his *Life*: 'His private opinion was, that Religion, at last (e.g. a hundred yeares hence – would come to settlement and that in a kind of ingeniose Quakerisme.'; a Puritan writer on royalist heresies, however, wrote in *The Cavaliers Bible* (1644) of 'Gnostici . . . who attribute every thing to the Fates: as if there were so many masculine and feminine gods, as *Davenant* their Commander and the Poets have fained'.[5]

The year 1638 was notable in Davenant's professional career, with the production of two Court masques, *Britannia Triumphans* and *Luminalia,* and two plays, *The Unfortunate.Lovers* and *The Fair Favourite,* the publication of his first collection of poems and his appointment as poet laureate.

After the 'three yeares of intermission' in which the King and Queen made no 'Masques and intermedii', as Davenant puts it, they now resumed their custom of exchanging masques at Christmas and Shrovetide. Rubens's great canvases for the Banqueting House had actually been completed in his Antwerp studio by 1634, but trouble over export and import dues delayed their dispatch for a year;[6] his fee of £3,000 was paid in two instalments in 1637 and 1638, and he also received a gold chain.

A special entry in the large parchment roll covering expenditure by the Office of the Works from October 1637 to October 1638[7] describes the 'temporary room of timber' (which, as Davenant says, was completed in two months) as 'the greate new *MASKING ROOME ATT*

WHITEHALL': it was 112 feet long, 57 feet wide and 59 feet high, and thus slightly larger than the Banqueting House itself, which was 110 feet by 55 feet by 55 feet, a double cube.[8] The structure was built of oak, deal and fir, with brick from foundations to floor and with a roof of pantiles; it was 'supported with xij greate Butteresses' of fir, and there were 'fouer p[ai]res of staires to goe vpp into the same roome', and twenty windows of 'firtimber', ten in the upper and ten in the lower part of the building. A detailed list follows of all the materials used, down to '2 mopps' at twelve pence, and including twelve dozen candles at six pence a dozen, £72, and 'Blew cloth to cover the Ceeling of the said Masking roome', £22 5s 3d. The 'roome' stood in the Preaching Court behind (that is, on the river side of) the Banqueting House, and a contemporary describes it as being 'betwixt the Guard-Chamber and the Banqueting house'.[9]

Assessment of the Court masque has changed radically in the past century. The Victorian editors of Davenant's dramatic works write unsympathetically of Inigo Jones (especially, of course, in connexion with his relationship with Jonson); they speak[10] of Shakespeare's plays in their own day failing to command an audience 'unless aided by the artist's brush, an unlimited supply of Dutch metal, and the employment of mechanical appliances' – with the strong implication that these words apply equally to Jones. Now opinion has swung round: we appreciate the magnitude of Jones's achievement, and acknowledge that he was the principal 'inventor' of the masques, the texts being 'a relatively small part of a complex whole'.[11]

The central theme of Rubens's paintings for the Banqueting House, as commissioned by King Charles, is a declaration of the principles of government and religion for which he stood, and for which he was to die – and above all the principle of the Divine Right of Kings. Peace and prosperity, in his view, could be achieved only through wise monarchical rule. This is summed up in his words: 'We have no other intention but by our government to honour Him by Whom Kings reign and to procure the good of our people, and for this end to preserve the right and authority wherewith God hath vested us.'[12] Beside that must be set his view of the masques, as set out by William Davenant in the introduction to *Britannia Triumphans*: 'Princes of sweet and humane natures have ever, both amongst the ancients and moderns in the best times, presented spectacles and personal representations, to recreate their spirits wasted in grave affairs of State, and for the entertainment of their nobility, ladies, and court.' That is, the masques were *private*; and, alongside his conception of the duties of sovereignty, Charles believed equally in the absolute propriety of 'spectacles' intended to refresh the sovereign and to entertain his intimates. Stephen Orgel and Roy Strong, in their *Inigo Jones: The Theatre of the Stuart Court* (1973),[13] argue that the Caroline masques served as symbolic justification of the royal position on current issues, and that the King was, in part, using the spectacles to control the popular response to royal policy; and more recently, Orgel has written[14] that as the masque is viewed in political and social terms, 'the concept of flattery grows increasingly irrelevant ... praise of the monarch was educative and cautionary as well as complimentary', and the masques were 'often critical and satiric as well as laudatory'. This would seem to underplay the entirely private and 'recreative' nature of the performances: and the terms 'educative and cautionary' are not easily applied to the next two masques, *Britannia Triumphans* and *Luminalia,* although the last one of all, *Salmacida Spolia,* is undoubtedly written in more sober and less adulatory terms.

A burning topic in 1638, when *Britannia* was put on, was the hated ship-money tax, the ostensible reason for which was to clear the seas of pirates; and the subject of the masque is set out thus: 'Britanocles [the King], the glory of the western world, [who] hath by his wisdom, valour, and piety, not only vindicated his own, but far distant seas, infested with pirates, and reduc'd the land, by his example, to a real knowledge of all good acts and sciences.' Jones's opening scene, a prospect of London, is transformed to a 'horrid hell', where Merlin the magician summons up the antimasques – a ballad-singer, porter, kitchenmaid, crier of mouse-traps and the like, plus such historical 'rebellious Leaders in war' as Cade, Kett and Jack Straw. After a light-hearted mock romanza in a 'vast wood' with damsel and dwarf, knight and squire, and a giant, and including such pantomine lines as: 'I'll strike thee till thou sink where the abode is / Of wights that sneak below, called Antipodes', a gold and silver palace rises up; Fame sings: 'Breake forth thou Treasure of our sight ... Thou universall wonder'; and Britanocles, supported by his fourteen Lords, is revealed (his apparel alone cost £150).[15] The Chorus, of poets 'in rich habits of several colours', sings: '*Britanocles,* the great and good appeares, / His Person fils our eyes, his name our eares, / His vertue every drooping spirit cheers! ...', and the masque ends with dancing, and a 'great fleet' entering a haven to represent the King's alleged sovereignty of the seas.[16]

Nethercot[17] finds 'the malignity of the popular party' towards this masque 'somewhat hard to account for'; he does, however, concede that staging it on a Sunday – the Sunday after Twelfth Night – was not calculated to dispel criticism. Some years later, during the civil war, the Parliamentary news-sheet *Mercurius Britanicus* (1643) was to write caustically that it had been 'an old fashion at Court, amongst the Protestants there, to shut up the *Sabbath* with some wholesome Piece of *Ben Johnson* or *Davenant*, a kinde of *Comicall Divinity*'; and in 1645 it was alleged that the masques at Whitehall had been 'maintained with *Ship-money*'.[18]

The Queen commissioned from Inigo Jones her 'reply' to *Britannia Triumphans*: 'to make a new subject of a Masque for her selfe, that with high and hearty invention, might give occasion for variety of Scenes, strange aparitions, Songs, Musick and dancing of severall kinds . . .'.[19] The result was *Luminalia or The Festival of Light*, performed by Henrietta Maria and her ladies on the night of Shrove Tuesday, 6 February. The subject is the struggle between darkness and light, and the masque opens with a moonlit scene in which Night appears in a chariot 'drawne by two great Owles'. Aurcra and Hesperus debate in song the sun's delay:

> *Hesperus.* What is the cause he then so long doth stay?
> *Aurora.*   He hath resign'd the pow'r of making day
>   Throughout this Hemisphere,
>   To a terrestr'all beautie here . . .

at which Henrietta Maria is revealed seated at the back of the stage surrounded by splendidly dressed ladies; in the final transformation scene, Zephyrs dance on 'a bright and transparent cloud'.[20] *Luminalia* was Inigo Jones's most elaborate aerial spectacle.

After these two masques in January and February, Davenant's play *The Unfortunate Lovers*[21] was licensed on 16 April, acted before the Queen and Court at Blackfriars on the 23rd, performed at the Cockpit at Whitehall in May and at Hampton Court in September. It was revived at the Restoration – in 1660, and when Davenant secured the monopoly of his own plays, at his theatre in Lincoln's Inn Fields, where it became a stock piece. Pepys saw it four times – on 7 March 1663/4, when he was 'not much pleased with it; though I know not where to lay the fault – unless it was that the house was very empty, by reason of a new play at the other house' (the Theatre Royal, Drury Lane); on 11 September 1667; and twice in 1668, in April ('no extraordinary play methinks'), and December ('a mean play I think, but some parts very good, and excellently acted').[22] The performance he saw in April was on the 8th; on the 7th he had been at the rival theatre, and it was while he was in Mrs Knepp's dressing-room after the play that he heard the news that 'Sir W Davenant is just now dead'. (His company, in performing *The Unfortunate Lovers* on the 8th, were faithful to the principle that 'the show must go on').

Most modern readers would probably agree with Pepys that *The Unfortunate Lovers* is 'no extraordinary play': it has a highly involved plot, with much rather clumsy explanation by minor characters of developments off-stage, and a blood-stained ending leaving only one of the six principals alive. In this, and in the Italian setting (Verona), it harks back to such early plays as *Albovine* and *The Cruel Brother*. Duke Altophil kills the evil Galeotto, favourite of the Prince of Verona; Galeotto's daughter, Amaranta, feeling partly responsible for his death, runs on Altophil's sword; Arthiope, 'her hair hanging loose about her', tells Altophil how she has been raped by the invading King of Lombardy, Heildebrand (to whom Galeotto had betrayed the city); later she is revealed to a repentant Heildebrand ('her hair dishevelled as before'), and Altophil kills him; he has been wounded in the fight, and he and Arthiope, the 'Unfortunate Lovers', die in each others' arms, she from 'no other wound than grief'.[23]

Some light relief is provided by Friskin (or Frisklin, as he appears in the 1673 folio), 'an ambitious Taylor' (Davenant probably had his old enemy Urswick in mind), who is constantly trying to get paid by Rampino, 'a young gallant Soldier, much indebted and vexed by Creditors'. Rampino ('I wear my clothes as well as another man') wants to know 'What's in fashion now? the jacket way / Down to the hams?', and again 'How are their cloaks? / A square full cape?' – and he orders 'A pattern of a Polish coat, I'd wear it loose and short' (Act II, p. 36). When the King's tailor is reported dead ('He fell mad with studying of new fashions'), Rampino asks Friskin:

> You can i'th' long vacation ev'ry year
> Travel to Paris, and instruct your self
> In the newest model and best cut?

To which the tailor replies:

> I have a brother lives there, sir. He is
> A shoe-maker, and lately sent me post
> A pattern of the finest spur-leather;
> 'Twas so admired at court.
> *Rampino.* Write for him straight!   (Act III, pp. 52–3)

Thus had Davenant's godfather, in days gone by, made fun of the youth of England for aping foreign fashions.

The Fair Favourite[24] was licensed on 17 November, performed before the King and Queen at the Whitehall Cockpit on 20 November and 11 December, but not printed until after the author's death, in the 1673 folio. Here the plot is of the slightest: Eumena is the chaste favourite of a King married to a wife whom he does not love. In the end she is won by her brother's friend Amadora, and the King suddenly and conveniently, by a 'miracle of love' as he calls it, conceives a genuine affection for his faithful and neglected Queen:

> Proclaim a lasting joy to all that love,
> Or are belov'd! Send 'em a bounteous share
> Of mine! I have enough to furnish either sex.
> I am so light that I could tread on growing
> Flowers and never bend their stalks.
> Qu. My joy is such, that till this hour
> I never felt the like!   (Act V, p. 227)

It recalls the passage in *Albovine* in which Grimond expresses astonishment at the King's being 'now in love with his own wife'.

In the midst of all this activity in 1638 was published Davenant's first collection of poems, *Madagascar; With Other Poems*.[25] It is dedicated to his two 'Maecenases', 'If These Poems Live, May Their Memories, By Whom They Were Cherish'd, END. PORTER, H. JARMYN, Live With Them.'

There are five commendatory poems, one by Porter himself, two by Suckling – one for 'Madagascar' and one for the other poems – and one each by Carew and Habington. Porter's is in modest terms: some poet, he says, has cited him for a wit:

> Now God forgive him for that huge mistake!
> If hee did know, but with what paines I make
> A Verse, hee'ld pitie then my wretched case;
> For at the birth of each, I twist my Face
> As if I drew a Tooth . . .
> Yet something I must say, may it prove fit;
> I'le doe the best I can; and this is it . . .

Prince Rupert had arrived in England to join his brother Charles for a visit early in 1636, and the idea was mooted that he should lead an expedition to conquer Madagascar and establish an English colony (he that ruled the island, it was said at the time, might 'easily . . . be Emperour of all India'), and it was this scheme which prompted Davenant's poem, addressed to the Prince.[26] Employing knowledge acquired from returned travellers, he describes the wealth of the island – some are busy in 'virgin Mines where shining gold they spie', some strive 'To root up Corall Trees, where *Mermaids* lie, / Sighing beneath those Precious boughs, and die / For absence of their scaly Lovers lost / In midnight stormes, about the Indian coast', while others find huge pearls; some climb the rocks and find sapphires, rubies and diamonds; 'Black Suds of

Ambar-Greece float to the shoare'; and in the woods there are exotic
fruits, and the 'silken little Weavers' on mulberry leaves (ll. 365–408).

The poet writes in moving and prophetic terms of the pressures of
multiplying mankind:

> all was *Adams* when the world was new;
> Then strait that all succeeded to a few;
> Whilst men were in their size, not number strong;
> But since, each Couple is become a Throng;
> Which is the cause wee busie ev'ry winde
> (That studious Pilots in their compasse finde)
> For Lands unknowne; where those who first doe come
> Are not held strangers, but arrive at home:
> Yet he that next shall make his visit there,
> Is punish'd for a Spie and Wanderer.
> Not that Man's nature is averse from peace;
> But all are wisely jealous of increase:
> For Eaters grow so fast, that wee must drive
> Our friends away to keepe our selves alive:
> And Warr would be lesse needful, if to die
> Had bin as pleasant as to multiplie.   (ll. 301–16)

This passage, so infinitely more applicable to our own times, itself
resembles Ralegh's earlier words about 'the want of room upon the
earth' leading to war.[27]

There are forty-two poems in the collection in addition to 'Madagascar' itself, some of which have been mentioned already. Among them is
an Ode to the poet's godfather, 'In remembrance of Master William
Shakespeare':[28]

> Beware (delighted Poëts!) when you sing
> To welcome Nature in the early Spring,
>   Your num'rous Feet not tread
> The Banks of Avon; for each Flowre
> (As it nere knew a Sunne or Showre)
>   Hangs there, the pensive head . . .   ll. 1–6)

Seven poems are addressed to Endymion Porter, more than to anyone
else.[29] In the second, Davenant writes of 'My Man, hot and dry / With
fierce transcriptions of my Poesie' (ll. 25–6), and of his 'Wreaths of
living Bay' (l. 12), indicating that he is now, thanks to Endymion, a busy
and well-established Court poet and playwright, and perhaps that he
knows he is about to be appointed the laureate. But once again there is
talk of the fierce rivalry he has to face, as he asks what will become of
him when his patron dies:

The Cruell and the Envious then will say:
Since now his Lord is dead, he that did sway
Our publique smiles, opinion, and our praise,
Till wee this Childe of Poesie did raise
To Fame, and love, let's drowne him in our Inke;
Where like a lost dull Plummet let him sinke
From humane sight; from knowledge was he borne . . .   (ll. 51–7)

'From knowledge was he borne' presumably means that he was, or was held to be, of obscure birth, and this may provide another real or imagined reason for the envy and malice about which he complained so often.

Porter also figures prominently in the poem 'A Journey into Worcestershire' already mentioned, and he is given half the dialogue in a poem 'Written, when Collonell Goring Was beleev'd to be slaine, at the siege of Breda: His death lamented by Endimion, Arigo' – the latter being Henry Jermyn, to whom there is also a poem.[30] A famous piece is addressed to Endymion's wife: 'For the Lady, Olivia Porter. A present, upon a New-yeares day':[31]

Goe! hunt the whiter Ermine! and present
His wealthy skin, as this dayes Tribute sent
To my *Endimion's* Love; Though she be farre
More gentle smooth, more soft than Ermines are!
Goe! climbe that Rock! and when thou there hast found
A Starre, contracted in a Diamond,
Give it *Endimion's* Love; whose glorious Eyes
Darken the Starry Jewells of the Skies! . . .   (ll. 1–8)

Five poems are addressed to the Queen:[32] the opening lines of the first, which begins 'Faire as unshaded Light; or as the Day / In its first birth, when all the Yeare was May', were subsequently borrowed by Pope in *Eloisa to Abelard*. The last, addressed 'upon a New-yeares day', contains several examples of the extravagant expressions of praise which Davenant humorously repents of in a later poem to her, 'A New-years-Gift to the Queen, in the Year 1643':[33]

First, I confess I did you wrong,
When rashly in each Lyrick Song,
I said your Native Beauty did belong
Unto some Planet of the Night:
As if I fondly could surmise
You had such weak and needy Eyes,
As borrow'd to maintain their light . . .   (ll. 15–21)

The tone indicates the easy and affectionate relationship between the Queen and her servant.

The poems published with 'Madagascar' are far from being a comprehensive collection of those almost certainly written before 1638:[34] and some of the early works omitted are among Davenant's most familiar, for example, the lovely song[35] – which owes a good deal to Shakespeare – 'The Lark now leaves his watry Nest', which must be known to a great many people who would not readily attribute it to William Davenant. Gibbs gives two musical settings, by John Wilson, both beginning with the refrain – 'Awake, awake, the Morn shall never rise' – one for solo soprano, the other for two sopranos and a bass; and also a setting by William Lawes, of the song as written, for soprano and baritone.[36] Two other well-known songs omitted from the collection are 'The Philosopher and the Lover', already mentioned, and the poignant 'The Souldier going to the Field:[37]

> For I must go where lazy Peace
>   Will hide her drouzy head;
> And, for the sport of Kings, encrease
>   The number of the Dead . . .   (ll. 9–12)

The final poem is addressed 'To Doctor Duppa, Deane of Christ-Church, and Tutor to the Prince [of Wales]. An acknowledgment for his collection, in Honour of Ben. Johnson's memory.'[38] Brian Duppa was chaplain to the fourth Earl of Dorset to whom Davenant wrote two poems mentioned earlier, and it was through the Earl that he had become Dean of Christ Church in 1628; he succeeded Dr John Davenant as Bishop of Salisbury in 1641. His collection of poems *Jonsonus Virbius*, referred to by Davenant, appeared probably at the beginning of March 1638.

Jonson had suffered a paralytic stroke, and become as he said a 'bed-rid wit', in 1628: but his mind was undamaged, and the Caroline poets Carew, Herrick and many others, including no doubt William Davenant, continued to call on him at his lodgings at Westminster until his death on 6 August 1637. When Davenant was buried near him in the Abbey thirty-one years later, the inscription 'O RARE Sr WILLIAM DAVENANT' was deliberately chosen to copy his O RARE BEN: IOHNSON'; and a contemporary elegy declared:

> Now roosting in yᵉ Poets nest,
> Amongst his kindred he doth rest . . .
> First in yᵉ broad Elysian streets
> Hee his old *Father Johnson* meets;
> Then him his *cousin Shakespeare* greets,
> But his *Freind Suckline* lent him sheets . . .[39]

thus firmly placing him among the 'Sons of Ben'. (A later and less solemn line added that 'Naso has lent him half his *nose*'.)

There has been much debate about whether William Davenant was ever in truth poet laureate. In 1616, the year in which the folio edition of Jonson's *Works* was published, Ben was granted a royal pension of a hundred marks a year, making him what has generally been recognised as the first (unofficial) laureate in England: the pension was raised to £100 in 1630. In the summer of 1637, Suckling wrote his irreverent 'The Wits' or 'A Session of the Poets'.[40] This is not a serious attempt to choose the man best qualified to succeed Jonson as laureate – indeed, Ben is still alive, or written of as though he were – and some of the score of other men named would never have been seriously considered as candidates; rather, to quote Suckling's most recent editor, Thomas Clayton, Suckling 'introduced a much-imitated minor genre – "the trial of the bays" – into English poetry'.[41] Ben himself speaks first, in characteristically blunt terms:

> he told them plainly he deserv'd the Bayes
> For his were called Works, where others were but Plaies . . .   (ll. 19–20)

– a glance at the current mockery of Jonson's alleged presumption in presenting mere plays as 'works'.

Well up among the candidates comes Davenant:

> *Will. Davenant* asham'd of a foolish mischance,
> That he had got lately travelling in *France,*
> Modestly hoped the handsomenesse of's Muse
> Might any deformity about him excuse.
> Surely the Company would have been content,
> If they could have found any President;
> But in all their Records either in Verse or prose,
> There was not one Laureat without a nose . . .   (ll. 41–8)

Finally an Alderman appears, 'At which *Will. Davenant* began to snear' (l. 104); but Apollo, presiding over the debate as the god of poetry, rules that ' 'twas the best signe, / Of good store of wit to have good store of coyn', and to the amazement of the assembled wits, crowns him with the laurels.

Nose or no nose, the real choice fell upon William Davenant, and the royal pension of £100 a year, backdated to 25 March 1638,[42] was awarded to him. How much money he ever received is another matter: certainly all payment would have ceased at the outbreak of the civil war, and there is no evidence of payments at the Restoration.

One may wonder why Davenant had not contributed to Dr Duppa's *Jonsonus Virbius:* the answer can probably be found in lines 39–40 of the poem to Duppa, which read: '. . . I now may erne my Bayes /

Without the taint of flatterie in prayse'. He may mean that it would have seemed sycophantic and improper to write in praise of Jonson before he was assured that he was to succeed him as laureate. He begins the poem in terms of warmest admiration for Ben:

> How shall I sleepe tonight, that am to pay
> By a bold vow, a mighty Debt ere Day?
> Which all the Poets of this Island owe: . . .
> This Debt hereditary is, and more
> Than can be pay'd for such an Ancestor . . .　　(ll. 1–3, 9–10)

For all practical purposes, Davenant was poet laureate from March 1638 until his death thirty years later, and was regarded as such by his contemporaries. Henry Herringman, editor of the 1673 folio, says in his printed address to the reader: 'My Author was *Poet Laureate* to two Great Kings.'[43] John Aubrey heads his *Life* 'Sr William Davenant knight, Poet Laureate', and immediately after a reference to 'Madagascar', firmly states: 'After the death of Ben: Johnson, he was made in his place Poet Laureat.' And the printed *Calendar of Treasury Books* 1669–72[44] includes the following entry, dated 27 January 1670/1: 'Money warrant for £500 to John Dryden Poet Laureate and Historiographer Royal, in full of what has grown due on his pension of £200 per annum granted by letters patent 18 August last, payable from the Feast of St John the Baptist next after the death of Sir William Davenant, it appearing by certificate that he was buried in the Abbey 9 April 1668.' This makes it clear that Dryden was the first Poet Laureate to have the title conferred by letters patent, but also that Davenant was officially recognised as his predecessor.

Davenant would have known Van Dyck and his work very well (he mentions the King's commissioning of portraits from the artist in 'A Journey into Worcestershire'), for Endymion Porter was one of his closest friends and patrons: he painted Porter at least four times, and in one of the portraits, now in the Prado, he includes himself – 'a unique and charming gesture of friendship', to quote Oliver Millar; he also painted Porter's wife Olivia.[45] And the eighteenth-century art historian George Vertue, writing about sixty years after William Davenant's death, reports: 'its said he had his picture drawn by Vandyke before the accident to his Nose'.[46] It was most probably in 1638, the year of his appointment as laureate, that he commissioned the portrait by the English painter, John Greenhill – in which he wears the laurels.[47] It was certainly in that year that Thomas Killigrew (who at the Restoration was to become, with Davenant, the only licensed theatre manager in London) sat to Van Dyck;[48] and 1638 is also thought to be the year in which Suckling commissioned his portrait (the only authenticated one of him) by the master.[49] Suckling had had his first play, *Aglaura,* put on at Court and at Blackfriars, at his own great expense, in the preceding winter of 1637–8. Aubrey says of the production: 'It had some scaenes to it, which in those dayes were only used at Masques' – an interesting implied comment on the innovations later introduced by Davenant at his commercial theatre. Aubrey is the first to mention the Van Dyck portrait of Suckling, which he says is 'like him' – here again he is presumably quoting Davenant, since he himself was only fifteen when Suckling died and had probably never seen him. At the time of writing, the portrait was in the Bishopsgate Street home of the poet's favourite sister Martha, Lady Southcot, and Aubrey describes Suckling as 'leaning against a rock, with a play-booke, contemplating'. He is in fact holding a copy of a folio edition of Shakespeare's plays – it must be the First, of 1623, or the Second, of 1632 – and opening it at *Hamlet.* The meaning of the picture, and its probable links with *Aglaura,* and with Inigo Jones, have recently been discussed in detail by Malcolm Rogers of the National Portrait Gallery:[50] Rogers argues persuasively that the painting is in part a propaganda statement in the war between the Ancients and the Moderns – and he links this with the account by Nicholas Rowe, in his life of Shakespeare preceding his 1709 edition of the works, of an alleged conversation between Suckling, Davenant, Endymion Porter, John Hales of Eton and Ben Jonson, in which Suckling stoutly defended Shakespeare against Ben's familiar charges of want of learning and ignorance of classical literature.

On 26 March 1639 a petition by Davenant was granted,[51] to put up a '*Theatre or Playhouse, with necessary tireing and retiring Rooms and other places convenient*' behind the Three Kings Ordinary in Fleet Street, and to '*gather together, entertain, govern, privilege and keep, such and so many Players and Persons, to exercise Action, musical Presentments, Scenes, Dancing and the like*' (my italics) as he should think fit, 'for the honest recreation of such as shall desire to see the same'. The 'Outwalls' were to be 'made or built of Brick or Stone' (as a precaution, of course, against fire). Charges for attendance would be as at other similar places. Davenant had clearly been inspired by experience gained under the directing genius of Inigo Jones in the presentation of masques at Court (and would have remembered the use of 'scaenes' by his friend Suckling in his play the year before); and although the time was not ripe for the commercial project which he now had in mind, the terms of the patent exactly foreshadow what he would achieve at the Restoration in his own theatre at Lincoln's Inn Fields – a theatre which he would manage, a company of players whom he would direct, and shows, musical or otherwise, of which an essential ingredient would be 'scenes', one of his most important innovations in the history of the English stage.

Immediately after the grant of the licence to build, Davenant became involved, as did most of the men about the Court, in what has become rather grandly known as the First Bishops' War – the first military revolt against the authoritarianism of King Charles. (Davenant's younger brother Nicholas also took part in the campaign.)[52] The attempt to force Anglican prelates and prayer book upon Scotland had resulted in the formation of the Covenant, and by what amounted to a declaration of war, the Church Assembly in Glasgow declared episcopacy abolished and presbyterianism restored. Thus the Great Rebellion may be said to have begun not in England but in Scotland. By the beginning of 1639, the King began recruiting men to make a show of force, and on 27 March – the day after the granting of Davenant's theatre petition – he began the march north, reaching York at the end of the month. Endymion Porter was of course in his train; and Davenant served under the Master General of the Ordnance, the Earl of Newport – whose wife Anne was a sister of Olivia Porter; Earl and Countess had both taken part in Davenant's first Court masque The Temple of Love four years before. The Earl was Mountjoy Blount, an illegitimate son of Penelope Devereux, sister of Queen Elizabeth's favourite, the second Earl of Essex; her nephew the third Earl was to become a Parliamentary general in the civil war.

Suckling had been one of the first to volunteer for royal service, and his Life by Aubrey includes a picturesque account – no doubt based on what Davenant had told him – of the troop of horse which he contributed: 'a Troope of 100 very handsome young proper men, whom he clad in white doubletts & scarlett breeches, and scarlet Coates, hatts, and . . . [Aubrey could not remember what kind] feathers, well horsed & armed. They say 'twas one of the finest sights in thos days.'

The first military necessity was to strengthen Berwick-on-Tweed, but the town was in sympathy with the Covenanters, and was in any case too small to accommodate the King's army; so they camped outside it to the south, Charles living under canvas with his men. The whole campaign was confused and ill-organised, and after the Earl of Holland – Henry Rich, a legitimate son of Penelope Devereux – had led an unsuccessful advance of a thousand cavalry towards Kelso, the so-called Pacification of Berwick was signed on 18 June. A letter written by Suckling shortly before that date[53] reveals another facet of Davenant's many-sided interests. He writes: 'The little stops or progresses . . . in the treaty now on foot arrive at one so slowly, that unless I had one of Mr Davenants Barbary pigeons (and he now employs them all, he says, himself for the queens use [presumably to send her messages to the King]) I durst not venture to send them, sir, to you, lest, coming to your hands so late, you should call for the map to see whether my quarters were in England or in Barbary . . .'. Davenant had already shown his interest in carrier-pigeons four years earlier: in the first scene of *The Platonic Lovers*, there is talk of sending messages 'in a little letter tied to / A Tartarian arrow. . . . / Or 'bout the neck of a Barbary pigeon'.

Further evidence of Davenant's service in the First Bishops' War comes in a petition by a tailor called James Fawcett, against whom Lord Newport had brought suit in the Court of Star Chamber alleging 'insolent speeches'. Fawcett stated that in May 1639, about four hundred horses used for drawing the royal ordnance had been put on land belonging to him at Goswick (Harbage and Nethercot say that this is near York: in fact it is six miles down the coast from Berwick, and close to Holy Island). He had been promised twelve pence per day and night for each horse, but had received only three pence each, 'and half of that unpaid'; much damage had been done to his corn, and 'William Davenant, the pay-master', had accused him of injuring some of the horses when he turned them off his land. Fawcett was summoned to the bar of the Upper House in London, where depositions were read: one alleged that he had described those proceeding against him as 'Knaves', another that he had claimed to have served the King better than the Earl or Mr Davenant, 'and they were base Fellows for prosecuting the case against him'. Davenant, of course, was of no direct interest to the Lords: they were concerned with the alleged insults to their fellow-peer. Fawcett was ordered to make humble submission to him 'at the Bar, upon his Knee', to do the same publicly at York, and to pay the Earl £500 damages.[54]

By the autumn of 1639, everyone on the royalist side of the northern campaign was back in London. Among those accompanying the King had been James Stuart, Duke of Lennox and later Duke of Richmond (a nephew of Davenant's first employer in London): he had returned by 16 April, for on that day Endymion Porter wrote to one of his employees in the capital instructing him to seek help from the Duke in furthering Davenant's plan for a theatre in Fleet Street.[55] But once again 'the Cruell and the Envious' seem to have been at work, for on 2 October, permission for the plan was withdrawn.[56] In a poem addressed 'To the Duke of Richmond, in the year 1639',[57] Davenant writes of the Court, in seagoing terms,

Where he that feels a wild ambitious spirit,
And nourishes desires above his merit,
Is lost when he imagines to prevail,
Because his little ship bears too much sayl . . .   (ll. 5–8)

He speaks darkly of 'Informers', and of finding his sails 'all rumpled and the Cordage slack', through the malice of 'some perverse and undiscovered hand' (ll. 25, 46–7) – Nethercot plausibly suggests that the hand may have been that of his old antagonist, Sir Henry Herbert.

In May 1640, a play critical of the King, which Herbert had declined to license, was acted by the King's and Queen's Servants, or 'Beeston's Boys', at the Cockpit in Drury Lane,[58] and on 27 June it was recorded in the Lord Chamberlain's Office Book that 'William Davenant, Gent., one of Her Majesty's Servants', should take over the theatre (perhaps the King, prompted by Porter, had come to his aid as he had over the censoring of *The Wits*). But Davenant had no chance to do this immediately, for that summer he was up north again for the Second Bishops' War (in which Porter's son Charles was killed), and once again in the ordnance department coping with horses: this campaign ended equally dismally. The State Papers, as before, are full of accounts of the general confusion: a letter from Sir Jacob Astley dated Selby, 30 June, for example,[59] describes the 'men already come' as 'good bodied but extremely unruly, so that they break open all prisons and are ready to strike their officers'; and one from Lord Conway in Newcastle to Secretary Windebank in London, dated 17 July,[60] declares that the lack of money will put them all into disorder:

> I haue borrowed of the Sheriffe of Durham and the Maior of Newcastle soe mutch as I hope will pay this moneth, but the Maior and his brethren would not lend any out of theire own Purse, it is shipping money therefore Sr William Vuedale must pay it againe to the Treasorer of the Nauy; There are 400. draught horses comme hither 800. more will be heere within fowre dayes, there is noe order taken for theire payment or any man that knowes what to doe with them, there is only one sent downe [i.e. from London] a deputy to Mr Dauenant, if another man should doe soe he would put it into a play; Sr Jacob Ashley [sic] must haue Martiall lawe in his power or he will neuer be able to gouerne those unruly men; . . .'

Davenant has been described as 'irresponsible' and 'inefficient', but surely unjustly:[61] Conway's scathing remarks about him are typical condemnation of the amateur, after the manner of Iago on the subject of Michael Cassio. Those close to the King devoted themselves unhesitatingly to his cause, but the great majority were inevitably amateurs in war. Lines of communication were overlong, the centre of the army

organisation was partly in London, and – as Conway's letter empha-
sises – there was always an acute shortage of cash. This is further
underlined in a letter from an understandably disgruntled Davenant,
written – in remarkably sharp terms – to Lord Conway from Newcastle
on 24 August:[62]

> May it please your lordship I find a command sent hither to despatch from
> hence three hundred and 50 horse for draught of the artillery towards Hull,
> and with all possible hast; but unless your Lo^p send money (according to
> your own computation) for theire charges thither, and mony for more iron
> to shoe them, and a warrant for theire weekly pay who attend them, it is
> impossible to sett them forward. ... Your Lo^p is to consider how many
> dayes be allowed them for their journey to Hull; how much shall be allow^d
> each horse when they travaile, and w^t to draw after their journey; 350 being
> the number, besides their carters and conductors, and mony for their shoe-
> ing ...

The winter of 1639–40, between the First and Second Bishops' Wars,
saw the licensing, on 30 November, of the last play written by William
Davenant before Parliament closed the theatres, and the last of all the
Caroline masques.

The play was called *The Spanish Lovers*,[63] and was not published
until the 1673 folio – where it is supposed to be the piece called *The
Distresses*. There is no positive evidence that it was ever performed,
although Davenant perhaps put it on at the Cockpit in Drury Lane
when he returned from the north. For once, as the title indicates, the
play is set not in Italy but in Spain (Cordova), and it principally
concerns the adventures of two beautiful girls, Amiana and Claramante; it is again very complicated – 'plotty' is Harbage's word for it.
The cast includes 'Musicians', and a part-song, sung at the behest of
Orgemon beneath the window of his mistress Claramante,[64] is rather in
the manner of Davenant's 'Vacation' poem of 1635:

> None but my self my heart did keep,
> When I on Cowslip-Bed did sleep,
>   Neer to a pleasant Bog:
>   Whilst you my pretty Rogue,
> With Knuckle knocking at my Brest,
> Did ask for my Three corner'd Ghest
> And whispering soft (as soft as voice could be)
> Did say come out thou little Heart to me. ....
>
> This Heart for joy, from me did leap,
> And follow'd thee even step by step,
> Till tir'd, it ask'd to rest
> A while within thy Brest.

'Twas thick, and fat, and plump before,
Weighing a full pound weight and more.
But now (alas) 'tis wasted to the Skin,
And grown no bigger then the Head of Pin . . .   (ll. 1–8, 13–20)

And later in Act II (p. 305) 'a merry gentleman', Orco, sings 'A Mock-song to a Ballad Tune' for which words are not provided: the theme is suggested by the two following lines of dialogue:

Good morrow to the Honorable *Dona Amiana*
And to th'Right Worshipful her little Dog.

The last of all the Caroline masques was *Salmacida Spolia*,[65] and according to the printed text of 1640 – this and the two previous masques are not included in the 1673 folio – it was generally considered the best: 'the noblest and most ingenious that hath been done here in that kind'. The 'spoils' (ironically, in view of what was to come) are peace, and the reference is to the fountain of Salmacis in Caria, whose waters were reputed to have had the power to win over barbarians *sine sanguine sine sudore*, without blood and sweat, to the virtues of civilisation and law. The text exactly defines the roles of the creators:

The invention, ornament, scenes and apparitions, with their descriptions, were made by INIGO JONES, *Surveyor General of his Majesty's works.*
What was spoken or sung, by WILLIAM D'AVENANT, *her Majesty's servant.*
The subject was set down by them both.
The music was composed by LEWIS RICHARD, *Master of her Majesty's Music.*

Both King and Queen took part, and by the beginning of December rehearsals were in full swing. The Earl of Northumberland wrote to his sister the Countess of Leicester:[66] 'I assure you their Majesties are not less busy now than formerly you have seen them at the like exercise.' Of the other performers, he wrote: 'A company of worse faces did I never see assembled than the Queen has got together for this occasion; not one new woman amongst them.' One was Lady Carnarvon, who had 'become so devout' that she had said she would not take part if the masque were performed on a Sunday – 'now she will neither dance nor see a play upon the Sabbath'. In the end she found herself able to participate, since the first performance was on Tuesday 21 January (the masque was repeated at Shrovetide). Among others taking part were Lord Newport – Davenant's commander in the northern campaigns – and the Duke and Duchess of Lennox.

It is not difficult, in later and changed times, to condemn the Court of

King Charles: Davenant's nineteenth-century editors declare (in tortuous language): 'The state of the metropolis antecedent to the republi-
can explosion shows the pains that had been taken to stimulate the
people to acts of violence, which, from London, their centre, spread
over the whole nation.';[67] and Harbage struggles to absolve Davenant
of being (in terms his own times would not have understood) 'a sinner
against democracy', presenting him as 'a thinking man constrained to
allegiance to an irrational cause' and taking refuge in a kind of political
sentimentalism. Nevertheless, as Nethercot remarks, Jones and Davenant were by no means oblivious of the sombre world beyond the
Court: in *Salmacida Spolia*, the confident and celebratory tone of
Britannia Triumphans is replaced by an acknowledgment that the King
– Philogenes, 'the lover of his people' – is constrained 'to rule in adverse
times, / When wisdome must awhile give place to crimes'. The masque
opens with 'a horrid scene . . . of storm and tempest', and Discord, a
Fury, sings a song of lamentation that the world 'should everywhere be
vext' (although she adds 'save only here'). Then, in a scene of 'calm',
Concord and the 'Good Genius of Great Britain' descend in a silver
chariot, singing of the great and wise Philogenes:

> O who but he could thus endure
>   To live, and governe in a sulleine age,
> When it is harder far to cure
>   The Peoples folly than resist their rage?   (ll. 23–6)

In one of the antimasques, the dwarf Jeffery makes his last appearance,
playing 'a little Swiss'. One song is addressed to Henrietta Maria's
mother, Marie de' Medici, widow of Henri IV of France, who was
present: this includes a reference to 'those groweing comforts', her three
grandchildren – Prince Charles (then nearly nine), Mary (eight) and
James (six). The King and his Lords are revealed, arrayed in blue richly
embroidered with silver, with long white stockings, their caps silver,
with scrolls of gold and plumes of white feathers. The King is a 'secret
Wisdom', one whose power is now endurance, and his virtue, patience:

> If it be Kingly patience to out last
>   Those stormes the peoples giddy fury rayse,
> Till like fantastick windes themselves they waste,
>   The wisedome of that patience is thy prayse . . .   (ll. 5–8)

While this chorus is being sung, the Queen and her ladies descend
from above on a 'huge cloud of various colours', arrayed 'in Amazonian
habits of carnation, embroidered with silver, with plumed helms',
antique swords hanging by their sides. Henrietta Maria was pregnant at

the time (Henry Duke of Gloucester was born on 8 July): nothing could better illustrate the chasm between Elizabethan and Caroline Court behaviour. Finally the whole company addresses the King and Queen in song:

> All that are harsh, all that are rude,
> Are by your harmony subdu'd;
> Yet so into obedience wrought,
> As if not forc'd to it, but taught . . .   (ll. 5–8)

Thus, in a brilliant spectacle before the approaching storm of rebellion, the small figures of Charles and Henrietta Maria performed for the last time in the candlelit Masking Room of Whitehall Palace. Nine years later, the King would walk from Inigo Jones's great Banqueting House on to a very different stage, the platform erected for his execution.[68]

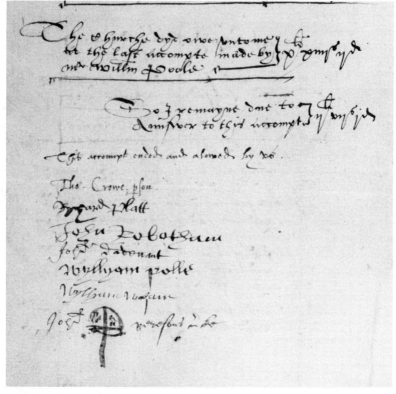

John Davenant, Sir William's grandfather: as a leading parishioner of St James Garlickhithe, he signs the churchwardens' accounts of 1583–4 as an auditor, see p. 11. Guildhall Library, MS 4810/1, f. 66v.

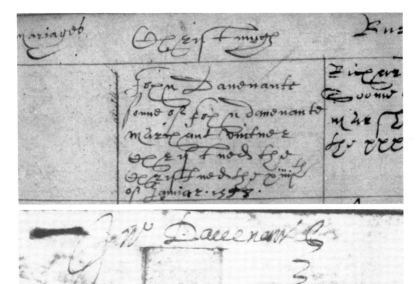

[top] John Davenant, Sir William's father: entered as 'Marchant Vintner' at the baptism at St James Garlickhithe of a son John on 14 January 1598/9, *see pp. 11, 12.* From Guildhall Library MS 9138. 1 and 2 reproduced by permission of the Rector and Churchwardens of St James Garlickhithe.

[centre] Signature of Sir William's father on an Oxford subsidy roll of 1610, as one of two collectors appointed to assess and tax the inhabitants of the city and suburbs, *see p. 221 n. 48.* From E/179/163/434, permission of the Public Record Office, London.

[right] Jane/Jennet Davenant *née* Sheppard, Sir William's mother, consults Simon Forman on 16 January 1597/8, *see p. 12.* From MS Ashmole 226, f. 287r, permission of the Bodleian Library, Oxford.

Royal warrant of 1607–8 authorising livery for life for Sir William's uncle Richard Sheppard as *Sufftor Domini Regis*, The King's Perfumer, *see p. 8.* From MS A03/1116, permission of the Public Record Office, London.

[*below*] Endymion Porter by William Dobson: courtier, connoisseur of the arts, and Davenant's patron and friend, *see p. 31.* Permission of the Tate Gallery, London.

[*right*] Sir John Suckling by Van Dyck: Davenant's close friend in pre-war years, *see pp. 74–5.* Copyright the Frick Collection, New York.

Letter from Davenant to Prince Rupert 13 June 1644, advising him on his next move in the civil war, *see pp. 94–5*. MS Addl. 20,723, f. 20, permission of the Department of MSS, British Library.

CHAPTER SIX

1 6 4 1 – 9
Civil War general and
gun-runner; exile in France

William Davenant had little or no opportunity to take up, or resume, his management of the Cockpit playhouse in Drury Lane,[1] for in the spring of 1641 he become involved in the abortive attempt to 'seduce the army against the parliament', to quote Anthony Wood. One cautious group was made up principally of young officers, and the attempt became known as the Army Plot; the other and more reckless consisted mainly of some of the Queen's courtiers, who planned to replace Northumberland, the Lord General in the north, with Newcastle, and for the army to march on London, free Strafford (whose trial was in progress) and dissolve Parliament.

On 5 May, Lords and Commons foregathered in the Painted Chamber at Westminster,[2] so that the Commons could report on 'the late discovered Plot'. Certain persons had been sent for to be examined, but were not to be found, and there was 'great cause to believe' they had fled: they were named as Henry Percy Esquire (Northumberland's younger brother), Henry Jermyn Esquire the Queen's favourite, Sir John Suckling, William Davenant and Captain Billingsley. On the 6th, Northumberland signed an order at York House for the ports to be stopped, and the five men brought to Westminster for examination.[3] On the 7th the order was renewed, the five to be examined 'concerning Designs of great Danger to the State, and mischievous Ways to prevent the happy Success and Conclusion of this Parliament';[4] on the same day Sir Henry Vane wrote in some puzzlement to Sir Thomas Roe, of 'Wm. Davenant the poet' and his fellows: 'It is strangely thought on, this their so sudden flight, and they are esteemed much more culpable than I hope they are. The truth is the design has been ill carried, whatsoever it hath been . . .'.[5]

Another letter-writer[6] arrived at a similar conclusion: the fact that the accused had all run away argued that they were 'the wise and active agents in this treacherous employment'. A Puritan sympathiser had no

doubts: he wrote of 'the greatest treason discovered this week that was
in England since the powder plot . . . the conspirators were Mr Jermyn,
Mr Percy, Sir John Suckling, Davenent the poet, and such youths . . . as
my lord of Essex called them in the House, the new Juntillio. They are
all fled . . .'.[7]

Davenant is frequently described thus in the contemporary accounts
– as 'the poet'; and as usual, the professionals were contemptuous of the
amateurs – one, Captain Hugh Pollard, declared in his deposition
during the subsequent parliamentary enquiry: 'Wee did not very well
like the men, for *Suckling*, Jermaine and Davenant were in it.'[8]

There is often something irresistibly comic about the story of William
Davenant, and this episode is no exception: Suckling and the others
managed to get away to the continent, but the poet was recognised and
caught in Kent, with his servant Elias Wallen. Predictably it was written,

> Soon as in *Kent* they saw the Bard,
> (As to say truth, it is not hard,
> For *Will.* has in his face, the flawes
> Of wounds receiv'd in Countreys Cause:)
> They flew on him, like Lions passant,
> And tore his Nose, as much as was on't;
> They call'd him Superstitious Groom,
> And Popish dog, and Curre of *Rome* . . .[9]

' 'Twas surely the first time', Aubrey remarks, 'that Wills Religion was a
Crime.' Although Davenant did eventually embrace the church of
Rome, there is no evidence that he had actually done so at this date;
however, his close adherence to the Queen was more than enough to
provoke the charge. The same doggerel verse speaks of Davenant's
'lolling' in his bed in Covent Garden, which chimes with a 1641 list of
Westminster tax defaulters, showing him, along with Captain Endymion Porter, Dr Theodore Mayerne and other leading royalists, as a
parishioner of St Martin-in-the-Fields.[10]

The Commons Journal for 15 May – two days before Strafford's
execution – notes that Davenant and his servant Wallen were to be sent
for 'as Delinquents' by the Serjeant-at-Arms:[11] he was kept in custody,
and examined by Parliament several times. And by 29 June, Thomas
Smith was writing to Sir John Penington: ' 'Tis thought Jermyn,
Suckling and Davenant will be judged guilty of death.'[12] There seems to
have been considerable sympathy for the poet, and one doggerel writer
declared:

> we hope hee'le scape the rope,
> That now him so doth fright-a:
> The Parliament being content
> That he this fact should write-a.[13]

Davenant himself promptly composed, and had printed, a 'Humble Remonstrance' addressed to the Commons.[14] He cheerfully begins: 'I humbly beseech you to conceive, that I have absented to appeare before this honourable Assembly, rather from a befitting bashfulnesse, as being an ill object, then of outward sence of guilt, as being a delinquent. I did beleeve, if I were layed aside a while, my Cause would be forgotten, because I knew nothing stronger but suspicions and meere opinions can be brought against me . . . it is possible I may be guilty of some mis-becoming words, yet not words made in dangerous principles or maximes, but loose Arguments, disputed at Table perhaps, with too much fancy and heat. And as in speaking, so in writing, I meane in Letters, I have perhaps committed errours, but never irreverently or maliciously against Parliamentary government.' 'Befitting bashful-nesse', and being 'absented' and 'layed aside', are characteristically bland Davenant euphemisms for attempted flight to foreign parts.

He makes no attempt to deny his friendship with 'Master *Iarmin* and Sir Iohn *Suckling*'; but 'they were strangely altered, and in a very short time, if it were possible they could design any thing against your happy and glorious proceedings, who . . . have so often extold the naturall necessity of Parliaments here, with extreame scorne upon the incapacity of any that should perswade the King he could be fortunate without them. And it is not long since I wrote to the Queens Majesty in praise of her inclination to become this way the Peoples advocate, the which they presented to her . . .'.

He repeats that his disobedience in not appearing before the Commons 'did rather proceed from a reverend awe your displeasure bred in me', and ends by begging them to 'leave me to posterity as a marke of your compassion, and let not my flight or other indiscretions be my ruine, though contrary to *Davids* opinion, I have fled from Divine power, which is yours by derivation, and chose to fall into the hands of men, which are your Officers that apprehended me.'

Davenant's statement about writing to the Queen refers to a poem[15] which reads in part:

> Madam; so much peculiar and alone
> Are Kings, so uncompanion'd in a Throne,
> That through the want of some equality
> (Familiar Guides, who lead them to comply)
> They may offend by being so sublime,

As if to be a King might be a crime . . .
To cure this high obnoxious singleness
(Yet not to make their power but danger less)
Were Queens ordain'd . . .
You are become (which doth augment your state)
The Judges Judge, and Peoples Advocate . . .

As Gibbs remarks, this criticism of the King's uncompromising policy towards Parliament makes the poem an interesting political piece; but it is doubtful whether the democratic sympathies which the poet ascribes to Henrietta Maria were anything more than a passing phase, for during the civil war she was even more inflexibly opposed to compromise with Parliament than Charles himself.

Harbage finds unconscious humour in Davenant's Humble Remonstrance, but it seems rather conscious than otherwise: one can detect the customary twinkle in the eye of a man never inclined to take himself too seriously. Certainly his Remonstrance must have touched the collective heart of Members, for on 8 July, upon hearing it read, they decided to release the poet on bail of £4,000 – £2,000 of his own, and a further £1,000 each from sureties.[16]

On 12 August Suckling, Percy and Jermyn were found guilty of high treason, but the House 'falling out about Mr Davenant there was great debate, but broke off till further consideration of the evidence against him'.[17] He had expressed the hope that his 'Cause would be forgotten', and it seems likely that this is what happened.[18]

On 4 January 1642 the King made his disastrous attempt to arrest the Five Members, thereafter departing from the House of Commons and from London, never to return until his trial and execution. Davenant was still lodging nearby at the time of the attempted arrest – his daughter Mary was baptised at St Martin-in-the-Fields a week later. The playhouses had begun performing again after a closure because of plague, for at the beginning of February Puritans made a 'great complaint' about them in the Commons, and sought their suppression.[19] But William Davenant had seen the last of the London stage for some years to come. The King had fled to the north, where his support was strongest, and the Queen departed for the continent to begin her efforts to raise money and adherents for her husband's cause. Her servant Davenant probably accompanied her; certainly by July he was at The Hague.[20] His friend the poet Carew was already dead, and at some time in the summer John Suckling also died, in Paris, and probably by his own hand.[21]

Before the King and Queen parted, they had devised an ingenious cipher for their communications, consisting of a combination of letters of the alphabet, figures and symbols, and they and their principal adherents assumed the names of leading figures on the other side (the Queen, for example, was 'Pym').[22] In August they devised a second cipher, Charles raised his standard at Nottingham on the 22nd, and the Great Civil War began. On 2 September Parliament formally banned all stage plays, 'to appease and avert the Wrath of God . . . publike Sports doe not well agree with publike Calamities, nor publike Stage-playes with the Seasons of Humiliation . . . Spectacles of pleasure too commonly expressing laciuious Mirth and Levitie'. Many of the actors, notably the King's Servants at the Blackfriars and Globe, enlisted on the royalist side, selling off their stock of 'Apparell, hangings, books, & other goods'.[23]

In the north the standard was raised, and a royalist force assembled, by the Earl of Newcastle as Lord General. George Lord Goring was his General of the Horse, and General of the Ordnance was his own son, Viscount Mansfield. Davenant had already been acting as one of the Queen's agents in trying to pawn jewels in Amsterdam,[24] but at an early stage he joined Lord Newcastle, for Henrietta Maria wrote to the Earl 'I have received your requests by Davenant and Cook . . .', and a little later, on 11 October:

> I beg you not to make any promise in the army that you are raising, for the place of master of the artillery, for I have it in my thoughts to propose you one whom I think very fit for it, and with whom you will be satisfied . . .[25]

This was William Davenant, and he served under the Earl as Lieutenant-General of the Ordnance for nine months, until August 1643 – Newcastle's only successful period, during which he subdued most of the north of England. General Davenant probably made use of his Barbary pigeons to communicate with the King and Queen. No details of his service survive – which suggests that it was satisfactory, since critics of 'Davenant the poet' would not have been slow to pick on shortcomings – apart from one anecdote recounted by Aubrey, whose informant was presumably Davenant himself. As Aubrey tells it, the poet had charge of two aldermen of York, who had been taken prisoner and proved themselves 'somewhat stubborne', in that they would not pay a ransom. Davenant 'used them civilly and treated them in his Tent, and sate them at the upper end of his Table à la mode de France'; but having done this for some time at his own expense, he told them privately that he could not keep it up any longer, and 'bade them take an opportunity to escape [typical Davenant behaviour]; wch they did; but having been gon a little way they considered with themselves that in gratitude they ought to goe back and give Sr William their Thankes, wch they did' – thus risking recapture. However, they managed to get away to York.

Of Davenant's time in the north, Aubrey writes: 'I have heard his brother Robert say, for that service there was owing to him by King Charles ye first 10000^{li}.' His commander, the Lord General, William Cavendish, was one of the most attractive figures on the royalist side, and he and Davenant were kindred spirits. Cavendish was himself a poet and playwright (*Mercurius Britanicus* later described him unkindly as 'one that in time of peace tired the stage in *Black-Fryers* with his *Comedies*'),[26] a brilliant horseman, and the author of two renowned books on horsemanship, an art which he had taught to the young Prince Charles while he was his tutor. A not entirely sympathetic contemporary describes him as 'a Gentleman of grandeur, generosity, loyalty, and steddy and forward courage . . . he had a tincture of a Romantick spirit, and . . . somewhat of the Poet in him; so as he chose Sir William Davenant, an eminent good Poet, and loyall Gentleman, to be Lieutenant-generall of his Ordinance'.[27]

Edgehill, the first great battle of the war, took place on 23 October; and on the 29th, as Anthony Wood vividly describes (no doubt as an eyewitness), King Charles came to Oxford toward the evening, riding in at the North Gate with his foot soldiers, and accompanied by his nephews Rupert and Maurice and his young sons Charles and James. 'They came in their full march into the towne, with about 60 or 70 cullours borne before them which they had taken at the saide battell of Edgehill from the parlament's forces.' They advanced along Cornmarket, past the Cross inn and the Davenant tavern – the poet's sister Jane Hallam watching the splendid sight – to Carfax, where the mayor and townsmen greeted the King and 'presented him with a summe of money, as I heard'.[28]

Soon Walter Strickland was writing to John Pym: 'Mr Percy [who had joined the Queen on the continent] is gone to England, to [Lord] Newcastle I think. So is Davenant . . . they say that Lord Newcastle will raise 8,000 or 10,000 troops'; and a little later he reported that the Queen was planning to follow, 'but it is thought she will not until she has heard from England by Davenant, Percy, Philpot or Sir Thomas Dorvill . . . I hear that the Queen intends to take over horses and ammunition. Great endeavours are made to raise money by borrowing and pawning jewels.'[29] By the beginning of 1643 she had raised on the Crown jewels, partly in the Spanish Netherlands and partly in the United Provinces, loans totalling the enormous sum of about £180,000; she had assembled several shiploads of arms; and a number of distinguished professional soldiers were waiting to sail for England under the escort of Admiral Tromp.[30]

The Queen was held up by storms, but she robustly assured her ladies that Queens of England never drowned, and in late February Lord Newcastle was able to greet her at Bridlington and conduct her to York. Davenant's poem 'A New-years-gift to the Queen, in the Year 1643' (that is, New Year's day Old Style, 25 March 1643), already mentioned, reflects the generally buoyant mood of the northern royalists at this time.[31] In the summer Newcastle provided a large force to escort the Queen to Oxford, where she rejoined her husband on 14 July, having been met at Stratford by Prince Rupert and stayed at New Place as the guest of Shakespeare's daughter Mrs Hall.[32]

Davenant followed soon after with dispatches, for on 13 August Henrietta Maria wrote to Lord Newcastle from Oxford: 'Davenant has arrived; I have not yet spoken to him. On his return, he will inform you of some things which cannot be written.' The King had moved on to Gloucester – much against his wife's advice: 'The king is gone himself in person to Gloucester, which gives no small dissatisfaction to everybody here, and with reason too, to see him take such sudden counsels.'[33] In fact, Davenant never did return to the north. No doubt he stayed with his sister at the tavern while he was at Oxford; but soon he too moved on to Gloucester, where in September, being then 'in great renown for his loyalty and poetry', as Wood puts it, he was knighted by King Charles – Aubrey and Wood wrongly say this was done by Lord Newcastle on commission. (The parliamentary siege of Gloucester was conducted by the third Earl of Essex – the son of Queen Elizabeth's favourite – who some years before had stood godfather to Davenant's nephew Essex Sherborne, son of his sister Alice.)

The King returned to Oxford to take up winter quarters, and parliamentary attacks on the alleged conduct of the Court continued: there were the customary gibes about masques – although it was thought the Queen would not be able to have as many at Christmas and Shrovetide as in former years, 'because *Inigo Jones* cannot conveniently make such Heavens and Paradises at *Oxford* as he did at White-hall; and because the Poets are dead, beggered, or run away'.[34] Jones's former collaborator William Davenant, far from having 'run away', had returned to the continent to continue his efforts to raise money and munitions on behalf of the Queen – which he did to such effect that one news writer in Rotterdam described '*Davenet* the Poet (now Knighted)' as the chief royalist agent there.[35] In March 1644, the House of Commons, having heard the report of an agent recently returned from Holland 'concerning the conveying of Arms and Ammunition to the Kings Quarters', approved a resolution that Davenant be accused of high treason, and ordered articles of impeachment to be prepared.[36]

At about this time, during a return to Oxford, Davenant addressed a poem 'To the Queen; Entertain'd at Night. In the year 1644'.[37] The buoyant tone of the earlier poem has disappeared, and the piece begins:

> Unhappy Excellence, what make you here?
>> Had you had sin enough to be afraid,
> Or we the vertue not to cause that feare,
>> You had not hither come to be betray'd.

The parliamentary victory at Alresford at the end of March constituted a serious threat to Oxford, and this is taken to be what Davenant is referring to. He writes bitterly:

> Your patience, now our Drums are silent grown,
>> We give to Souldiers, who in fury are,
> To find the profit of their Trade is gone,
>> And Lawyers still grow rich by Civil War.

The 'entertainment' given for the Queen must have taken place before 17 April, for on that date she left Oxford for the west country and the continent: the King, with their two sons, escorted her as far as Abingdon. She was ill, and pregnant (Princess Henrietta was born at Exeter on 16 June), and she and her husband were never to meet again. The royal miniaturist Laurence Hilliard, son of Nicholas, was one of those who served her and her family at Exeter, thereafter incurring debts on her behalf and being forced to 'fly into France and the West Indies for shelter' until better times should come.[38] In London, two days before the Queen's departure from Oxford, another relic of the pre-war world of the theatre disappeared, when the second Globe playhouse was pulled down after a life of only thirty years, 'to make tenements in the room of it'.[39]

The King had resumed campaigning, and on 29 June at Cropredy Bridge near Banbury he inflicted a substantial defeat on the parliamentary forces.[40] Prince Rupert was now in control of Chester, and a fortnight before, Davenant had addressed a shrewd letter of advice to him.[41] The Prince was faced with a choice: should he relieve Lord Newcastle, who had been forced by a Scottish invasion to withdraw to York, or should he move south to support the King? Davenant strongly advised the former, on the ground that loss of the north would be fatal to the royalist cause. If the rumour current at Chester – that he was going off to join his uncle – were to reach York, it would be even more damaging to the royalist forces there than their lack of food and the continuing enemy pressure. Alternatively, if the pressures upon the

King forced him to march northward, he would 'hardly be follow'd by those Armys which consist of Londoners; for it was never heard that any force or inclination could leade them so farre from home'. Then, if the Prince were 'invited towards the King', he would immediately lose eight thousand foot soldiers in York, plus others who might be spared from the garrisons of Newcastle and elsewhere in the north – the whole constituting 'a much greater Army than ever the South will be able to rayse in his Maties behalfe'. Furthermore, the enemy would be able to gain control of 'the 3 great mines of England' – the resources of alum, coal and lead – and would be able to convert them into 'a constant treasure' in a way that Lord Newcastle, for lack of shipping, had never been able to do. 'They having the advantage of the sea will make those Mines a better maintenance to their cause than London hath binne.' The letter is endorsed: 'Prince hastned to York June 13 1644' – the day of Davenant's letter – but he may have decided to do so anyway, and there is no proof that the letter arrived before he left. He reached York at the end of the month and, with the help of some of Goring's cavalry, relieved the city. Then – against the advice of the Lord General, who strongly urged him to await reinforcements – he marched out to Marston Moor, where on 2 July the parliamentary forces inflicted their first major defeat of the war. There is no evidence that Davenant took part in the battle, but *The Parliament Scout* reported that among those royalists killed was '*Daunant* the Poet', an indication of the importance they attached to him. Lord Newcastle, disgusted and disheartened, departed with his sons for the continent, going first to Hamburg, and then to Paris where in April of the following year he joined Prince Charles: as *Mercurius Britanicus* unkindly put it, he 'help't *Rupert* to a sound beating, and Exit'.[42]

The Queen sailed once more for the continent, accompanied by Henry Jermyn (now Baron Jermyn of St Edmundsbury), who was to preside over her household for many years. The King decided to lead his army to Cornwall in pursuit of Essex, and William Davenant was with him: on 16 August he was at Boconnoc near Lostwithiel, whence Lord Digby addressed a letter to Colonel Edward Seymour, Governor of Dartmouth, by 'this bearer, Sir William Davenant, my very good friend'.[43] Three days later Sir Hugh Pollard wrote to Seymour from Exeter:

> I join with Sir William Davenant in desiring you to let him know whether you have any ship or bark in your harbour that will transport him into France; that secrecy and speedy answer is likewise desired, and I am sure when you consider whose business he carries with him, you will need no quickening to afford him all the accommodation you possibly can . . . upon

notice from you, Sir William will be instantly with you . . .

(Pollard's tone had markedly changed from the days when he was so rude about Davenant during the Army Plot.)

The letter shows that Davenant was now to engage in gun-running, conveying munitions sent by the Queen through the parliamentary blockade to the royalist forces in the west. For the rest of 1644, and the whole of 1645, he continued this highly important and dangerous activity – a contribution to the royalist cause which has been much under-valued. Contemporaries were in no doubt: Jermyn, in a letter to Digby from Paris,[44] wrote: 'This bearer, Sir William Davenant, is infinitely faithful to the Kings cause; he hath been lately in Holland, so that he met there with the knowledge of our treaty, so that it was neither possible nor needful to conceal it from him [a reference to the Queen's attempt to secure military aid from the Dutch, in return for a marriage contract between her son and the Princess of Orange]. . . . Pray if Davenant have need of your favour in anything use him very kindly for my sake'. (This letter, partially in cipher, was subsequently captured, and read to Parliament in November 1645.)[45] An agent on the parliamentary side, in a letter to Oliver St John, wrote of 'Sir William Davenant, the poet – now the great pirott – and he that was the agent in projecting and bringing up the northerne army three years since', and said he 'would be put into the exceptions for life. No man hath don you more hurt, and hath been a greater enemy to the parliament'.[46]

In all, Davenant is said to have succeeded in delivering more than £13,000 worth of arms and ammunition – plus ammunition worth more than £1,000, probably paid for by himself, for which he unsuccessfully sought repayment at the Restoration.[47]

All this effort was in vain. The royalists were heavily defeated at Naseby in mid-June 1645. The London actors – Davenant's former colleagues – who had joined up so loyally at the outbreak of war, were now utterly discouraged. To quote the cavalier *Mercurius anti-britanicus*, 'when the Stage at *Westminster* . . . is once more restored back againe to *Black-Fryers,* they hope they shall returne to their old harmlesse profession of killing Men in Tragedies without Manslaughter'. But now they left the Court at Oxford, returned to London, and threw themselves on the mercy of Parliament, offering to take the Covenant and '(if they may be accepted) are willing to put themselves into their service'. [48] The last royalist stronghold between London and the west, Basing House near Basingstoke, fell in October after a long siege: this was the seat of the Marquess of Winchester, who had given sanctuary to many of the artistic fraternity. In London three months before, the great Masking Room, scene of Inigo Jones's last triumphs before the outbreak of war, had been pulled down – and now, with the breaking of the siege of Basing, the old man suffered the indignity of being carried out of the house naked in a blanket. The engraver William Faithorne (who was later to engrave Davenant's portrait by Greenhill) was transported to France, and did not return until 1650; the greater engraver Wenceslaus Hollar escaped to Antwerp, returning in 1652; the actor William Robbins or Robinson was shot dead.[49] In the previous month, it will be recalled, the Court composer William Lawes had been killed at Chester while the King was attempting to relieve the garrison there.

Goring, who had taken over in the west country as General of the Horse, remained inactive, and departed for France at the end of the year – escorted by Davenant to Le Havre, Rouen and Paris.[50] A plan by the Queen, to ship several thousand troops from France to Newhaven, thence to be escorted by Davenant to Dartmouth, came to nothing.[51] On 5 May 1646 the King gave himself up to the Scots at Southwell near Newark. Sir William Davenant, who throughout had been so 'infinitely faithful to the Kings cause', finally took up residence at St Germain-en-Laye near Paris with the exiled Court of the Queen and Prince of Wales, where he was once again in touch with his old friend and patron Endymion Porter.

That once beloved courtier had, like so many others, fallen on hard times: he wrote to his old friend Nicholas:[52] 'I am in so much necessity, that were it not for an Irish barber that was once my servant, I might have starved for want of bread. He hath lent me some money that will last me for a fortnight longer . . . I am so retired into the streets of a suburb that I scarce know what they do at the Louvre, and I want clothes for a Court, having but that poor riding suit I came out of England in.' And again to Nicholas:[53] 'Here in our Court no man looks on me, and the Queen thinks I lost my estates for want of wit rather than from my loyalty to my master.' (Henrietta Maria must have been sorely jealous of him.) Davenant's poem 'To all Poets upon the recovery of Endimion Porter from a long Sickness'[54] probably refers to this time. He adjures his fellow-poets:

Arise! bring out your Wealth! perhaps some Twigge
Of Bay, and a few Mirtle Sprigs
Is all you have: but these ought to suffice,
Where spacious hearts make up the Sacrifice.
Be these your Off'ring as your utmost Wealth,
To shew your joy for lov'd *Endimions* Health . . .

The poet refers to the illness in a letter written on 1 September from St Germain to a friend in Paris: 'I promised to wait upon my lord of Brainford on Sunday night at St Looe, resolving to have given you notice of it that we might have enjoyed your good company there, but I am likewise void of that happiness by reason of Mr Porters indisposition of body . . .'.

John Evelyn was visiting Paris that summer, and he became very fond of the family of His Majesty's Resident at the Court of France, Sir Richard Browne, 'and particularly set my affections on a daughter'; on 10 June 'we concluded about my marriage, in order to which I went to St Germains, where His Majesty, then Prince of Wales, had his court'. A few weeks later, on 14 August, William Davenant addressed a letter from St Germain to the Resident which has caused much debate. In the usual jaunty Davenant manner, he begins: 'I understand I have 2 Children newly arrived at Paris, which a servant of my wives hath stolne from an obscure Country education in which they have continued during this Parliament neere London.' The wording seems to suggest that the poet's first wife is still living. Her son William was now twenty-two, too old to be still at school – he had probably joined his aunt Jane at the Oxford tavern where he was to die five years later; his sister Mary, who as we now know was only four in 1646, was probably there too. In any case, if Davenant had by then only these two offspring, one would have expected him to write of 'my 2 Children' rather than '2 Children'; altogether it seems probable that the ones now arrived at Paris were two more hitherto unknown members of his family. In some vestry minutes of St Sepulchre's in Holborn which, unlike the registers, survived the Fire, I have found references to a John and Richard Davenant who, in 1654 and 1655 respectively, received bibles under bequests by former godly parishioners, and perhaps these two boys were Sir William's. We know that he, and presumably his wife, had lived in Holborn at times, and it seems likely that she stayed on in St Sepulchre's parish: if so, the loss of the pre-Fire registers would explain why it has not been possible to trace her date of death.

In the letter about the two children, Davenant writes to Browne:

I shall desire you will be pleased to contribute a litle of your care toward the provision of such necesserie things as shall refine their Bodys, and for their mindes, I will provide a Magician of mine owne. M^m Porter [Endymion's wife] tells me Mistresse Sayers will upon your intreaty take this paynes: and I will intreat you to give her mony to furnish them cheap and handsomely which upon sight of your hand shall be returnd you by

Your most humble and affectionate servant
Will: Davenant[55]

Shortly after this, Davenant was entrusted with an important political commission – albeit one foredoomed to failure. He was sent to Newcastle from Paris as the Queen's emissary, to try to persuade King Charles to make a token acceptance of the Covenant. Edward Hyde's assessment has been much quoted, that he was 'an honest man and a witty, but in all respects inferior to such a trust'; but he himself concedes that the King was already very well aware of his wife's views ('the Queen had enough declared her opinion to his majesty, that he should part with the church for his peace and security'). No emissary could prevail upon King Charles to change his mind when she herself had failed.

Hyde's account of the episode is heavily weighted in his own favour – he has the King describing Lord Jermyn as not understanding 'any thing of the church', and Lord Colepeper as having 'no religion', while declaring 'the chancellor' (that is, Hyde himself) to be 'an honest man, and would never desert him, nor the prince, nor the church'. He then states that Davenant 'mentioned the church slightingly' to the King, at which Charles was 'transported with so much passion and indignation, that he gave him more reproachful terms, and a sharper reprehension, than he did ever towards any other man; and forbad him to presume to come again into his presence. Whereupon the poor man, who had in truth very good affections, was exceedingly dejected and afflicted, and returned into France, to give an account of his ill success to those who sent him.'[56]

That this account is grossly exaggerated, and in part untrue, is demonstrated by three letters written by the King shortly afterwards (and among State Papers later collected by Hyde himself). The first, dated 3 October and addressed to Jermyn, Colepeper and John Ashburnham,[57] speaks of the emissary in temperate terms: 'I found Davenants instructions to be such both for matter and circumstance, that my just greife for them had been unsuportable, but that the extraordinary and severall kynde expressions of my Wyfe . . . abated the sharpnesse of my sorrow. . . . Only one particular I must mention, wherwith Davenant hath threatened me; which is 351 [the Queen] retyring from all businesses into a monastery. This if it fall out, (which God forbid) is so distructife to all my affaires – I say no more of it; my hart is too bigg . . .'. The second, written to the same trio on the 10th,[58] restates the King's immovable position on the church: 'you are monstrously mistaken in beliving that the question is simply between Episcopal and Presbiterian governement; For nothing less then the change of the whole frame of Religion is now in dispute . . .'. The third, dated the 16th and addressed to the Queen,[59] is perhaps the most significant in the present context. 'I asseure thee', Charles tells his wife, 'that the absolute establishing of Presbiteriall governement would make me but a titulary King. And that this is so, both the Wills, Davenant and Murray confesses; but then they say, that a present absolut concession is the only way to reduce the governement, as I would have it . . .'. Charles endorsed this on the 17th to be delivered to Henrietta Maria by Davenant himself. The affectionate reference to 'both the Wills', the acknowledgement in the words 'Davenants instructions' that the poet was simply a mouth-piece, the fact that he was accompanied by Murray, Earl of Dysart, and the obvious implication that there was more than one meeting between the three men – all this entirely undermines Hyde's overheated account.

On the poet's return to Paris, Henrietta Maria wrote to her husband: 'Davenant hath given me a large account of the business where you are, upon which I must conclude with more fear than hope . . .'.[60] And on 5 December Charles wrote to her: 'I have, as thou desired me, done my part concerning Davenants Proposition for the sending of persons from thee to me, with fitt asseurances for theire safty'[61] – additional evidence that his confidence in Davenant remained unimpaired.

On his return to Paris after the mission to the King, Davenant took up residence in the Louvre with Lord Jermyn. The Prince of Wales had for a time maintained a company of players there to entertain the exiled English, and Davenant's former commander Lord Newcastle 'writ severall things' for it; but in November 1646 it was 'for want of pay dissolved'. A detailed account survives of a masque put on by the courtiers at New Year 1647, and the Queen had two plays performed during the following Christmas season;[62] her servant Davenant probably had a hand in the writing, but positive evidence is lacking. In London, public performances were still taking place from time to time at the Cockpit, Fortune and Salisbury Court playhouses, in defiance of the parliamentary ban and in spite of frequent raids by soldiery, and the King's Servants were preparing their old Blackfriars theatre for a hoped-for reopening. The appeal of the theatre remained strong: on a Sunday in January 1648, for example, 'there were ten Coaches to heare Doctor *Ushur* [preach] at *Lincolns* Inne, but . . . above sixscore Coaches on the last Thursday in Golden Lane to heare the Players at the Fortune'.[63] On 5 February John Evelyn 'saw a tragi-comedy acted in the Cockpit'.

The compulsive writer exiled in France was cut off from all this theatrical activity, so he embarked on a new venture: *Gondibert: An Heroick Poem*. There must have been many interruptions, for the ambitious men surrounding the heir apparent had little to do but indulge their jealousies and jockeyings for position, and inevitably William Davenant, the close associate of the head of the Queen's household Lord Jermyn, aroused hostility. In the winter of 1647–8 the two men travelled to Calais, where the Prince hoped to take command of some ships which had broken away from the parliamentary fleet. Davenant protected Jermyn from attack by an ambitious Captain Griffin, who subsequently followed the pair to Paris threatening to 'cause Davenant to be pistolled and Lord Jermin to be gelt'. A few months later Lord Digby, offended at Jermyn's pre-eminence, challenged him to a duel with swords: this was to have taken place at Nanterre, and would have involved Davenant – Jermyn's chosen second – in a duel with the challenger's brother, Sir Kenelm. However, no one seemed over-anxious for a fight, and Sir Kenelm departed disgruntled. Another outraged courtier, Sir Balthazar Gerbier, composed a hysterical thirty-six-page *Manifestation* ('printed for the Authour' in London in 1651) in which he sought to defend himself against a string of real or imagined accusations. He declared that he had had 'a great deal of right to claim favour' at the exiled Court; but 'a secret cabale, which envied me, moved against me' (the tone recalls Davenant's frequent complaints in earlier years about hostile factions). One subject of complaint was that an alleged attack on him between Rouen and Dieppe instigated by the 'cabale' had been dismissed as 'a fixion'; and 'who should be the authour of this abominable falsehood, but William Crafts [Crofts] and Davenant the poet, who reported it frequently at the Louvre, and up and down Paris. Neither were they [it is not altogether clear whether 'they' still include the poet] contented to disperse the said calumny throughout France, but they published it into all other parts by their letters, insomuch as that Westminster Hall was filled with the same, and it was the common talk about London, how that I had committed horrid things with some of my own family . . .'. Poor Gerbier seems to have been afflicted with persecution mania.[64]

On 30 January 1649, with the execution in London of King Charles, his eighteen-year-old son became the King in exile; and in August Endymion Porter, his old and faithful friend, and patron of so many painters and writers including William Davenant, died in penury. He had recently been allowed to return to England, and was buried at St Martin-in-the-Fields. His widow continued to live at their house in the Strand, which had been much damaged by soldiers who had been quartered there, until her death soon after the Restoration. Davenant's 'Song. Endimion Porter, and Olivia'[65] stands as a monument to their love. It reflects, as do many of Davenant's poems, speculation and doubt about an after-life, and reads in part:

ENDIMION.

Olivia, 'tis no fault of Love
To loose our selves in death, but O, I fear,
    When Life and Knowledge is above
Restor'd to us, I shall not know thee there.

OLIVIA.

Call it not Heaven (my Love) where we
Our selves shall see, and yet each other miss:
    So much of Heaven I find in thee
As, thou unknown, all else privation is.

Olivia's singing voice was reputed to be 'the rarest in the world', and the poem ends with Endymion's declaring:

I need not seek thee in the Heavenly Quire;
For I shall know *Olivia* by her Voice.

CHAPTER SEVEN

1649–55
Gondibert; imprisonment
in the Tower

It was on his return to Paris at the collapse of the royalist cause that, according to Anthony Wood, William Davenant 'changed his religion to that of Rome'. Soon he almost changed the pattern of his life by settling in the New World.

After the execution of King Charles, the English colonists in America remained divided in their political loyalties. In September 1649 a commission was made out appointing Davenant Treasurer of Virginia; a second commission, in the following February, named him instead as Lieutenant-Governor of Maryland to replace Lord Baltimore, who did 'visibly adhere to the Rebells of England'; finally, a commission dated Breda, 3 June 1650, appointed him one of sixteen members of the Council of Virginia under the governor, Sir William Berkeley, who were to build castles and forts at the charge of the colonists 'for the better suppressing of such of Our subjects as shall at any time rebel against Us or Our Royal Governor there'.[1]

Davenant had sailed for Jersey in January, *en route* for America; and early in May he left for the Atlantic crossing (still supposing, of course, that he was bound for Maryland rather than Virginia), in a vessel provided by the governor of the island, Sir George Carteret. The colonies were in urgent need of skilled craftsmen, and John Aubrey explains that as part of Davenant's mission, he had

> layd an ingeniose Designe to carry a considerable number of Artificers, (chiefly Weavers) from hence [France] to Virginia; and by Mary [Henrietta Maria] the Q. mothers meanes, he got favour from the K. of France to goe into the Prisons, & pick & choose, so when the poor dammed wretches understood what the Designe was, the[y] cryed uno ore Tout Tisseran. we are all Weavers. Will. [took] 36, as I remember if not more, and shipped them . . .

It seems highly probable that Henrietta Maria had engineered her servant's appointment to America, as she had done his service under Newcastle in the civil war. As his body-servant, Sir William took a Frenchman, Jean Bernard, and as secretary, Thomas Cross, who would soon become his stepson by his second marriage.[2]

On 10 May, the poet Abraham Cowley wrote anxiously from Paris to Henry Bennet, the future Earl of Arlington: 'We have not heard one word from Sir W. Davenant since he left us; be pleas'd to give me some account of him and his Voyage.' The news when it came was bad: Davenant had been captured in the Channel by one Captain John Green, commanding the frigate *Fortune,* and imprisoned in Cowes Castle (Wood and Aubrey wrongly say he was taken to Carisbrooke). In Aubrey's words: 'he & his Tisseran were all taken by the Shippes then belonging to the Parliament of England, the Slaves I suppose they sold . . .'. Cowley wrote to Bennet towards the end of the month that the laureate was 'now Prisoner with all his Men in the Isle of Wight. We are strangely pursu'd in all things, and all places, by our evil Fortune, even our retreats to the other World (except by death) are cutt off'. (Thomas Cross, who according to himself had been sent out by his mother 'in very good Equipage', managed to get away to Barbados, where he became secretary to the governor.)[3] News travelled slowly about the continent: when Davenant's appointment to the Council of Virginia was made on 3 June, it was evidently not known in Breda that he had been captured, and it was not until 12 July that Edward Hyde, writing a letter to Cowley from Madrid, added a postscript which eloquently expresses his real affection for his old friend: 'I am exceedingly afflicted for the misfortune of poore will Davenant. I beseech you lett me know w^t is become of him, for I heare no more then y^t he was taken prisoner and carried to ye Isle of Wight.'[4]

When Davenant set out on his abortive voyage to America in May, he had taken with him the manuscript of the first two completed Books of *Gondibert,* and probably also part of the third; for although his publisher Henry Herringman's gloss on the third says it was 'Written by the Author during his imprisonment', he himself states in the *Preface* – published 'from the Louvre' before his departure from Paris, on 2 January – that a 'little time would . . . make it fit for the Press', which suggests that the period between his capture in the Channel in May and the *Postscript* dated '*Cowes-Castle in the Isle of* Wight, *October 22*'[5] was spent in revising his draft rather than in original writing.

The *Preface* is addressed to the author's '*much Honour'd* FRIEND M^r. HOBS'. It occupies the first twenty pages of the 1673 folio edition of the *Works,* and Davenant states in his opening sentence that the philosopher had done him the honour of allowing *Gondibert* 'a daily examination as it was written'. Reaffirming his gratitude in a later passage, he writes: 'I cannot forbear to thank you in publick, for examining, correcting and allowing [approving] this Poem in parcels ere it arriv'd at the contexture: by which you have perform'd the just degrees of proceeding with Poets; who during the gayety and wantonness of the Muse, are but as children to Philosophers . . .'.

The *Preface* is an interesting document in which this thoughtful and realistic man speaks to us (to quote his recent editor David Gladish)[6] 'from the threshold of our own era'. Employing the word 'philosophy' in the broad sense, it reflects many of the ideas current in mid-seventeenth-century England, and recalls in particular Bacon's treatment of the faculties of memory, imagination and reason in *The Advancement of Learning* (published in 1605). The account of the 'House of Astragon' in Book II of *Gondibert* owes something to Bacon's 'Solomon's House' in *The New Atlantis*; and the *Preface* as a whole breathes the seventeenth-century spirit of enquiry which pervades Pepys's *Diary* and which in a decade would lead to the establishment of the Royal Society.[7] In composing the *Preface*, Davenant achieves an engagingly colloquial and discursive style which seems to echo the debates enjoyed in Paris by the middle-aged poet and the elderly philosopher, debates probably often joined by fellow-exiles. Sometimes one can almost catch the author's actual tone of voice – as in this robust passage about his poem:

> I have found Friends as ready as Books to regulate my conceptions, or make them more correct, easie, and apparent. But though I am become so wise, by knowing my self, as to believe, the thoughts of divers transcend the best which *I* have written; yet I have admitted from no man any change of my Design, nor very seldom of my sense: for *I* resolv'd to have this Poem subsist and continue throughout with the same complexion and spirit [Davenant's italics]; though it appear but like a plain Family, of a neighbourly alliance, who marry into the same moderate quality and garbe, and are fearful of introducing strangers of greater ranke, lest the shining presence of such, might seem to upbraid, and put all about them out of countenance.

Explaining why he has 'taken so much paines to become an Author' (as distinct from a poet and playwright), Davenant writes that 'Men are chiefly provok'd to the toyl of compiling Books, by love of Fame, and often by officiousness of Conscience, but seldom with expectation of Riches. . . . Those that write by the command of Conscience (thinking themselves able to instruct others, and consequently oblig'd to it) grow commonly the most voluminous; because the pressures of Conscience are so incessant, that she is never satisfy'd with doing enough: . . . And this may be the cause why Libraries are more than double lin'd with

Spiritual Books.' He repeats that for himself, Fame (which he describes as 'reputation' for the living, and 'a musical glory' for the dead) is the spur; and in his 'riper age' he has chosen to seek it more especially 'by an Heroical Poem', this being generally 'allow'd to be the most beautiful of Poems'. He writes of his purpose throughout in a tone of high serious-ness, and it was evidently not for want of effort that – like many another author – his eventual 'Fame' owed little to his most grandiose project.

The *Preface* opens with a survey of the classical practitioners of the epic poem – Homer, Virgil, Lucan and Statius – followed by 'the first of the Moderns', Tasso – recalling in each case what 'the Curious have against them'; last comes Spenser, criticised for his 'obsolete Language'. Then the laureate turns to his own work, 'my new Building', explaining – in a defence of artistic as against historical truth – why he has set it 'in a Century so far remov'd': the aim is to

> preserve me from their improper examinations, who know not the requisites of a Poem, nor how much pleasure they lose . . . who take away the liberty of the Poet, and fetter his feet in the shackles of an Historian: for why should a Poet doubt in Story to mend the intrigues of Fortune by more delightful conveyances of probable fictions, because austere Historians have enter'd into bond to truth . . . Truth narrative, and past, is the Idol of Historians (who worship a dead thing) and truth operative, and by effects continually alive, is the Mistris of Poets, who hath not her existence in matter, but in reason.

The author turns to 'the forme' of his 'Building'. Experienced play-wright as he is, he explains: 'I cannot discern . . . that any Nation hath in representment of great actions (either by *Heroicks* or *Dramaticks*) digested Story into so pleasant and instructive a method as the English by their *Drama*'; so his epic poem will have five Books, corresponding to the five Acts of a play, with Cantos corresponding to Scenes '(the *Scenes* having their number ever govern'd by occasion)'. As for the decision to use what he calls

> my interwoven *Stanza* of four . . . numbers in Verse must, like distinct kind of Musick, be exposed to the uncertain and different taste of several Ears. Yet I may declare, that I believ'd it would be more pleasant to the Reader, in a Work of length, to give this respite or pause, between every *Stanza* (having endeavored that each should contain a period) then to run him out of breath with continued *Couplets*. Nor doth alternate Rime by any lowliness of Cadence make the sound less Heroick, but rather adapt it to a plain and stately composing of Musick; and the brevity of the *Stanza* renders it less subtle to the Composer, and more easie to the Singer, which in *stilo recita-tivo*, when the Story is long, is chiefly requisite . . .

For he has so much 'heat' (pride) as to presume that his Cantos might (like the works of Homer 'ere they were joyn'd together and made a Volume') be 'sung at Village-feasts. . . . For so . . . did *Homer's* Spirit, long after his bodies rest, wander in musick about *Greece*'. The passage reflects Davenant's profound love of music, and foreshadows the innovative 'declamations with music' and 'operas' which he would soon be staging in London. John Dryden, who had a high regard for the older poet, writes in the *Preface* to his *Annus Mirabilis* (published by Henry Herringman in 1667, the year before Davenant's death) that he has chosen the same stanza form for *his* poem: 'I have chosen to write my poem in quatrains, or stanzas of four in alternate rhyme, because I have ever judged them more noble, and of greater dignity, both for the sound and number, than any other verse in use amongst us.' The *Preface* is addressed to his brother-in-law Sir Robert Howard, and in a direct tribute to Davenant he writes later: 'I have dwelt too long upon the choice of my stanza, which you may remember is much better defended in the preface to *Gondibert*.'[8]

Having dealt at length with his 'new Building', Davenant turns to 'the Builder', and sees fit to 'accuse and condemn, as papers unworthy of light, all those hasty digestions of thought which were published in my youth'. He has now gained experience, and has proceeded 'with a slow pace', following 'two great examples': Virgil, 'who was many years in doing honor to *Aeneas*', and Statius, who 'was twice Seaven years in renowning the war between *Argos* and *Thebes*'. Some upbraid 'painful' (painstaking) poets for the 'want of extemporary fury, or rather *inspiration*'; but 'inspiration' is 'a dangerous word . . . a spiritual Fitt'.

There follows a discussion of the place of the poet in society, a subject no doubt much discussed by the English poets exiled in Paris. The 'four chief aids of Government (*Religion, Armes, Policy* and *Law*)' have been defectively applied by their practitioners, the *Divines, Leaders of Armies, States-men* and *Lawyers*, for 'the People . . . are more unquiet then in former Ages'. Authority has attempted to prevail upon their bodies, whereas 'the subject on which they should work is the Minde; and the Minde can never be constrain'd, though it may be gain'd by perswasion'. And 'none are so fit aids to this important work as Poets'. It may be objected that the education of the People's minds by poetry is 'opposite to the receiv'd opinion, that the People ought to be continu'd in ignorance' – but ignorance is 'rude, censorious, jealous, obstinate, and proud; these being exactly the ingredients of which Disobedience is made'. It is absurd to criticise poets for praising Beauty, they are but praising the wonderful works of God; equally, those who accuse the poets as 'Inventors, or Provokers of that which by way of aspersion they call *Love*' are 'Enemies to Nature; and all affronts to Nature are offences to God'; for Love is 'Natur's Preparative to her greatest work, which is the making of *Life*'. Here, as elsewhere – notably in an earlier passage in which he writes of Love as 'the most acceptable imposition of Nature, the cause and preservation of Life, and the very healthfulness of the mind, as well as of the body' – the laureate reaffirms his deeply held belief that 'love' means sexual love. It recalls his baffled attempts to come to terms with the concept of platonic love, that 'new court epithet scarce understood', when in the 1630s he was writing *The Temple of Love* and *The Platonic Lovers* at the behest of Henrietta Maria.

Davenant concludes his *Preface* by promising to proceed with *Gondibert* unless Hobbes sends him 'a discouragement' after reading the first two Books; but he says he will delay publication of any part of the poem 'till I can send it you from *America,* whither I now speedily prepare; having the folly to hope, that when I am in another world (though not in the common sense of dying) I shall find my Readers (even the Poets of the present Age) as temperate, and benigne, as we are all to the Dead, whose remote excellence cannot hinder our reputation'.

'The ANSWER of Mr HOBBES' (pages 21–7 of the folio) is dated 10 January. The philosopher pleads 'incompetence' as a critic, being no poet himself: but he praises Davenant for the 'dignity and vigor' of his expression, and declares that he has 'performed all the parts of various experience, ready memory, clear judgement, swift and well govern'd fancy'. As for the verse-form: 'in an Epigram or a Sonnet, a man may vary his measures . . . but in so great and noble a work as is an Epique Poem, for a man to obstruct his own way with unprofitable difficulties, is great imprudence. So likewise to cho[o]se a needless and difficult correspondence of Rime, is but a difficult toy. . . . I cannot therefore but very much approve your *Stanza,* and the Rime Alternate'.

He writes of the honour done him by the poet in 'attributing in your Preface somewhat to my Judgment', and goes on: 'I have used your Judgment no less in many things of mine, which coming to light will thereby appear the better.' This has been taken as no more than an over-generous tribute from a friend, but there is reason to believe that in their intellectual exchanges at the exiled Court, the philosopher did indeed borrow from as well as give to the poet; in particular, it has recently been argued that 'Hobbes followed Davenant in regarding the moral and political education of the aristocracy as the essential task of government.'[9]

Davenant's *Preface,* when it was published in Paris in 1650, was accompanied by commendatory verses from Edmund Waller and Abraham Cowley on Books I and II of *Gondibert,* 'Finished before his

Voyage to *America*'.[10] Both commend the poet for his courage in going overseas: he excels 'No less in *Courage* then in *Singing* well,' Waller declares, and is demonstrating to his country 'that they have impov'-rished themselves, not you'; while Cowley writes of his 'Fancy, like a Flame' which 'leaves bright tracks for following Pens to take./Sure 'twas this noble boldness of the *Muse* / Did thy desire to seek new Worlds infuse; / And ne'r did Heaven so much a Voyage bless, / If thou canst Plant but there with like success'.

Books I and II of *Gondibert*, the uncompleted Book III ('I am heere arriv'd at the middle of the Third Book' as Davenant says in his *Postscript*), and the preliminary essays and commendatory poems, came out in London, in quarto and octavo editions, in 1651 (the year in which Hobbes's *Leviathan* also appeared). By publishing the *Preface* on its own in Paris in 1650, the poet had laid himself open to the 'envy' and ridicule of the exiled courtiers, and they seized the opportunity with cheerful gusto. *Certain Verses Written by Several of the Author's Friends: to Be Reprinted with the Second Edition of Gondibert* (London 1653) make fun of him on every predictable ground. The writers are anonymous, but Aubrey describes their effort as 'a very witty but satericall little booke . . . writt by G.D. of Bucks [George, second Duke of Buckingham], S^r Jo: Denham &c.'. There are two references in the poems to the laureate's 'four best friends', and he himself was no doubt well aware of all the rhymesters' identities, and their numbers.[11] They would have read parts at least of *Gondibert* as the writing progressed (the author claims in his *Preface* that 'divers with no ill satisfaction have had a taste of it', and Aubrey says he was 'very fond of it', so he was no doubt not averse to passing it round), but the fact that the *Preface* was published in isolation allowed them to scoff:

> A Preface to no Book, a Porch to no house:
> Here is the Mountain, but where is the Mouse?
> But, oh, America must breed up the Brat . . .
> For *Will* to Virginia is gone from among us,
> With thirty two slaves, to plant *Mundungus* [tobacco].

The commendatory poems by Waller and Cowley and the approval of 'old *Hobbs*' are mentioned only to be dismissed, and the author is criticised, with some justification, for pretentiousness, and in particular for the profusion of classical references in his work. There is a predicta-ble remark about his 'untaught Childhood', the customary taunt level-led at writers lacking a university education. No doubt, like his godfa-ther, Davenant had 'small Latin, and less Greek', and although he speaks of Homer, Virgil, Tasso and the rest, it is suggested that all are

'by *Will* unread, and most unseen'. His claims for his own epic are
extravagant: 'Down go the *Iliados,* down go the *Aneidos,* / All must give
way to the *Gondiberteidos.*' There are the inevitable references to the
poet's unfortunate nose, and disparaging remarks about his civil war
service: 'The King knights *Will* for fighting on his side, / Yet when *Will*
comes for fighting to be tri'd, / There is not one in all the Armies can /Say
they ere felt, or saw, this fighting man.'

The laureate is addressed as 'old *Daph*' or 'Daphne' (one verse is
addressed 'To DAPHNE *On his Incomparable Incomprehensible Poem*
GONDIBERT') – a neat play on both his name, and his office,
            , laurel.[12] Of the poem itself, the rhymesters complain
that he laboured at it incessantly in Paris, so as to 'sacrifice thy sleep, thy
diet, / Thy business; and what's more, our quiet. / And all this stir to
make a story, / Not much superior to *John Dory.*' His verse is described
as 'fustian', and his 'Rime' as poor; he is dismissed as a 'damn'd insipid
Poet'; and – unkindest cut of all – it is suggested that the pages of
Gondibert could best be employed to 'wipe the *Taile*'.

The fact that the epic is set in Lombardy prompts the final verse in the
collection – the one (quoted earlier) which ridicules Davenant for his
grandiose claim that his family came from there, and for his insertion of
the apostrophe into his surname: 'come from *Avenant,* means from
No-where. / Thus *Will* intending *D'Avenant* to grace / Has made a
Notch in's name, like that in's face . . .'.

Gondibert is not 'heroic' in any classical sense – and Dryden, in his
essay *Of Heroic Plays,*[13] recalling the author's decision to relate it to the
drama, with five Books each of several cantos, describes it as 'rather a
play in narrative . . . than an heroic poem'. It grows out of the tradition
of romance, and the theme is love rather than honour or ambition
(Gondibert, pledging his love to Birtha, (III, ii, sts. 74–5), declares: 'I
here to *Birtha* make / A vow, that *Rhodalind* I never sought, / Nor now
would with her love her greatness take. / Loves bonds are for her
greatness made too straight; / And me Ambition's pleasures cannot
please . . .)': the laureate, as in his play *Love and Honour,* was probably
responding once again to Henrietta Maria's proposal for a theme. He
writes only of mankind and the material environment: there is nothing
of the classical links between the worlds of men and gods. Hobbes
underlines this in his *Answer:* 'the subject of a Poem is the manners of
men'; and Waller and Cowley pick up the point in their verses. As
Waller puts it, the author writes of Love 'as th'antique World did know,
/ In such a stile as Courts may boast of now, / Which no bold tales of
Gods or *Monsters* swell, / But humane Passions, such as with us dwell. /

Man is thy theame, his Vertue or his rage'. And Cowley: 'Methinks
Heroick Poesie till now, / Like some fantastique Fairyland did show; /
. . . Thou like some worthy Knight, with sacred Arms / Dost drive the /
Monsters thence, and end the Charms: / Instead of these, dost *Men* and
Manners plant . . .'.

The completed part of *Gondibert* (pages 31–195 of the folio) is a
rambling affair – acknowledged by the author in his *Preface,* where he
expresses the hope that its 'Meanders' will prove 'as pleasant as a
summer passage on a crooked River, where going about, and turning
back is as delightful as the delays of parting Lovers'. As in a classical
epic, there are some elaborate set-pieces, the first an account of a
stag-hunt in a forest near Verona. The poet's sympathies, like those of
his godfather, are emphatically with the hunted rather than the hunter.
He writes (I, ii, sts. 36–8) of the huntsmen busily uncoupling the hounds
against the stag 'As if the world were by this Beast undone, / And they
against him hir'd as Nature's Foe'; and of how, at the sound of the horn,
all the beasts of the forest are 'Alarm'd by Eccho, Nature's Sentinel, /
Which shews that Murd'rous Man is come abroad. / Tyranique Man!
Thy subjects Enemy! / And more through wantonness then need or
hate'. And again, after the stag has resisted the hounds to the limit of his
strength, 'the Monarch Murderer comes in, / Destructive Man! whom
Nature would not arme, / As when in madness mischief is foreseen / We
leave it weaponless for fear of harme. / For she defenceless made him
that he might / Less readily offend; but Art Armes all, / From single strife
makes us in Numbers fight; / And by such art this Royall Stagg did fall'
(I, ii, sts. 52–3). Later, and in another context, he writes of 'anger, the
disease of Beasts untam'd; / Whose wrath is hunger, but in Men 'tis
pride, / Yet theirs is cruelty, ours courage nam'd' (II, i, st. 44). Here
speaks a sensitive and humane man, with views in tune with our time
rather than his own.

Princess Rhodalind (her name is a variant of Rhodolinda in *Albovine*
– the names Hermegild and Paradine also recur) is the only daughter of
Aribert, the aged King of Lombardy. Prince Oswald and Duke Gondibert are both of the Lombard royal line: Oswald aspires to the hand of
Rhodalind and the throne, but she and her father favour Gondibert.
After a battle and duel in which Oswald is killed, Book I ends with the
wounded Gondibert and his lieutenants being taken to the palace of
Astragon, a wealthy and famous philosopher. At the beginning of Book
II, the scene switches to Verona, and here the poet seems to be more at
ease. He writes – in a lively passage strongly reminiscent of his 'Vacation' poem of earlier years – of the town's awakening at dawn (II.i, sts.
14–19):

quickly ev'ry street
Does by an instant op'ning full appear,
When from their Dwellings busy Dwellers meet . . .

And here the early Lawyer mends his pace;
For whom the earlier Cliant waited long;
Here greedy Creditors their Debtors chace,
Who scape by herding in th'indebted Throng.

Th'advent'rous Merchant whom a Storm did wake,
(His Ships on *Adriatick* Billowes tost)
Does hope of Eastern windes from Steeples take,
And hastens there a Currier to the Coast.

Here through a secret Posterne issues out
The skar'd Adult'rer, who out-slept his time;
Day, and the Husbands Spie alike does doubt,
And with a half hid face would hide his crime.

There from sick mirth neglected Feasters reel,
Who cares of want in Wine's false *Lethe* steep.
There anxious empty Gamsters homeward steal,
And fear to wake, ere they begin to sleep . . .

'The City Morning' is among the descriptive passages singled out by
Hobbes for particular praise. Another is that of Oswald's funeral,
'grac'd with Roman Rites' (II, iv). Here, as earlier in describing the
history and architecture of Verona, the author's painstaking stanzas no
doubt reflect the extensive reading by which, as he explains in the
Preface, he had prepared himself for his task (he describes his sources as
'my Assistants . . . men of any Science, as well mechanical as liberal').

At II, v we return (with some relief) to 'The House of Astragon',
where everyone is 'as busie as intentive *Emmets* are'. Some go 'from the
Mine to the hot Furnace', some from 'flowry Fields to weeping Stills'
where 'hopefull *Chymicks*' extract 'Med'cine . . . for instant cure';
elsewhere divers and quarriers are busy. In 'Tow'rs of prodigious
height', philosophers study the cause and flight of meteors, while others
'with Optick Tubes the Moons scant face / . . . Attract through Glasses
to so near a space / As if they came not to survey, but prie'. Astragon
seeks 'the Stars remote societies'.

Man's pride (grown to Religion) he abates,
By moving our lov'd Earth; which we think fix'd;
Think all to it, and it to none relates;
With others motion scorn to have it mix'd;

As if 'twere great and stately to stand still
  Whilst other Orbes dance on; or else think all
Those vast bright Globes (to shew God's needless skill)
  Were made but to attend our little Ball . . .   (sts. 15–20)

Next we read of a building entitled *Great Nature's Office*, where *Nature's Registers* (zoologists) organise data collected by their *Intelligencers* (field-workers); *Nature's Nursery* (a botanical garden); *The Cabinet of Death*, an anatomical museum where hang 'Skelitons of ev'ry kinde'; and *The Monument of Vanish'd Mindes*, a huge library (sts. 21–68).

II, vii returns to the convalescent hero, who has fallen instantly in love with Astragon's only child, Birtha, and she with him. She is a 'Country Maid' of such remarkable beauty, virtue and innocence as to outstrip Miranda: 'she ne'r saw Courts', 'she never had in busie Cities bin', and 'not seeing punishment, could guess no Sin' (sts. 6–7). 'She thinks that Babes proceed from mingling Eyes, / Or Heav'n from Neighbourhood increase allows.' However, 'come they (as she hears) from Mothers pain, / . . . yet that she will sustain, / So they be like this Heav'nly Man she loves' (sts. 45–6). The course of true love naturally does not run smooth: news comes from court that Aribert has proclaimed Gondibert his successor and the future husband of Princess Rhodalind (III, ii). Our hero, torn between love and duty, takes from a heart-shaped casket an ancestral emerald for Birtha: it will lose its brilliance if he is ever unfaithful to her (III, iv, sts. 45–52). The couple 'seal their sacred plight' with kisses, 'Like Flowres still sweeter as they thicker grew' (st. 63), and Gondibert departs for Verona. The sorrowing Birtha is encouraged by her father to follow, and seek to serve Rhodalind: 'Your plighted Lord shall you ere long preferr / To neer attendance on this royal Maid' (III, v, 52).

Leaving his readers in suspense, the author dispatches Gondibert's lieutenants Goltho and Ulfinore to Verona as well; and in the final Canto (III, vi) '*Black Dalga's fatal beauty is reveal'd*' (to quote the 'Argument' which precedes it), and there is at last some light relief. The two young men ride in at the Western Gate as the sun is setting, but their progress to the Palace is delayed, 'For a black Beauty did her pride display / Through a large Window, and in Jewels shon' (st. 31). Having attracted the attention of the pair, 'She, with a wicked Woman's prosp'rous Art, / A seeming modesty, the Window clos'd' (st. 34). A 'little Page, / Clean and perfum'd', emerges to lead them upstairs, and the credulous Goltho is almost ensnared, in spite of Ulfinore's plea: 'Let's go! . . . Ere she shew cloven Feet' (st. 63). Suddenly there is a summons at the garden gate, and the resourceful beauty cries to Goltho (st. 67):

'My Mother, Sir! Alass! You must depart!' The watchful Ulfinore observes that the page gives admittance 'Not to a Matron, still prepar'd to die; / But to a Youth wholly design'd to live' (st. 72), and the chastened Goltho and Ulfinore ride on to the Duke's Palace, Ulfinore gravely advising his friend to 'fly from Lust's experiments!' (st. 80).

This episode is of particular interest, because it seems that for the young Goltho we can read the young Davenant: he told John Aubrey that when he wrote about Dalga, he had in mind the 'Black handsome wench that lay in Axe-yard' from whom he got the 'terrible clap . . . wch cost him his Nose'.

We do not know how *Gondibert* would have ended: in his *Preface,* Davenant says only that there would be 'an easie untying of those particular knots, which made a contexture of the whole; leaving such satisfaction of proba[bi]lities with the Spectator, as may perswade him that neither Fortune in the fate of the Persons, nor the Writer in the Representment, have been unnatural or exorbitant'. We may suppose that Gondibert and his Birtha are united.

Herringman, in his initial address to the reader in the 1673 folio, says that he is presenting 'a Collection of all those Pieces *Sir William D'ave-nant* ever design'd for the Press; In his Life-time he often express'd to me his great Desire to see them in *One Volume,* which (in Honor to his Memory) with a great deal of Care and Pains, I have now Accomplish'd'. The fact that *Gondibert* and its accompanying documents take precedence is no doubt in accordance with the author's wishes. Later on in the volume, as Herringman explains, are 'several Poems and Copies of Verses *never before Printed*; amongst them, there is the Death of *Astragon,* call'd, *The Philosophers Disquisition, directed to the dying Christian,* which the Author intended as an *Addition to Gondibert*'. It appears with *The Christians Reply to the Phylosopher.*[14]

As Davenant's editor Gibbs puts it, the two poems represent the laureate's 'fullest poetical meditation on religion', and express the desire of religious thinkers in the middle and later years of the seventeenth century, amidst the chaos of 'diff'ring Faiths, by adverse Pens perplext' (*Disquisition,* st. 32), to find a rational basis for religion, and to reconcile reason and faith.

The *Disquisition,* an impressive poem in ninety stanzas, begins with a general meditation on the errors of human learning and the limitations of human understanding. But it argues that knowledge must never be regarded as 'forbidden fruit': to denigrate knowledge is to denigrate its object, Nature. 'If Knowledge must, as evil, hidden lie / Then we, its object, Nature, seem to blame; / And whilst we banish Knowledge, as a Spy, / We but hide Nature as we cover shame.' (st. 18).

The central part of the poem, stanzas 24 to 59, is taken up with the Philosopher's enquiry into the relation of faith and reason. Faith unaided by Reason falls back on Tradition, and that 'presumptuous Antiquary' makes 'Strong Lawes of weak opinions of the Dead' and 'weares out Truth's best Stories into Tales' (sts. 51–2).

Finally the Philosopher puts a series of pertinent questions about the Christian religion itself:

> If, as Gods Students, we have leave to learne
>   His Truths, Why doth his Text oft need debate?
> Why, as through Mists, must we his Lawes discerne?   (st. 68)

> Tell me why Heav'n at first did suffer Sin? . . .
> Why, when the Soules first Fever did begin,
>   Was it not cur'd, which now a Plague is grown?   (st. 74)
> Why should our Sins, which not a moment last,
>   (For, to Eternity compar'd, extent
> Of Life is, e're we name it, stopt and past)
>   Receive a doome of endless punishment?   (st. 80)

> If Destiny be not, like humane Law,
>   To be repeal'd, what is the use of Prayer?   (st. 88)

The Christians Reply, in ten stanzas, views religion from the side of faith rather than reason:

> God bred the Arts to make us more believe
>   (By seeking Natures cover'd Misteries)
> His darker Workes, that Faith may thence conceive
>   He can do more then what our Reason sees.   (st. 3)

And stanza 5:

> Religion, e're impos'd, should first be taught;
>   Not seeme to dull obedience ready lay'd,
> Then swallow'd strait for ease, but long be sought;
>   And be by Reason councell'd, though not sway'd.

Waller's and Cowley's tributes to *Gondibert* were followed in 1651 by a commendatory poem in similar terms by Henry Vaughan ('To Sir William D'avenant, upon his *Gondibert*' in *Olor Iscanus*): 'where before *Heroick Poems* were / Made up of *Spirits, Prodigies,* and *fear,* / . . . Thou like the *Sun,* whose Eye brooks no disguise, / Hast Chas'd them hence . . .'. Vaughan writes of Davenant's fire breaking through 'the *ashes* of thy aged *Sire*', and this has sometimes been taken as a reference to Shakespeare; but the poet must intend a reference to the laureate as one of the 'Sons of Ben', since he goes on to speak of the 'sire's' '*bayes*', his crown of laurels. In the opinion of Thomas Rymer (1674), the *Preface* to *Gondibert* contains 'some strokes of an extra-ordinary judgement': Davenant is 'for *unbeaten tracks,* and *new wayes of thinking*', and if he had been able to finish his epic, he would not have been 'so open to the attack of Criticks'. Rymer does not, however, care for the choice of the stanza form, and nor does Richard Flecknoe (1668), who dismisses the laureate's Muse as 'none of the nine, but only a Mungrill'. Among admirers is the celebrated and eccentric Margaret Cavendish, herself a poet and playwright, and second wife of Lord Newcastle, Davenant's commander in the north in the civil war. '. . . of all the Heroick Poems I have read', she writes, 'I like Sir *W.D.s.* as being Most, and Nearest to the Natures, Humours, Actions, Practice, Designs, Effects, Faculties, and Natural Powers, and Abilities of Men or Human Life . . .'[15].

Among critics of later centuries, Alexander Pope·(1736) considers that *Gondibert,* while not a good poem, contains 'a great many good things'; and Sir Walter Scott declares (1808) that it often exhibits 'a majestic, dignified, and manly simplicity'. He gives qualified praise to the stanza form, describing its use as 'an advance towards true taste', and recalling that it was 'twice sanctioned by the practice of Dryden, upon occasions of uncommon solemnity'.[16]

On 17 May 1650, the new Council of State in London decided to instruct Colonel Sydenham to hold Davenant in Cowes Castle until further notice, 'he having been an active enemy to the common-wealth'.[17] Parliament was in an agitated state: Dr Dorislaus, their envoy to the States General, had recently been murdered by English or Scottish exiles, and just after Davenant's capture Antony Ascham, a second envoy, was murdered by exiles in Madrid. The new government had made provision for such royalists as wished to compound and live peacefully in England, but Davenant was one of the 'malignants' to whom the act did not apply. On 28 June the Council of State was asked to 'think of some Names of Persons to be brought to trial' in the High Court; four were chosen, and at the beginning of July six more were 'pitched on', including the laureate – '*Davenant,* called *Sir William Davenant*', as he is customarily described at the time. When his case came up in the House, 27 voted for him and 27 against – he was spared because 'Mr Speaker declared himself to be a No'. The news-sheet *Mercurius Politicus* could not resist reporting that 'some *Gentlemen,* out of pitty, were pleased to let him have the *Noes* of the House, because he had none of his own'. But on the following day, there was another vote, and Davenant's name was restored to the list. And on the 9th, an act was passed and ordered to be printed, naming Davenant and five others to be tried for their lives for 'all Treasons, Murthers, felonies, Crimes and offences', thus putting them into the same category as the murderers of Dorislaus and Ascham. Once again, as at the time of the Army Plot in 1641, there seems to have been considerable public sympathy for the poet: *Mercurius* hoped that '*Will. D'Avenant* may not dy, till he hath finished his own *Monument [Gondibert]*'.[18]

Davenant's 'POSTSCRIPT *To the* READER' (pages 196–8 of the folio), in which he speaks of his work on *Gondibert* being 'interrupted by so great an experiment as Dying', is dated Cowes Castle 22 October, which indicates that his removal to the Tower of London in preparation for the expected trial was imminent. He writes:

> 'tis high time to strike Sail, and cast Anchor (though I have run but halfe my Course [of *Gondibert*] when at the Helme I am threatened with Death; who, though he can visit us but once, seems troublesome; and even in the Innocent may beget such a gravity, as diverts the Musick of Verse. And I beseech thee (if thou art so civil as to be pleased with what is written) not to take ill, that I run not on till my last gasp. For though I intended in this POEM to strip Nature naked, and clothe her again in the perfect shape of Vertue; yet even in so worthy a Designe I shall ask leave to desist, when I am interrupted by so great an experiment as Dying: and 'tis an experiment to the most experienc'd; for no Man (though his Mortifications may be much greater then mine) can say, *He has already Dy'd.*
>
> It may be objected by some (who look not on Verse with the Eyes of the Ancients, nor with the reverence it still preserves among other Nations) that I beget a *Poem* in an unseasonable time. ... But I will gravely tell thee (*Reader*) he who writes an *Heroick Poem*, leaves an Estate entayl'd; and he gives a greater Gift to Posterity, then to the present Age ...

Legal proceedings seem to have been under way by December, but one of the relevant documents now in the Public Record Office[19] states explicity that 'no action was taken' against William Davenant. There has been much debate about who saved him from death. Wood reports that John Milton, and the two 'godly aldermen' of York whom he had kindly allowed to escape during the civil war, were among the saviours; and Aubrey – who reports that 'he expected no mercy from the Parliament, and had no hopes of escaping [with] his life' – says that when the aldermen heard he was in extreme danger, they hastened to London to petition the House on behalf of the man 'who had been so civill to them'. In a later addition in the margin, Aubrey writes: ' 'Twas Harry Martyn [Colonel Henry Marten] that saved Sr Wm Davenant's life in the Howse, when they were talking of sacrificing one, then s^d Hen: that In Sacrifices they always offerd pure, & without blemish, now yee talke of making a Sacrifice of an old rotten Rascall . . .'. He undermines his own anecdote by stating that Lord Falkland later saved Marten himself 'by this *very jest*' when he was tried as a regicide at the Restoration; but a letter which the poet wrote to Marten from the Tower on 8 July 1652 (shortly before his release on bail) indicates that he did play a part: 'I would it were worthy of you to know how often I have profess'd that I had rather owe my libertie to you than to any man, and that the obligation you lay upon me shall be for ever acknowledg'd.'[20]

The report about Milton's intervention has usually been dismissed, but perhaps too readily. Wood, with his close contacts with Sir William's relations at Oxford, should have known what he was talking about; nor should it be forgotten that in the City of London, the Davenants of Bow Lane and the Miltons of Bread Street had been very near neighbours in earlier times. Similarly, it would be rash to dismiss the reports that Davenant (and Marvell, who succeeded Milton as Latin secretary to the Cromwellian Council of State when the poet went blind) interceded for Milton at the Restoration.

Although Davenant escaped execution, he had to spend two years in the Tower – a period during which, understandably, he seems not to have had the heart to do much writing. Commendatory poems 'To my Friend Mr. Ogilby, Upon the Fables of Aesop Paraphras'd in Verse' and 'To Mr Benlowes, on his Divine Poem', were addressed from the Tower on 30 September 1651 and 13 May 1652 respectively.[21] Ogilby was an admired translator of Virgil, Aesop and Homer, and a successful publisher and cartographer; on the title-page of the 1673 edition of the *Fables* he describes himself as 'His MAJESTY'S *Cosmographer, Geographic Printer,* and *Master of the Revels* in the Kingdom of IRELAND'. (At the Restoration he and Davenant competed for the third position: Davenant obtained a warrant in November 1660, but Ogilby petitioned for reconsideration, and in May 1661 obtained the royal patent himself).

One gets the impression that, as at the time of the Army Plot, there had perhaps never been any real determination to execute 'Davenant the poet', and that the time he had to spend in the Tower was the result of bureaucracy and muddle rather than active malevolence.[22] In November 1651 there had been an agreement between the parliamentary governor of Guernsey, Colonel John Bingham, and the governor of Castle Cornet there, to exchange Davenant for a prisoner in the castle, Colonel John Clarke. This was approved by the parliamentary admiral and general-at-sea, General Blake, and Clarke was duly released, and returned to army service. But Davenant was not – although it was subsequently stated that he had not forfeited his chance of freedom by 'any hostility to Parliament'. It was not until 7 October 1652 that the Council of State finally ordered his release (the French servant who had set sail with him for America had been released from the Gatehouse at Westminster in June of the previous year).[23] Bulstrode Whitelocke, whom the poet had known from his Inns of Court days and who was now a member of the Council, must have spoken on his behalf, for Davenant wrote him an effusive letter of thanks on the 9th.[24]

Within the month, Davenant married the widow of Sir Thomas Cademan, the royal doctor who had cared for him during his bout of syphilis, and who had died in 1651. The exact date and place of the marriage are not to be found, no doubt because the parties were Catholics. Anne Cademan brought the penniless poet the best part of £800, left from the estate of her first husband, Thomas Cross; but although his only son William had died in the previous December at the family wine-tavern at Oxford, Chancery documents discovered by Leslie Hotson[25] show that she also brought him four young stepsons: Thomas, Paul and John Cross, aged twenty-two, sixteen and eleven, and nine-year-old Philip Cademan.

Not long after his release from the Tower on bail, the unfortunate laureate was arrested again, for debt. Finally, in desperation, in the early spring of 1654 he addressed an appeal to the Lord Protector, which was referred to a committee of the Council of State with relevant documents annexed. One was a telling letter, date 1 February, from Colonel Bingham, who wrote of the great concern he had felt at 'the blemish gen. Blake and I received, by the breach of conditions with Sir William Davenant. He has lately been made a prisoner for debt, whilst he remains a prisoner on bail to the Court of Articles, to return to the Tower when demanded; and thereby he cannot stir out of town to recover his debt. . . . I hope, in lieu of his two years imprisonment after exchange, the Court will allow him some further time to follow his occasions, as his sufferings, contrary to the articles of war, have been great.' Davenant himself made four specific requests: for full liberty, having been two years in the Tower and a year more under bail, 'not to stir from the town'; for a stay of the two writs whereby he had lately been arrested for debt, and 'made double prisoner'; for an extension, from six weeks to six months, of the period promised him to put his affairs in order; and for a general pardon, 'that I may live as a faithful subject'. Release and pardon were agreed on 27 June and finally approved on 22 July, a discharge warrant from Protector and Council was dated 1 August, and the laureate was finally released on 4 August.[26]

He seems to have settled at the Cademans' house in Tothill Street, Westminster, on his marriage; but the family probably moved later to

Holborn, for on 5 March 1654/5 Dame Anne was buried at St Andrew's Holborn 'out of Castle Yard' (now Furnival Street).[27] Nethercot[28] is perhaps unduly harsh about the marriage: 'whatever the precedent circumstances', he writes, 'her loss did not occasion her practical husband any prolonged fit of mourning. D'avenant, in spite of being a cavalier poet, never regarded the marriage relationship with even an ephemerally sentimental or romantic eye'. But 'sentiment' and 'romance' are not words usually applicable to a seventeenth-century marriage, and there is no need to assume that there had been no affection between William and Anne. In the *Preface* to *Gondibert,* for example, the poet writes of a man's 'darling Wife', and later, when he is describing Love as 'Natur's Preparative to her greatest work, which is the making of *Life'*, he goes on to write of the marriage of true minds: 'Marriage in Mankind were as rude and unprepar'd as the hasty elections of other Creatures, but for acquaintance, and conversation before it; and that must be an acquaintance of Mindes, not of Bodies.'

In any case, the needy laureate, with his houseful of stepsons, had to be 'practical', and speedily; and, resourceful as always, he lost no time in securing the support of another widow of means. On 10 August he obtained a pass to travel to France, and soon returned with a third (and final) wife. She was Henrietta-Maria du Tremblay, 'of an ancient family in St Germain-Beaupré [Anjou]';[29] no doubt the couple had met during Davenant's time at the exiled Court. Lady Davenant ('Dame Mary Davenant', as she was known in her day) was to bear her husband many sons, to be an extremely capable business partner during his years as a Restoration theatre manager, and to carry on the business after his death.

CHAPTER EIGHT

1656-60
Davenant the innovator
– the opera

⋆⟩∘⟨⋆

In spite of the parliamentary ordinances of 1642 and subsequent years banning stage plays, the actors contrived to carry on – after a fashion – in face of raids by soldiery, plundering of their costumes and props, fines and occasional imprisonment.[1] There was evidently considerable sympathy for the 'poor players', and even during the height of the civil war, plays were given with remarkable frequency at the regular play-houses in London. In 1647 the actors were openly resuming their profession at the Salisbury Court off Fleet Street, the Cockpit in Drury Lane and the Fortune in Golding Lane; but in March 1649, two months after the execution of King Charles, the interiors of all three theatres were dismantled by a company of soldiers. The Salisbury Court and Cockpit would later be refurbished and figure in Sir William Davenant's career, but the Fortune never reopened as a playhouse.

However, the Red Bull in St. John Street, Clerkenwell, to the north of the City, somehow kept going. This open-air theatre had originally been a haunt of 'citizens and the meaner sort of people' – 'the rabble', attending a place where only 'noise' prevailed, to quote Carew's commendatory verses about Davenant's early play *The Just Italian*. If audiences were displeased, 'the Benches, the tiles, the laths, the stones, Oranges, Apples, Nuts, flew about most liberally'. But now, the Red Bull began to be frequented by the nobility and gentry, since two other theatres had been lost. The second Globe on Bankside – for which Davenant had written his *News from Plymouth* in 1635 – had been pulled down in 1644, 'to make tenements in the roome of it'; and by 1653 the Blackfriars, the aristocratic, private indoor theatre, where the rest of his staged plays had achieved performance, was in a sad state. Richard Flecknoe wrote: 'Passing on to Black-fryers, and seeing never a *Play-bil* on the Gate, no *Coaches* on the place, nor *Doorkeeper* at the *Play-house* door, with his *Boxe* like a *Church-warden*, desiring you to remember the poor *Players*, I cannot but say for *Epilogue* to all the

Playes were ever Acted there (that the Puritans) Have made with their Raylings the *Players* as poore / As were the *Fryers* and *Poets* before.'[2]

In that year the devoted man of the theatre William Davenant was back in the Tower for the second time. Upon his final release in August 1654 he no doubt patronised such stage performances as were on offer: a brief reference survives to a visit to what seems to have been an expensive private show at the Red Bull, in company with Daniel Fleming and Sir George Fletcher, in February or March 1655[3] (probably in the latter month, after the death of his wife). Soon afterwards, on Monday 6 August, the Blackfriars theatre was finally demolished, and (as on the site of the Globe) 'tenements built in the room'.[4] Davenant was probably there to watch the melancholy sight, for it was not until four days later that he secured the pass to travel to France which enabled him to marry his third wife. And perhaps he was back by 14 September, when there was another spectacular raid by soldiers on the Red Bull. In the words of *The Weekly Intelligencer*: 'This day proved Tragical to the Players . . . the Soldiers secured the persons of some of them who were upon the Stage, and in the Tyrin[g]-house, they seized also upon their cloaths in which they acted; a great part whereof was very rich, it never fared worse with the spectators than at this present, for those who had monies payed their five shillings apeece, those who had none to satisfie their forfeits, did leave their Cloaks behind them, the Tragedy of the Actors, and the Spectators, was the Comedy of the soldiers. . . .' The raid inspired a ballad ending:

> The poor and the rich,
> The whore and the bitch,
>   Were every one at a losse,
> But the Players were all
> Turn'd (as weakest) to the wall,
>   And 'tis thought had the greatest losse.[5]

The irrepressible Davenant was nothing if not resourceful: during the regime of Cromwell (who had become Lord Protector in December 1653) plays were inadmissible, but as a subtle first step towards nothing less than the introduction of operatic drama (and ultimately the reintroduction of the drama proper) on the London stage, he now put on a form of medley consisting of 'declamations' interspersed with instrumental music and songs – not in a theatre, but in the 'back part' of his own home. He had acquired (perhaps with financial help from the barrister Sir John Maynard),[6] the residence of an early patron, Rutland House in upper Aldersgate Street near Charterhouse Square. A single sheet, now among the State Papers at the Public Record Office, bears the report of an anonymous official who attended to see what Davenant was up to:[7] it tells us that 'Vpon Friday the 23 of May 1656' that first momentous performance took place 'att the Charterhouse', and at a charge (five shillings a head) – thus making it something more than 'private'. Four hundred people had been expected to attend, 'but there appeered not above 150 auditors' (perhaps because of prudently modest advance publicity).

Davenant's venture, *The First Days Entertainment*, had been preceded by activities of some sort at four other places. The evidence is in a ballad entitled 'How Daphne [Davenant] pays his Debts', which was entered at Stationers' Hall on 17 March 1655/6. This shows that at unknown dates before then he had hired Apothecaries' Hall in Blackfriars for '. . . Masques / Made a la mode *de France*'; that the 'next house' he hired was at '*S. Jones's*'; and that he had also used 'houses' in Lincoln's Inn Fields and Drury Lane. Stanza 22 declares: 'Now in these houses he hath men, / And cloathes to make them trim; / For six good friends of his laid out / Six thousand pounds for him.' The reported use of Apothecaries' Hall makes sense, for we know that Davenant rehearsed there before opening at his Restoration theatre in Lincoln's Inn Fields; '*S. Jones's*' must mean the former priory of St John at Clerkenwell, which had long been used for rehearsals and to store costumes; the place in Lincoln's Inn Fields must be Gibbons's Tennis Court, later to be used by Killigrew's company as the first Theatre Royal (Lisle's Tennis Court, the one adapted by Davenant for *his* theatre, was not built until the autumn of 1656); the 'house' in Drury Lane is the Cockpit Theatre.[8]

The report about *The First Days Entertainment*, coupled with the text of the show as published at the time, and in the 1673 folio,[9] combine to give us a detailed account of what went on. The reporter says: 'The roome was narrow, at the end of which was a stage and on ether side two places railed in, Purpled and Guilt, the Curtayne also that drew before them was of cloth of gold and Purple. . . . The Musick was aboue in a Loouer hole railed about and couered wth Sarcenetts to conceale them,[10] before each speech was consort Musick.' He is somewhat dismissive about the singers, whom he lists as 'Cap[t]. Cooke, Ned Coleman and his wife, a nother wooman and other inconsiderable Voyces'. But from the printed text we learn that the vocal and instrumental music was composed by Dr Charles Coleman, Captain Henry Cooke, Henry Lawes and George Hudson – a most distinguished list. It is apparent that for Davenant, nothing but the best would do – and that he had had no qualms about enlisting the services of men who shared his royalist sympathies. Lawes's association with him, as with Milton, had probably begun in the 1630s, when with his brother William, he composed the music for the masque *The Triumphs of the Prince d'Amour*; he also set several of Davenant's songs to music, and for an unfinished satirical poem which, on internal evidence, can be dated to 1655, he set the first stanza as a part-song, for four and for three voices.[11] Of the other musicians associated with *The First Days Entertainment*, Charles Coleman, Doctor of Music, was a leading composer, singer and instrumentalist, and George Hudson primarily a composer, while Captain Cooke (whose title dated from military service in the civil war) was especially celebrated as a practitioner of the Italian style of singing, derived originally from the time when, as a chorister of the Chapel Royal, he had come under the influence of a pupil of Monteverdi. As Master of the Choristers of the Chapel at the Restoration, he introduced Italianate techniques of composition and singing there. His influence upon Davenant's introduction of opera to the English stage must have been considerable.[12] John Evelyn wrote that he was 'esteem'd the best singer, after the Italian manner, of any in England', and he appears frequently in the *Diary* of that passionate music-lover Samuel Pepys: on 27 July 1661, for example, the two repaired to a tavern with a friend 'and there he did give us a song or two; and without doubt, he hath the best manner of singing in the world'.[13] Pepys was also acquainted with Dr Coleman's son Edward (Ned), and his wife Catherine the actress and singer: the first *Diary* reference is on 30 October 1665, when at the invitation of the writer, Coleman (his wife was unwell and could not accompany him), Nicholas Lanier, then Master of the King's Musick, and Pepys's musical friend Thomas Hill spent the evening together: 'with whom, with their Lute, we had excellent company and good singing till midnight, and a good supper I did give them'.[14]

The full title of Davenant's show in 1656 is *The First Days Entertainment at Rutland-House, by Declamations and Musick: after the manner of the Ancients*, and the scene is Athens. (It is not of course an opera, as stated by the official observer, but an introduction to, or argument in favour of, opera.) After a 'flourish of music' the curtain is drawn back, and *Prologue* appears, to apologise for the 'narrowe room':

> We wish we could have found this roof so high,
> That each might be allow'd a canopy;
> And could the walls to such a wideness draw,
> That all might sit at ease in *chaise a bras*.
> But though you cannot front our cup-board scene,
> Nor sit so eas'ly as to stretch and lean,
> Yet you are so divided and so plac'd,

That half are freely by the other fac'd; . . .
Think this your passage, and the narrow way
To our Elyzian field, the *Opera*. . . .

(the first use of the magic word: in the first edition, and the 1673 folio, it is printed in bold type). The last two lines are the only ones mentioned by the reporter, who obviously realised their significance.

Diogenes and Aristophanes now appear, seated 'in two gilded rostras . . . in habits agreeable to their country and professions; who declaim against, and for, public entertainment by moral representations'. This is followed by the first song, 'Did ever War so cease / That all might Olive wear?'[15] – which, the reporter tells us, was composed by Lawes. After further instrumental music, the curtain is drawn back again to reveal a Parisian and a Londoner seated 'in the rostras', in the appropriate 'livery robes'. Each sets out the defects of the other's city – which allows Davenant to write, in the lively descriptive manner at which he excelled, of the two capitals he knew so well. The Parisian ('speaking broken English', the reporter tells us) criticises London's narrow, dark streets and jumbled, low-ceilinged houses, the 'importunate noise' of the Thames watermen, the 'bread too heavy', 'drink too thick' and beds 'no bigger than coffins'. As for the children: to them 'you are so terrible, that you seem to make use of authority whilst they are young, as if you knew it would not continue till their manhood. . . . When they encrease in years, you make them strangers . . .'. However, the English sometimes have the sense to send their children abroad to learn the behaviour of other nations, and 'to Paris they come, the school of Europe'. The Parisian would now like to make a safe retreat, but is 'stopt by one of your heroic games, call'd foot-ball, which I conceive – under your favour – not very conveniently civil in the streets'.

The Londoner (who, the reporter predictably concludes, 'had the better of itt') criticises the tall Parisian tenement buildings, where whole families are stuffed into single rooms; each creates 'a chorus of clamour' – whereas there is 'dead silence' in the kitchens, where the cooks are 'considering how to reform the mistakes of nature in the original compositions of flesh and fish'. In lodging-houses the beds, though large, have to be shared with fleas, 'those dexterous little persecutors'. As for the Seine boatman, he herds his passengers (all standing) like cattle, and there are no walled banks or stairs (as, by implication, there are on the Thames), so that people have to 'crawl through the mud like cray-fish' to embark and disembark. The Parisian is no doubt affronted because the Londoner does not 'point with great wonder at the Louvre' (where of course Davenant had lodged with Lord Jermyn); but it has 'a very singular way of being wonderful; the fame of the palace consisting more in the vast design of what it was meant to be, than in the largeness of what it is'. On the upbringing of children, 'Your sons you dignify betimes with a taste of pleasure and liberty', which tends to make them, when they are men, 'turbulent to supreme authority'; he suggests that 'the ancient jurisdiction of parents and masters, when it was severe', perhaps made 'all degrees of human life more quiet and delightful'.

The Parisian had twice spoken of London's notorious sea–coal smog, and the declamations of the two citizens are followed by a song on the subject (composed, says the reporter, by Dr Coleman): 'London is smother'd with sulph'rous fires; . . . But she is cool'd and clens'd by streams / Of flowing and of ebbing Thames. / Though Paris may boast a clearer Sky, / Yet wanting flows and ebbs of Sene, / To keep her clean, / She ever seems choakt when she is dry . . .'. The song recalls Davenant's earlier poem to 'The Queene, returning to London after a long absence', which begins with a reference to the 'Mists of Sea–coale–smoake' in the capital.[16]

On a Sunday evening in 1664 Elizabeth Pepys was unwell, and her husband sat at her bedside and read to her ('with great mirth') 'Sir W Davenents two speeches in dispraise of London and Paris, by way of reproach one to the other', to cheer her up.[17] The French wives of diarist and poet would have enjoyed the joke.

The *Epilogue* to *The First Days Entertainment* speaks of its lasting 'some two hours', but the observer says that in fact it ran for an hour and a half – 'and is to continue for 10 dayes by wch time other Declamations wilbee ready'; no more is known for certain of them.[18] He also reports something that does not appear in the printed text: that at the end of the performance on 23 May 'were songs relating to the Victor (the Protector)', which apparently immediately preceded the one about the London smog. The author was obviously doing everything possible to conciliate the authorities; and it will be noticed that his 'entertainment' was quite unlike a stage play, with seated declaimers, and no dialogue, elaborate costumes or props.

Encouraged by the fact that the show prompted no official displeasure, Davenant now went ahead with his epoch-making first attempt at an opera – what ultimately became Part I of *The Siege of Rhodes*. It obviously derived from the Court masques, but differed from them in having a unified, romantic plot on a modern, heroic subject – the siege of Christian Rhodes by the Turkish monarch, Solyman the Magnificent, in 1522.[19] It was completed before 17 August 1656, the date of the address 'To the Reader' preceding the text as published in that year.[20] It is divided into five 'Entries' rather than Acts (again to

jokes about 'a *Monkey* dancing his Trick-a-tee on a Rope, for want of *strong Lines* from the Poets pen', and 'deluding an ignorant Rabble with the sad presentment of a roasted Savage'.[40] The last Entry features a (painted) army of English mariners and Peruvians – the former naturally in the van – and Davenant cheerfully defends his use of poetic licence: 'These imaginary English Forces may seem improper, because the *English* had made no discovery of *Peru*, at the time of the *Spaniards* first invasion there; but yet in Poeticall Representations of this nature, it may pass as a Vision discern'd by the Priest of the Sun, before the matter was extant, in order to his Prophecy.' After the Restoration, his old adversary Sir Henry Herbert, restored to the office of Master of the Revels, was to speak caustically of the playwright as 'a person who . . . wrote the First and Second Parts of Peru, acted at the Cockpitt, in Oliuers tyme, and soly in his fauour; wherein hee sett of[f] the justice of Oliuers actinges, by comparison with the Spaniards, and endeavoured thereby to make Oliuers crueltyes appeare mercyes, in respect of the Spaniards crueltyes. . . .'[41]

Davenant's boldness was increasing: *The History of Sir Francis Drake*, which followed *Peru* and was based on the voyage to Panama in 1572, is much more of a drama, with several characters, some dialogue and a certain amount of action and plot – although it is still divided into 'Entries' and not Acts. It subsequently became the third Act of *The Playhouse to be Let*.[42] One rollicking song is sung by the steersman, with a chorus of rowers, and begins thus:

Aloof! and aloof! and steady I steer!
    'Tis a Boat to our wish,
    And she slides like a Fish,
When chearily stem'd, and when you row clear.
    She now has her trimme!
    Away let her swim.
Mackerels are swift in the shine of the Moon;
    And Herrings in Gales when they wind us,
But, timeing our Oars, so smoothly we run,
    That we leave them in shoals behind us . . .

In the Second Entry, four 'Symerons' (Cimaroons), described by the author as 'a Moorish people, brought formerly to *Peru* by the Spaniards, as their Slaves, to dig in Mines', 'dance a *Morisco* for joy of the arrival of S^r. *Francis Drake*'. In John Playford's *Courtly Masquing Ayres* published in 1662 are three pieces by Matthew Locke entitled 'The Apes Dance', 'The Symerons Dance' and 'Antick Dance', and no doubt the first two at least were composed for *Peru* and *Drake* respectively.[43]

The text includes several references to the use of 'noises off' in this production. In the First Entry the boatswain 'within' speaks of a ship approaching, towing a prize; and one mariner calls to another 'what canst thou see / From the top-Gallant of that Tree?', to which the other 'within' replies: 'The ship does Anchor cast; / And now her Boat does haste / To reach the Shore . . .'. Pepys (as one would expect) must have seen the production, for he later wrote of a visit to Clothworkers' Hall where he watched an 'entertainment' with 'very good Musique', and was 'pleased that I could find out a man by his voice, whom I had never seen before, to be one that sung *behind the Curtaine formerly at Sir W. Davenants opera* [my italics]'.[44] During the Second Entry of *Drake*, the 'Symerons Dance' is followed by a chorus of mariners 'within'; the last includes a (painted) train of mules 'loaden with Wedges of Silver and Ingots of Gold', and 'the Bells of the Mules are heard from within', and later a 'clashing of arms is heard afar off'.

On 5 May John Evelyn noted in his *Diary*: 'I went to visit my brother in London; and, next day, to see a new opera, after the Italian way, in recitative music and scenes, much inferior to the Italian composure and magnificence; but it was prodigious [extraordinary] that in a time of such public consternation such a vanity should be kept up, or permitted. I, being engaged with company, could not decently resist the going to see it, though my heart smote me for it.' As the show was 'new', it must have been *Drake* – the most recently produced at the time; if only Pepys had begun his *Diary* by 1659, we would no doubt have a much more precise, and less grudging, account from him.

Part II of *The Siege of Rhodes* was entered at Stationers' Hall at the end of the month – on the 30th.[45] It is not known in what month of 1659 it was staged, but it was probably June; and we cannot be certain of its then form, since (unlike Part I) no version was published until 1663. It has recently been stated[46] that when Part I was put on at the Cockpit after its transfer from Rutland House, 'it was presented as a spoken drama', and that Part II was then staged in the same form. I do not think this is a safe assumption: the Restoration version of Part I published in 1663 is specifically described on the title-page as 'lately [recently] Enlarg'd'; and Dryden states in his essay *Of Heroic Plays* that it was *after* the Restoration that Davenant 'reviewed his *Siege of Rhodes*, and caused it to be acted as a just drama [i.e. a straight play]'.

Part II as given in the latter half of 1659 marks the final stage of Davenant's steady progression towards restoration of the drama. John Aubrey sums up his achievement to date: 'Being freed from Imprisonment, because Playes (Scil: Trag[edie]s & Comoedies were in those Presbyterian times scandalous), he contrives to set-up an Opera stylo recitativo, wherin S^{r}jeant Maynard & severall Citizens were engagers, it began at Rutland house in Charter-house yard. next A^o . . . [he could not remember the year] at the Cock-pitt in Drury-Lane, where were acted very well stylo recitativo, Sr Francis Drake, . . . [his memory fails him again], and the Siege of Rhodes, 1st & 2^d part. It did affect the Eie and eare extremely. This first brought Scenes in fashion in England. before, at playes, was only a Hanging.'

Naturally Davenant's activities did not escape criticism. This had been muted during Cromwell's lifetime, when they were no doubt presumed to be officially condoned: but the Protector had died in September 1658, and during Evelyn's 'time of consternation' which followed, the criticism became sharper. By December someone was predicting that the opera would 'speedily go down; the godly party are so much discontented with it', and Richard Cromwell and the Council of State were ordering 'the Poet and Actors' to explain by what authority their opera was being given publicly; in February 1659 the House of Lords ordered an enquiry, and in April the matter came up in the Commons. No one was in much doubt that the opera at Drury Lane was being 'showne in imetation of a play', as one correspondent put it; but there is no evidence that it was ever suppressed. In August, Davenant (with others) was briefly imprisoned for alleged complicity in a royalist plot, but he was released on the 16th. Sentiment in favour of Charles II's return was growing, and by March 1660 the poet was hailing with a 'Panegyrick', the arrival in London of Lord General Monck, whose moderation is emphasised in the poem: 'you . . . / Call in the firm support of Church and Lawes / . . . You court the City, and the Nation too . . .'. In the same month Davenant secured a lease of Lisle's Tennis Court, in preparation for its conversion into his Restoration theatre; and on the 17th he secured a pass to travel to France, presumably to join King Charles.[47]

Let Davenant's future collaborator John Dryden sum up the state of the English stage at the close of the interregnum, as written in his essay *Of Heroic Plays* published four years after the laureate's death:[48]

The first sight we had of them, on the English theatre, was from the late Sir William D'Avenant. It being forbidden him in the rebellious times to act tragedies and comedies, because they contained matter of scandal to those good people, who could more easily dispossess their lawful sovereign than endure a wanton jest, he was forced to turn his thoughts another way, and to introduce the examples of moral virtue, writ in verse. and performed in recitative music. The original of this music, and of the scenes which adorned his work, he had from the Italian operas; but he heightened his characters (as I may probably imagine) from the example of Corneille and some French poets. In this condition did this part of poetry remain at His Majesty's return. . . . We who come after him have received the advantage from that excellent groundwork, which he laid.

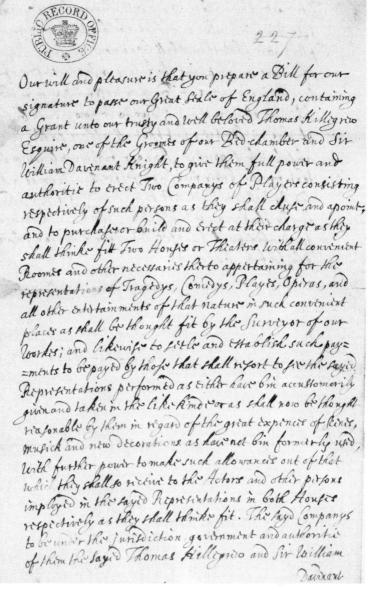

Warrant of 1660 granting the London stage monopoly to Davenant and Thomas Killigrew: first page as drafted and written by Davenant for the Attorney General, *see pp.* 143–4, SP29/8/no. 1, permission of the Public Record Office, London.

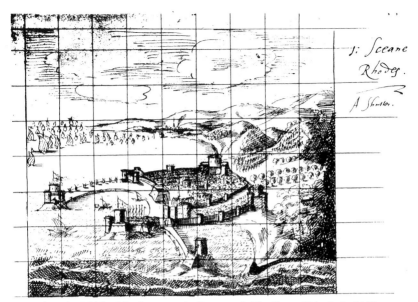

Design by John Webb of the first scene for Davenant's *The Siege of Rhodes* in 1656, generally regarded as the first opera in England, *see p. 127*. Devonshire Collection, Chatsworth.

[*below*] Engraving by Hollar of part of west London, *c.* 1658, showing the tennis court buildings used by Davenant and Killigrew respectively as their first playhouses, *see pp. 146, 154*. [*right*] Lisle's tennis court: first Duke's Theatre. [*left*] Gibbons's tennis court: first Theatre Royal. Permission of the Department of Prints and Drawings, British Museum. *See also Leslie Hotson's plan of Davenant's conversion of Lisle's tennis court, Lincoln's Inn Fields, p. 178.*

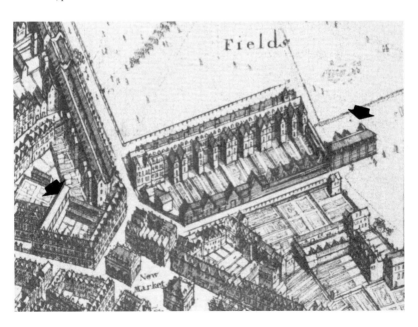

[*left*] Thomas Killigrew by William Sheppard, 1650, Venice. Permission of the National Portrait Gallery, London.

Samuel Pepys by John Hayls, 1666: the diarist holds part of his setting of 'Beauty retire . . .' from Act IV of Davenant's *The Siege of Rhodes Part II, see p. 164.* Permission of the National Portrait Gallery, London.

Davenant's leading actors, Thomas Betterton, Kneller studio, and [*right*] Henry Harris, by John Greenhill, *see pp. 156, 185*. The Harris, showing him as Wolsey in Davenant's revival of *Henry VIII*, is the first known representation of an English actor in a Shakespearean role. Permission of the National Portrait Gallery, London, and the Ashmolean Museum, Oxford.

CHAPTER NINE

1660–1
The Davenant/Killigrew
stage monopoly established

◦➤◦⊂◦

In February 1660 Sir William Davenant reached the age of fifty-four. During the remaining eight years of his life he was to make his most important contribution to the development of the English theatre, when as manager and director (in the modern sense) he presided over a company which, in the words of a recent commentator, deservedly enjoyed a 'brilliant and sustained success'.[1]

Fewer than a hundred years lay between the erection by James Burbage of The Theatre in Shoreditch – which 'permitted strollers to become citizens, and pastime to become art'[2] – and the establishment of the two Restoration monopoly theatres whose leading players ranked as gentlemen. The laureate's father John Davenant, that 'admirer and lover of plays and play-makers, especially Shakespeare', had had strong links with the Elizabethan theatre, and had moved to Oxford in time to see Inigo Jones's first involvement with the planning of a new kind of stage for drama, as distinct from masque (in Christ Church Hall, for the visit of King James in August 1605).[3] Some thirty years later, his son William worked with Jones and John Webb before the outbreak of the civil war, and then, as the only significant playwright to bridge the gap, carried the practice of music, scenes and 'machines' from the Caroline Court masque through the interregnum to the Restoration professional theatre. His importance as a champion of continuity can hardly be over-estimated. When he came to direct Shakespeare plays and adaptations at his own theatre in Lincoln's Inn Fields, he stood at the centre of the transmission of acting traditions going back to Elizabethan days.[4] He had known the actor and theatre owner Christopher Beeston, a member of Shakespeare's company, and was well acquainted with his son William (who outlived Davenant); another important informant was John Lowin, one of the twenty-six 'Principall Actors' named in the First Folio. 'John Lowen the Player' was buried at St Clement Danes on 24 August 1653,[5] while Davenant was immured in the Tower, but they had known each other well before that: Lowin spoke the Prologue to Davenant's *Platonic Lovers* at the Blackfriars in 1635; and when the laureate, who was an excellent instructor of actors although he never acted himself, came to direct *Henry VIII*, he would use Lowin's account of Shakespeare's direction of the play.

Not only was Davenant the trustee of acting traditions. Sir Edmund Chambers, in his magisterial account of the growth of the 'Shakespeare-Mythos' from the seventeenth century to the mid-nineteenth, writes of the three streams of tradition deriving respectively from London, from Oxford and from Stratford: the London tradition is mainly theatrical, and Chambers declares unhesitatingly that 'the main channel of transmission' seems to have been Sir William Davenant, followed by Thomas Betterton – who visited Stratford on behalf of Nicholas Rowe, author of the first considered attempt at a life of Shakespeare (1709). From Betterton the tradition passed through Pope and his circle, including the antiquary Oldys who also learnt something from Aubrey, Shadwell, the actor John Lacy and William Beeston. The Oxford tradition concerns itself only with the relations between Shakespeare and the Davenants, and soon much was being written about the playwright's possible begetting of Davenant. As Chambers soberly remarks, 'it is possible to underestimate the value of biographical tradition'; and he makes the cogent point that 'provincial memories are long-lived, and so are those of professions which, like that of the stage, are largely recruited as hereditary castes'.[6]

Although Davenant was the principal custodian of stage tradition, he was also well aware of changing public tastes. He was a man of remarkable foresight and persistence, and realised very early that playgoers would soon be demanding scenic theatre; his pre-war plan for a playhouse in the Strand offering 'Action, musical Presentments, Scenes, Dancing and the like' came to nothing in those inauspicious times, but now, nearly a quarter of a century later, his ideas were to be realised. In spite of the repressive measures advocated, although not always effectively enforced, against the London theatre during the war and interregnum, the appetite for plays was as lively as ever, and by 1659 – when it was apparent that the return of King Charles would not be long delayed – there was feverish manoeuvring among theatre people, to plan for what was obviously going to be a profitable activity. Davenant and Thomas Killigrew eventually came out on top, although not without considerable difficulties and opposition, notably from Sir Henry Herbert and the player George Jolly. Herbert resumed his office of Master of the Revels at the Restoration, but in spite of prolonged and vigorous efforts, inside and outside the courts, he was never again able to exercise his previous sweeping powers to the full. Davenant and Killigrew were not close friends: indeed, while they were both at the exiled Court in the 1650s, Killigrew once listed himself, together with Sir John Denham and his own brother-in-law, William Crofts, as one of the 'dire foes' of Davenant's *Gondibert*. But they were shrewd enough to exploit their contacts with the King to pursue their campaign for a theatre monopoly.[7] Killigrew was six years younger than Davenant, of better family, and personally a good deal closer to Charles II – Pepys, on board ship with him in the Channel in the days immediately preceding the Restoration, describes him as 'a merry droll, but a gentleman of great esteem with the King';[8] after the return to London, he – unlike Davenant – was appointed a Groom of the Bedchamber in the Royal Household. He soon secured the reversion of the office of Master of the Revels (to which he succeeded at Herbert's death in 1673); Davenant went through the motions of applying for the parallel office of Master of the Revels in Ireland, but as we know, lost it to John Ogilby.[9]

King Charles entered his capital on 29 May, his thirtieth birthday. And shortly afterwards, Davenant produced a long panegyrical 'Poem upon His Sacred Majestie's most happy Return to his Dominions'.[10] During the laureate's absence on the continent, John Rhodes had been running a company of young actors at the Cockpit in Drury Lane – although all the evidence is against John Downes's statement in *Roscius Anglicanus*, that he had secured a licence from General Monck to do so.[11] Pepys went to the Cockpit on 18 August – the first play he had had 'time to see since my coming from sea'; the piece was Fletcher's *The Loyal Subject*, 'where one Kinaston, a boy, acted the Dukes sister but made the loveliest lady that ever I saw in my life – only, her voice was not very good'; after the performance, Pepys and his friends were joined by Edward Kynaston and another actor in the company, probably Thomas Betterton, for a drink.[12] This young group was to become the nucleus of Davenant's company – although Kynaston, one of the last actors to play feminine roles in the Elizabethan tradition, joined Killigrew's, and went on to be a distinguished adult actor of male parts.

While Rhodes's men were performing at the Cockpit during the summer, an older and more experienced company under Major Michael Mohun (who had served as a captain in the civil war and ranked as major during subsequent service in Flanders) were at the Red Bull in Clerkenwell. William Beeston tried to carry on at Salisbury Court for a time, then and later, without authority:[13] he had acquired this playhouse, dismantled in 1649, in 1652, and subsequently restored and partly rebuilt it. The long and tortuous story of his negotiations with the Sackvilles over the lease of the theatre, and of his restoration work, is recounted in detail by Hotson.[14]

George Jolly, the most active opponent of Davenant and Killigrew apart from Herbert, was one of the last of the English strolling players who had for so long exercised a powerful influence upon the German drama. By 1654 – two years before Davenant's first staging of opera in England – Jolly on the continent was offering (in a letter to the Council of Basle) a 'well-practised company' performing 'good instructive stories ... with repeated changes of expensive costumes and a theatre decorated in the Italian manner, with beautiful English music and skilful women'; and when he was in Frankfurt, he too used a tennis court building as a theatre. In September 1655 young King Charles travelled incognito with a small royal group from Paris to Frankfurt Fair and evidently much enjoyed what he saw. Jolly, fairly assessed by Hotson on all the evidence as a 'typical violent and rapacious actor–manager', had a stormy time in Germany, culminating in expulsion from Nuremberg at the beginning of 1660: he returned to England soon after the Restoration to seek a share in the expected theatrical revival.[15]

In London, Killigrew secured a warrant from King Charles on 9 July to form the King's Company of players,[16] one of the two companies now envisaged; Davenant naturally regarded as inadequate the indirect authority granted to him by Charles I in 1639 for the then projected playhouse, and on 19 July he drafted a document which would set in train a sequence of events influencing the pattern of metropolitan theatre in England right up to the present day. The draft, which is in his own hand, is now among the State Papers at the Public Record Office,[17] and reads thus:

> Our will and pleasure is that you prepare a Bill for our signature to passe our Great Seale of England, containing a Grant unto our trusty and well beloved Thomas Killegrew Esquire, one of the Grooms of our Bed chamber and Sir William Davenant Knight, to give them full power and authoritie to erect Two Companys of Players consisting respectively of such persons as they shall chuse and apoint; and to purchase or build and erect at their charge as they shall thinke fitt Two Houses or Theaters with all convenient Roomes and other necessaries therto appertaining for the representations of Tragedys, Comedys, Playes, Operas, and all other entertainments of that nature in such convenient places as shall be thought fit by the Surveyor of our Workes; and likewise to setle and establish such payments to be payed by those that shall resort to see the sayed Representations performed as either have bin accustomarily given and taken in the like kinde or as shall now be thought reasonable by them in regard of *the great expences of scenes, musick and*

new decorations as have not bin formerly used [my italics – one can hear the
voice of Davenant, speaking from experience], With further power to make
such allowances out of that which they shall so receive to the Actors and
other persons imployed in the said Representations in both Houses
respectively as they shall thinke fit. The sayd Companys to be under the
jurisdiction, government and authoritie of them the sayed Thomas Killegrew
and Sir William D'avenant. And in regard of the extraordinary lisence that
hath bin lately used in things of this Nature our pleasure is that there shall be
no more places of Representations or Companys of Actors or Representers
of Sceanes in the Cittys of London or Westminster or in the liberties of them
then the Two to be now erected by virtue of this authoritie, but that all others
shall be absolutely suppressed. And our further pleasure is that for the better
inabling of the sayed Thomas Killegrew and Sir William D'avenant to
performe what Wee intend hereby that you add to the sayed Grant such
other Clauses as you shall thinke fitt.

The draft is addressed, in Davenant's hand, to the Attorney General.

He demurred at the plan for a royal grant establishing a monopoly of
stage plays, but after Davenant and Killigrew had complained to the
King, he acquiesced, writing on 12 August that he had simply felt 'that
the matter was more proper for A tolleration; then A Grant under the
greate Seale of England';[18] and on the 21st the warrant for which
Davenant had provided the model passed the privy signet (the last stage
of a patent before the Seal).[19] Its text differs very little from Davenant's
draft, although the crucial passage 'that there shall be no more Places of
Representations. . . .' has been made a little more specific, so that it now
reads: 'nor Companies of Actors of Playes, or Operas by Recitative
musick, or Representations by danceing and Scenes, or any other
Entertainments on the Stage . . .'. And it now includes an important
clause, as provided for in Davenant's draft, authorizing the two
managers 'to peruse all playes that haue been formerly written, and to
expunge all Prophanesse and Scurrility from the same, before they be
represented or Acted' (one can surmise that Davenant's hand had been
at work again). This clause particularly incensed Sir Henry Herbert,
since it encroached upon his previous powers of censorship.

Davenant and Killigrew have been described in recent years as a 'pair
of scheming adventurers', and as having indulged in 'bribery, skuldug-
gery and force' in their pursuit of monopoly,[20] but this seems to
overstate the case (and to ignore Davenant's overriding claim to predo-
minance, by virtue of length and breadth of metropolitan theatre
experience).

As well as visiting Frankfurt Fair during his exile and seeing what
Jolly had to offer, King Charles and his courtiers had enjoyed the plays
and players of Paris, and during short visits to Bruges and Brussels had

seen how tennis court buildings and other enclosed halls could be adapted as scenic theatres.[21] The King was now impatient to have similar things in London, and two months after granting the Davenant/Killigrew monopoly, he cheerfully allowed a licence to one Giulio Gentileschi 'to build a theatre for an Italian band of Musicians whom he is bringing into England'; in fact, nothing came of this, but on 24 December he granted a licence to Jolly, to set up a company and acquire or build a theatre, 'notwithstanding any former grant made by us to our trusty and well beloved Servant Thomas Killegrew Esqr and Sir William Davenant K$^{nt.}$'.[22] The two monopolists had reason to feel aggrieved – although the way in which they were later to treat Jolly, over a period of several years, left a good deal to be desired.

Killigrew and Davenant eventually received definitive patents under the Great Seal on 25 April 1662 and 15 January 1662/3 respectively (some time after they had both been in full production); and it was probably then that Davenant wrote the long poem 'To the Kings most Sacred Majesty', in the course of which he dwells at some length on Charles's patronage of 'the *Theatre* (the Poets Magic-Glass)' and on how 'the *Scene* [has] so various now become'.[23] The modern Theatre Royal Drury Lane and the Royal Opera House Covent Garden enjoy the distinction of being the only two theatres in the capital to derive their rights not from licences issued by the Lord Chamberlain or local authorities, but by direct grant from the Crown: Killigrew's patent is in the possession of the lessees of the Theatre Royal, and the rights of the Royal Opera House stem directly from Davenant's patent, although his document is lost. The Davenant/Killigrew dual monopoly, although often evaded, persisted in London for some 180 years, until the passing of the Act of 1843 for regulating theatres.[24]

The royal grant of 21 August 1660 had in effect given Davenant and Killigrew authority to proceed with their plans, and as soon as it passed the privy signet they pressed ahead, assembling the best actors in London from the Cockpit and Red Bull groups; and for a short time, from 8 October until at least the 16th,[25] they ran a joint company at the Cockpit which they leased from John Rhodes. (When Herbert demanded to know, on the 8th, by what authority Rhodes was using the building as a theatre, he tersely replied – as Herbert noted on the back of his own message – 'That the King did authorize him'.)[26] The joint company included Mohun and Charles Hart from the Red Bull and Betterton and Kynaston from the Cockpit.

Pepys was there twice during the month: on the 11th he saw *Othello*, 'well done', and on the 30th 'a very fine play', again 'very well acted', Fletcher's *The Woman's Prize, or The Tamer Tamed*, which had been

designed as a sequel to Shakespeare's *The Taming of the Shrew*. He also
called there on the 16th, but understanding that Fletcher's *Wit Without
Money* was to be performed, 'would not stay, but went home again by
water'.[27]

On Monday 5 November – an auspicious date, for by this time it was
well established as a public holiday – the company formally divided into
two, Killigrew's thereafter enjoying the patronage of the King, and his
theatre known as the Theatre Royal – first of the succession of Theatre
Royals near and in Drury Lane extending to our own day – while
Davenant's patron was the Duke of York, the future James II, and his
company and theatre known as the Duke's. Pepys noted that this
particular 5 November was 'observed exceeding well in the City; and at
night great bonefires and fireworks'.[28] Killigrew's first playhouse was
the former Gibbons's Tennis Court in Vere Street near Lincoln's Inn
Fields (where his clandestine production of his own play *Claracilla* in
1653 had been broken up by soldiers tipped off by one of the actors);
Davenant used the Salisbury Court theatre between Fleet Street and the
river until his conversion of Lisle's Tennis Court, just east of Gibbons's,
should be completed. Killigrew had made virtually no alterations to his
building, which probably measured about 70 by 25 feet and seated at
most five hundred spectators.[29] Very unwisely he had – unlike Davenant – made no provision for scenery.

It has repeatedly been stated that both groups, Davenant's and
Killigrew's, began performing immediately. In 1790 Edmond Malone
published a list of plays, put on at this time by Killigrew, which Herbert
had noted down, presumably 'in order to ascertain the fees due to him,
whenever he should establish his claim': this shows that Killigrew
staged *Wit Without Money*, Shirley's *The Traitor* and Fletcher and
Massinger's *The Beggars' Bush* (at the Red Bull) on the Monday,
Tuesday and Wednesday respectively and then opened at Vere Street
with *Henry IV Part I* on Thursday 8 November. He was able to start
without delay because his theatre was ready, but Davenant was in no
position to do so. Killigrew had secured a monopoly of almost all
existing plays – including, ironically, Davenant's own – on the ground
that his company was the successor to the pre-war King's Men, so that
Davenant had almost nothing to stage.[30]

On 19 November the first performance of a play at the Restoration
Court took place – an entertainment offered by General Monck, newly
created Duke of Albemarle: Killigrew's company performed Jonson's
Epicoene, or The Silent Woman (which they had done at Vere Street on
the 10th, says Herbert's list), and Davenant wrote the Prologue, which
describes the stage as 'the Mirror of the times'. An actor stepped

forward and began:

> Greatest of Monarchs, welcome to this place
> Which *Majesty* so oft was wont to grace
> Before our Exile, to divert the Court,
> And ballance weighty Cares with harmless sport.
> This truth we can to our advantage say,
> They that would have no KING, would have no *Play*:
> The *Laurel* and the *Crown* together went,
> Had the same *Foes*, and the same *Banishment* . . .[31]

The morning after the performance at Court, Pepys found 'my Lord' – his relative and patron Edward Mountagu, newly created Earl of Sandwich – 'in bed late, he having been with the King, Queene [the Queen Mother, Henrietta Maria, who had returned to London earlier in the month], and Princesse at the Cockpitt [the Cockpit-in-Court theatre], all night, where Generall Monke treated them; and after supper, a play – where the King did put a great affront upon Singleton's Musique, he bidding them stop and bade the French Musique play – which my Lord says doth much out-do all ours'.[32] Charles, son of a French mother, had developed a great love of French music during his exile.

Killigrew's company were having a busy time, for Herbert's list shows that on the afternoon of the 19th, before giving the play at Court, they had put on Davenant's *The Unfortunate Lovers* at Vere Street (with Kynaston playing Arthiope); and after being up all night at Court they then played *The Beggars' Bush* again on the 20th. This was Pepys's first visit: 'Mr Sheply and I to the new Play-house near Lincolnes Inn fields (which was formerly Gibbons's tennis-court), where the play of *Beggers' Bush* was newly begun. . . . It was well acted (and here I saw the first time one Moone [Mohun], who is said to be the best actor in the world, lately come over with the King); and endeed it is the finest play-house, I believe, that ever was in England.'[33] If it was, which is unlikely, it was soon to be outstripped by Davenant's.

Thereafter Pepys visited Killigrew's theatre four more times before the end of the year – describing it each time as 'the new theatre' or 'the new playhouse', a practice he dropped in January. On 22 November he saw part of Shirley's *The Traitor* (having earlier been to Court and thought Henrietta Maria 'a very little plain old woman'), and admired the piece and Mohun's playing of the title-role; on the 27th he noted, without comment, that he had seen Beaumont and Fletcher's comedy *The Scornful Lady*; on 4 December *The Silent Woman* was on again, but he did not go; on the 5th he saw *The Merry Wives of Windsor* – 'The humours of the Country gentleman and the French Doctor very well done; but the rest but very poorly, and Sir J. Falstaffe [probably played by William Cartwright] as bad as any'; and on the 31st, *Henry IV Part I*.[34]

It is a striking fact that the diarist did not visit Salisbury Court before the end of the year. I think the conclusion must be that it had not yet opened to the public.[35] It was not until 12 December that Davenant secured exclusive rights from the Lord Chamberlain's office to a certain number of plays, no doubt after pressing for some justice. These were: Shakespeare's *The Tempest*, *Measure for Measure*, *Much Ado*, *Romeo and Juliet*, *Twelfth Night*, *Henry VIII*, *Lear*, *Macbeth* and *Hamlet* (which of course still left many more to Killigrew), Webster's *Duchess of Malfi*, Denham's *The Sophy*, and his own works. Of the plays performed by his actors before he took over their control, only two – *The Changeling* by Middleton and Rowley, and Massinger's *The Bondman* – were now legally theirs. The warrant closes by allowing Davenant to keep six other plays from their repertory for two months more (some of which his company continued to perform long after the time-limit had expired): Fletcher's *The Mad Lover*, *The Loyal Subject* and *Rule a Wife and Have a Wife*, *The Maid in the Mill* by Fletcher and Rowley, *The Spanish Curate* by Fletcher and Massinger, and Shakespeare's *Pericles*.[36] Davenant would certainly have needed until at least the end of the year for rehearsals – especially as the interruption of the Christmas season was approaching; his actors were young and relatively inexperienced, and – complete professional that he was – he would not have wished to expose them to public view prematurely.

Pepys saw *The Beggars' Bush* again at Vere Street on 3 January, and it was 'here for the first time that ever I saw Women come upon the stage'.[37] So it seems that Killigrew was ahead of Davenant by about six months in putting on actresses. His women included Mrs Knepp, of whom Pepys was so fond – he used to call her 'Bab Allen' after one of her songs; Nell Gwyn, who was only about ten years old at this time, did not join the company until it had moved to the new Theatre Royal in 1663, starting as an orange-girl – she is said to have been introduced by Charles Hart.

Pepys visited 'the Theatre' five more times during January 1661 – on the 4th he saw *The Scornful Lady* again, 'acted very well'; on the 7th, to celebrate 'Twelfeday', he took his wife and his brother Tom to *The Silent Woman* – 'the first time that ever I did see it and it is an excellent play'. Once again he was much impressed by young Edward Kynaston: 'Kinaston the boy hath the good turn to appear in three shapes: I, as a poor woman in ordinary clothes to please Morose; then in fine clothes as a gallant, and in them was clearly the prettiest woman in the whole house – and lastly, as a man; and then likewise did appear the handsomest man in the house.' Next day, the 8th, he 'took my Lord Hinchingbrooke and Mr Sidny [Mountagu's boys Edward and Sidney] to the Theatre and showed them *The Widdow* [by Middleton], an indifferent good play, but wronged by the womens being much to seek in their parts' – evidence that Killigrew's actresses were under-rehearsed, and that he had been ill-advised to put them on so soon. On the 19th the diarist saw Sir William Berkeley's tragi-comedy *The Lost Lady*, which did not much please him – and he was 'troubled', a characteristic Pepysian word, 'to be seen by four of our office Clerkes, which sat in the half-Crowne box and I in the 1s.6d.'. (Above the pit there were usually three tiers of seats; the boxes, where a seat cost four shillings, the middle gallery – where Pepys was sitting – and the top gallery. His clerks were probably in a special box in the middle gallery.) Finally, on 28 January, Pepys saw *The Lost Lady* again, enjoying it more this time; he was sitting 'behind in a dark place' and a lady, not seeing him, 'spat backward' upon him by mistake. 'But after seeing her to be a very pretty lady, I was not troubled at it at all.'[38]

Now at last, on the next day, 29 January, the diarist went with 'my Lord' and Mountagu's man of business, a lawyer called Henry Moore, to the Salisbury Court theatre – 'the first time that ever I was there since plays begun', and Pepys being Pepys, surely very near the start of Davenant's season. The manager was having teething troubles, for Pepys speaks of exercising 'great patience' and having 'little expectacions from so poor beginnings', but finally he saw the first three acts of *The Maid in the Mill*, the comedy by Fletcher and Rowley, to his 'great content'; by then it was getting late, and he went home.[39]

The Salisbury Court theatre was off the south side of the Strand, near the present Salisbury Square, and almost opposite the site on the north side 'behind the Three Kings Ordinary', between Fetter Lane and Shoe Lane,[40] where Davenant had been planning to build a theatre in 1639. In those days it was variously known as 'Salisbury Court' (the Bishops of Salisbury had had their London inn on the site); 'Whitefriars', recalling the former monastery; and 'Dorset Garden' (the Sackvilles, Earls of Dorset, had had their town house there): all three names, Salisbury, Whitefriars and Dorset, are preserved today on and near the site.

On 31 January Pepys was back at Vere Street for a first (post-Restoration) performance: Henry Glapthorne's romantic pastoral play *Argalus and Parthenia*: 'the house was exceeding full', but – as often with the diarist – the piece was 'wronged by my over-great expectacions'. On

5 February he saw it again, but 'though pleasant for the dancing and singing, I do not find good for any wit or design therein'. On the 9th he liked 'pretty well', Davenant's production of Fletcher's *The Mad Lover*; on the 12th he and two friends went first to Salisbury Court but then changed their minds and took coach to Vere Street, where Pepys was seeing *The Scornful Lady* for the third time – but 'now done by a woman, which makes the play appear much better then ever it did to me'. On the 16th, at Vere Street again, he saw *The Virgin Martyr*, a tragedy by Dekker and Massinger – 'a good but too sober a play for the company'.[41]

On the 23rd it was the diarist's twenty-eighth birthday – and he chose to celebrate the occasion by going to Davenant's production of Middleton and Rowley's tragedy *The Changeling*: 'the first time it hath been acted these 20 yeeres – and it takes exceedingly'. (Downes notes that Thomas Sheppey played Antonio in this play, and that Betterton was much praised for his acting of De Flores.) Pepys here reports that 'the gallants do begin to be tyred with the Vanity and pride of the Theatre-actors, who are endeed grown very proud and rich'.[42] He was exaggerating their wealth, but perhaps they were 'proud' in their bearing, and Davenant always ensured that his players' stage costumes were 'rich'.

On 1 March Pepys was back at Davenant's theatre, where he saw Massinger's tragi-comedy *The Bondman* for the first time: during the period of the diary he records that he saw it, in whole or in part, no fewer than seven times in all. On this first occasion the verdict was: 'an excellent play and well done – but above all that ever I saw, Baterton doth the Bondman the best'. This is his first reference to the great man, then twenty-five years old, whom – as he recorded later in the year – he and Elizabeth always considered 'the best actor in the world'. Mrs Pepys had a dog called Betterton in 1664.[43]

Next day, 2 March, Pepys went to Vere Street – 'where I find so few people (which is strange, and the reason I did not know) that I went out again; and so to Salsbury Court – where the house as full as could be; and it seems it was a new play – *The Queenes Mask* [Heywood's allegorical drama *Love's Mistress, or The Queen's Masque*]. Wherein there is some good humours. . . . But above all, it was strange to see so little a boy as that was to act Cupid, which is one of the greatest parts in it.' On the 11th he saw Killigrew's production of this piece, but preferred Davenant's. On the 14th he considered Beaumont and Fletcher's *King and No King* at Vere Street 'well acted'; but on the 16th did not greatly enjoy Fletcher and Massinger's *The Spanish Curate* at Salisbury Court.[44]

On the 19th he was back there to see *The Bondman* again, 'acted most excellently; . . . I am every time more and more pleased with Batterton's action'; and on the 25th, part of Davenant's production of *Love's Mistress* again. Next day, the 26th, was 'my great day', the third anniversary of his successful operation for the stone, which he celebrated each year. After a 'very merry' dinner at his father's house (his birthplace, which was very near the theatre) the diarist, with Elizabeth and another couple, saw *The Bondman* yet again, 'done to admiration'. On the 28th he went to Killigrew's production of Fletcher's *The Bloody Brother* (one of the models for Davenant's early play *The Cruel Brother*), but although the cast included Hart and Kynaston, he considered it 'ill acted'.[45]

During March, on the 23rd, he had been out to the Red Bull in Clerkenwell, where George Jolly (presumably)[46] was making one of his intermittent attempts to compete with the two monopolists. For a man who loved order and efficiency, it was a most depressing visit, which graphically underlined how Davenant and Killigrew were now dominating the London theatre world. 'I was led by a seaman that knew me, that is here as a servant, up to the tireing-room; where strange the confusion and disorder that there is among them in fitting themselfs; especially here, where the clothes are very poore and the actors but common fellows.' 'At last', the diarist concludes, 'into the pitt, where I think there was not above ten more then myself, and not 100 in the whole house – and the play (which is called *All's lost by Lust* [a tragedy by Rowley]) poorly done – and with so much disorder; among others, that in the Musique-room, the boy that was to sing a song not singing it right, his master fell about his ears and beat him so, that put the whole house into an uprore.'[47]

On 1 April Pepys was back at Salisbury Court, where he saw part of the comedy *Rule a Wife and Have a Wife* – the first time he had seen it. Although he did not care for it, it proved to be one of John Fletcher's most popular plays during the seventeenth century. Next day he went to the theatre again, for the same playwright's *The Night Walker, or The Little Thief*: 'a very merry and pretty play – and the little boy [perhaps the one he had seen playing Cupid on 2 March] doth very well'.[48]

On the 6th he saw an unidentified play which he calls *Loves Quarrell*.[49] That was his last visit to Salisbury Court, from which I deduce that Davenant was about to close the doors, and concentrate on intensive preparations for the grand opening at Lincoln's Inn Fields at the end of June. There was much to be done: scenery, wigs and costumes to be completed, actors and musicians to be rehearsed; and his young actresses to be intensively schooled for their first public performances.

Hitherto Davenant had been making do with the meagre repertory of old plays allowed him by the Lord Chamberlain's office – and it will be noticed that he had prudently concentrated on the ones with which his young players were already familiar: he now planned to open at his new Duke's Playhouse with two major productions of his own work – *The Siege of Rhodes* and *The Wits*. Downes tells us that for rehearsals he used Apothecaries' Hall – the former Cobham House in Blackfriars, which had been bought by the Society from Lady Ann Howard of Effingham in 1632 to serve as their Hall:[50] it will be remembered that the ballad about 'Daphne' and his debts says Sir William had presented – or planned to present – masques there for 'the Ladies' in the 1650s.

During this period Killigrew was of course carrying on as usual at Vere Street. On 20 April he gave a command performance (which Pepys did not greatly admire) of Fletcher's *The Humorous Lieutenant, or Demetrius and Enanthe*, before the King at the Cockpit-in-Court.[51] After that everything stopped for the coronation: the great 'Shew' – the traditional royal progress from the Tower to Whitehall – on the 22nd; the coronation itself on the 23rd; and on the 24th, fireworks on the river before the King. Pepys enjoyed all these 'glorious things' so much that he was sure he would never see the like again.

Thereafter, being deprived of any productions by Davenant, he visited Killigrew's theatre seven times between 27 April and 27 June – the eve of Davenant's opening at Lincoln's Inn Fields. On 27 April he saw Fletcher's *The Chances*; on 16 May the latter part of Beaumont and Fletcher's *The Maid's Tragedy*, but thought it 'too sad and melancholy'; on the 25th, again, *The Silent Woman*; on 4 June *Henry IV Part I*, 'a good play'; on the 8th, the first post-Restoration performance of *Bartholomew Fair*, 'a most admirable play, and well acted; but too much profane and abusive'; on the 22nd *The Alchemist* (the first specific reference to a post-Restoration production), 'a most incomparable play'; and on the 27th, in a party of two coachloads, *Bartholomew Fair* again.[52] Killigrew enjoyed a monopoly of Jonson's plays at this time, and was clearly exploiting it to the full while Davenant was out of commission.

From 29 January to 6 April, the dates of Pepys's first and last visits to Salisbury Court, he went twelve times to Davenant's productions and seven to Killigrew's – clear evidence that in his estimation, Davenant's were superior; and he chose to go to Salisbury Court to celebrate his two special days that spring, his birthday on 23 February and the anniversary of his life-saving operation on 26 March.

We owe the diarist a great deal for helping us to chart the progress of Davenant's activities preceding the opening of the Duke's Playhouse.

The present Pepys Librarian sums him up as 'a considering, though inconsistent, critic' – not critically prescient, but one who had real feeling for the 'design' and 'wit' of plays and who was equally responsive to singing, dancing, or a well-spoken scene. Although his 'expectation' was sometimes unfulfilled, the avidity of his appetite for the drama is never in question; and Dr Luckett makes the point that his admiration for Jonson is unsurprising, since it was Jonson who had established the terms of 'critical learning' – 'plot', 'design', 'wit', 'humour', 'language' – which Pepys customarily deployed, and which had been taken up by those 'exceedingly influential "sons of Ben"', Sir William Davenant and Thomas Hobbes', in the *Prefaces* to Davenant's *Gondibert* 'which initiated, for England, an entirely new style of critical discourse'.[53]

Sir William was now ready to play his trump-card, the opening of the Duke's Playhouse in Lincoln's Inn Fields. The articles of agreement under which he ran his company, signed on 5 November 1660 (the date of the formal establishment of the King's and Duke's) is a text of great importance. The agreement is tripartite, between himself and his ten principal players: Thomas Betterton, Thomas Sheppey, the brothers Robert and James Nokes, Thomas Lovell, John Moseley, Cave Underhill, Robert Turner and Thomas Lilliston, plus Henry Harris who was recruited separately and is here described as 'painter' (perhaps he had earlier been employed as a scene-painter). Davenant constituted the players into a company, to act at Salisbury Court or elsewhere in London or Westminster until he provided his 'newe Theatre with Scenes'; during the preliminary period, shares were divided into fourteen, of which Davenant had four and the company the rest, Betterton, James Nokes and Sheppey acting as his deputies; he undertook to provide a 'Consort of Musiciens', paid out of gross receipts at not more than thirty shillings a day. At one week's notice the actors would move to the new theatre, 'with other men *and women* [my italics]' provided by Davenant, to perform 'Tragedies, Comedies, Playes and representacions'. From then on, profits would be divided into fifteen shares, two going to Davenant for 'house-rent, buildinge, scaffoldinge, and makeing of fframes for Scenes', one for 'Habittes, Properties, and scenes', and seven for him 'to mainteine [that is, to pay directly] all the Women that are to performe or represent Womens partes . . . And in consideration of erectinge and establishinge them to bee a [separate] Companie, and his the said Sir William's paines and expences to that purpose for many yeeres'. The remaining five shares would go to the actors. Davenant would appoint three men to receive the admission money in a room adjoining the theatre, and the actors would choose two or three of the company to supervise, receipts to be paid nightly to the manager. He would appoint half the doorkeepers, the wardrobe keeper, the barber, and all other necessary staff; choose the successor to any actor-sharer who died; and fix the wages of the men-hirelings (the non-sharers). He would not supply 'Hattes, feathers, Gloues, ribbons, sworde belts, bandes, stockinges, or shoes' for any of the men, 'Vnlesse it be to Properties'. A private box to hold six people would be made available to Killigrew (there is no evidence of a reciprocal arrangement for Davenant at the Theatre Royal). The actor-sharers were bound in the sum of £500 each to keep the terms of the agreement. Finally it was 'mutually agreed . . . That the said Sir William Dauenant alone shalbee Master and Superior'.[54]

Lady Davenant's Bill of Complaint in the Court of Chancery in 1684, already mentioned, and the Answer of her late husband's stepsons Thomas and Paul Cross,[55] provide further information about the conduct of the playhouse. It will be remembered that Thomas Cross had set off with Davenant in 1650 as his secretary on the abortive voyage to Maryland; after the capture in the Channel, he secured employment as secretary to the governor of Barbados, and then became 'Receiver of the proffits of the operas and the Representacons' put on in London by his stepfather before the Restoration. Thereafter, until 1675, he filled the same post with the Duke's Company. Although, by the nature of the document, he is almost certainly exaggerating the extent of the 'businesse heaped upon him', as he puts it, his account gives a good idea of some of the complexities of running a Restoration theatre. As well as checking receipts against tickets sold at the end of each day, he says, he 'had the sole trouble of paying the whole charge of the House weekly that is to say the Salaries of all hireling Players both men and Woemen, Musick Masters, Dancing Masters, Scene men, Barbers, Wardrobe keepers, Dorekeepers and Soldiers, besides Bills of all kinds, as for Scenes, Habits, Properties, Candles, Oile and other things, and in making and paying, if called for, all the Dividends of the Sharers . . .'.

We do not know who converted the tennis court building for Sir William, but it seems reasonable to surmise that he and John Webb continued their collaboration. Wenceslaus Hollar's famous engraving of west London c. 1658 shows Lisle's just before new houses were built on its northern side, and its subsequent conversion into a playhouse: it juts out into the Fields, where people are strolling about, women are laying out washing to dry, a London train-band is exercising, and a coach is drawn up at the door of the Grange Inn, where Davenant's players drank after performances.[56] A plan drawn by Hotson shows that the theatre was about the same size as Killigrew's in Vere Street. Davenant had a scene-room and his own lodgings built as annexes, so that he could exercise tight control as manager. We also do not know how he raised money for the venture. The theatre was clearly handsome – by January 1661 its royal patron was already showing the designs with pride to the Florentine agent in London, Giovanni Salvetti, who reported home in a dispatch: '[The Duke of York] showed me the design of a large room he has begun to build in the Italian style in which they intend to put on shows as they do there [in Italy], with scenes and machines'; and in spite of the usual narrow rectangular shape of the site, the interior was ingeniously designed to convey the impression that it was based on a circular plan, as another Italian visitor, Lorenzo Magalotti, travelling in the train of Cosimo de' Medici, later reported: 'The theatre is practically round in plan, surrounded within by separate compartments in which there are several degrees of seating for the greater comfort of the ladies and gentlemen who, according to the liberal custom of the country, share the same boxes. Down below there remains a broad space for other members of the audience. The scenery is entirely changeable, with various transformations and lovely perspectives.'[57]

The figure mentioned for help with Davenant's earlier activities, in the ballad about 'Daphne' and his debts – £6,000 – is no doubt as much exaggerated as the story (later to be attributed to Davenant) that the Earl of Southampton once gave young Shakespeare £1,000 to 'make a Purchase which he heard he had a mind to': but Aubrey speaks of 'severall Citizens' who then lent a hand, and Hotson supplies some names;[58] perhaps some of the same men rallied round in 1660–1. It can be assumed, too, that Davenant's wife was a woman of means: he would hardly have hastened to France to marry her had it been otherwise. But the Duke's Playhouse was a much more ambitious project than anything he had attempted before, and by March 1661 he had begun selling off shares in what was clearly an attractive enterprise: half a share went to Richard Alchorne Esquire of Sussex, a whole one to Sir William Russell of Worcestershire, and a further half was put in trust for Endymion Porter's widow; in June, the month in which the theatre opened, further shares were disposed of, including a half to Endymion's son George; in September John Ashburnham's younger brother William, the Cofferer at Court (whose wife was a sister of Mrs Porter) bought a thousand-year interest in another share; and further sales were made later. Davenant made over one half-share to his old friend the poet Abraham Cowley, for 'Assistance & Judgment in Writing Correcting & providing Tragedies Comedies And other Poetic Entertainments for the stage'.[59]

The terms of the agreement between Davenant and his actor-sharers had set the Duke's Company on a stable footing, with the manager in undisputed control and closely involved in day-to-day business. This, together with his great theatrical expertise and no doubt his qualities of character, ensured that his company was infinitely more successful than Killigrew's: his rival neither possessed nor developed managerial skills, never lived on his premises as Davenant did, and delegated most of his functions to his leading actors. His actresses, unlike Davenant's, were recruited as hirelings, and there is no evidence of a sharing agreement with the actors until after the ground had been secured for the new Theatre Royal.[60] The King's Company, wracked by dissension, greed and bad management, eventually disintegrated, to be 'swallowed alive' (Hotson's words) by the rival Duke's Company fourteen years after Davenant's death.[61]

The laureate's company was as harmonious and cohesive as his godfather's company the Chamberlain's/King's Men had been; and as they had had their Richard Burbage, so Davenant's now had the universally admired Thomas Betterton – later to be succinctly assessed thus by Colley Cibber: 'Betterton was an *Actor*, as *Shakespear* was an Author: both without Competitors.' Towards the end of his long life, Betterton paid a notable tribute to his old director as a disciplinarian: 'When I was a young Player under *Sir William Davenant*, we were obliged to make our Study our Business, which our young Men do not think it their duty now to do, for they now scarce ever mind a word of their Parts but only at *Rehearsals*.' After a month or two they imagined themselves masters of an art which in truth took 'a whole life of application'. Charles Gildon had gone down to visit the great actor in 1709, the year before his death, at his country house at Reading, where – after they had 'sate down in an agreeable Shade' in the garden with a glass of wine – Betterton 'fell into a Discourse of *Acting*'. He repeatedly asserted his belief in naturalistic playing (or what passed for it at the time), condemning 'bawling Actors', advocating moderation in gestures and facial expression, and insisting that the actor 'must transform himself into every Person he represents'. He quoted with vehement approval all Hamlet's celebrated observations about acting, commending in particular the advice to 'speak the speech trippingly on the tongue'.[62]

As the painting after Kneller in the National Portrait Gallery shows, Betterton was a man of sturdy build – a contemporary 'Satyr upon the Players' speaks of him as 'Brawny *Tom*'[63] – but he played all kinds of part, both tragic and comic. Gildon lists some sixty plays in which he 'made some considerable Figure'.[64]

The actor was a son, by a second wife, of Matthew Betterton, who worked in the catering department of the Household of Charles I. He lived in a house in Tothill Street, Westminster, given him by his father-in-law Thomas Flowerdew, a wealthy vintner. There Thomas was born in 1635, and baptised at St Margaret's Westminster on 11 August.[65] As we know, the Cademans also lived in Tothill Street, and Davenant may well have met young Betterton there in the 1650s. His father apprenticed him to a bookseller, and there has been much debate as to whether his master was John Holden or John Rhodes. Some writers have stated positively that it was Holden – who briefly kept a bookshop, from 1650 to 1651, at the sign of the Blue Anchor in the Lower Walk of the New Exchange in the Strand, and published Davenant's *Gondibert* in 1651: he was succeeded there by the distinguished Henry Herringman, who published nearly all Davenant's subsequent works. It has further been stated that the 'Mrs Holden' named by Downes as one of Davenant's actresses was Holden's daughter. I have established that none of this is true. Holden died young and unmarried in 1652, and could not have been Betterton's master; he made his unmarried sister Susanna his executrix, and possibly she was Davenant's actress, but there is as yet no evidence.[66] Betterton's (and apparently Kynaston's) master was undoubtedly John Rhodes, for whom Betterton had been acting at the Cockpit before the formation of the Duke's Company. Rhodes was about the same age as Davenant; as well as being a bookseller for a time – at the sign of The Bible at Charing Cross, says Gildon – he was a freeman of the Drapers' Company, and Downes was told that in pre-war days he had been wardrobe-keeper at the Blackfriars Theatre – so that Davenant would probably have known him from the late 1620s, when his early plays were put on there.[67]

The wording of Davenant's agreement with the actors makes it quite clear that he did not employ actresses until the opening of the Duke's Theatre in June 1661. Downes[68] provides us with the names of the girls he chose: the Mistresses Davenport, Saunderson, Ann Gibbs, Norris, Davis, Long, Holden and Jennings, adding the invaluable information that the first four 'being his Principal Actresses, he boarded them at his own House'. It must have been a crowded establishment: in addition to the four Cross and Cademan stepsons (who probably lodged nearby, but would have been constantly in and out), Lady Davenant bore the laureate nine sons in quick succession – named by his eldest grandson (for the College of Arms pedigree) as Charles, Edmund, William, Alexander, Augustin, Thomas, Nicholas, George and Richard. As can be seen in the Hotson plan, the theatre and lodgings were just within the parish of St Clement Danes, with St Giles-in-the-Fields immediately to the north. No baptisms are to be found in either set of registers – no doubt because the parents were Catholics; however, for some unknown reason, Thomas *was* baptised at an anglican church, St Giles Cripplegate, on 31 January 1663/4.[69] The Ralph Davenant who later became a treasurer of the playhouse is sometimes said to have been a tenth son of Sir William, but he was in fact a nephew – one of the eight children of the laureate's brother Dr Robert down in Wiltshire (he had been created Doctor of Divinity at Oxford on 2 August 1660).[70] The Davenant babies would have been put out to nurse, but presumably returned home later. And Sir William had many friends to entertain, among them Aubrey, Samuel Butler the author of *Hudibras*, the royal doctor Gideon de Laune, Evelyn and Pepys, Dryden, Cowley (who died the year before him), and Hobbes and Waller who outlived him.[71] In a prominent place in the house, or perhaps in the playhouse, hung the portrait of Shakespeare, the only one with a real claim to have been painted during the poet's lifetime, which Davenant had inherited in the 1650s; it was bought by Betterton after his death, and now hangs in the National Portrait Gallery.[72]

CHAPTER TEN

1661–2
Theatre manager
and stage director

◦❧◦⟨❧◦

It is generally agreed that William Davenant opened at the Duke's Playhouse in Lincoln's Inn Fields on Friday 28 June 1661, because when Pepys 'took Coach and went to Sir Wm. Davenant's opera' on Tuesday 2 July, he said it was 'the fourth day that it hath begun, and the first that I have seen it. Today was acted the second part of *The Siege of Rhodes*'. If John Downes is right in saying that that performance of Part II was 'the very first Day', it implies that Part I had been given on the three previous days. Downes further reports that the productions of both parts, and of *The Wits* which followed, had 'new Scenes and Decorations, being the first that e're were Introduc'd in *England*': the exact truth, of course, is that the Duke's was the first public theatre in the country in which painted scenery was regularly used.[1] The manager had set the model for the modern stage, with proscenium arch (frontispiece'), proscenium doors and movable scenery, and specially built tiring-rooms and scene-store.

In the 'Enlarg'd' text of *Rhodes* Part I, published with Part II in 1663[2] – with a respectful dedication to the author's old friend Edward Hyde, now Lord Clarendon and Lord Chancellor – Ianthe appears earlier than in the 1656 version, and Roxolana is introduced into Part I for the first time. Ianthe, originally performed by Catherine Coleman, was now played by Mary Saunderson, and Roxolana by Hester Davenport: from then on Pepys usually refers to the two actresses as 'Ianthe' and 'Roxolana' (or 'Roxalana' as he often spells it) whenever he mentions them, regardless of what piece they happen to be in at the time. The part of Solyman the Magnificent, sung by Captain Cooke in 1656, was now performed by Thomas Betterton, making his first appearance at the Duke's Playhouse; Alphonso, originally sung by Ned Coleman, was played by Henry Harris, who was to become, with Betterton, one of Davenant's leading actors. Although it has recently been argued[3] that the Restoration performances of Part I, like Part II, were presented as

spoken drama, the choruses remain in the printed text: I conclude that
all or most of the dialogue – now performed by actors and actresses, not
musicians – was spoken, but that the choruses were done in recitative. It
is difficult to imagine, for example, that the Chorus of Soldiers in the
Fifth Entry would have rendered 'With a fine merry gale, / Fit to fill ev'ry
sail, / They did cut the smooth sea / That our skins they might flea . . .' in
straight speech; and the Chorus of Wives in the Fourth is actually
printed thus:

1

1. This cursed jealousy, what is't?
2. 'Tis love that has lost it self in a mist.
3. 'Tis love being frighted out of his wits.
4. 'Tis love that has a fever got;
Love that is violently hot;
But troubled with cold and trembling fits.
'Tis yet a more unnatural evil:
CHORUS
'Tis the God of Love, 'tis the God of Love, possest with a Devil. . . .

which surely indicates an exchange in recitative by four voices. (Pepys
was later moved to set this chorus to music.)[4] Alphonso, too, has some
lines which would seem better fitted to recitative than to straight speech
– for example, his 'How bravely fought the fiery French, / Their bul-
wark being stormed! . . .' in the Second Entry, and his exchange with
Ianthe in the Third beginning: 'Indeed I think, Ianthe, few / So young
and flourishing as you . . .' (to which she responds: 'When you, my
Lord, are shut up here . . .'). Harris was much admired as a singer and
dancer as well as an actor, and Pepys was later to write of Mary
Saunderson's 'sweet voice', so both players would have been capable of
recitative; and we know that musicians were present, because each
Entry was 'prepared by Instrumental Musick'.[5]

   Rhodes Part II was certainly done as 'a just drama', in Dryden's
words: the only mention of music in the text is in Act V, where 'A
Symphony expressing a Battel is play'd a while', and later 'A Symphony
sounds a Battel agen'.[6] For the first performance on 2 July 1661,
Davenant wrote a *Prologue*[7] advising the distinguished audience:

Hope little from our Poets wither'd Wit;
From Infant-Players, scarce grown Puppets yet.
Hope from our Women less, whose bashful fear,
Wondred to see me dare to enter here:
Each took her leave, and wisht my danger past;
And though I come back safe and undisgrac'd,
Yet when they spie the WITS here, then I doubt

No *Amazon* can make 'em venture out.
Though I advis'd 'em not to fear you much;
For I presume not half of you are such . . .

The author speaks of 'many Trav'lers, from *Paris*, *Florence*, *Venice* and from *Rome*' having come 'as Judges'. He then, through *Prologue*, makes the customary apology for the 'narrow Place', and continues – in terms markedly reminiscent of the *Prologue* to the original production of *Rhodes* I at Rutland House in 1656:

Oh Money! Money! if the WITS would dress,
With Ornaments, the present face of Peace;
And to our Poet half that Treasure spare,
Which Faction gets from Fools to nourish War;
Then his contracted Scenes should wider be,
And move by greater Engines, till you see
(Whilst you Securely sit) fierce Armies meet,
And raging Seas disperse a fighting Fleet . . .

Having made the author's point for him, *Prologue* bids the audience 'entertain' themselves, and gracefully retires 'like an old Rat . . . to Parmizan'.

Davenant must have been supremely confident about the quality of the entertainment he was about to offer, or he would never have risked such a mock-modest *Prologue*. And his *Epilogue* is in similar terms:

Though, bashfully, we fear to give offence;
Yet, pray allow our Poet confidence.
He has the priv'lege of old servants got;
Who are conniv'd at, and have leave to Doat . . .

The poet recalls how

he serv'd your Fathers many years.
He says he pleas'd them too, but he may find,
You Witts, not of your Duller-Fathers mind.
Which, well consider'd Mistress-*Muse* will then
Wish for her old Gallánts at Fri'rs agen;

As old mistresses console themselves

With thoughts of former Lovers they have had:
Even so poor Madam-*Muse* this night must bear,
With equal pulse, the fits of hope and fear;
And never will against your Passion strive:
But, being old, and therefore Narrative,
Comfort her self with telling Tales, too long,
Of many Plaudits had when she was young.

Madam-*Muse* had no need to worry: *The Siege of Rhodes* Part II was an instant and continuing success; and when Pepys visited Vere Street two days later, to see a performance of the rival manager's play *Claracilla*, it was 'strange to see this house, that use to be so thronged, now empty since the opera begun – and so will continue for a while I believe'.[8]

John Downes reports that *Rhodes* 'continu'd Acting 12 days without Interruption [apart from Sunday 7 July of course] with great Applause' – an exceptionally long run for those days; and it had many later revivals. Pepys's account of the first performance is well-known: 'We stayed a very great while for the King and the Queene of Bohemia. And by the breaking of a board over our heads, we had a great deal of dust fell into the ladies' necks and the men's haire, which made good sport. The King being come, the Scene opened; which endeed is very fine and magnificent, and well acted, all but the Eunuches [part], who was so much out that he was hissed off the stage.' The unfortunate man who dried, having been cast for the very small part of Haly the eunuch, was John Downes himself: he explains (later) that – in addition to King Charles and his aunt – 'the Duke of *York*, and all the Nobility [were] in the House, and the first time the King was in a Publick Theatre', and that 'the sight of that *August* presence, spoil'd me for an Actor'.[9] His loss was our gain, for kindly Davenant transferred him, as he tells his readers, to the very responsible post of book-keeper and prompter, so that for many years he was 'Conversant with the Plays and Actors . . . Writing out all the Parts in each Play; and Attending every Morning the Actors Rehearsals, and their Performances in Afternoons'. Although he is not always accurate, he supplies much information not available elsewhere.

Hester Davenport was one of three of Davenant's actresses who, in Downes's words, were 'by force of Love . . . Erept the Stage' (the others were Moll Davis and Mrs Jennings).[10] On 15 November 1661 Pepys saw *Rhodes* II again, saying simply that it was 'very well done'; but by February 1662 he was writing regretfully of the 'losse of Roxalana'. Aubrey de Vere, Earl of Oxford, had fallen in love with the twenty-year-old actress, and when she resisted his advances, was compelled to offer marriage. He then resorted to the well-worn trick of a bogus ceremony, arriving at her lodgings with his trumpeter (or, according to another account, his kettledrummer), robed as a priest.[11] When the Pepyses went to *Rhodes* II on 20 May, they thought it 'not so well done as when Roxalana was there – who, it is said, is now owned by my Lord of Oxford'; however, by 27 December they considered 'the new Roxalana', Mary Norton, 'rather better in all respects, for person, voice and judgment, then the first Roxalana' (Davenant had no doubt been rehearsing her intensively). They were 'not so well pleased with the company at the house today, which was full of Citizens, there hardly being a gentleman or woman in the house, but a couple of pretty ladies by us, that made sport at it, being jostled and crowded by prentices' – a comment showing that Davenant's audiences were usually much more high-class. When Pepys later met Mrs Norton, he described her as 'a fine woman, indifferent handsome, good body and hand – and good mine [mien]; and pretends to sing, but doth it not excellently'.[12]

On 1 January 1663 he saw Hester Davenport 'in the chief box' at Davenant's playhouse (which was again 'full of Citizens' and so 'less pleasing' than usual); she was 'in a velvet gowne as the fashion is and very handsome, at which I was glad'. There is no evidence that she ever again appeared on the stage. She bore the earl a son in 1664, and later lived obscurely; 'Hester, call^d Countess of Oxford' was buried at St Anne Westminster (now Soho) on 20 November 1717.[13]

Pepys never mentions *Rhodes* Part I, and it seems likely that it was not put on very often. His last reference to Part II during the diary period is on 21 May 1667: this was a royal command performance at the theatre. He saw 'my Lady Castlemaynes coach and many great coaches' at the door, and could hardly bear to go away: but he had vowed not to visit a playhouse again until Whitsun, and 'did command myself; and so home to my office and there did much business to my good content, much better then going to a play' – he stoically concludes. There was also at least one command performance at Court, for Davenant's specially written 'Epilogue to the King at Whitehall, at the Acting of *The Siege of Rhodes*' survives;[14] there may have been more, since the Lord Chamberlains' records are not complete. Altogether King Charles did Davenant signal honour: in spite of the fact that it was Killigrew's company and theatre which enjoyed his patronage, when he made his first visit to a public theatre in his own country, Davenant's was the one he had chosen.

Pepys greatly admired *Rhodes* as a piece of literature as well as a play: he naturally bought both parts when they were published in 1663 (and his copy of the 1673 folio edition of the *Works*, which also contains them, is still in the Pepys Library at Magdalene College, Cambridge).[15] On 23 September 1664 he had a nasty cold, and Elizabeth too was not well: he sat up late reading to her from the work. On Sunday 1 October 1665 he was on board the King's yacht *Bezan*, which he used that year as a floating office on several trips down-river from the Bridge; he and the captain 'spent most of the morning talking, and reading of *The Siege of Rhodes*, which is certainly (the more I read it the more I think so) the best poem that ever was wrote'. After playing cards in the evening they read some more, before turning in. On a fine Sunday afternoon in the following August, the diary evokes an idyllic scene: Samuel and Elizabeth took a boat-trip upstream as far as Mortlake, 'with great pleasure', accompanied by Mrs Pepys's waiting-woman Mary Mercer and the Pepyses' beloved servant Jane Birch – 'reading over the second part of *The Siege of Rhodes* with great delight'. And on 19 December 1668 Mrs Pepys read from the opera to her husband before supper and bed.[16]

The diarist was particularly interested in the music which had been composed for the original production of *Rhodes* I in 1656 (none of which can now be traced): when 'Darnell the Fidler', one of the Duke of York's household, called on him on 22 January 1667, he asked about it, 'which he tells me he can get me, which I am mighty glad of'. On 31 October 1665 (for the second evening running) he had given a musical evening: it was attended by, among others, Ned and Catherine Coleman, and after the dancing, Mrs Coleman – whom Pepys describes as 'a pleasant jolly woman' – sang 'very finely, though her voice is decayed as to strength; but mighty sweet, though saft [*sic*]'. They got her to sing 'part of the Opera' (in her own original role of Ianthe), after which she took off 'most excellently', part of Captain Cooke's role as Solyman (she had presumably retired from the professional stage).[17]

On the following 6 December, Pepys 'spent the afternoon upon a song of Solyman's words to Roxolana that I have set'; this was his setting of the passage from *Rhodes* Part II, Act IV, beginning:

Beauty, retire! Thou dost my pity move!
Believe my pity, and then trust my love!

He was very proud of what was to become his best-known musical composition; it is now in the Pepys Library, and the diarist is holding a copy of it in the familiar portrait of him in his 'Indian gown' done by John Hayls in 1666, and now in the National Portrait Gallery.[18]

On 13 February 1667,[19] Samuel and Elizabeth went to a party given by Dr Timothy Clarke, physician to the King's Household. Among their fellow-guests was Captain Cooke, who greatly displeased the diarist: he 'had the arrogance to say that he was fain to direct Sir W Davenant [at the original 1656 production of *Rhodes* I] in the breaking of his verses into such and such lengths, according as would be fit for music, and how he used to swear at Davenant and command him that way when W. Davenant would be angry, and find fault with this or that note'. 'A vain coxcomb I perceive he is', Pepys disgustedly concludes, 'though he sings and composes so well.' Most of the 'discourse' at the party was about plays and the opera, and Pepys was astonished when their host (of whom he was very fond) declared that Davenant was 'no good judge of a dramatic poem', finding fault with his choice of Lord Orrery's *Henry V* and other plays for the stage – 'when I do think', Pepys reaffirms, 'and he confesses the *Siege of Rhodes* as good as ever was writ'. After dinner Cooke and two of his boys sang, and again Pepys praises his singing: but he then reverts to the attack on Davenant – a man for whom he had a high regard: Cooke's 'bragging that he doth understand tones and sounds as well as any man in the world, and better then Sir W. Davenant or anybody else, I do not like by no means; but was sick of it and him for it'. It was a bad day for the diarist: an 'ill and little mean' meal, dingy table-linen, tiresome company, and when it was time to go, the weather was 'foul' and he had great difficulty in securing a coach to get home 'over the ruins' left by the Fire – and when he did, had to sit with his sword drawn, his customary practice after dark at that troubled time.

Pepys's assessment of *The Siege of Rhodes* reflected the general reaction to the piece, which provided a resounding start to Davenant's regime as a theatre manager: one theatregoer, in a rambling report in doggerel verse to a friend in the country about shows on in London, wrote: 'all say / It is an everlasting play' (conceding, however, that 'The ffirst [Part] did not satisfy soe fully'). But Dryden considered that the work lacked 'the fulness of a plot, and the variety of characters' which Davenant could have provided had he lived longer; and Buckingham makes a similar point in the *Epilogue* to *The Rehearsal*: 'The Play is at an end, but where is the Plot? / That circumstance our Poet *Bayes* forgot . . .', one of several obvious references to *Rhodes* which he allowed to remain in the text, although his play was not put on at the Theatre Royal until the end of 1671 – thereby indicating the continuing popularity of Davenant's work nearly four years after his death.[20]

Richard Flecknoe, a man not often disposed to praise Davenant, was to insert into the raillery of his own Sr *William D'avenant's Voyage To The Other World* some lines by an anonymous poet describing the laureate as one who 'in this later Age' had 'chiefly civiliz'd the Stage', and declaring that *The Siege of Rhodes* 'out-goes all the rest' of his plays.[21] Its influence persisted in such works as Dryden's *The Conquest of Granada* and John Hughes's *The Siege of Damascus* well on into the eighteenth century.

The twelve consecutive performances of *The Siege of Rhodes* in the summer of 1661 took the company up to the middle of July. There was then a pause to allow for rehearsals and changes of scenery, after which, as Pepys records on Thursday 15 August: 'Thence to the Opera [as he continues to call Davenant's theatre], which begins again today with *The Witts*, never acted yet with Scenes . . . and endeed, it is a most excellent play – and admirable Scenes'.[22] The cast was headed by

Betterton and Harris as the Elder and Young Pallatine, with Cave Underhill as Sir Morglay Thwack and Hester Davenport as Lady Ample. Once again the first performance was graced by royalty, for the King and the Duke and Duchess of York attended. As Downes reports, there were eight consecutive performances – and as we know, Pepys enjoyed the play so much that he was at two more of them, on Saturday the 17th, when the Queen of Bohemia and Lord Craven were present, and on Friday the 23rd for the last of the initial run. In April 1667 the Pepyses saw the piece twice, now 'corrected and enlarged': on the 18th the diarist was not so pleased with the play, although he admired the acting, but on the 20th 'it likes me better then it did the other day, having much wit in it'. There was a command performance at Court in the following month, on 2 May.[23] The Pepyses saw the play once more during the diary period, on 18 January 1669, when the diarist described it as 'a medley of things, but some similes mighty good, though ill mixed'. It was still being revived at Lincoln's Inn Fields as late as 1726.[24]

The afternoon immediately following the end of the first run of *The Wits*, Saturday 24 August, saw Davenant's revival of *Hamlet*, and John Downes declares: 'No succeeding Tragedy for several Years got more Reputation, or Money to the Company than this.' Pepys, naturally, was present, and wrote that it was 'done with Scenes very well'. The cast on this great occasion was headed by Betterton – now twenty-six years old – as the Prince, with Harris playing Horatio, Lilliston as Claudius, Hester Davenport as Gertrude and Mary Saunderson as Ophelia.[25]

The production was notable above all for Betterton: his interpretation was generally considered to be the greatest of his long career. Pepys, on that first afternoon, declared: 'Batterton did the Prince's part beyond imagination'; a performance in May 1663 provided 'fresh reason never to think enough of Baterton'; and when the diarist and his wife, with Deb Willet and Mary Mercer, their neighbour the wine-merchant William Batelier, and Pepys's lifelong friend and colleague Will Hewer, saw the play in August 1668, they were 'mightily pleased with it; but above all with Batterton, the best part, I believe, that ever man acted'.[26] There can be little doubt that Betterton's interpretation derived ultimately from Shakespeare, by way of Davenant, for Downes says that 'Sir *William* (having seen Mr. *Taylor* of the *Black-Fryars* Company Act it, who being Instructed by the Author Mr. *Shaksepeur*) taught Mr. *Betterton* in every Particle of it; which by his exact Performance of it, gain'd him Esteem and Reputation, Superlative to all other Plays'. There must be something wrong about this story, for Joseph

Taylor did not join the King's Men until three years after Shakespeare's death; but that is no reason for doubting that Betterton inherited the tradition of the original Shakespeare/Burbage interpretation. Steele, who saw Betterton's last recorded performance in the role, in 1709 when he was over seventy, wrote in the *Tatler* that he portrayed the Prince as 'a young man of great expectation, vivacity, and enterprize', which gives a hint of his reading of the part; Rowe, in his *Life* of Shakespeare published in the same year, spoke of 'the Advantage with which we have seen this Master-piece of *Shakespear* distinguish itself upon the Stage, by Mr *Betterton's* fine Performance of that Part'.[27]

Another notable feature of the Davenant production, of course, was Mary Saunderson's playing of Ophelia – her first Shakespearean role in a career which, to quote Cibber, 'was to the last, the Admiration of all true Judges of Nature and Lovers of Shakespeare, in whose Plays she chiefly excell'd, and without a Rival'.[28] She was without doubt the first leading English professional actress: Catherine Coleman maintains her claim to have been the first identified actress, but as Malone remarks, 'the little she had to say [in *Rhodes* in 1656] was spoken in recitative'.[29] There has been much debate about a small collection of poems entitled *A Royal Arbor of Loyal Poesie*, published in 1664 by the minor actor and poet Thomas Jordan, who had strong links with the Red Bull playhouse.[30] Some eight pages of the collection consist of prologues and epilogues relating to theatrical performances both dated and undated – the former, although not in strict chronological order, belonging to 1660 and 1661. One *undated* item (pp. 21–2) is entitled 'A Prologue to introduce the first Woman that came to Act on the Stage in the Tragedy, call'd *The Moor of Venice*'; Herbert's list of plays put on by Killigrew in 1660, as published by Malone, includes a reference to *The Moor of Venice* on 8 December, and most commentators, including Malone himself, have concluded that this was the occasion of the appearance of the 'first Woman'. A surviving series of letters from this period, written by Andrew Newport in London to Sir Richard Leveson in the country,[31] may be relevant. They are full of unrelated bits of news from the capital; in one dated 6 December Newport speaks of 'Plays at Court every week'; and on 15 December – that is, a week after the performance of *Othello* at Vere Street – he writes: 'Upon our stages [*sic*] we have women-actors, as beyond sea' – implying that this is something brand-new. Quite possibly the 'first Woman' did perform on 8 December; but if she did, she is unnamed, and so cannot rival Mary Saunderson as the first identified player of great female Shakespearean roles. The introduction of professional actresses upon the English stage had really become inevitable: war and interregnum had brutally halted

the theatrical training process whereby boy playing girl progressed to
man playing man, so that at the Restoration the profession was faced –
to quote the prologue about the 'first Woman' – with the ludicrous
situation that men of forty or fifty were playing 'Wenches of fifteen':

> With bone so large, and nerve so incomplyant,
> When you call *Desdemona*, enter Giant.

Davenant's revival of *Hamlet* included the appearance of Cave
Underhill (or 'Undril', as his name is sometimes printed, indicating the
contemporary pronunciation) as First Gravedigger. It was his most
famous role, and he monopolised it for most of his long life, returning to
play it one last time at a benefit performance at Drury Lane, when
pitifully 'worn and disabled', in 1709. I find that Underhill's birthplace,
on 17 March 1633/4, was Robin Hood Court at the top end of Shoe
Lane, which lay within the parish of St Andrew Holborn (the bottom
end was in that of St Bride Fleet Street): he was baptised at St Andrew's
on 23 March, the son and grandson of musicians.[32] The 'Satyr upon the
Players' has a few scurrilous lines about 'Roaring Mad *Cave* . . . / Drunk
every night . . . / Who strove so long a Fool to be believ'd, / That at the
last he is a Fool indeed'; Cibber, more generously and no doubt more
accurately, describes him as a 'correct and natural comedian', with a
'face full and long', who could appear 'the most lumpish moping
mortal' when he wanted to.[33]

   '*The Tragedy of Hamlet Prince of Denmark*. As it is now Acted at His
Highnes the Duke of *York's* Theatre' was not printed until 1676 (by
Andrew Clark, for its publishers Martyn and Herringman, at the Bell in
St Paul's Churchyard and the Blue Anchor in the New Exchange
respectively) – fifteen years after Davenant's revival of the play, and
eight years after his death. So it is not absolutely certain that the 1676
edition exactly reproduces the Davenant version. However, the
immediate and continuing success of the play upon the Restoration
stage suggests that it does so. The play-text is given in full, with verbal
alterations aimed principally at clarity, and the cuts made for the acting
version are indicated with inverted-comma signs. As a notice *To the
Reader* explains: 'This Play being too long to be conveniently Acted,
such Places as might be least prejudicial to the Plot or Sense; are left out
upon the Stage: but that we may no way wrong the incomparable
Author [whose name appears in capitals on the title-page], are here
inserted according to the Original Copy . . .'. On the whole the extensive cuts have been made with care and sensitivity, to provide a version
recently described as 'swift-moving and a good vehicle for Betterton'.[34]
Valtemand, Cornelius and Reynaldo disappear; so do Polonius's words

of advice to Laertes, and Hamlet's to the players; many of the longer speeches are shortened, and one soliloquy – 'How all occasions do inform against me' – is omitted, as in the Folio text of the play. 'To be or not to be' survives intact. On 13 November 1664 Pepys and his wife spent a Sunday afternoon indoors learning it by heart; it has been suggested that a musical setting of it for a single voice, which is in the Pepys Library, may hint at Betterton's mode of delivery on stage.[35]

William Davenant has often been ridiculed and reviled for what he did to Shakespeare: but for nearly twenty years the public had been deprived of the opportunity of seeing the plays in performance, and he was the man above all others who restored them to the English stage, and prepared the way for the bardolatry that would soon set in. He must also have stimulated the interest of the reader: Pepys's expressed admiration for *The Siege of Rhodes* as both play and 'poem' illustrates the constant interaction between theatre and bookshop in late seventeenth-century England. There is no doubting Davenant's profound veneration for his godfather; but he was well aware that 'native wood-notes wild', exalted poetry, flights of fancy, examination of the profundities of the human mind and soul, and of the oddities and inconsistencies of human behaviour, were not altogether to the taste of his contemporaries. Nor did romance greatly appeal (*As You Like It*, *Love's Labour's Lost*, *All's Well* and *The Winter's Tale*, for example, were never staged during the Restoration period). The taste of the time was for action, 'design', symmetry, orderly plots, reward for the just and retribution for the unjust. That was what Davenant usually aimed at providing. But in the case of *Hamlet* he did not attempt 'reformation': and the overwhelming impact of Betterton's portrayal of the Prince is sufficient evidence that the power of the play was unimpaired. It was years after Davenant's death, and after the secession of Betterton and others from the United Company in 1695, that Cibber was to write of 'rude and riotous havock' at Drury Lane, and of how 'Shakespeare was defaced and tortured in every signal character. – Hamlet and Othello lost in one hour all their good sense, their dignity, and fame'.[36]

Hamlet, of course has nearly always been found 'too long to be conveniently Acted', and each generation has made what cuts it considers appropriate. The play has long been so famous that the excellence of the actual story it has to tell is often taken too much for granted. Early directors, including Davenant, were largely concerned to promote the clarity of the 'Plot or Sense', for audiences coming to the play for the first time.

Davenant's production of *Hamlet* in August 1661 was followed in September by one of *Twelfth Night*. Pepys, who happened to be

G

walking through Lincoln's Inn Fields on the 11th, discovered that it was the first performance, and that the King was present. But although characteristically he 'could not forbear to go in', he was not in the mood: he was 'troubled' because he had promised Elizabeth that he would never again go to a play without her, and did not enjoy it at all. Betterton and Harris were cast as Sir Toby Belch and Sir Andrew Aguecheek, with Underhill as Feste; Thomas Lovell played Malvolio, and the sixteen-year-old Ann Gibbs, Olivia – from which it is apparent that the whole emphasis was on comedy rather than romance. Downes does not mention Viola and Orsino at all. He reports that the play had 'mighty Success by its well Performance', adding that it had been 'got up on purpose to be Acted on Twelfth Night'. Pepys went to a performance on the Twelfth Night not of 1662 but of 1663, but then considered the play, although well acted, to be 'silly [which he always uses in its sense 'simple'] . . . and not relating at all to the name or day'; and when he saw it again some years later (possibly much altered), it seemed to him 'one of the weakest plays that ever I saw on the stage'. We do not know what text was used: the Davenant version was never printed.[37]

In October 1661, Davenant revived his own *Love and Honour* with great success. Downes reports[38] that the production was 'Richly Cloath'd': Betterton, Harris and Joseph Price, playing Alvaro, Prospero and Leonell, were allowed to wear the coronation suits of the King, the Duke of York and the Earl of Oxford respectively; Hester Davenport (the Earl's future mistress) played Evandra. 'The Play having a great run, produc'd to the Company great Gain and Estimation from the Town.' It will be remembered that Pepys was there for all three first performances, on Monday the 21st and on the 23rd and 25th: his only criticism was of the scenes, which he thought had been altered for the worse.

Hamlet was on again that winter: Pepys saw it on 27 November and 5 December.[39] Earlier, on 4 November, he and Elizabeth had been to another revival of *The Bondman*, the play which they 'both did so doate on': this was the occasion on which the diarist called Betterton 'the best actor in the world'.

On 16 December, the couple were at the first public performance of a 'very good' play by the manager's old friend Abraham Cowley, *The Cutter of Coleman Street* – a comedy based on the author's play *The Guardian* which had been acted before Prince Charles at Trinity College, Cambridge in 1641 and published in 1650. In his revision, Cowley shifted the scene to London in 1658, so that it now included 'reflection much upon the late times', to quote Pepys, satirising the Puritans and the type of cavalier who succumbed to their influence. The cast included Betterton, Harris, James Nokes (one of the company's best comedians), Mary Saunderson, Ann Gibbs and Mrs Long (who was to become the mistress of the Duke of Richmond). Underhill was in the title-role, and the character of Captain Worm, which Downes says was 'not a little injurious to the Cavalier Indigent Officers', was played by Samuel Sandford – his first mention of a fine actor who had joined Davenant's company a little after its formation. As was customary at a first performance, the seat-prices were doubled, so the Pepyses went up to the gallery (for two shillings each), where they 'saw very well'. Downes says the play was 'Acted so perfectly well and Exact, it was perform'd a whole week with a full Audience'.[40]

Sir William Davenant's sustained success at the Duke's Playhouse forced Thomas Killigrew to plan a better and larger theatre, where he too could offer scenery. On 20 December a plot of ground was secured from the Earl of Bedford called the Riding Yard, lying between Drury Lane and Bridges (now Catherine) Street and measuring 112 by 58 or 59 feet; on this would be built the first of the Theatre Royals which have stood there up to our own day. The plot was leased to two trustees, William Hewett and Robert Clayton, for forty-one years, and they in turn made it over to Sir Robert Howard, Killigrew and eight members of the company – Charles Hart, Nicholas Burt, John Lacy, Michael Mohun, Robert Shatterel, Walter Clun, William Cartright and William Wintershall. A theatre was to be built on the site by Christmas 1662 at a cost of £1,500, and the ground-rent was set at £50 a year. The interest in the land was divided between the 'building sharers' in thirty-six shares, of which to begin with Howard and Killigrew had nine each, Lacy four and the others two each. The acting company, made up of the eight players already named plus five more – Theophilus Bird, Richard Baxter, Edward Kynaston, Nicholas Blagden and Thomas Loveday – undertook to act in the projected theatre and no other, and to pay the building sharers £3 10s 0d for each acting day. (Contrary to Davenant's arrangement, whereby the actresses were formed into a separate company, Killigrew evidently treated his women as hirelings.) The building shares were based on the amounts of money invested in the building, while the acting shares were allotted according to the value of an actor to the company. To begin with, Mohun, Hart and Lacy each had one-and-a-quarter acting shares, and five others – Wintershall, Cartwright, Burt, Clun and Bird – had one each. By the time the Theatre Royal was finished, the cost had risen from the estimated £1,500 to £2,400.[41]

His professional future assured, on 27 February 1661/2 the beautiful Edward Kynaston 'of the parish of St Giles in the Fields gentleman' secured a licence to marry: his bride was Mary, daughter of Henry Carter, of the same parish, and the couple were married there on 6 March.[42] Since all the leading London players knew each other well, and some – including Betterton and the bridegroom – had previously acted together, no doubt members of the Duke's company joined those of the King's for the celebrations.

Work on the new Theatre Royal continued throughout 1662, and Killigrew had to carry on for the time being at Vere Street: the theatregoer who had written of Davenant's *Rhodes* II as 'an everlasting play' remarked to his friend in the country that at the King's 'one would imagine Playes should be better', but that it was not so – 'the Knight with his Scenes' was having much more success at the rival theatre. The first new play at Vere Street, he notes, had been the manager's own *The Princess: or, Love at First Sight* – which Pepys saw on 29 November 1661, when the playhouse was so full that he and Sir William Penn (Navy Commissioner, and father of the founder of Pennsylvania) could hardly get in: Penn went up to one of the boxes, and Pepys 'into the 18*d* places' in the middle gallery. It was the first time the play had been put on 'since before the troubles; and great expectation there was, but I find the play to be a poor thing; and so I perceive everybody else do' (it lasted only two days). The other new plays mentioned by the theatregoer are Sir Robert Howard's *The Surprisal* (first staged on 25 April 1662), which 'took well enough', thanks mainly to Lacy's playing of Brancadoro, 'a rich Senator's Son'; Sir William Berkeley's *Cornelia* (1 June), which had 'abundance of witt', indeed was 'too witty for the vulgar sort'; and *Selindra* (3 March), by the manager's elder brother Sir William Killigrew, which had less wit, but a good plot.[43]

In February 1662 Davenant had his first less than successful production at the Duke's Playhouse: *The Law Against Lovers*,[44] his own ill-advised adaptation of *Measure for Measure* into which he imported Beatrice, Benedick (who becomes Angelo's brother), and the singing Balthazar from *Much Ado*, and from which he removed Mistress Overdone the bawd. A new character, Viola, 'sister to Beatrice; very young', is given a few lines; has a song in Act III, 'Wake all the dead!', which proved very effective; makes an entrance in Act IV 'dancing a saraband, awhile with castanietos'; and in Act V follows Lucio, Beatrice and Benedick in singing each a solo verse, interspersed with a chorus.[45] Pepys was particularly impressed with the 'Little Girle', as he calls her, '(who I never saw act before) dancing and singing': in his opinion, she redeemed the play which would otherwise have been spoiled by the recent loss of Hester Davenport. It has been suggested that the girl was Mary Norton, but this cannot be so as she was the leading actress who had just become the 'second Roxolana'; another suggestion is that she was Ann Gibbs, but this also will not do, for she was now seventeen, no longer a 'little girl', and Pepys had already seen her in December, in *The Cutter of Coleman Street*; the most plausible suggestion is that he was having his first sight of Moll or Mall Davis, who was to become so famous for her singing and dancing, and later for the way in which she captivated King Charles. On 23 February 1663 the Pepyses saw a new play, Sir Robert Stapylton's *The Slighted Maid*, with Betterton and Harris as usual leading the cast, and the diarist enjoyed seeing 'the little girl dance in boy's apparel, she having very fine legs'; by 8 March 1664, when they saw a version of Corneille's tragedy *Heraclius*, he thought 'the little guirle is come to act very prettily and spoke the epilogue most admirably'. Later, on 17 April 1666, he was given a false report that 'Mall Davis, the pretty girl that sang and danced so well at the Duke's house', had died.[46]

When Davenant first staged *The Law Against Lovers* in 1662, the theatregoer dismissed it as 'the worst that ever you saw', but Evelyn saw it done before the King on 17 December. However, it never became one of the company's stock plays, and Downes simply mentions it along with other also-rans, as he does Stapylton's *The Slighted Maid*;[47] Pepys, who thought it 'a good play', was in the minority.

On 1 March the Pepyses were at the first performance of Davenant's revival of *Romeo and Juliet* (which was never printed), with Harris and Mary Saunderson in the title-roles and Betterton playing Mercutio. Downes is somewhat confused about the plot, or perhaps it had been altered, to keep Betterton on stage: he writes of 'a Fight and Scuffle in this Play, between the House of *Capulet*, and House of *Paris*', and has Mrs Holden playing the non-existent part of the wife of Paris. He is presumably referring to III.i, where after the stabbing of Mercutio and Tybalt, Shakespeare has Lady Capulet enter crying: 'Tybalt, my cousin, O my brother's child! / O prince! O husband! . . .' This performance provided Mrs Holden with her only claim to fame (or notoriety), for she 'enter'd in a *Hurry*, Crying, O my Dear *Count*! She Inadvertently left out, O, in the pronuntiation of the Word *Count*! giving it a Vehement Accent, put the House into such a Laughter, that *London Bridge at low Water was silence to it*'. The episode may go some way to explaining Pepys's extraordinarily severe dismissal of the whole performance: 'It is the play of itself the worst that ever I heard in my life, and the worst acted that ever I saw these people [who included his most admired performers] do; and I am resolved to go no more to see the first time of acting, for they were all of them out more or less.' (It has been charitably remarked that the diarist had 'various domestic differences' at the time, and was 'in a thoroughly bad humour.')[48]

Downes reports that *Romeo and Juliet* was later made into a tragi-comedy by James Howard, 'he preserving *Romeo* and *Juliet* alive'; the piece was then played alternately as tragical and tragi-comical 'for several Days together' – he does not say with what success.

During the previous year a well-known French provincial company, the Comédiens de Mademoiselle d'Orléans, had put on spectacular works by Chapoton and Gabriel Gilbert at the Cockpit in Drury Lane after visiting Brussels, Ghent and Rouen. The Pepyses went to a performance on 30 August,[49] which the diarist thought 'so ill done and the Scenes and company and everything else so nasty and out of order and poor, that I was sick all the while in my mind to be there'; but the Florentine agent in London reported that the King, the Queen and the Duke and Duchess of York had greatly enjoyed performances in August and September. Both Charles II and Davenant were well aware how far the English stage had fallen behind technically since the imposition of the parliamentary ban twenty years before, and soon the King dispatched Betterton to Paris to study and report on developments there: he probably went after the production of *Romeo and Juliet* in the spring of 1662, since he is not heard of again until 4 July, when Sir Henry Herbert sent a warrant, in accordance with an earlier writ, to try to stop the Duke's company performing. Twelve members of the company, headed by Betterton (and all described as 'late of St Clement Danes, gentlemen') assaulted Herbert's messenger: they came up at Middlesex sessions on the 18th, and were each fined 3s 4d.[50]

On 1 April Charles, son of Sir Charles Harbord, 'that lately came with letters from my Lord Sandwich to the King', dined with the Pepyses, and then all three, with 'the two young ladies' – Sandwich's daughters Jemima and Paulina – went to Davenant's production of Fletcher and Rowley's *The Maid in the Mill*, 'a pretty good play'; after that the diarist took the party for a walk in the fields at Islington, followed by cheesecake at his favourite inn, The King's Head.[51] (It will be remembered that Pepys had seen part of the play on 29 January 1661, the first time he went to Davenant's season at Salisbury Court.)[52] Next month, on 23 May, after dinner with Sandwich, the Pepyses 'slunk away' to Davenant's theatre to see the first performance of Henry Glapthorne's comedy *Wit in a Constable* – 'so silly a play I never saw I think in my life' – after which they went to the puppet play at Covent Garden.[53]

On 30 September they saw Davenant's production of Webster's *The Duchess of Malfi*, with Mary Saunderson in the title-role and Betterton as Bosola; Harris played Ferdinand, William Smith (another fine actor who had joined the company shortly after its formation) played Antonio, and Ann Gibbs, Julia. Downes reports: 'This Play was so exceeding Excellently *Acted* in all Parts; chiefly, Duke *Ferdinand* and *Bosola*: It fill'd the House 8 Days Successively, it proving one of the Best of Stock Tragedies.'[54] On 12 July, Thomas Gaudy Esquire of the prominent Norfolk family had secured a licence to marry Ann Gibbs, then aged about seventeen, at St Clement Danes, with the consent of her father Thomas Gibbs of Norwich, gentleman, and the allegation by her brother Thomas, gentleman of Furnival's Inn. It has always been assumed that the marriage took place on the same day (which would have been fairly unusual), but it does not appear in the St Clement's register: either it took place elsewhere, or it did not take place at all. Downes continues to call the actress 'Gibbs' and not 'Gaudy', but that does not necessarily prove anything.[55]

Pepys thought *Malfi* was well acted by the whole cast, 'but Baterton and Ianthe to admiration'. He was somewhat disturbed to find 'how easily my mind doth revert to its former practice of loving plays and wine, having given myself a liberty to them both these two days' (on the 29th he had seen *A Midsummer Night's Dream* at Vere Street – 'the most insipid ridiculous play that ever I saw in my life'): he now resolved to foreswear the theatre until Christmas.[56] Clearly he was not attuned to Shakespearean romantic comedy (or tragedy) – *Romeo and Juliet* had been 'the worst that ever I heard in my life', *Twelfth Night* was 'silly', and now *The Dream* 'insipid' and 'ridiculous'. In common with many of his contemporaries, for whom the works of Shakespeare were an accepted staple of the stage, he perhaps took their excellences for granted, and tended to remark only upon what he regarded as weaknesses: but all in all his taste in the drama was, in the words of the Pepys Librarian, 'something of a random phenomenon', and his reaction to individual performances was always much influenced by his mood on the day.

On Saturday 18 October 1662, Davenant – loyal as ever to the family of his beloved Maecenas, the late Endymion Porter – put on the first of four plays written by Porter's son Tom, *The Villain*, with a cast headed as usual by Betterton, Harris and Mary Saunderson. Downes reports that it did much better than the company expected, running for ten days with full houses. Pepys noted on the Monday that three people had highly recommended it to him during the weekend, and he promptly took Elizabeth that afternoon (having called on Lely in the morning, and been greatly impressed at the 'pomp' with which his table was set for the midday meal). Pepys did not enjoy the play (which had 'good singing and dancing, yet no fancy'), but put this down partly to his conscience, which was reproaching him for having broken his recent vow.[57] He enjoyed the play much more when he saw it on 26 December – thanking God for enabling him to curb his 'natural desire to pleasure' by his late oath: he would take another oath soon – 'after two or three plays more'; and when he saw it on 1 January 1663, he remarked 'the more I see it, the more I am offended at my first undervaluing the play, it being very good and pleasant and yet a true and allowable Tragedy' – a good example of Pepys's ruthless honesty with himself, and a warning against putting too much weight on his individual assessments of plays.[58] Davenant gave at least one command performance of *The Villain* at Court, on 1 January 1667.[59]

Rumours had begun to circulate during the autumn of 1662 that Betterton and Mary Saunderson were married. The actress was probably very attractive: Dryden is thought to have had her in mind when he wrote the description of Elvira in *The Spanish Friar* – of medium height, with dark hair, 'bewitching' eyes, cheeks which dimpled when she smiled, and 'her smiles would tempt a hermit'. Pepys's barber Tom Benier, a man 'acquainted with all the players', assured him that no marriage had taken place – adding that the great actor was 'a very sober, serious man, and studious and humble, fallowing [sic] of his study, and is rich already with what he gets and saves'. However, Gildon reports that he had begun to 'cast his Eyes on *Mrs Saunderson*, who was no less excellent among the Female Players, and who being bred in the House of the Patentee [Davenant], improv'd her self daily in her Art'; she was a virtuous woman (unlike some of the other actresses), and Betterton admired her qualities of 'Mind, as well as Person'.[60]

As usual the company were hectically busy: on 1 November some of them performed in a translation by Ferdinando Parkhurst (apparently under John Rhodes's direction) of a play *Ignoramus, or The Academical Lawyer* before the King and Queen at the Cockpit-in-Court, having previously done it at the Drury Lane Cockpit; on 1 December Pepys was at Court for the company's performance of *The Valiant Cid*, an English version of Corneille's tragedy *Le Cid*, with 'Baterton and my Ianthe' and the 'fine wench' Mary Norton heading the cast;[61] and during the month the company were rehearsing a new tragi-comedy by Sir Samuel Tuke, *The Adventures of Five Hours* (Evelyn went to a rehearsal with the author on 23 December 'to hear the comedians con and repeat his new comedy'). Tuke wrote the play, which is in the main a translation of a Spanish comedy of intrigue, at the suggestion of King Charles. The Pepyses saw the first public performance at the theatre on 8 January:[62] the house was so full that although they arrived early, they had to sit 'almost out of sight' of the stage at the end of one of the backless benches near the front of the pit. The play became one of the greatest successes of the early Restoration stage, and Pepys declared it to be 'the best, for the variety and the most excellent continuance of the plot to the very end, that ever I saw or think ever shall'; here his taste reflected the demands of contemporary neo-classical criticism, but he was probably at variance with the majority of his fellow-playgoers in rejoicing that there was not 'one word of ribaldry'. The cast, headed as usual by Betterton and Harris, with Mary Saunderson as Portia, were all clothed 'Excellently Fine in proper Habits', and the piece ran for thirteen days. Davenant was continually adding to his collection of scenes: for *The Villain* there had been 'the New Scene of the Hall', and *The Adventures* included a novel scenic effect, 'The Rising Moon', while the stage directions indicate that among new scenes were 'Don Henrique's House', 'Don Octavio's House', 'Don Carlos's House', 'a Garden' and 'The City of Sevil' – many of which could be used later in other productions.[63] On 2 February (the feast of Candlemas) the company gave a private performance at the Inner Temple, with Lord Clarendon present as guest of honour; in a special *Prologue*, Davenant recalled: 'My Lord, you in your early youth did sit, / As Patron and as Censor too of Wit; / When onely that which you approved could please / In Theaters, the Muses Palaces. / As you were then our Judge, so now we come, / In yearly trial to receive our doom. . . .'[64]

During all this activity in the winter of 1662–3, Betterton had managed to snatch time on Christmas Eve to secure a licence to marry Mary Saunderson: he is described in the document as a 'gentleman of Westminster [his birthplace]', and Mary, aged about twenty-five, as the daughter of a widow living in the parish of St Giles Cripplegate. The widow was supported in the application by Enoch Darrack, who came of a substantial family living in the parish of St Pancras Soper Lane, Cheapside. They are entered in the registers variously as Darrack, Darak, Darack, Darick, Derick, Derrick and Dorick, and Enoch's father Mr William 'Derrick' was a freeman of the Grocers' Company, which ranks second of the Great Twelve. I suspect that the family were of Protestant immigrant stock – William and his wife Mary gave their children the uncompromising Old Testament names Enoch, Elisha, Caleb, Hester and Deborah, and William was probably the son of an alien called William Derrick who was living in Bermondsey in the 1590s.[65]

The wedding of Thomas Betterton and Mary Saunderson took place on Christmas Eve, immediately after the issuing of the licence (as they would not have been married on Christmas Day), at the popular village church of St Mary Islington;[66] no doubt the whole company drove out there to celebrate. The couple spent a long and happy life together: they had no children, but in the 1670s they adopted Anne Bracegirdle, who would also become a celebrated actress.[67]

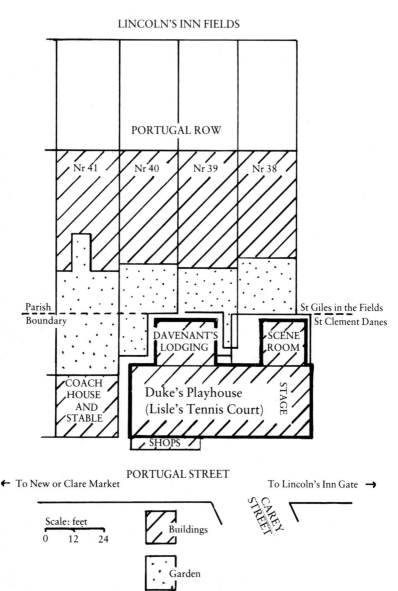

From Leslie Hotson's plan of Davenant's conversion of Lisle's tennis court, Lincoln's Inn Fields, drawn by him for his *The Commonwealth and Restoration Stage* (1928): by permission of Harvard University Press.

CHAPTER ELEVEN

1663–8:
'A man of quick imagination'

❧∞❧

The two theatre managers were still trying to remove George Jolly from the capital. Evidence of his activities is sparse, but he was presumably responsible for a production of Marlowe's *Doctor Faustus* which the Pepyses saw at the Red Bull on 26 May 1662 – 'so wretchedly and poorly done, that we were sick of it';[1] it must have been as bad as his production of Rowley's *All's Lost by Lust* which the diarist had seen there in March of the year before.

On 1 January 1662/3 Jolly was granted a licence by the Master of the Revels, Sir Henry Herbert, to take a company on tour in the country – having secured an undertaking (as he believed) two days earlier from Davenant and Killigrew, to rent his original London licence of 24 December 1660 for £4 a week. Jolly's departure engineered, the managers told the King that they had *bought* his London licence, and asked for one to be made out in their names, permitting them to run a third metropolitan playhouse in addition to the two they had already: it was understood that this would be a 'nursery' for training young actors. A warrant was duly drafted, and Jolly's original licence was declared revoked; Davenant and Killigrew then arranged with Colonel William Legge (who like Killigrew was a Groom of the Bedchamber) that the new licence should be made out in his name, and petitioned the King to make him the nominal licensee. This passed the privy seal on 30 March 1664, Legge being authorised to launch a 'nursery for breeding players' on behalf of the managers. The document stated that Jolly's London licence of 1660 had been surrendered to them 'with the full use and benefit thereof', which of course was not true; it further stated that Jolly had made 'noe use' of it, which was also untrue. An angry Jolly returned to London, perhaps in 1664, and attempted to resume performances at the Drury Lane Cockpit – until in 1665 all theatre activity was halted by the outbreak of the plague.[2]

In 1663 the old Red Bull in Clerkenwell ceased to be used as a theatre:

the House-Keeper in Davenant's *The Playhouse to be Let*, which was probably put on in August, remarks on the arrival of 'Two very hot Fencers without doublets' who want to hire the Duke's house 'For a School, where they'd teach the Art of Duel', to which one of the Players retorts: 'Tell 'em the *Red Bull* stands empty for Fencers. / There are no Tenents in it but old Spiders: / Go and bid the men of wrath allay their heat / With Prizes there' – which is what was happening. The Red Bull was being hired out for fencing-matches, or 'prize-fights' as they were then called – the Pepyses went to part of one on 25 April 1664.[3]

When Tom Killigrew was young and poor – he was the fourth son of a somewhat neglectful father – he used to get in to plays at the Red Bull for nothing when boys were called for to volunteer to 'be a divell' in performances requiring diabolical apparitions; now times were much changed, and on 7 May he opened as manager of the new Theatre Royal Drury Lane – the first purpose-built theatre of the Restoration period. (Downes, never strong on dates, later wrote that Davenant opened at Lincoln's Inn Fields in 1662 instead of 1661, and Killigrew at Drury Lane on 8 April instead of 7 May 1663.) The new theatre must have been a handsome place, its boxes lined with gilt leather and its stage equipped with trap-doors, flying machines and other scenic devices; it probably held from seven hundred to a thousand spectators.[4] No drawings survive of the interior, but contemporary prints show its glazed cupola above the pit, which provided light, but imperfect protection from the weather. During a performance on 1 June 1664 of *The Silent Woman* (with Knepp playing the title-role formerly taken by Kynaston), the whole place was thrown into 'disorder' by a hail-storm half-way through, and the Pepyses had to take refuge in a little alehouse nearby; there was 'disorder in the pit' again on 1 May 1668, during a performance of Sir Robert Howard's *The Surprisal*, when the rain came in – 'it being a very foul day and cold', typical May Day weather.[5]

Pepys (surprisingly) was too busy to attend the opening performance at Drury Lane on 7 May 1663, but noted in the *Diary*: 'This day the new Theatre Royall begins to act with scenes'; he went on the following day, and considered that the house was 'made with extraordinary good contrivance'; however, it had some faults, 'as the narrowness of the passages in and out of the pit, and the distance from the stage to the boxes, which I am confident cannot hear . . . above all, the Musique being below, and most of it sounding under the very stage, there is no hearing of the bases at all, nor very well of the trebles, which sure must be mended'.[6] (Alterations were made while the theatre was closed because of the plague.)

Killigrew might have been expected to open with a new, or newish, play, as Davenant had done at Lincoln's Inn Fields: but he put on Fletcher's *The Humorous Lieutenant*, which in the opinion of Pepys 'hath little good in it'. It must have been a favourite with the King, and presumably he ordered it. Killigrew had already given a command performance at Court on 20 April 1661, before the King, and the Duke and Duchess of York. The title-role was usually played by Walter Clun, but by Charles's order, one of his favourite actors, John Lacy, took it at the opening of the new theatre.[7]

Clun was murdered in the following year, on 2 August: he was set upon near Tottenham Court and 'most cruelly butchered and bound' as he was riding home to his country house at Kentish Town after playing Subtle in *The Alchemist*: Pepys, who heard the news two days later, was sure the King's company would 'have a great miss' of this actor, and was still bemoaning his loss five years later, and especially his Subtle and Iago.[8]

The murder of Clun removed one of the building sharers from Killigrew's company; and shortly before the new theatre opened, one of the acting sharers, Theophilus Bird, died – 'Mr Theophilus Bird' was buried at St Giles-in-the-Fields on 31 March 1663. He belonged to one of the great stage families of the period, for he had married Christopher Beeston's daughter Anne, and his will reveals that his own eldest daughter Anne had become the wife of Michael Mohun. The will does not mention his acting share, but he bequeaths to his sons Thomas and George 'all my playes and play bookes that are mine by payment and Survivor Shipp'.[9]

Davenant was undoubtedly contemplating a new, more spacious and better-equipped playhouse, to rival Killigrew's: but the sumptuous Dorset Garden Theatre which would house the Duke's company was not built until after his sudden death in 1668, and he had to carry on at his 'narrow Place' in Lincoln's Inn Fields. His two principal players provided a striking contrast, both on stage and off: Betterton, as we know, was sober, serious and humble, whereas Harris is described by Pepys, in a vivid phrase, as 'a more ayery man'. And he was certainly far from humble. Pepys was two years older than Betterton, but always speaks of him almost with awe: Harris, on the other hand, he later got to know well during the player's 'full schedule of acting and socializing'.[10] On 22 July 1663, before they had met, the diarist called on his shoemaker William Wotton in Fleet Street – a good source of theatre news: he 'tells me the reason of Harris's going from Sir W. Davenant's house – that he grew very proud and demanded 20*l* for himself extraordinary there, [more] then Batterton or anybody else, upon every new play, and 10*l* upon every Revive – which, with other things, Sir W

Davenant would not give him; and so he swore he would never act there more – in expectation of being received in the other House; but the King will not suffer it, upon Sir W. Davenants desire that he would not'. Davenant himself told the diarist that Harris's departure was 'a great loss . . . And that he fears that he hath a stipend from the other House privately'. Davenant repeated that 'the fellow grew very proud of late, the King and everybody else crying him up so high, and that above Baterton . . . but yet Baterton, he says, they all say doth act some parts that none but himself can do'.[11]

On 24 October Pepys, who had called at Wotton's to try on some shoes, learned that 'by the Duke of Yorkes persuasion, Harris is come again to Sir W. Davenant upon his terms that he demanded, which will make him very high and proud'.[12] As the actor was obviously well aware, this was a crucial time for Davenant, who was faced with much stronger rivalry from Killigrew than before.

Inventive as always, Davenant put on – almost certainly in August – an example of the behind-the-scenes or rehearsal pieces which have been consistently popular with audiences ever since. The vacation stimulated him: he wrote *News from Plymouth* for the Globe in the summer of 1635, and also almost certainly his poem 'The Long Vacation in London, in Verse Burlesque'; now he staged *The Playhouse to be Let*. Pepys does not mention it: like the earlier play, it was aimed at 'citizens' and not the gentry, who were mostly out of town, and would not have appealed to him at all. In any case, Elizabeth was away during the first half of August, and Pepys himself seems to have been exceptionally busy with Navy Office affairs, and making frequent trips downriver to Deptford, Greenwich, Woolwich, Gravesend and Chatham; on the 31st, however, he does note 'my wife after dinner going with my brother to see a play', and probably this was Davenant's piece.[13]

The Playhouse to be Let[14] opens with the House-Keeper and a Player of the Duke's company awaiting responses to their advertisement on the door. First comes a Monsieur, manager of a French touring company, who in comic broken English invites them to take a farce. The Player is doubtful: 'I believe all *French* Farces are / Prohibited Commodities, and will / Not pass current in *England*.' He wonders how an English audience will follow the proposed piece, since 'all our travell'd Customers are gone / To take the Air with their own Wives, beyond / *Hide-Park* a great way' – leaving behind, as he says later, people who simply want to be 'merry at such obvious things / As not constrain 'em to the pains of thinking' (as· he had written in the *Prologue* to *News from Plymouth*, 'This . . . season does more promise shows, / Dancing, and buckler fights, than art or wit'). The Player goes on to renew the complaint about the company's 'narrow Place':

> We'll let this Theatre and build another, where,
> At a cheaper rate, we may have Room for Scenes.
> *Brainford's* [Brentford's] the place!
> Perhaps 'tis now somewhat too far i'th' Suburbs;
> But the mode is for Builders to work slight and fast;
> And they proceed so with new houses
> That old *London* will quickly overtake us.

Next comes a Musician with instrument-cases offering (and demonstrating) 'a Novelty . . . Heroique story / In *Stilo Recitativo*'; he explains that

> Recitative Musick is not compos'd
> Of matter so familiar, as may serve
> For every low occasion of discourse.
> In Tragedy, the language of the Stage
> Is rais'd above the common dialect;
> Our passions rising with the height of Verse;
> And Vocal Musick adds new wings to all
> The flights of Poetry.

The Musician proposes to tune his instruments in the women's tiring-room, to which the Player responds: 'You may; for they are all gon, Sir, to rob Orchards, / And get the Green-sickness in the Country.' After reported approaches by a German fool, opera-puppets from Norwich, an old gentlewoman with a rope-dance, a Turk 'that flies without wings', jugglers, tumblers and the like, a Dancing-Master offers 'Historical dancing' with choruses, while another man wants to hire the company's turban, sceptre and throne used by Solyman in *The Siege of Rhodes* (such transactions were a way of making a little money during the 'dead vacation', as the Player calls it: Restoration players usually wore contemporary clothes on stage, but sometimes with appropriate additions such as the turban, a practice which of course went back to Elizabethan days).

Lastly the Player accepts a piece submitted by a Poet – having invited him to send his 'lean and empty' followers to 'our House-inn, the *Grange*' across the way. The Poet has proposed 'Romances travesti', presenting 'The actions of the Heroes, / (Which are the chiefest Theams of Tragedy) / In Verse Burlesque'. (The author, with a little joke against himself, has him insist that something new is needed – 'Your old great Images of / Love and Honour are esteem'd but by some / Antiquaries now'.) Pressed further, the Poet explains that he is offering 'the

Mock-heroique', and the Player invites him to conduct his 'mock-bur-lesquers' to the wardrobe to choose costumes and props. It is striking evidence of Davenant's enterprise and versatility, and of his feeling for changing tastes, that only a few years after laying the foundations of English opera with *The Siege of Rhodes*, he was now helping to pro-mote the burlesque and mock-heroic as popular forms in the Restora-tion period.[15]

Act II of *The Playhouse* consists of the French farce – a free transla-tion (presumably by Davenant himself) of Molière's *Sganarelle, ou le Cocu Imaginaire*, ending with a dance *à la ronde*, a jig, and a song, 'Ah, Love is a delicate ting, / Ah, Love is a delicate ting, / In Vinter it gives de new Spring . . .;[16] this was sung by Winifred Gosnell, who for a very brief period the year before had been employed as companion to Elizabeth Pepys. Act III, the 'heroique story in *Stilo Recitativo*', turns out to be Davenant's *The History of Sir Francis Drake*; Act IV (the Dancing-Master's offering) is *The Cruelty of the Spaniards in Peru* (the original scenery from the 1650s was used in both Acts); finally, Act V, the Poet's offering, treats of Antony and Cleopatra in the kind of burlesque verse which Davenant had been one of the first writers to use some thirty years before. A dance of gypsies is followed by exchanges by two eunuchs: Mark Antony, says one, 'Is here arriv'd for love of our black *Gypsy*, / On *Cleopatra* he has cast a Sheeps-eye. / And *Caesar* too with many a stout *Terpawling* [sailor], / Landed with him and comes a Catterwawling', at which the other declares: 'How she will simper, at the sight of *Caesar*! / And oh, how trusty *Tony* means to tease her! . . .' and so on. The little piece ends with Cleopatra calling for the fiddlers; after a dance, the company repair to the alehouse, where (Caesar assures them) the tapsters know him and 'Fat Hostess will trust'.

Davenant's *Playhouse* is supposed to have prompted Buckingham (perhaps with others) to start work on *The Rehearsal*, which would probably have been on soon afterwards if it had not been for the plague and fire. His Act II ends with jaunty Mr Bayes tripping up, and exclaiming: 'Ah, gadsookers, I have broke my Nose', and coming on at the beginning of Act III 'with a papyr on his *Nose*'. He then explains to the gentlemen, Mr Johnson and Mr Smith, that his 'fancie' in the play he is rehearsing 'is to end every Act with a Dance', presumably a glance at *The Playhouse*. Later he declares: 'I'm the strangest person in the whole world. For what care I for my money? I gad, I write for Fame and Reputation'[17] – an obvious reference to Davenant's passage in the *Preface* to *Gondibert*, explaining why he has 'taken so much paines to become an Author. . . . Men are chiefly provok'd to the toyl of compil-ing Books, by love of Fame . . . but seldom with expectation of Riches'.

Davenant may have put on another play by Sir Robert Stapylton, *The Stepmother*, shortly after *The Playhouse*.[18] But the spectacular event at the Duke's that autumn, and one obviously intended to meet the competition from the new Theatre Royal, was his revival of *Henry VIII* – a play in which the element of pageant has always been exploited.[19] He did not neglect advance publicity: when Pepys called at his shoemaker's on 10 December, he was told – again – that Henry Harris had returned to the Duke's, 'and of a rare play to be acted this week of Sir Wm. Davenant's, the story of Henry the 8th with all his wifes'. In fact, the play has the original quota of two, Katharine of Aragon and Anne Boleyn. No expense had been spared, and Downes is lyrical about the result. 'This Play, by Order of Sir *William Davenant*, was all new Cloath'd in proper Habits: the King's was new, all the Lords, the Cardinals, the Bishops, the Doctors, Proctors, Lawyers, Tip-staves, new Scenes; the part of the King was so right and justly done by Mr. *Betterton*, he being Instructed in it by Sir *William*, who had it from Old Mr. *Lowen*, that had his Instructions from Mr. *Shakespear* himself, that I dare and will aver, none can, or will come near him in this Age, in the performance of that part.' Harris's playing of Wolsey (the actor had obviously realised the wisdom of returning to his company) 'was little Inferior to that, he doing it with such just State, Port and Mein, that I dare affirm, none hitherto has Equall'd him'. Four years later Pepys wrote of his fame in the part – and Greenhill portrayed him more than once in the Cardinal's robes. A portrait in the Ashmolean Museum at Oxford, in coloured chalks with some wash on buff paper, and a version, dated 1664, at the President's Lodgings at Magdalen College, are the earliest known representations of an English actor in a Shakespearean role.[20]

Mary Betterton played Queen Katharine in Davenant's production; other members of the cast were William Smith as Buckingham, James Nokes and Lilliston as Norfolk and Suffolk, and Underhill as Bishop Gardiner. Every part, says Downes, 'by the great Care of Sir *William*', was 'exactly perform'd', and the piece ran for fifteen days. On 22 December poor Pepys, driving with Elizabeth by coach to Westminster, saw 'the King and Duke and all the Court' on their way to it; he himself was bound not to visit any playhouse until after Christmas – 'But Lord, to see how near I was to have broken my oath or run the hazard of 20*s* loss, so much my nature was hot to have gone thither'. He finally took Elizabeth on 1 January – but, as so often with him, 'expectation' was unfulfilled, and although he was determined to enjoy the play, he thought it 'so simple a thing, made up of a great many patches, that, besides the shows and processions in it, there is nothing in the world good or well done'. On the 27th, the Pepyses drove to 'the French house' in Covent Garden to buy a mask for Elizabeth, and on the way saw 'the street full of coaches' for Killigrew's counterblast at the Theatre Royal – 'which for show, they say, exceeds *Henry the 8th*': this was *The Indian Queen* by Dryden and his brother-in-law Sir Robert Howard, which had been put on on the 25th. Their rhymed heroic tragedy was indeed notable for its scenery; according to a most unusually enthusiastic John Evelyn (*Diary*, 5 February), it was 'so beautiful with rich scenes as the like had never been seen here, or haply (except rarely) elsewhere on a mercenary theatre'. The Pepyses saw *Henry VIII* once more during the diary period, on 30 December 1668 – and this time, the diarist was 'mightily pleased, better then I ever expected, with the history and shows of it'. The production was so spectacular that it was talked about for years. In *The Rehearsal*, Mr Bayes tells Johnson and Smith: 'Now, Gentlemen, I will be bold to say, I'l shew you the greatest Scene that ever *England* saw: I mean not for words, for those I do not value; but for state, shew, and magnificence. In fine, I'l justifie it to be as grand to the eye every whit, I gad, as that great Scene in *Harry* the Eight, and grander too, I gad. . . .'[21] (Presumably Buckingham's liberal use of 'gadsookers' and 'I gad' is intended to echo Davenant's way of talking.)

It was on 14 January 1664 that the Davenants' son Thomas was born, and unaccountably baptised at St Giles Cripplegate on the 31st: perhaps the family had temporarily moved out of their home at the theatre, for the convenience of Lady Davenant and to allow the company more room for manoeuvre during the elaborate production of *Henry VIII*.

On 7 March the Pepyses saw the manager's revival of his own play *The Unfortunate Lovers*. The diarist did not enjoy it at all, but thought that was perhaps because 'the house was very empty, by reason of a new play at the other house'; one consolation was that the beautiful Lady Castlemaine was present in a box. Edward Angel made a great success of Friskin the 'ambitious Taylor', and at his death an *Elegy* declared: 'Adieu, dear *Friskin*: Unfort'nate Lovers weep. / Your mirth is fled, and now i'th' Grave must sleep.'[22] In the *Prologue*, as written for the Blackfriars and repeated, slightly revised, in the 1660s, Davenant reminds the audience how their 'silly Ancestors . . . / Good easie judging Souls', had been content to miss dinner to get to the playhouse early to secure the best seats, and to sit on 'benches not adorn'd with Mats', and had politely doffed their high-crowned hats 'to every halfe-dress'd Player', as he peeped through the hangings to see the house filling up. In the *Epilogue* he writes: ''Las, Gentlemen, he knows, to cry Plays down / Is half the business Termers have in Town'.[23]

Johnson defended it on the ground that the original text – not restored until the nineteenth century – was too painful. Presumably Davenant's audiences felt the same.[48]

It was not until November 1666 that the London theatres were able to reopen, and then only by promising large donations to charity. It seems that these were stopped, but the King gave a lead by commanding plays at Court. On 11 October Killigrew's company presented Fletcher's comedy, *Wit Without Money*, there; John Evelyn saw Davenant's company give *Mustapha* on the 18th; and Pepys saw their *Love in a Tub* on the 29th – the first time he had visited the new Hall Theatre. On 7 December he saw part of Beaumont and Fletcher's *The Maids Tragedy* at Drury Lane, his first visit to either public playhouse since the outbreak of plague the year before: he noted that they had been in action for about a fortnight.[49]

On 5 January 1667 the Pepyses saw *Mustapha* again at the Duke's; on 4 February, the house was full for Corneille's *Heraclius*, with many of the great ladies wearing their hair 'done up in puffs' (rolls); on 21 March the diarist watched a performance by young members of the company, who were being allowed to put on some plays during Lent 'for their own profit'; and on the 30th he saw *The Humorous Lovers* by Davenant's old civil war commander Lord Newcastle, which he thought very silly. Davenant revived *The Wits* in April – Pepys saw it on the 18th and 20th, and there was a command performance at Court on 2 May; and there was a command performance of *The Siege of Rhodes* at the theatre on the 21st. There were apparently no performances at either theatre during June and part of July.[50]

Now began the shortlived but memorable period of collaboration between Sir William Davenant and his successor as poet laureate, John Dryden. There was a connexion between the two men which may seem tenuous now, but would have been of importance at a time when local ties were strong. Judith Davenant (1576–1632), a sister of Dr John Davenant the Bishop of Salisbury, married as her second husband Dr Thomas Fuller, who had a living at the Northamptonshire village of Aldwincle near Oundle; their son Thomas, author of *The Worthies of England*, was born there in 1608 – and so was John Dryden, in 1631 (as Anthony Wood sees fit to note in his entry on William Davenant – 'the very same place that gave breath to Dr. Tho. Fuller the historian').[51]

In August 1667 Davenant staged Dryden's comedy *Sir Martin Mar-all* with great success. James Nokes, one of the leading comedians of the period, was famous for his portrayal of the title-role, which Dryden had written for him – and, says Downes, all the parts were 'very Just and Exactly perform'd, 'specially Sir *Martin* and his Man, Mr. [William]

Smith. . . . This Comedy was Crown'd with an Excellent Entry; In the last Act at the Mask, by Mr. *Priest* and Madam *Davies* [Moll]; This, and Love in a Tub, got the Company more Money than any preceding Comedy'.[52] Pepys saw it eight times, in whole or in part, in a matter of months. He was unable to get into the first performance, on 15 August, at which the King and Court were present, but succeeded next day: 'It is the most entire piece of Mirth, a complete Farce from one end to the other, that certainly was ever writ. I never laughed so in all my life . . . and at very good wit therein, not fooling.' There were command performances, at the theatre, on 21 August, 4 October and 5 November 1667, and 8 January and 18 April 1668, and one at Court on 3 February.[53]

On 4 September 1667 Davenant had *Mustapha* on again, and on the following day *Heraclius*; and on the 12th Pepys saw the first Restoration performance of an old comedy by John Cooke, *Tu Quoque*, 'with some alterations' by Davenant. The diarist thought this very silly – 'but it will please the citizens'.[54] On 5 October the Pepyses tried to get into another new play at the Duke's, *The Coffee House*, a comedy by Sir Thomas St Serfe; but again the house was full, so they went to Drury Lane, where Knepp took them up into the tiring-rooms, all round the auditorium and 'below into the Scene-room'. Pepys was shocked at the 'base company of men' that came among the actresses, and their lewd talk; he was also struck again by stage illusion – what poor clothes the actors had, 'and yet what a show they make on the stage by candle-light'. He heard Nell Gwyn cursing because there were so few customers in the pit – 'the other House carrying away all the people at the new play, and is said nowadays to have generally most company, as being better players'. This is one of seven references in the *Diary* – ranging from 1663 to 1667 – to the superiority of Davenant's players, both men and women, as compared to Killigrew's.[55]

On 15 October the Pepyses did manage to see *The Coffee House* ('ridiculous' and 'insipid' the diarist thought it) – after a long wait for the King and his brother to arrive. Betterton was not in it, and probably he was unwell, for on the 16th and 24th, and again on 6 November, Pepys notes that he was absent through illness.[56] He would have made a point of getting back on the following day, 7 November, for it was then that the celebrated adaptation of *The Tempest* by Davenant and Dryden had its first performance. (The complete cast-list is not known, but he probably played Prospero.)

'*The Tempest, or The Enchanted Island*. A Comedy. As it is now Acted at His Highnes the Duke of York's Theatre' was published by Herringman in 1670, with a *Preface* composed by John Dryden. Ever

since then, Davenant's part in this notable Shakespearean adaptation
has been obscured, or even denied. To put the record straight, it is
necessary to quote Dryden at some length. He begins by expressing his
gratitude to Davenant for doing him the honour of inviting him to
collaborate on altering this play by the poet 'whom he first taught me to
admire'. Davenant, 'a Man of quick and piercing imagination', had

> design'd the Counterpart to *Shakespear's* Plot, namely, that of a *Man* who
> had never seen a Woman; that by this means those two Characters of
> Innocence and Love might the more illustrate and commend each other. This
> excellent contrivance he was pleas'd to communicate to me, and to desire my
> assistance with it. I confess that from the very first moment it so pleas'd me,
> that I never writ anything with more delight. I must likewise do him that
> justice to acknowledge, that my writing received daily his amendments, and
> that is the reason why it is not so faulty, as the rest which I have done without
> the help or correction of so judicious a Friend. The Comical parts of the
> Saylors were also of his Invention, and for the most part his Writing, as you
> will easily discover by the Style.

When Dryden worked with Davenant on *The Tempest*, he was able to
observe him closely, and

> I found him then of so quick a Fancy, that nothing was propos'd to him, on
> which he could not suddenly produce a thought extreamly pleasant and
> surprising... And as his fancy was quick, so likewise were the products of it
> remote and new. .... His corrections were sober and judicious: and he
> corrected his own Writings much more severely than those of another man,
> bestowing twice the time and labour in polishing, which he us'd in invention.
> [Dryden continues:] It had perhaps been easie enough for me to have
> arrogated more to my self than was my due in the writing of this Play, and to
> have pass'd by his name with silence in the publication of it, with the same
> ingratitude which others have us'd to him, whose Writings he hath not only
> corrected, as he hath done this, but has had a greater inspection over them,
> and sometimes added whole Scenes together, which may as easily be distin-
> guish'd from the rest, as true Gold from counterfeit by the weight.

But quite apart from the unworthiness of any such action, he concludes:
'I could never have receiv'd so much honour in being thought the
Author of any Poem how excellent soever, as I shall from the joining my
Imperfections with the merit and name of *Shakespear* and Sir *William
Davenant*.'

It is clear that the conception, and a considerable part of the execution, were Davenant's. Dryden cannot be accused of trying to flatter
him, because the *Preface* is dated 1 December 1669, and by then
Davenant had been dead for over a year and a half.

The Davenant/Dryden *Tempest* formed the foundation for the fully operatic version which was staged at Dorset Garden in April 1674, and published by Herringman in 1674. The Davenant/Dryden version was only reprinted once, until our own century – in the Dryden folio (Tonson, two volumes) in 1701, the year after Dryden's death. It is the 1674 version – partially rewritten and, in Downes's words, 'made into an Opera' by Shadwell – which has subsequently been included in all editions of Dryden's works; and it is the 1674 edition which Davenant's nineteenth-century editors print among his dramatic works. As recently as 1985, the Dryden entry in the new edition of *The Oxford Companion to English Literature* makes no mention of Davenant, referring simply to Dryden's 'perceptive adaptation of *The Tempest* (1667)'. Justice to Sir William Davenant is three centuries overdue.[57]

The classical order and symmetry which he had sought to impose upon *Macbeth* were modest compared to what he imported into *The Tempest*. Miranda is provided with a sister, Dorinda, so that there are now two girls 'that never saw Man'; there is a new young man, Hippolito, 'that never saw Woman'; Caliban is given a twin sister, Sycorax, to make 'two Monsters of the Isle'; even Ariel, at the end, is provided with 'a gentle Spirit for my Love', Milcha, with whom he dances a sarabande. Indeed, as Nicoll remarks, 'our only surprise is that the happy thought did not come to D'Avenant of providing Prospero with a female counterpart'. Dorinda – in character and lines – bears a marked resemblance to the artless Birtha in *Gondibert,* and Hippolito to Gridonell, another young man who had never seen a woman, whom Davenant had introduced years before into *The Platonic Lovers* (reprinted, with *The Wits,* in 1665). Dorinda and Hippolito did not disappear until Macready's production of the play in 1838.

Stephano (played by Edward Angel) becomes the ship's master, and Trincalo (*sic*) – played by Underhill – becomes the boatswain; two new characters, the mate, Mustacho, and Ventoso, a mariner, are introduced. Towards the end Ariel, owing much to Puck in *The Dream,* flies 'o'er almost all the habitable world' to collect herbs (including 'purple Panacea' from the British Isles) to salve a wound suffered by Hippolito in a sword-fight with Ferdinand (Henry Harris). The part of Prospero is much diminished, and there are no cloud-capped towers and gorgeous palaces.

Pepys was at the first performance, and describes the piece as 'the most innocent play that ever I saw'; the house was crowded, with the King and Court and quantities of 'great ones' present. The diarist was particularly taken with 'a curious piece of Musique in an Echo of half-sentences . . . which is mighty pretty'. This was the song 'Go thy way' (III.iv), sung by Ferdinand and echoed by Ariel (?Moll Davis): the music, which survives, was composed by John Banister. He had been in the band for Davenant's *Siege of Rhodes* in 1656; for a time he directed King Charles's string orchestra, and in December 1661 – shortly before Betterton's mission to Paris – the King had sent him there, to look at Louis XIV's musical establishment. When Pepys met him at Knepp's lodging, a few months after the first performance of *The Tempest* in 1667, he got him to prick down the notes of the echo-song, and four days after that, when he saw the play again, he sought out Harris between acts and took down the words from him. In all he went to *The Tempest* eight times in a little over a year (including Twelfth Night 1668) – applauding its 'variety', as he had that of Davenant's *Macbeth*. On 11 May 1668 – the day he went backstage to get the words of the echo-song – he 'had the pleasure to see the Actors in their several dresses, especially the seamen and monster, which were very droll'. On that occasion, too, he had trouble with the orange-woman, who pursued him into the pit and claimed that he had failed to pay her for an order for some ladies in a box on an earlier date: 'I did deny it and did not pay her, but for quiet did buy 4s worth of oranges of her – at 6d a piece.'[58]

By the successive efforts of Davenant and Shadwell, *The Tempest* was now, even more than *Macbeth* had been, a musical variation on a Shakespearean theme. In November 1674, a few months after the staging of the Shadwell version, the Theatre Royal put on another burlesque by Thomas Duffett, *The Mock-Tempest, or The Enchanted Castle*. (It was always the Duke's company that initiated, and the King's that imitated.) Shadwell no more intended disrespect to Shakespeare than Davenant had done: as John Aubrey writes in his *Brief Life* of the playwright: 'I have heard S^r Wm. Davenant and M^r. Thomas Shadwell (who is counted the best Comoedian we have now) say that he had a most prodigious Witt, and did admire his naturall parts beyond all other Dramaticall writers. . . . His Comoedies will remain witt, as long as the English tongue is understood.'[59]

In the first months of 1668 Davenant was as active as ever. On 2 February, the feast of Candlemas, his company gave Etherege's *Love in a Tub* at the Inner Temple; and four days later, the King was present at the theatre for another new play by the same author, *She Would If She Could*. According to Pepys, a thousand people had to be turned away from the pit, and he had to go into 'the 18d box' in the middle gallery where he 'could see but little and hear not all'. The cast included Smith as Courtall, Harris as Sir Joslin Jolly, Moll Davis as Gatty and Mrs Shadwell as Lady Cockwood: Downes says the play 'took well, but Inferior to Love in a Tub'. Many people stayed on after the performance

H

because it was raining, including (in the pit) Buckingham, Buckhurst, Sir Charles Sedley, and the author – and Pepys says everyone was critical, especially Etherege, who complained that the players were under-rehearsed, and that Harris could not even 'sing a Ketch'. However, the diarist – who, as we know, did not appreciate the play-wright – was no doubt exaggerating the general reaction, for there were command performances of the play at the theatre on 25 February, 7 March and 20 April, and one at Court on 29 May, the King's birthday.[60]

At some unknown date, Davenant's actress Ann Gibbs had become the wife of Thomas Shadwell: Downes first calls her 'Mrs Shadwell' in giving the cast of *She Would If She Could* – and 'Mrs Shadwell' has replaced 'Mrs Betterton' in the cast-list of *The Rivals* published in the same year, 1668.

On 11 February, Davenant had *Mustapha* on again – Pepys particularly enjoyed Smith's performance as Zanger; on the 22nd he saw the second performance of *Albumazar*, a revival of an old comedy by Thomas Tomkis, at which the King was present, and everyone enjoyed the 'mimique tricks' of Edward Angel in the principal comic part.[61]

On 26 March King Charles was at the theatre again, for Davenant's play *The Man's the Master,* a farcical comedy of intrigue, translated by Davenant and based on Paul Scarron's *Jodelet, ou le Maistre Valet.* Downes especially commends the playing of the title-roles by Harris and Underhill, and adds that Harris and Sandford sang the *Epilogue* 'like two Street Ballad-Singers'. This tells the audience 'because in all Plays / You still look for new ways / We mean now to sing what ought to be spoken'. There are some shrewd digs at 'Town-Gallants' who put 'half-Crowns of Brass' instead of 'true Coyne' into the box; bully the theatre attendants ('make our Guards quail'); or pretend 'but to speak with a friend' and get in for nothing. 'O little *England*! speak, is it not pity, / That Gallants ev'n here, and in thy chief City, / Should under great Peruques have heads so small, / As they must steal wit, or have none at all?' After the play – which he did not much care for at first, although by 7 May he thought it 'very good' – Pepys gave a splendid party at a nearby ordinary (which cost him nearly four pounds); they were joined by Harris, who brought with him 'Mr. Banester, the great maister of Musique' who had composed the songs for the play. There was a command performance at the theatre on 23 April.[62]

On 3 April Pepys saw the play for the second time. On the 7th, he was at the Theatre Royal, and went down after the performance to call on Knepp, who was being 'undressed' by so pretty a maid that she told Pepys she did not intend to keep her, 'for fear of her being undone . . . by coming to the playhouse' – another revealing comment on the Restoration theatre. As they were chatting, news came 'that Sir W Davenant is just now dead'.[63]

The funeral took place two days later, and is reported for us by two of the most acute observers of the day. Pepys, after midday dinner and a visit to his bookseller, went to the Duke's Playhouse 'there to see . . . Sir W Davenant's corps carried out toward Westminster. . . . Here were many coaches, and six horses and many hackneys, that made it look, methought, as if it were the burial of a poor poett. He seemed to have many children by five or six in the first mourning-coach, all boys.' Aubrey went to Westminster: 'I was at his funerall, he had a coffin of Walnutt tree, Sr John Denham sayde twas the best [crossed out] finest coffin that ever he sawe, His body was carried in a Herse from the Play-house to Westminster abbey, where at the great West dore he was received by the Sing[ing]men & Choristers, who sang the Service of the Church (I am the Resurrection &c.:) to his Grave,* [in the margin: '* which is neer to the Monument of Dr Isaac Barrow.'] which is in the South crosse aisle, on which on a paving stone of marble is writt in imitation of y^e [one] on Ben: Johnson, *o rare Sr Will: Davenant* . . . he had severall children, I sawe some very young ones at the Funerall.' He comments (not in the *Brief Life*, as is usually stated, but in a subsequent letter to Wood): 'But me thought it had been proper that a laurell should have been sett on his coffin – which was not donne.' Wood, in *Athenae Oxonienses*, picks up Aubrey's note and says that the funeral took place 'without any lawrel upon his coffin, which, I presume, was forgotten'. Finally, John Downes adds his report: Sir William 'was Bury'd . . . near Mr. *Chaucer's* Monument, Our whole Company attending his Funerall'.[64]

CHAPTER TWELVE

Epilogue

Sir William Davenant, who died intestate, left his company a legacy of good management, and production continued smoothly under Betterton and Harris, acting as artistic directors on behalf of his widow. On the day intervening between his death and burial the company staged his *Unfortunate Lovers,* and by 2 May they were performing the first play by Thomas Shadwell, *The Sullen Lovers, or The Impertinents,* before the King and the Duke of York (Pepys had prudently paid a poor man to keep a seat for him). Harris played Sir Positive At-all, Nokes 'Poet *Ninny*', and Smith and the author's wife the lovers, and Downes reports that the piece – which had probably been in rehearsal before Davenant's death – had 'wonderful Success', running for twelve days.[1]

Davenant's record at the Duke's Playhouse is remarkable. In not much over five years' actual playing time he put on some fifty productions: opera, tragedy, comedy, tragi-comedy, rhymed heroic drama, farce, burlesque; old plays and new plays; adaptations from the French and from Spanish romantic comedy; Shakespeare plays straight, and Shakespeare plays 'alter'd' and with singing and dancing. He directed the first two plays by George Etherege, thereby promoting the development of the English comedy of manners; a comedy by John Dryden; also new pieces by Tuke, Orrery, Tom Porter, Stapylton and others. He built up an excellent troupe of actors and actresses, pioneered the use of scenery, and commissioned the best composers, dancing-masters and costume-designers. With so many productions, not only at the theatre but also at Court and sometimes at the Inns of Court, and such a rapidly changing repertory, enormous demands were made upon the players, and it is no wonder that they were sometimes 'out'. In September 1667, during a performance of *Mustapha,* Betterton and Harris could not stop laughing, during a serious part of the play, at a 'ridiculous mistake' by another actor, and next day, during *Heraclius,* the whole company were laughing and 'out': Pepys's outrage, coupled with his comment that he had never before seen such behaviour at the Duke's Playhouse, testify to the customary professionalism of Davenant's company.[2]

It is impossible to estimate profits: clearly many productions were very successful, but costs were high;[3] and although, in theory, £10 was paid for each command performance at the theatre, and £20 for each one at Court, it is doubtful whether payment was prompt. Much has also been made of the fact that Davenant was never reimbursed for losses incurred during the civil war, and that at the Restoration, the annuity granted to him by Charles I was not renewed. However, in this he suffered no more than many others: as soon as Charles II returned to his kingdom, he was bombarded with hundreds of petitions from people claiming recompense for past royal service and consequent hardship, some of it going back very many years; he could not possibly have met a fraction of the claims. The proposition that the King was unsympathetic towards Davenant, and considered him 'old-fashioned', does not seem to be borne out by the records.

His old friend and colleague Abraham Cowley had died, at Chertsey in Surrey, a few months before him, on 28 July 1667 – having bequeathed £20 each to several friends, including Davenant, and his 'share and interest' in the Duke's Playhouse to the Hon. John Hervey of Ickworth, Suffolk.[4] Soon after Sir William's death, the company began to look for a site for a new theatre where they might 'with more Conveniency Act', and in August 1670 they leased a plot in Dorset Garden – near Salisbury Court, but on the river – at an annual rent of £130. Davenant's brother Nicholas (who is said by Aubrey to have become an attorney) was involved in the business arrangements, as was his stepson Thomas Cross, the theatre treasurer. The estimated cost of this, the finest playhouse yet built in the capital, was £3,000, the actual cost £9,000; it measured 140 by 57 feet, and is said to have been designed by Wren. An indication of its splendours is given by the fact that Betterton – an early admirer of Grinling Gibbons – commissioned him 'to Carve for him the Ornements & decorations of that house particularly the Capitals cornishes & Eagles'; Lely admired Gibbons's work so much that, having found out from Betterton who he was, he recommended him to King Charles. The company opened at Dorset Garden on 9 November 1671 with Dryden's *Sir Martin Mar-all,* which – Downes reports – ran for three days to full houses, 'notwithstanding it had been *Acted* 30 Days before in *Lincolns-Inn-Fields,* and above 4 times at Court'.[5]

Thomas Betterton followed Davenant's example and lived on the premises, in a lodging in the upper part of the front of the building overlooking the river, and was later to claim that 'by his nearness and diligence' he had several times saved the theatre from being burnt down: on the following 25 January, the first Theatre Royal Drury Lane – where there was no such prudent management – *was* burnt to the ground, and the whole stock of scenes and costumes destroyed. Ignominiously, Killigrew moved his company to the premises in Lincoln's Inn Fields so recently vacated by his rivals; the next Theatre Royal, designed by Wren, was ready for use by March 1674. From about 1667 George Jolly had been running a nursery at Hatton Garden as deputy to Davenant and Killigrew, taking two-thirds of the income, but by early in 1669 this moved to Killigrew's original playhouse in Vere Street: later Lady Davenant started another nursery, in Barbican, which continued for some years.[6]

Davenant had probably begun planning before his death to have his *Works* published, for on 19 August 1667 Herringman entered a collection of his 'Maskes, Playes and Poems' at Stationers' Hall. Lady Davenant collaborated with him to bring out the handsome volume – dedicated to the Duke of York – in 1673. In June, she handed over nominal control of the playhouse to her eldest son Charles, who was now about seventeen; in the same year Philip Cademan was accidentally 'with a sharp Foil pierc'd near the Eye' and incapacitated in a fight with Henry Harris, during a performance of his late stepfather's *The Man's the Master*.[7] In 1678, the company's player Michael Medbourne – one of Davenant's early recruits, and a staunch Roman Catholic – was arrested on a false charge of being implicated in the Popish Plot and imprisoned in Newgate, where he died in March 1679. Killigrew's player William Wintershall died in the same year, and was buried at St Paul Covent Garden on 8 July.[8]

The 1680s saw the deaths of seven leading figures in the theatre world, six of them Killigrew's men – John Lacy, William Beeston (who had joined the King's company on the opening of the first Theatre Royal Drury Lane in 1663), Charles Hart, Michael Mohun, Robert Shatterel and William Cartwright – and the seventh Killigrew himself. Lacy died intestate on 17 September 1681 and was buried at St Martin-in-the-Fields two days later.[9] Thomas Killigrew died on 19 March 1682/3; and Charles Hart, who had retired to a gentleman's country house at Stanmore Magna in Middlesex, died on 18 August, and was buried on the 20th. He bequeathed money for mourning to a number of 'loving friends', including £5 each to Betterton and Smith of the Duke's company; and to Edward Kynaston, his thirty-sixth share in the Theatre Royal 'in the parishes of St Martin in the Fields and St Paul Covent Garden' (the old parish of St Martin then extended as far east as Drury Lane, the new parish of St Paul having been carved out of the middle of it earlier in the century).[10] 'Mr Michael Mohun', who died intestate, was buried at St Giles-in-the-Fields on 11 October 1684 from his home in Brownlow (now Betterton) Street off Drury Lane; his widow Anne, daughter of Theophilus Bird and grand-daughter of Christopher Beeston, was buried there on 2 January 1701/2. In her will – the will of a woman of property – she describes Elizabeth Boutell (presumably the actress) as her niece. Her bequests include one to her daughter Elizabeth Leserture/Lesserteur of 'her grandmothers Picture', and in the following year her son Henry, an apothecary of the parish of St James Westminster (now Piccadilly) left Elizabeth 'my Grandfather's picture sett in gold': these would have been miniatures of Theophilus Bird and Anne *née* Beeston.[11] The player Robert Shatterel, the more prominent of the two brothers, died intestate like Mohun, and in the same year, 1684: he had evidently retired to the village of Islington. William Cartwright, gentleman of St Giles-in-the-Fields, died in December 1686, and his body was 'carried away' on the 20th for burial elsewhere.[12]

Perhaps the most interesting of this group is William Beeston: his death in 1682 rounded off the century of stage history from the building of the first theatres in London and the arrival of Shakespeare to the formation of the United Company under Betterton which would exercise a monopoly in the capital for thirteen years. Beeston had returned to the cradle of the theatre – the parish of St Leonard Shoreditch – and was living in Holywell Street. I find that he occupied one of the tenements in King's Head Yard inherited from his father Christopher: this was in the manor of Norton Folgate, just within the southern boundary of the parish and on the corner of Hog Lane and the west side of Holywell Street – exactly where John Aubrey, in pursuit of material about Shakespeare for *Brief Lives,* was told that Beeston was to be found. It was the player Lacy who told Aubrey that 'Mr Beeston . . . knows most of him'. The antiquary's first visit to him probably took place in August 1681 – he caught both his informants just in time, for Lacy died in the following month and Beeston in the following year. Beeston's information about Shakespeare must have a strong claim to accuracy, and what he told Aubrey has the ring of truth: the young man (Aubrey jotted down) was 'the more to be admired q[uia] he was not a company keeper / lived in Shoreditch, wouldnt be debauched, & if invited to / writ: he was in paine'. It was probably at a further meeting that Beeston told Aubrey that Shakespeare 'understood Latine pretty well: for he had been in his younger yeares a Schoolmaster in the Countrey'. No other report about the 'lost years' comes with better authority, or seems more probable.[13]

Christopher Beeston had been buried at St Giles-in-the-Fields on

15 October 1638; on 15 July 1642 his son William married there Alice, widow of Thomas Bowen, mercer. William was buried at St Leonard Shoreditch on 4 September 1682, and Alice on 16 October 1686. I have found William's original will, a handsome document with a fine signature, an almost perfect seal and also the signature of the player Thomas Sheppey (originally with Davenant's company, later an actor-sharer and building-sharer in the Theatre Royal Drury Lane, and one of those who signed the lease of the theatre to Charles Davenant in 1682): Sheppey was a witness of Beeston's will, and executor of his widow's. Beeston's mentions his son Sackville ('Sackfeild') and Benaiah, reputed son of his son George. With the will is a brief inventory, taken on 28 April 1683, which shows that the couple had been living in very modest circumstances, in a tenement consisting of cellar, kitchen, two chambers and a garret, contents valued at £12 7s 8d: the only item of any conceivable interest is '4 old pictures', but the subjects are not specified.[14]

Six leading theatre people, all connected with Davenant, died during the 1690s – Shadwell, William Mountfort, William Smith, James Nokes, Ralph Davenant and Samuel Sandford. Thomas Shadwell died at his home in Chelsea in 1692, and his will was witnessed by the players Anthony Leigh and his wife Elinor, who were in the United Company under Betterton – Leigh himself died later in the year. Shadwell describes his wife Ann *née* Gibbs, Davenant's former actress, as a 'dilligent careful and provident woeman, and very indulgent to her Children': he bequeaths to her his two tenements in Dorset Garden alias Salisbury Court 'by the Theatre', and the rent he purchased of Lady Davenant and Cave Underhill 'issueing out of the dayly proffitts of the said Theatre'. His father-in-law Thomas Gibbs of Norwich was, he says, 'Proctor and publick Notary': thus Ann was of somewhat higher social standing than many of the Restoration actresses. Thomas Jordan, in the *Prologue* about the 'first Woman', had been at pains to emphasise that 'a vertuous woman' could 'abhor all forms of looseness' and yet appear on the stage, and had begged the gentlemen in the pit to 'have modest thoughts' of the actress playing Desdemona, and 'not run / To give her visits when the play is done'; and in the *Epilogue,* he assured the gentlewomen in the audience that she was 'not a Whore'. It was a sensitive subject. Nell Gwyn, with her customary frankness, had no hesitation in declaring that she had been brought up in a brothel; and Moll Davis, who bore King Charles his fourteenth and last child in 1673, is said to have been the illegitimate daughter of one of the Howard family, Earls of Berkshire, who had a seat at Charlton near Marlborough in Wiltshire – or, alternatively, daughter of a blacksmith

there. Probably nearly all the actresses were of modest means: Mary
Betterton was an orphan, Anne Bracegirdle the daughter of a
Northamptonshire man who had fallen on hard times, Elizabeth Barry
the daughter of a barrister who had ruined himself by raising a
regiment for the King in the civil war. Sir William and Lady Davenant
took in Elizabeth Barry – the manager had probably met her father
during the war. All the actresses had to rely on their talent and charm to
make their way in the world, and there is ample evidence, not least
from Pepys, that they were very vulnerable to 'visits' in their
dressing-rooms (no doubt often with their active encouragement). It
was not unknown for gallants to bribe the theatre staff to admit them
backstage; and a warrant of 1665 speaks of complaints of great
disorders at the Duke's playhouse caused by the entry into the
tiring-rooms of people unconnected with the company.[15]

William Smith, the distinguished actor recruited by Davenant shortly
after he formed his original company, died in 1695 – he is described as
a gentleman of the parish of St Bride (where he had lodged in Fleet
Street for many years with a Mr and Mrs Audley), but was buried on 29
December at St Giles Cripplegate, perhaps the parish of his birth. He
had once had the misfortune to kill another player on stage, but soon
returned to acting; after Davenant's death, Betterton and Harris shared
the artistic direction of the Duke's until 1677, when Harris withdrew
and was replaced by Smith. In his will he calls Betterton his 'friend and
eldest acquaintance', and leaves him £100, plus £6 for mourning, and
ten shillings each to him and Mrs Betterton for mourning rings; there
are further bequests of rings to Charles, Alexander and Thomas
Davenant and Philip Cademan, Sir William's sons and stepson. Smith
also leaves £50 to Dr Davenant's 'pretty prateing eldest [surviving]
daughter': this was Charlotte, who was three and a half years old when
the actor made his will in November 1688. Smith had one young son,
Francis, whom he commits to the care of Dr Davenant, Betterton and
others.[16]

James Nokes (or Noke), one of Davenant's original players, died on
8 September 1696 at his country house at Totteridge in Hertfordshire:
The Protestant Mercury, reporting the death of this 'famous
Comedian' on the following day, said he had left 'a considerable Estate'
(it was valued at more than £1,500), although 'he had not frequented
the Play-house constantly for some years'. He bequeaths a thirty-sixth
share in Sir Hugh Myddelton's New River Company, which conveyed
water from the county to London.[17]

Two theatre people met violent deaths during the decade. On 9
December 1692, young William Mountfort of the Duke's was

murdered by Captain Richard Hill as he was returning home to his lodgings in Norfolk Street: Hill had intended to abduct Anne Bracegirdle when she came away from rehearsals, and suspected that Mountfort 'stood between him' and her: this event caused a great stir. (On 2 July 1686 Mountfort had secured a licence to marry the actress Susanna Percival, whose father was also a player; after his murder she married another promising young actor, John Verbruggen.)[18] Late at night on 18 May 1698, Sir William Davenant's nephew Ralph, treasurer of the playhouse, was attacked by three soldiers as he was on his way home to his lodgings in Gray's Inn Lane (now Road) in the parish of St Andrew Holborn: he was taken back to Charles Davenant's home in the parish of St Bride, where he managed to utter a brief nuncupative will, making his brother William his executor, and was buried at St Bride's on the 22nd.[19] In the following year came the death of Samuel Sandford – another of Davenant's early recruits, and a man who had specialised in playing villains. He is described in the will as a gentleman of St Clement Danes.[20]

By this time the United Company, formed under Betterton in 1682, had come to an end. Betterton and his adherents broke away in 1695, hired Davenant's old playhouse in Lincoln's Inn Fields, and had it reconverted from a tennis court; on 25 March they were granted a separate licence, ending the one-company monopoly; and on 29 April they opened with Congreve's *Love for Love*. In 1704 Vanbrugh built the Queen's Theatre in Haymarket and took over Betterton's manager's licence, and the theatre opened on 9 April 1705.[21]

Henry Harris died in 1704, Betterton in 1710, his widow and the player Kynaston in 1712, and Elizabeth Barry and Cave Underhill in 1713.

We have a uniquely rounded picture of Davenant's former leading player Henry Harris – that talented, fashionable and raffish Restoration player so greatly admired for his acting, singing and dancing – from the *Diary* of Samuel Pepys, who got to know him well: he was a man after the diarist's own heart, of enquiring mind and wide interests. Harris was a guest at two big evening parties which Pepys gave on 24 January 1667 and Twelfth Night 1668: he found the actor 'very understanding . . . in all, pictures and other things . . . a very excellent person, such as in my whole [life] I do not know another better qualified for converse, whether in things of his own trade or of other kinds, a man of great understanding and observation, and very agreeable in the manner of his discourse'. In April 1668, three weeks after Davenant's death, Pepys went up to Harris's dressing-room for the first time (perhaps discipline imposed by the late manager had been relaxed), and observed 'much company come to him, and the Witts to talk after the play is done and to assign meetings'. A month later he went with Harris and others to Vauxhall gardens, where they met some raffish young blades and supped in an arbour. 'But Lord, what loose cursed company was this that I was in tonight; though full of wit and worth a man's being in for once, to know the nature of it and their manner of talk and lives.'

The summer of that year was notable for some much more decorous meetings, which arose out of the interest in painting shared by diarist and player. On Sunday 29 March (three days after the first performance of Davenant's *The Man's the Master,* when Harris and Banister joined Pepys's party at the ordinary), the diarist entertained the two men to dinner – 'most extraordinary company both, the latter for music of all sorts, the former for everything'. Harris commended a portrait of Elizabeth by Hayls, and Pepys decided to commission the artist to do a portrait of Harris for himself; Harris then persuaded the diarist to get Samuel Cooper to limn Elizabeth, and thereafter she sat several times for the miniature (now lost) for which her husband paid £30. It was during this period, on Sunday 19 July, that Pepys gave a notable midday dinner party attended by Cooper and his cousin John Hoskins the miniaturists, Hayls the portrait-painter, Harris, Samuel Butler, and Richard Reeve, a leading maker of optical instruments – 'all eminent men in their way', as the host observes. In the following month Pepys entertained Harris to dinner again, after which they went to inspect Barber-Surgeons' Hall which was being rebuilt after the Fire, and also 'their great picture of Holben's' – the large panel, still at the Hall, showing Henry VIII with freemen of the Company.[22]

During the 1670s Harris spent less and less time acting. It was probably he who married Anne Sears at St Marylebone on Twelfth Night 1671/2: thereafter he was continually being proceeded against by creditors, and his wife sued him for maintenance more than once; by 1678 Nell Gwyn was writing that Lord Dorset 'drinkes aile with Shadwell & Mr. Haris at the Dukes House all day long'. Anne Harris was buried at St Paul Covent Garden on 13 August 1689; Henry died on 3 August 1704, and was buried there on the 6th.[23]

Thomas Betterton died intestate on 28 April 1710, and was buried at the south end of the east cloister of Westminster Abbey on 2 May. We learn from Vertue that he left a collection of 'pictures', including a great many crayon drawings of famous players which were bought by the print-seller John Bullfinch. In the year before his death there had been a benefit performance of *Love for Love* at the Theatre Royal, at which Anne Bracegirdle and Elizabeth Barry, standing on either side of the old man, spoke a specially written *Prologue* by Congreve and *Epilogue* by

Rowe: in the words of the latter: 'Had you with-held your Favours on this Night, / Old SHAKESPEAR's Ghost had ris'n to do him Right', and according to Gildon the distinguished audience 'paid a particular Deference to him by making his Day worth 500 *l.*'. His widow was buried beside him on 13 April 1712.[24]

Edward Kynaston died in his parish of St Giles-in-the-Fields three months later, and his body was 'carried away' for burial at St Paul Covent Garden on 30 July. His first wife, by whom he had had several children, had died in April 1682: the actor soon married again, and is subsequently entered in the register as living in Great Queen Street.[25] Elizabeth Barry, who had been brought up by Lady Davenant, died on 7 November 1713: she had been a parishioner of St Mary Savoy, but retired to Acton where she lies buried.[26] Seventeen-thirteen was also the year of Cave Underhill's death. He had married firstly Sarah Kittermaster at St Bride Fleet Street in 1655, and a daughter Mary was born and baptised on 29 March 1656; Underhill married secondly Elizabeth Robinson at St James Clerkenwell on 17 November 1664, and in the following year – when a second daughter was born – he is recorded as living in the parish of St Vedast Foster Lane off Cheapside, in a sizeable house with nine hearths taxable. By 1695, the year he and the rest of Betterton's group broke away from the United Company and returned to Lincoln's Inn Fields, he was living as a widower in the parish of St Andrew-by-the-Wardrobe between St Paul's and the river: his body was taken from Carter Lane to be buried in the parish of his birth, St Andrew Holborn, on 26 May 1713.[27]

Moll Davis also lived on into the eighteenth century (it used to be supposed that she died in 1687). In December 1686 she had become the wife of James Paisible, a French-born composer and woodwind player living in London; he was employed at Court, and composed instrumental music for the Theatre Royal Drury Lane.[28]

Of Sir William Davenant's brothers and sisters, *Elizabeth* (born ?1601) married firstly Gabriel Bridges, fellow of Corpus Christi College, Oxford, and Rector of Letcombe Basset near Wantage, and secondly Richard Bristow (died 1664), Rector of Didcot; she and *Jane* (born 1602) lived as widows (presumably together) in the parish of St Peter-le-Bailey, Oxford, and were buried at St Martin Carfax, Jane on 27 September 1667 and Elizabeth on 11 May 1672.[29] *Robert* (born 1603) of Merchant Taylors' School and St John's College, Oxford, became Rector of Talbenny, Pembrokeshire (1631) and of West Kington, Wiltshire (1633). In 1649 he married Jane, daughter of John Harward, Vicar of Wanborough, Wiltshire. He was appointed D.D. (1660), and

Rector of Dauntsey, Wiltshire (1663).[30] *Alice* (born 1604) married Dr
William Sherborne (1594–1679), of Merchant Taylors' School and St
John's College, Oxford. He was Rector of Talbenny (1625–31) and,
having entered the suite of Robert Devereux, third Earl of Essex, in
1631 became Rector of Pembridge, Herefordshire, where the Earl
owned the manor; prebendary of Hereford and Chancellor of Llandaff;
he suffered for his royalist sympathies during the civil war. Pembridge
Court – where Alice died in 1660 – was the family seat during the 17th
and 18th centuries. The Sherbornes had numerous daughters, and one
son, Essex – godson of the Earl, born 1636, who is described as of
'Clearbrook' (anglicisation of 'Sherborne'), Pembridge. 'Davenant' was
maintained in the family for some time as a Christian name, and when
the male line died out, the Clearbrook estate passed to Sir William
Davenant's grandson James by his son George. Colonel James Davenant died at Pembridge in 1776.[31] *John* (born 1607) may have died in
London in 1634; *Nicholas* (born 1611) served in the First Bishops'
War; lived for a time with the Sherbornes at Pembridge in the 1650s;
was active in London in 1662; and is presumed to have been involved in
the theatre business.[32]

Sir William Davenant had at least three children by his first wife –
William, Elizabeth and Mary – and perhaps two more (?John and
?Richard), the ones who travelled to Paris in 1646; 'a stillborn child of
William Davonett', buried at St Giles-in-the-Fields on 10 September
1639, was probably his also. *Mary,* who had been living with her aunt
Jane Hallam at the Oxford wine-tavern, became the wife of Thomas
Swift, an uncle of Jonathan, who graduated from Balliol in 1656 (M.A.
1659). At the Restoration Thomas failed in an attempt to become
Rector of Thorpe Mandeville in Northamptonshire. He and Mary had a
daughter, Elizabeth, who died young, and a son, also Thomas – Sir
William Davenant's first surviving grandchild: he, his cousin Jonathan
Swift, and William Congreve were all educated at Kilkenny School and
Trinity College, Dublin.[33] Thomas became Rector of Puttenham near
Guildford.

Of the nine Anglo-French sons of the third marriage, eight survived at
Sir William's death in 1668: the one who did not must have been
Edmund or Augustin. *Charles* (born *c.* 1656), LL.D., M.P., commissioner of the excise, writer on political economy, and much involved in
the theatre business, died intestate on 7 November 1714, and was
buried at St Bride Fleet Street on the 9th.[34] Davenant had married into
the distinguished Molins family of surgeons, who had lived for many
years in Shoe Lane in the parish of St Andrew Holborn. Dr James
Molins I (died 1638) married Aurelia, a daughter of John Florio; of

their large family, the second son, Edward (died 1663) – referred to by Pepys as 'the famous Ned Mullins' – succeeded his father as surgeon at St Thomas's Hospital and lithotomist at St Thomas's and St Bartholomew's, and Edward's son James (1631–87) became surgeon-in-ordinary to Charles II and James II. James lived in Salisbury Court, and it was his only child and heir, Frances, whom Charles Davenant married, probably in 1678. In 1687 James Molins bequeathed fifty guineas each to his daughter and son-in-law (having already made full provision for Frances) in token of his love and esteem; his tenement in Shoe Lane to his wife; all other properties to his dear grandson, Henry Molins Davenant. There is a reference to his two-year-old granddaughter Charlotte, the 'pretty prateing' child of William Smith's will.[35] The link between the Davenant and Molins families helps to explain Vertue's strange notion that John Florio was Sir William's maternal grandfather.

William (born *c*. 1657) went up to Oxford, was ordained and given a living in Surrey, travelled with his patron to France and was drowned in the summer of 1681 while swimming in the Seine near Paris.[36] *Alexander* supplanted his stepbrother Thomas Cross as treasurer of the playhouse in November 1675, appointed his younger brother Thomas manager over the heads of Betterton and Smith in 1688, and having defrauded various shareholders, decamped for the Canary Islands in 1693.[37] *Thomas* (born 1664) died, unmarried and intestate, at Moor Park in Hertfordshire in 1698.[38] *Nicholas* (born ?1665–6) was probably the godson of Sir William's brother of that name. *Richard* (born *c*. 1667) was page to the Duke of Monmouth, and was with him on the scaffold. He served as a lieutenant-colonel in several campaigns under King William, and married a widow, Judith Halford, daugher of Thomas Boothby of Tooley in Leicestershire, by licence at St Bride Fleet Street on 5 February 1700/1. He died on 11 June 1745 aged seventy-eight and was buried at St Martin-in-the-Fields on the 15th; 'Richard D'Avenant Esquire of Whitehall', as he appears in the will, leaves everything to unmarried daughters Susannah and Mary.[39] *George* (born ?1668) is described in his will as 'George D'Avenant of St Martin in the Fields Esquire', and was buried there on 19 March 1709/10. He names a wife Mary, said to have been a daughter of John Ford, alderman of Bath, and son James: it was this son to whom the Sherborne estate in Herefordshire descended. Two of his sons, Colonel Thomas Davenant, and Henry Davenant of Surrey, are said to have been living in 1786, each with a son.[40]

Lady Davenant was buried in the old vault of St Bride Fleet Street on 24 February 1690/1, having made a will on 19 November 1686 in which she bequeaths £20 each for memorial rings to Charles and his wife, £200 each to Nicholas, George and Richard, £400 to Thomas, the rest to Alexander who is appointed executor.[41]

ABBREVIATIONS

BL	The British Library
CJ	*House of Commons Journals*
CLRO	Corporation of London Records Office, City of London
CRO	County Record Office
CSPD	*Calendar of State Papers Domestic*
CSP Col.	*Calendar of State Papers Colonial*
DNB	*The Dictionary of National Biography*
ERO	Essex Record Office, Chelmsford
GL	Guildhall Library, City of London
GLC	Greater London Council
GLRO	Greater London Record Office
Harl. Soc.	The Harleian Society, publications of
HLRO	House of Lords Record Office
HMC	The Historical Manuscripts Commission, publications of
HMSO	Her Majesty's Stationery Office
Hug. Soc.	The Huguenot Society, publications of
L. & P.	*Letters and Papers, Foreign and Domestic, of the Reign of Henry VIII*
LCC	London County Council
LJ	*House of Lords Journals*
MLR	*Modern Language Review*
N. & Q.	*Notes and Queries*
NPG	The National Portrait Gallery
OHS	Oxford Historical Society, publications of
PCC	Prerogative Court of Canterbury (wills)
PRO	The Public Record Office
SP	MS State Papers, PRO
SR	*Stationers' Company Registers*
TLS	*The Times Literary Supplement*
VCH	*Victoria County History* series
WCL	Westminster City Library (Archives), Buckingham Palace Road

NOTES

CHAPTER ONE

1 T/P 195/12, ERO.

2 4D 14, ff. 176–7: printed by A. H. Nethercot, *Sir William D'avenant: Poet Laureate and Playwright-Manager* (1938), Appendix II. In addition to Holman and Mawson, five other Davenant pedigrees, of varying degrees of inaccuracy, exist: (1) in a MS Essex Visitation of 1614, College of Arms; (2) *Visitation of Essex 1634*, I, Harl. Soc. XIII, 388; (3) Harl. MS 1398, BL, done 'up to 1667 by Mr John Withie'; (4) by George Matcham in section on Hundred of Frustfield in Sir Richard Colt Hoare's *History of Modern Wiltshire* (1844); (5) in *The Life of Thomas Fuller, D.D., with Notices of his Books, his Kinsmen and his Friends,* ed. J. E. Bailey (1874), p. 35.

3 D/DVZ 85, ERO.

4 Will, D/ABW 12/23, ERO.

5 See C24/7 (1544), PRO.

6 PCC 79 Drake, Prob.11/88/79, PRO.

7 Registers of Allhallows Bread Street, Harl. Soc., XLIII.

8 PCC 2 Tashe, Prob.11/36/2, PRO.

9 *MS List of Freemen 1530–1648* at Company's Hall in Threadneedle Street, and microfilm and modern index at GL.

10 *The Diary of Henry Machyn 1550–1563,* ed. J. G. Nichols, Camden Soc. XLII, 27.

11 In Aubrey's *Life* of Edward's eldest son, Dr Edward Davenant, vicar of Gillingham in Dorset, MS Aubrey 6, f. 43, Bodleian Library.

12 *Ed. cit.,* p. 300.

13 Until now it has been supposed that the two Sparkes were the same man: cf. T. S. Willan, *The Muscovy Merchants of 1555* (1953) and *The Early History of the Russia Company 1553–1603* (1956), and *Early Voyages and Travels to Russia and Persia,* ed. Morgan and Coote, Hakluyt Soc., LXXII and LXXIII (1886), 1st Series, I and II.

14 For Southam's report to headquarters in London, Hakluyt's *Voyages* (Everyman ed.,), II, 57–65, and *Early Voyages,* Camden LXXIII, II, 190–206.

15 *Voyages,* II, 269; will, PCC 4 Darcy, Prob.11/63/4, PRO. These freedoms were personal grants to individual Englishmen, which explains why they could bequeath them.

16 *Early Voyages,* Camden LXXIII, II, 338–9. In the introduction, Camden LXXII, I, li, it is wrongly stated that Sparke 'met with his end at the burning of Moscow in 1571'.

17 Registered copy, PCC 5 Darcy, Prob.11/63/5, and original of elder Sparke's will at PRO; younger Sparke's original will at GL.

18 *Memorials of St Margaret's Church Westminster,* ed. A. M. Burke (1914), pp. 27, 427.

19 Will, PCC 39 Bakon, Prob.11/61/39, PRO; and, at York, Prerogative Court (Borthwick Institute), XXI, ff. 286v–287.

20 See *Visitations of Yorkshire 1584–5 and 1612,* ed. Joseph Foster (1875).
21 Will, PCC 19 Butts, Prob.11/66/19, PRO.
22 See *L. & P.,* ed. James Gairdner, XVII (1900), 704; and VCH, *North Riding,* I (1914), 64–6, 134–8.
23 For William, see E179/70/115, PRO. He died abroad unmarried in 1626, *PCC Admons. 1620–30,* f. 111.
24 Marriage licence, Harl. Soc., XXV, 109.
25 Forman casebook, MS Ashmole 226, ff. 153–153v, 221, 245v, 309; for burial, GL MS 6538.
26 *HMC, De L'Isle and Dudley (Penshurst) Papers,* II, 200–1.
27 *HMC, Salisbury,* XIV, 281; *Cecil Papers* at Hatfield, petition no. 1096.
28 LC2/4(4), PRO.
29 *Copies of Warrants 1603–30* (Great Wardrobe), LC5/50, ff. 32–3, PRO.
30 LC2/4(5), PRO.
31 AO3/1115 (Audit Office accounts, various), PRO.
32 *HMC, De L'Isle and Dudley,* III, 134.
33 GL MS 6538.
34 LC5/50, f. 58; *CSPD 1603–10,* p. 396; SP38/9 (docquet), PRO.
35 AO3/1116 (1607–11), PRO. Thereafter Richard Sheppard appears regularly in the accounts, E351/3083 (1608–9); E351/3084 (1610–11); E351/3086 (1611–12); E351/3087 (1612–13); AO3/1117 (1611–14).
36 E351/3087 for the wedding; and for 1614, AO3/1117.
37 PCC 110 Weldon, Prob.11/130/110, PRO.
38 Allotted cloth for mourning livery at King James's funeral, LC2/6, and see two Certificates of Residence, E115/377/31 and E115/358/122; and, for the royal debt, his will, PCC 48 Hele, Prob.11/148/48 – all PRO.
39 St Martin's churchwardens' accounts, MS F2, WCL.

CHAPTER TWO

1 First register, GL MS 9138 (paper), MS 9140 (parchment).
2 E. P. Hart, *Merchant Taylors' School Register 1561–1934* (2 vols., 1936), I; C. J. Robinson, *Merchant Taylors' School Register 1562–1874* (2 vols., 1882–3).
3 F. W. M. Draper, *Four Centuries of Merchant Taylors' School 1561–1961* (1962); E. K. Chambers, *The Elizabethan Stage* (4 vols., 1923), II, 75–6; A. Feuillerat, *Documents Relating to the Office of the Revels in the Time of Queen Elizabeth* (1908).
4 His freedom has been wrongly given as dating to 1589, but he must be the John 'son of John' freed by patrimony in 1590: see Company's list of freemen, and their *Court Minute Books* (MSS at their Hall, microfilm at GL). Nethercot, Ch. II, 'The Facts', is inaccurate at many points.
5 John Stow, *Survey of London* (2 vols., 1908), ed. C. L. Kingsford, I, 238–9.
6 See *Vintners' Account Book I* (1522–1582), GL MS 15,333/1, p. 651 (covering 1580–2), and *Book II* (1582–1617), MS 15,333/2, pp. 5, 20, 43, 69, 87, 107, 126, 144, 163, 179, 192, 208, 220, 232, 248, 268, 288, 308

(last entry covers 1601–2). There are also entries about John Davenant senior in the first *Book of Apprentice Bindings and Freedom Admissions* (1428–1602), GL MS 15,211/1, ff. 199 and 218v, relating to the lease of his house and to a tierce of wine. For St James Garlickhithe the churchwardens' accounts, GL MS 4810/1.

7 T. S. Willan, *A Tudor Book of Rates* (1962), p. xii.

8 E190/9/7 and E190/10/4, PRO.

9 Aldermen's *Repertories 19, 515,* CLRO. Among numerous references to brokers in the MS City records, one relating to 1618, Court of Common Council *Journal 31,* ff. 73–74v, reports a hearing of English brokers petitioning that the number of foreign brokers be reduced to four, while the number of English brokers would stand at twenty. This serves to show the importance of the job the John Davenants had been doing.

10 Cf. MS Lansdowne 18, f. 39, BL.

11 See Req.2/197/28; C24/208; and C2Jas.I/G16/75, all at PRO. I am indebted to Leslie Hotson for the third reference.

12 MS Ashmole 226, f. 287, Bodleian Library. Jane consulted Forman on 16 January.

13 *Survey,* I, 239, 248, 253 and II, 328 (he calls it 'Kerion' or 'Kirion' Lane). See also H. A. Harben, *A Dictionary of London* (1918), p. 377, on Maiden Lane (1).

14 See MS *Liber Probationis Scholae Mercatorum Scissorum* at Company's Hall. For his possible burial, St Michael Wood Street register, GL MS 6530, entry for 27 February 1633/4: 'Iohn Dauenant, Prisoner buried.'

15 E179/146/388, PRO. Father and son are entered again in the roll for the following October, E179/146/374, but the 'affi' by their names means that the collectors had sworn out an affidavit that they had not paid; in John junior's case this may be because he had already left London for Oxford.

16 E. K. Chambers, *William Shakespeare* (2 vols., 1930), I, 572, and Nethercot, p. 13. In general, Chambers's details about the Oxford Davenants, pp. 571–6, are somewhat inaccurate.

17 The St Martin Carfax registers are now in CRO, County Hall.

18 The quotation has been crossed out in Aubrey's MS, presumably by Wood who perhaps considered it trivial or frivolous. Robert Davenant was for many years rector of West Kington in Wiltshire, which is very near Aubrey's birthplace at Easton Pierse, Kington St Michael.

19 MS Aubrey 6, ff. 46–47v, Bodleian Library.

20 See, for example, S. Schoenbaum, *Shakespeare's Lives* (1970), pp. 101–2.

21 Anthony Wood, *Athenae Oxonienses,* ed. P. Bliss (4 vols., 1813–1820): Wood's passage on the Davenants is in III (1817), 802–9.

22 See nuncupative wills, now in CRO, of Jane Hallam and Elizabeth Bristow, who were buried at St Martin Carfax on 27 September 1667 and 11 May 1672. With Mrs Bristow's will is a bond signed by her nephew 'Ch: D'Avenant'. At some unknown date in or after 1672, Charles, described by Wood as 'a yong poet . . . lately gentleman commoner of Balliol col.', had a marble monument placed on the wall of the north aisle of St Martin's commemorating Sir William's parents, brother John, eldest son William, brother-in-law and sister Hallam, sister Bristow and grand-daughter Swift (his daughter Mary's daughter, who according to Wood died *c.* 1670), see Wood, *Survey of Oxford* (OHS, 3 vols., ed. Andrew Clark) III, 173. This

might be taken to mean that John, like the others, was buried at St Martin's, but (as Wood rightly notes) his name 'non occurrit in registro'. The wall-monument was moved to All Saints when St Martin's was demolished; now, with the recent transformation of All Saints Church to Lincoln College Library, the monument has been remounted near the south door.

23 Vertue, *Notebooks II,* Walpole Soc., XX, 80; Acheson, *Mistress Davenant* (1913), p. 175. Shaw's play was put on and published in 1910: see 1932 ed., pp. 205, 203.

24 *Ministers' and Receivers' Accounts,* SC6.Jas.I/1646, ff. 28v, 29, PRO.

25 MS Ashmole 226, f. 254v (22 November 1597); MS 411, f. 150 (7 October 1601); and MS 226, f. 13v (5 February 1596/7), Bodleian Library.

26 MS Ashmole 219, f. 101v (7 July 1599), Bodleian Library.

27 For the Gores see, in particular, the wills of Gerard, PCC 7 Windebanck, Prob.11/111/7, and his wife Ellen *née* Davenant, PCC 32 Windebanck, Prob.11/111/32, PRO; Gore's funeral certificate at the College of Arms, printed in *Miscellanea Genealogica et Heraldica,* 2nd Series, II, 225; and T. S. Willan, *Studies in Elizabethan Foreign Trade* (1959).

28 Will, PCC 4 Windsor, Prob.11/69/4, PRO.

29 Aldermen's *Repertories 26,* II, 451 (9 October 1604), CLRO.

30 PCC 53 Byrde, Prob.11/143/53, PRO.

31 Will, PCC 10 Butts, Prob.11/66/10, PRO, and see the Gore funeral certificate mentioned at n. 27 above.

32 *The Elizabethan Stage,* II, 346–7.

33 See Chambers, *William Shakespeare,* II, 53, 66–7.

34 For a detailed account of the properties, with inventories, plans and photographs, see W. A. Pantin and E. Clive Rouse, 'The Golden Cross, Oxford', *Oxoniensia XX* (1955).

35 Cf. Nethercot, pp. 17–18, and Schoenbaum, *Shakespeare's Lives,* p. 99.

36 7. Edw. VI. cap. 5.

37 The distinction between inn and tavern is succinctly stated in the *Shorter OED,* 'inn', 3. For the particular case of the Cornmarket inn and tavern, see *Oxoniensia XX,* 62, 71, for a 1623 inventory of the Cross listing forty-seven beds; the terms of John Davenant's will of 1622 show that the tavern was to go on being run as a place to serve wines, not to provide accommodation – compare the quotation, for which see H. E. Salter, *Oxford City Properties,* Appendix III (OHS, 1926), 348. As Chambers points out, *William Shakespeare,* I, 574, there was town-and-gown rivalry at Oxford over the issuing of wine licences, but that does not mean that there were more than three wine-taverns (as laid down by the 1553 Act).

38 Schoenbaum, *William Shakespeare: A Documentary Life* (1975), p. 164.

39 E. T. Leeds, *Oxoniensia I* (1936), p. 148.

40 New College *Leasebook V* (1562–1585), ff. 109v, 223–223v, 231v, 239v; H. E. Salter, *Survey of Oxford I* (OHS, 1926), New Series XIV, ed. W. A. Pantin, 6–10; and E. T. Leeds, *Oxoniensia I*; the All Saints registers are in CRO.

41 The tavern had previously been run by John and Elizabeth Tattleton – she was Thomas Underhill's widow – who were buried at St Martin Carfax on 20 February and 27 June 1581 (Chambers, *William Shakespeare,* I, 574, supposed that Elizabeth was still alive in 1583); the tavern was known for years as 'Tattleton's', even after 1581. For the fact that Mrs Underhill

married Tattleton, see a Bill of Complaint by her daughter Joan, C2Eliz./ S16/23 (1601), PRO.

42 New College *Leasebook VI* (1585–1601), pp. 223, 234–5, at College.

43 Entry in churchwardens' accounts (1592–3), about Hough senior's burial; his will, *MS Wills Oxon.*, 189, f. 21, proved 11 May 1594 (Chambers, *op. cit.*, I, 574, supposed that he died 'about 1596'). William junior was buried at St Martin Carfax on 7 July 1595, for which see churchwardens' accounts, but his will, PCC 87 Stafford, Prob.11/108/87, PRO, was not proved until 1606, which led Chambers to think that he died in about that year.

44 For transfer of Cross lease from Staunton to Pierce Underhill, see Pierce's will, PCC 23 Harte, Prob.11/103/23; for the Vine, see Staunton's will, PCC 64 Kidd, Prob.11/94/64 (1599), both PRO; for the Angel, Stow, *Survey*, I, 170–1, and Aldermen's *Repertories 34*, f. 129v, CLRO. Chambers, I, 575, did not realise that Staunton was a London man, and thought that Joan was still at the Oxford tavern in 1601.

45 See subsidy rolls E179/163/389, E179/163/393 and E179/163/400, PRO; and for the office of college manciple, Carl I. Hammer Jr., 'Some Social and Institutional Aspects of Town-Gown Relations in Late Mediaeval and Tudor Oxford' (D.Phil. thesis, Toronto, 1973) – I am grateful for this reference to Dr Penry Williams.

46 See Plate XII, *Oxoniensia XX.*

47 Pierce is said to have been older than his brother John, who is described as being about thirty-four in a Chancery deposition of October 1579, C24/139/W, PRO. For the 'unquiett life', see their sister Joan's Chancery deposition , C24/328/L (1606), PRO, and J. H. Morrison, *The Underhills of Warwickshire* (1932).

48 See E179/163/396, PRO. Davenant appears in all subsequent rolls during his lifetime, E179/163/433, E179/163/434 – which he signs, as one of the two collectors for the city – and E179/163/437. Grice had arrived by 1599 – he had a daughter baptised at St Martin Carfax in August.

49 See n. 41 above, and Joan's deposition at n. 47 above.

50 After the death of her husband William Hough in 1593, she would have stayed on to help with the inn and tavern until after the death in July 1595 of her son William, who was unmarried and only twenty-three years old – he was baptised at All Saints in November 1571. The Angel inn was administered by the Bridgemasters, and the first time that Staunton appears in their account books as the lessee is in 1595–6, *Bridge House Account Book XIV*, BHA/C 10, CLRO.

51 Smith appears in early seventeenth-century customs lists as a buyer of wine, e.g. E190/12/4 and E190/13/1, PRO; his will, PCC 12 Ridley, Prob.11/155/12 (1629), PRO. See Ruth Fasnacht, *A History of the City of Oxford* (1954), p. 154, for sending goods from London to Oxford by barge.

52 The two men were of an age: Grice became a freeman of the Vintners' in 1589, GL MS, 15, 211/1, ff. 157, 191v, Davenant of the Merchant Taylors' in 1590. Grice had been apprenticed to Thomas Hollinshed, who kept a well-known Holborn tavern called the Greyhound, for which see his will, 33 Rutland, Prob.11/72/33; it was a recognised starting-place for the journey by road from London to Oxford, See *The Life and Times of Anthony*

Wood 1623–95, ed. Andrew Clark (OHS, 5 vols., 1891–5), II, 155, 221; for the Three Tuns at Oxford, E. T. Leeds, Appendix to Arthur Acheson, *Shakespeare's Sonnet Story 1592–1598* (1922), p. 604.

53 For Donne's birth, see R. C. Bald, *John Donne: A Life* (1970), p. 35; *DNB* and Chambers wrongly date the Bishop's birth to 1576.

54 Sir Richard Baker, *Chronicles* (1643), quoted by Bald, p. 72.

55 Bald, pp. 31, 44, 561.

56 The Dawsons appear in the college leasebooks.

57 See his will, now in Oxford CRO; it was made in 1623 – he was buried at St Martin Carfax in September – but not proved until 1627.

58 At the time, babies were usually named after the principal godparent. No William has been found among former friends and colleagues in London or near neighbours in Oxford who might have been expected to provide a godparent; among the Davenants themselves, the name persisted only in the Essex/Suffolk branch of the family, and no evidence has been found that Sir William's branch kept in touch with them.

59 The *DNB* entry on Sir William Davenant omits John, and includes a 'George', who in fact was one of Davenant's apprentices, see Leeds Appendix as at n. 52 above, p. 620.

60 *Oxford City Council Act Book II* (1591–1628), Town Hall, A.5.6, f. 94. In the following year the city chamberlain's accounts note ten shillings 'paid for wine and sugar to Mr Davenaunte . . . bestowed upon Mr Recorder'.

61 Davenant surrendered his city wine-licence on 19 October 1620, see H. E. Salter, *Survey of Oxford I* (ed. Pantin, OHS, new series, XIV), quoting *Reg. Oxon.* II, i, ed. Boase and Clark, 322, so he must have retained the University one, acquired from Pierce Underhill, until the end of his life. Thomas Hallam was admitted a freeman of the city four months after his former master's death, on 20 August 1622 (entry in *Oxford Council Acts*); he and Jane had a University wine-licence dating from 15 April 1623 – see *University Register,* ed. Clark – which would have replaced the one held by Davenant; and on 25 May 1627 Hallam paid £6 13s 4d for a city one, see H. E. Salter, *Oxford City Properties* (OHS, 1926), Appendix III.

The New College leasebooks have only one reference to Davenant as tenant of the tavern (dated 8 July 1613, *Leasebook VII*, pp. 404–5), which caused Chambers some concern, but the books, as well as being written up at fairly long intervals, were often inaccurate and out-of-date. For example, in the entry about Davenant, the tavern is referred to as 'Tattletons howse', although both Tattletons had been dead for thirty-two years; and in November 1616 the tenement between inn and tavern is said to be 'nowe' in the tenure or occupation of *William* Hough, B.D. of Lincoln College (*Leasebook VIII*, p. 61). William – no B.D. – had by then been dead for twenty-one years, and the man intended was his younger brother Daniel (the man under whom Sir William Davenant studied briefly). After William Hough junior had signed the lease in July 1592, the tavern is not mentioned again until December 1602 (*Leasebook VII*, pp. 61–2), when it is described as being in the tenure or occupation of William (dead since 1595) 'or his assigns' (presumably Davenant).

62 See MS *Council Act Book II,* Town Hall, A.5.6, for instructions, in an entry dated 6 June 1605; and Anthony Nixon, *Oxfords Triumph* (1605).

63 Robert presented Ralegh's *History of the World,* and John a MS volume

containing Richard Rolle of Hampole's *Prick of Conscience;* a list of Mayors and Sheriffs of London from the reign of Richard I to that of Henry VI, illustrated with a chronicle of events; a poem by Chaucer, *Chorus avium* or *Scipionis Somnium;* and Regulations for the army by Henry V: 'These been the statutis and ordenauncis to be kept in the hoqst . . .'. A nicely varied collection; I am indebted to the college Librarian for the details.

64 Aubrey inserted 'Charles', but it should be 'Edward', for whom see Nethercot, pp. 23–6, 29, and Harbage, pp. 20–1.

65 PCC 113 Savile, Prob.11/140/113, PRO.

66 MS *Draft Council Minutes 1615–1634,* Town Hall, A.4.2.

67 Quoted by J. O. Halliwell-Phillipps, *Outlines of the Life of Shakespeare* (7th ed., 1887), pp. 43–4; and see Harbage, pp. 14–15, and Nethercot, p. 34.

68 *Draft Council Minutes,* Town Hall, ff. 111v–112.

69 Elaborate theories have been built round this woman, Mrs Joan Hatton, and it has been alleged that Davenant married twice, Jane being his second wife – see Chambers, *William Shakespeare,* I, 571–2, for a summary of the 'Anne Sachfeilde' story. In fact, Mrs Hatton was the widow of Timothy, a mercer and embroiderer who was buried at St Martin Carfax on 5 November 1616 (his will in CRO); their home was on the Carfax side of the tavern. Mrs Hatton was the aunt of Mr Thomas Davies, who was one of the overseers of Davenant's will, and who had become lessee of the Cross inn in about 1613, see his Chancery suit, C3/400/33, and will, PCC 137 Twisse, Prob.11/197/137, PRO. I am grateful to Dr Hotson for the Chancery reference.

70 Daniel, for whom see n. 61 above. Chambers, *op. cit.,* I, 575, found 'a little puzzle' in the entry in Davenant's will, because he believed that the Houghs had no interest in the tavern in 1622. But an entry for 1621 – not 1627 as Chambers supposed – describes the tavern as being then in the occupation of Hough 'or his assigns' (i.e. Davenant), see *Leasebook VIII,* 174.

71 Nethercot, p. 35, wrongly accused the couple of being 'precipitate': but see n. 61 above. They could not have married while Hallam was still an apprentice. On 23 March 1634/5 Hallam became a freeman of the Merchant Taylors' Company in London, 'by vertue of his service with John Davenant deceased', *Court Minute Book VIIIa.*

72 Company's *Apprentice Bindings Book IX* (1623–8), 4; apprenticed to John Elliot of Watling Street on 1 November for eight years; he seems not to have completed his term.

CHAPTER THREE

1 C2.Chas.I/D5/65, *Davenant v. Urswick,* PRO, printed by Nethercot, Appendix III, 433–41.

2 *Complete Peerage,* VII, 605–7.

3 *CSPD 1623–5,* p. 441: SP14/181/ no. 29, PRO.

4 *Complete Peerage,* VI, 506; Harl. Soc., XXIII, 13.

5 MS Ashmole 226, ff. 103, 170v, Bodleian Library.
6 Cf. Nethercot, p. 41; *Complete Peerage*, VI, 506.
7 PCC 81 Leicester, Prob.11/74/81, PRO; Vintners' *Freedom Book* (1428–1602), GL MS 15,211/1, *passim*.
8 Venn, J. and J. A., *Alumni Cantabrigienses 1261–1751* (4 vols., 1922–7).
9 Will, PCC 93 Kidd, Prob.11/94/93, PRO.
10 Harl. Soc., IX, 99.
11 St Benet Paul's Wharf, Harl. Soc., XLI, 17; St Martin-in-the-Fields, MS register 3 (1636–1653), WCL; Davenant had also been entered as a Westminster tax defaulter a few months earlier.
12 Printed by Leslie Hotson, *The Commonwealth and Restoration Stage* (1928), pp. 356–63.
13 With her brother Charles, Mary Swift signs the bond with the nuncupative will of their aunt Mrs Bristow who died in 1672, See Ch. Two, n. 22.
14 *Athenae Oxonienses*, III, 803.
15 Many authors dedicated works to Porter, among them (in 1631) the Reverend Giles Widdowes: he was rector of the parish where Davenant was born, St Martin Carfax at Oxford, and Gibbs (for whom see n. 16 below), p. 339, makes the interesting suggestion that Davenant may have become acquainted with Porter before he went to London. This is perhaps strengthened by the fact that in the St Martin's register, Widdowes has entered – out of date order – the fact that in June 1621 he baptised Endymion's son George (to whom Davenant was later to address a poem, see Gibbs pp. 162–6, 421–2) in Gloucestershire, Porter's county. Someone else, and someone with an obvious interest in the Davenants, has added to the entry: 'How comes this to be put here' – and has added also 'Widdow' after the burial entry for Sir William's sister Mrs Hallam in 1667 and 'an ancient woman, daughter of Mr John Davenant, sometime of this parish' after the burial entry for his sister Mrs Bristow in 1672.
16 A. M. Gibbs, *Sir William Davenant: The Shorter Poems and Songs from the Plays and Masques* (1972); for the poem 'To Lord B.', see pp. 34–5, 362.
17 For the plays, see *The Dramatic Works of Sir William D'Avenant*, with prefatory memoir and notes, (5 vols., 1872–4), ed. James Maidment and W. H. Logan. Quotations from the plays are taken from this edition.
18 For the licensing of the plays, see *The Dramatic Records of Sir Henry Herbert Master of the Revels 1623–1673*, ed. Joseph Quincy Adams (1917): entry for *The Cruel Brother*, p. 31.
19 See Mary Edmond, 'In Search of John Webster', *TLS*, 24 December 1976.
20 *Dramatic Works*, I, 109–97.
21 Gibbs, pp. 206, 440.
22 *Ibid.*, pp. 22–3, 350–1; 172–3.
23 SP16/100/ f. 59; and quoted in full by Nethercot, pp. 59–60, and Harbage, p. 39.
24 See will of Agnes/Anne Davenant, PCC 95 Weldon, Prob.11/130/95, PRO; and C2.Chas.I/D60/28 (for which I have to thank Dr Hotson).
25 E157/16/ f. 29, PRO.
26 D/ABW 57/41, ERO.
27 See Ch. One, n. 6.
28 PCC 101 Evelyn, Prob.11/186/101, PRO.
29 SP16/126/42 and *CSPD 1628–9*, p. 435; quoted in full by Harbage, p. 38.

30 From his *Life,* quoted by Nethercot, pp. 67–8 and n. 4.

31 Will of Gerard Gore, PCC 31 Lawe, Prob.11/123/31, PRO.

32 *John Webster: Citizen and Dramatist* (1980), Ch. II.

33 Quoted by Nethercot, pp. 9–10 and n. 2.

34 For a later poem by Habington 'To My Friend, Will. Davenant', see Gibbs, pp. 8–9, 342: he supports Nethercot's suggestion that Habington was the 'W.H.' who, during Davenant's absence in the civil war, dedicated *The Unfortunate Lovers* to Philip Herbert, Earl of Pembroke in 1643.

35 A letter from Suckling to a friend 'Will', written from Leyden on 18 November 1629, was previously thought – see Harbage, pp. 43–4, and Nethercot, pp. 85–6 – to have been addressed to Davenant, but see Gibbs, p. 341. See also Gibbs, p. 410, for the text of Suckling's poem 'To Mr. Davenant For Absence'.

36 For the Inns of Court group, *Alumni Cantabrigienses*; *Alumni Oxonienses*; *Gray's Inn Admission Register 1521–1889*, ed. Joseph Foster (1889); *Records of the Honourable Society of Lincoln's Inn* (2 vols., 1896); *Register of Middle Temple Admissions*, ed. H. A. C. Sturgess (3 vols., 1949); *DNB*; wills of Henry Prannell senior and junior, see nn. 7 and 9 above, and of Griffith Ellice, PCC 76 Clarke, Prob.11/146/76, PRO; W. A. Shaw, *The Knights of England* (2 vols., 1906); and registers of St Mary-le-Bow, Harl. Soc., XLIV, XLV.

37 *Dramatic Works*, I, 1–107.

38 See *The Dramatic Works of John Ford*, ed. William Gifford with additions by A. Dyce (1895) and *The Broken Heart*, ed. Brian Morris (1965). Morris, p. xi and n. 1, points out that the method of killing Ithocles was based on a real event in Antwerp in the 1550s which was widely reported, notably in Matteo Bandello's *Novelle*, IV. Thomas Ellice of Gray's Inn contributed commendatory verses to *Albovine* (pub. 1629) and *The Broken Heart* (1633).

39 Quoted by Nethercot, p. 53 and n. 26.

40 Sophia B. Blaydes and Philip Bordinat, *Sir William Davenant: An Annotated Bibliography, 1629–1985* (1986), items 539, 545.

41 Nethercot, pp. 79, 84, and Harbage, pp. 228–9 and nn. 10, 11.

42 *Dramatic Works*, I, 199–280.

43 Gibbs, pp. 68–9, 386–7.

44 *Ibid.*, pp. 167–8, 423.

45 Clarendon later wrote contemptuously of him, but Ben Jonson addressed several complimentary poems to him. Davenant wrote a poem 'To the Earle of Portland, Lord Treasurer; on the mariage of his Sonne', see Gibbs, pp. 45–6, 371–2.

46 *Ibid.*, pp. 77, 342, 390.

47 *Ibid.*, pp. 175, 427–8.

48 See Appendix B, pp. 289–338, ed. by Judy Blezzard, and pp. lxxxiii–lxxxvi.

49 Gibbs, pp. 31–2, 359–60.

50 *Ibid.*, pp. 37–43, 363–7.

CHAPTER FOUR

1 The mock-epic 'Jeffereidos' had been completed early in the year, see Gibbs, p. 364.

2 *The Diary of Samuel Pepys*, ed. Robert Latham and William Matthews (11 vols., 1970–83), I, xxiii, and X, 15.

3 See Gibbs, pp. 24–6, 352–4; he favours 1632 as a date for the poem, but Davenant is likely to have been still ill that summer. See also the poem 'In celebration of the yearely Preserver of the Games at Cotswald', Gibbs, pp. 53–4, 377–80, which may be connected with the trip to Worcestershire.

4 See Nethercot, p. 90 and n. 1.

5 See *The Works of Sir John Suckling: I: The Non-Dramatic Works*, ed. Thomas Clayton (1971), pp. 32, 239–40.

6 Gibbs, pp. 51–2, 375–6.

7 P. 93.

8 Gibbs, pp. 44–5, 369–71. He identifies 'I.C.'.

9 *Ibid.*, pp. 49–50, 374.

10 *Ibid.*, pp. 29–30, 357–9. He thinks this might have been written in 1636, during a recurrence of illness.

11 Gibbs, pp. 26–7, 355.

12 The parish registers for the Savoy Chapel do not survive further back than 1680.

13 See his letter of 1 August 1634, now in PRO, SP16/273/3, addressed to his wife 'at my howse in the strand ouer against Durramhowse gate'.

14 *Dramatic Works*, II, 107–244.

15 Pp. 90–107.

16 Pp. 100–1, n. 18.

17 See 'Davenant Exonerated', *MLR* (July 1963), pp. 335–42.

18 P. 100, n. 15.

19 Nethercot prints the English texts, Appendix IV, pp. 443–7.

20 Harbage, pp. 65–7, is aware of the wife's petition, although not of the other documents about the murder of Warren, but he thinks that the husband William must be the poet because the wife's name is given as Mary, whereas the other William married an Elizabeth. (He secured a licence on 1 March 1632/3, Harl. Soc., XXIV, 29, and the couple were married at St Bride Fleet Street on 4 March, GL MS 6537: the securing of the licence, allowing marriage to take place without delay, suggests that William's sentence of transportation was just about to take effect.) Harbage quotes the wife's petition for pardon in 1638 as being headed 'The humble petition of Mary: Davenant'. But he does not mention that the petition is not the signed original, but an unsigned copy (SP16/323, f. 269): and the copying clerk, entering up many petitions covering some six months of 1638, was clearly in a muddle, since he wrote and then crossed out 'Will' and 'Johis' before entering 'Mary:' above the surname. It is permissible to surmise that either he made a mistake about the wife's name, or this William Davenant married again between March 1633 and 1638.

   The petition refers to the husband's 'lands' being held by 'certain meane Lords': Davenant the poet had no lands, then or at any time.

21 P. 106, n. 24.

22 Indictment, Quarter Sessions, 30 September 1602, Q/SR 159/111, ERO.

He is described as 'of Poslingford, gentleman', where his father had bought property and where he was born: on 16 March 1601/2, at Danbury, he mortally wounded William Toftes with a sword.

23 John Downes, *Roscius Anglicanus, or, an Historical Review of the Stage from 1660 to 1706*, ed. Joseph Knight (facsimile reprint, 1886), p. 21.

24 *Diary*, II, 155, 156, 160.

25 Herbert, p. 22.

26 *The King's Peace 1637–1641* (1955), p. 67.

27 Herbert, p. 54.

28 Gibbs, pp. 52–3, 376–7.

29 *Ibid.*, pp. 143, 413–14.

30 Cf. Ch. Three, p. 54 and n. 44.

31 See Gibbs, p. 144 and *Dramatic Works*, II, 225; the *Epilogue* spoken when the play was brought back at the Restoration, *Dramatic Works*, II, 243, was much longer and in quite different terms.

32 *Dramatic Works*, III, 91–192.

33 *Diary*, II, 200, 201.

34 For two catches in *The Wits* sung by Snore and the watch – one in Act V when the play was first put on, the other added for the numerous revivals during the Restoration – see Gibbs, pp. 206–7, 440–1. For *Love and Honour*, a song entitled 'To Two Lovers Condemn'd to die' was printed in the first edition of 1649 (Act V, pp. 173–4), but omitted from the text of the play in the 1673 folio, see Gibbs, pp. 156, 420 – and, for a musical setting by William Lawes, pp. 294–5. For two songs for the sub-plot, 'No morning red and blushing faire' (Act IV, pp. 155–6) and 'With cable and thong he drew her along', see Gibbs, pp. 208–9, 441–2. For the *Epilogue*, Gibbs, pp. 66, 385. He makes the point that the play is important historically for its anticipation of favourite themes in Restoration heroic drama.

35 See Marchette Chute, *Ben Jonson of Westminster* (1953), pp. 323–6; Nethercot, p. 118 and n. 17; Anne Barton, *Ben Jonson, dramatist* (1984), pp. 26, 237, 333.

36 *Coelum Britannicum* was staged on 18 February 1633/4. It is included in the 1673 edition of Davenant's works, but see Nethercot, p. 117, and *Dramatic Works*, I, ix.

37 *Ben Jonson*, p. 264.

38 Later in the year, Elizabeth of Bohemia and Wentworth, then Lord Deputy of Ireland, also received letters on the subject, see Harbage, p. 56 and nn. 19 and 20, and Nethercot, p. 117, and nn. 16 and 18.

39 *Dramatic Works*, I, 281–316.

40 *Florimène* was not performed in the Banqueting House, as stated by Nethercot, p. 120, n. 22, but in the Great Hall of Whitehall Palace.

41 For the songs, see Gibbs, pp. 209–15, 442–5; and John Harris, Stephen Orgel and Roy Strong, *The King's Arcadia: Inigo Jones and the Stuart Court* (1973), pp. 166, 177.

42 *Dramatic Works*, II, 1–105.

43 Quoted in *Dramatic Works*, I, vi; from her dedication of the 1673 folio edition to the Duke of York. She speaks, as her husband had so often done, of 'the envy and malice' of the censorious age.

44 *Dramatic Works*, IV, 105–99, and for the *Epilogue*, Gibbs pp. 67, 385–6.

45 See Gibbs, pp. 215–16, 444–5.

46 Although it did not appear in print until 1656 – in a collection by several 'admirable wits' entitled *Wit and Drollery, Jovial Poems . . .*, see Gibbs, pp. 125–30, 403–7, and for the 1656 text, Appendix A, pp. 285–8; see also pp. xlviii–ix for the importance of the poem in the development of English burlesque literature. A different version of the poem is in the 1673 folio.

47 Compare *News from Plymouth,* Act V, p. 182, where Cable learns from letters from London that during the vacation, 'the / Distress'd daughters of old Eve, . . . lie windbound / About Fleet-Ditch' – a further indication that the play and the 'Vacation' poem were written in the same summer.

48 *Dramatic Works,* I, 317–340, 349–52.

49 See Nethercot, pp. 135–6.

50 See *The New Grove Dictionary of Music and Musicians,* ed. Stanley Sadie, X, 557–8, note on Henry Lawes by Ian Spink, and pp. 558–66, note on William Lawes by Murray Lefkowitz.

51 Herbert, p. 56.

CHAPTER FIVE

1 *Arcadia,* p. 163.

2 *Dramatic Works,* II, 245–300.

3 MS Aubrey 6, ff. 110–110v, Bodleian Library.

4 See Nethercot, pp. 156–7.

5 Quoted by Leslie Hotson in an unpublished Harvard Ph.D. thesis (1923), p. 67; see Nethercot, p. 157 and n. 19.

6 For this and further details, see John Charlton, *The Banqueting House Whitehall* (1964) – published to mark its reopening.

7 E351/3271, mems. 15–15v.

8 Hotson, p. 72, n. 34, gives 115 feet for the length of the Banqueting House, and 60 feet for its width – he may be speaking of its exterior, as distinct from the interior measurements as given by Charlton, see n. 6 above.

9 Quoted by Hotson, p. 12. Here he wrongly gives the length of the new building as 120 feet. A separate entry in the Works roll, mem. 4, speaks of fitting and preparing the room 'for Two Masks': this presumably refers to the two immediate ones, *Britannia* and *Luminalia* – *Salmacida Spolia* was also performed there, and it was not until 1645 that Parliament ordered the structure to be demolished, see Hotson pp. 13, and 72, n. 40.

10 *Dramatic Works,* II, 251–2.

11 See Harris, Orgel and Strong, *The King's Arcadia* and Orgel and Strong, *Inigo Jones: The Theatre of the Stuart Court* (2 vols., 1973), also Graham Parry, *The Golden Age Restor'd* (1981).

12 Quoted by Wedgwood, *The King's Peace,* p. 19.

13 Two vols., 1973: see in particular I, Ch. IV, 'Platonic Politics'.

14 See n. 11 above.

15 *CSPD 1637–8,* p. 19.

16 For songs see Gibbs, pp. 222–6, 447–8.

17 See pp. 160–1 and n. 27.

18 See Hotson, pp. 9 and 71–2, nn. 25, 27.
19 See Gibbs, p. 448.
20 *Ibid.*, pp. 226–34, 448–50.
21 *Dramatic Works*, III, 1–90.
22 *Diary*, V, 77; VIII, 433 (where Pepys calls it *The Ungratefull Lovers*); and IX, 157, 383.
23 The play was published in 1643 and 1649. For dedication in 1643 to the Earl of Pembroke see Ch. Three, n. 34. See Gibbs, pp. 140–2, 234–5, 413, 451, and also two musical settings by William Lawes and Alphonso Marsh, pp. 298–302 and 331–6.
24 *Dramatic Works*, IV, 200–80.
25 Gibbs, pp. 1–80. A second edition appeared in 1648, see Gibbs, p. xxv.
26 *Ibid.*, pp. 10–21, 342–50.
27 See Gibbs, p. 348, note to ll. 281–316.
28 *Ibid.*, pp. 28–9, 356–7.
29 *Ibid.*, pp. 26–7, 355; 35–7, 362–3; 49–50, 374; 52–3, 376–7; 55–6, 381; 58–9, 382; 64, 384.
30 *Ibid.*, pp. 69–73, 387–9; 75–7, 389–90.
31 *Ibid.*, pp. 43, 367–9.
32 *Ibid.*, pp. 28, 355–6, and 296–7 for a musical setting by William Lawes; 32–4, 360–2; 47, 373; 61–2, 383; 67–8, 386. In the second (l. 36), the poet writes of his harp hanging silently 'since my *Euridices* sad day', which has led previous writers (cf. Nethercot, pp. 225–6, and Gibbs, pp. xxiii, 361) to conclude that Davenant's first wife had died by 1638 (which could mean that he married four times in all). This cannot be the meaning of the line: as already noted on pp. 30, 90, Mary, daughter of William and Mary Davenant, was baptised in January 1641/2, and the poet's widow (who must have known the facts) explicitly described her as the daughter of the *first* wife.
33 Gibbs, pp. 134–6, 411.
34 See Gibbs, pp. xxv–xxvi, and n. 1 on xxvi.
35 *Ibid.*, pp. 173, 425–6.
36 See Gibbs, Appendix B, 'Musical Settings', ed. Judy Blezzard, pp. 322–30, 290–2.
37 Gibbs, pp. 175–6, 428–9.
38 *Ibid.*, pp. 78–80, 390.
39 In an elegy on Davenant, written in a contemporary hand in poems by Sir John Denham published in 1668; first printed in recent times in *N. & Q.*, 4th series, V, 576 (January–June 1870). Also in *Dramatic Works*, I (1872), lxxxvii–lxxxix.
40 Thomas Clayton, *The Works of Sir John Suckling: I: The Non-Dramatic Works*, pp. 71–6, 266–78, argues (p. 274) that Suckling's poem should be entitled 'Sessions' (meaning 'trial') rather than 'Session' ('sitting'); but against that, it will be remembered that in the *Prologue* to *The Wits*, Davenant writes of 'A *Session* [my italics], and a Faction at his Play, / To judge, and to condemn', see Ch. Four, p. 70.
41 *Ibid.*, p. 266.
42 *CSPD 1638–9*, p. 161, 11 December (docquet), and patent roll entry, 13 December, for which see Harbage, p. 65 and n. 39.
43 Quoted in *Dramatic Works*, I, vii.

44 II, 72.

45 See Oliver Millar, *Van Dyck in England* (catalogue for NPG exhibition, 1982–3), pp. 32–3, and Fig. 33 for the Prado portrait, and p. 78, no. 36, for the one of Olivia.

46 *Notebooks II,* Walpole Soc., XX, 80.

47 Vertue, see n. 46 above, also reports seeing 'at Mr D'Avenants' (perhaps one of Sir William's sons) a three-quarter length of him by Greenhill, 'more a profil' than the portrait from which Faithorne's engraving for the 1673 folio was taken. Elsewhere, *Notebooks I,* Walpole Soc., XVIII, 79, he writes of going to the house in Great Marlborough Street of a Commodore Carr, 'he lately dead', and seeing 'a small painting in chiaro-scuro. on board' of Davenant: 'on the back is writt his Name & painted Sr P. Lilly, but I rather believe it was done by. Baptist Gaspars'.

48 NPG catalogue, see n. 45 above, no. 39 and pp. 81–2, and colour plate VIII.

49 NPG catalogue, pp. 101–2 and Fig. 48. The portrait is now in the Frick Collection in New York.

50 Malcolm Rogers, 'The Meaning of Van Dyck's Portrait of Sir John Suckling', *The Burlington Magazine* CXX (1978), 741–5; see also Clayton, pp. lxii–lxiii and n. 4.

51 Printed by Thomas Rymer, *Foedera XX* (1735), pp. 377–8; and see *CSPD 1638–9,* p. 604 (docquet).

52 There is a contemporary reference to 'Coll. Massey' (Sir Edward Massey, for whom see *DNB*) being 'made Capt. of Pyoneeres by Nicholas Davenant, poet Davenant's brother': Massey later went over to Parliament. In this paper, dated 1648, Nicholas Davenant is said to be 'now in London at the Feathers in Long Aker, as is thought . . . expecting a com̃and from Massey'. See Clarke Papers, II, Camden Soc. publications, New Series, LIV (1894), ed. C. H. Firth, p. 159. And see Nethercot, p. 280, n. 43.

53 See *The Works of Sir John Suckling in Prose and Verse,* ed. A. H. Thompson (1910), pp. 333–4, 415–16. Gibbs, pp. xxvi–xxvii, n. 5, considers, I think wrongly, that Suckling's letter can be dated to 'about the end of June'.

54 See *HMC,* 4th Report (vol. 3.i), 35, and *LJ IV* (1628–42), pp. 118, 131. The legal aftermath of the event took place at the end of 1640 and beginning of 1641. See also Harbage, pp. 71–2, Nethercot, pp. 184–5, and Gibbs, pp. xxvi–xxvii and n. 5; Nethercot calls Fawcett a 'yeoman' and Gibbs a 'farmer', but he is put down as a tailor in the *HMC* report of Newport's complaint.

55 *CSPD 1639,* p. 49, quoted by Harbage, p. 67 and n. 43; a newsletter dated 23 April (see *CSPD 1639,* p. 72) says Lennox had returned to London from York 'last Thursday'.

56 See Harbage, p. 68 and n. 45 and Nethercot, pp. 172–3 and n. 6.

57 Gibbs, pp. 132–3, 408–9.

58 Harbage, p. 72 and n. 52; Nethercot, pp. 180–1; Hotson, p. 129, n. 36.

59 *CSPD 1640,* p. 365.

60 *CSPD 1640,* p. 483; SP16/460/25, PRO.

61 Cf. Wedgwood, p. 408 and Nethercot, p. 187.

62 *Catalogue of Collection of Autograph Letters and Historical Documents,* 2nd series, III (D), (1896), ed. Alfred Morrison; quoted by Nethercot, pp. 187–8.

63 *Dramatic Works,* IV, 281–363.

64 Act II, p. 299; Gibbs, pp. 236, 451.
65 *Dramatic Works*, II, 301–31; and see *Salmacida Spolia*, ed. T. J. B. Spencer, in *A Book of Masques: In Honour of Allardyce Nicoll* (1967), pp. 337–70. For the songs, Gibbs, pp. 237–43, 452–5.
66 *HMC*, 3rd Report, letter of 5 December 1639.
67 *Dramatic Works*, II, 304.
68 For a survey of the contributions of Davenant and his contemporaries to the Caroline masque, and to drama and poetry at Court, see Parry, *op. cit.*, pp. 184–213.

CHAPTER SIX

1 Hotson, p. 129, n. 36 assumes that he actually managed the theatre from 27 June 1640, the date of his licence, but as we now know, he was away in the north taking part in the Second Bishops' War in the summer, and was then concerned with the production of *Salmacida Spolia* at Court.
2 *LJ IV*, pp. 236–7.
3 *HMC 5th Report*, I, 413.
4 *LJ IV*, p. 238.
5 *CSPD 1640–1*, p. 571.
6 Arthur Brett to the Earl of Middlesex, *HMC 4th Report*, p. 295.
7 *HMC 63 (Egmont)*, I, i, 134; Nethercot, pp. 191–2; Harbage, p. 81.
8 *HMC 29 (Portland)*, I, 17; Nethercot, pp. 192–3; Harbage, p. 82.
9 Aubrey, *Life*; Nethercot, p. 190; Harbage, p. 82; Wood, III, 804, n. 3.
10 E179/143/338, PRO.
11 *CJ II*, p. 147.
12 *CSPD 1641–3*, p. 29.
13 Nethercot, p. 196; Harbage, p. 83.
14 *HMC 4*, p. 307; quoted in full by Harbage, pp. 84–5, and in part by Nethercot, pp. 193–5.
15 Gibbs, pp. 139–40, 412.
16 *CJ II*, p. 203.
17 Nethercot, p. 198; Harbage, p. 86.
18 According to Wood, Davenant had been caught at Faversham in Kent – and then, after the imposition of bail, had tried to escape again and been caught at Canterbury; but he is unlikely to have jumped bail, and there is nowhere else any suggestion that he absconded twice. Wood was probably misled because Aubrey named Canterbury as the place of his (single) apprehension.
19 Hotson, p. 5.
20 Nethercot, p. 198.
21 Aubrey, and family tradition, say it was suicide; Wood, III, 803, footnote, speaks of 'his endeavours not meeting with success' at which he died 'seized of a fever'; others reported that a man-servant, having cheated him and been found out, placed an open razor or a penknife in his boot which severed an artery. His most recent editor, Clayton, pp. lvii–lix, favours

suicide, and says there is good evidence that he was alive only as late as 23 July.

22 *Letters of Queen Henrietta Maria*, ed. Mary A. E. Green (1857), viii, 173.
23 Hotson, pp. 5–6, 13, 32, 71.
24 Harbage, p. 88 and n. 26.
25 *Letters*, pp. 121, 134.
26 Hotson, p. 20.
27 Harbage, p. 89 and n. 30.
28 Wood,/*Life and Times*, I, 67–8.
29 *HMC 15*, p. 89.
30 C. V. Wedgwood, *The King's War 1641–1647* (1958), p. 174.
31 Gibbs, pp. 134–6, 411; Nethercot, p. 210, wrongly interprets the date as 1644.
32 Wedgwood, pp. 221, 225, 231; Schoenbaum, *Shakespeare's Lives,* p. 30 and *William Shakespeare: A Documentary Life,* p. 249; Chambers, II, 98; Harbage, p. 90.
33 *Letters*, pp. 224–5.
34 Hotson, pp. 9, 71.
35 Nethercot, p. 210 and n. 22; Harbage, pp. 91–2.
36 *CJ III*, p. 421; Nethercot, p. 212.
37 Gibbs, pp. 136–9, 411–12.
38 Mary Edmond, *Hilliard and Oliver* (1983), p. 188.
39 Hotson, pp. 18, 74.
40 There is no evidence that Davenant took part, as stated by Harbage, p. 92.
41 BL Addl. MS 20,723, f. 20. Written on 13 June from 'Haleford'. There are three Halfords in England: he must have been writing from the one in Shropshire – the first sentence of the letter shows that he was near enough to Chester to be in touch with opinion there. See Nethercot, pp. 214–15, and Harbage, p. 93, on the letter.
42 Nethercot, p. 215, and Harbage, p. 93, for *The Parliament Scout*; Hotson, p. 20, for *Mercurius Britanicus*.
43 *HMC 43*, pp. 78–9; Nethercot, p. 216; Harbage, p. 94.
44 *CSPD 1644 and 1645,* pp. 429–31.
45 *CJ IV*, pp. 329, 332; Nethercot, p. 218; Harbage, p. 95.
46 *HMC 29 (Portland)*, I, 323–4; Nethercot, p. 221; Harbage, p. 95; Gibbs, p. xxviii.
47 *HMC 70 (Pepys)*, p. 302; *CSPD 1661–2,* p. 359; Nethercot, p. 251; Harbage, pp. 94–5.
48 Hotson, pp. 19, 74.
49 *Ibid.,* pp. 13, 72.
50 *HMC 6*, p. 453; Harbage, p. 96.
51 *HMC 29*, I, 335.
52 Nethercot, pp. 222–3.
53 Gibbs, p. 430.
54 *Ibid.,* pp. 180, 430.
55 MS Montague, d.l., f. 40, Bodleian Library. Nethercot, pp. 224–6, and Harbage, p. 104, comment on the letter. For the vestry minutes, GL MS 3149/1, 4, 51–2.
56 Hyde, Edward, *The History of the Rebellion and Civil Wars in England* (7 vols., 1849), IV, 223–5.

57 Hyde, Edward, *State Papers Collected by Edward, Earl of Clarendon* (3 vols., 1767–86), II, 270.
58 *Ibid.*, p. 273.
59 *Ibid.*, pp. 277–8.
60 *Letters*, pp. 329–31.
61 Hyde, *State Papers*, II, 304–6.
62 Hotson, pp. 21–3, 74.
63 *Ibid.*, pp. 24–7, 29, 74, 76.
64 See Nethercot, pp. 245–9, and Harbage, pp. 106–8; Gerbier's *Manifestation* is quoted at length in *Dramatic Works*, II, 256–63.
65 Gibbs, pp. 173–4, 426–7.

CHAPTER SEVEN

1 Harbage, pp. 110–11; Nethercot, pp. 252–61; Gibbs, p. xxx; *CSP Col. 1574–1660*, p. 340; *HMC 70 (Pepys)*, p. 302.
2 Davenant's 'Epitaph on Mrs. Katherine Cross buried in France' – for which see Gibbs, pp. 144–5, 414 – was probably addressed to a sister of Thomas.
3 Harbage, pp. 112–13; Nethercot, pp. 261–4; Hotson, p. 367.
4 The letter, in the Bodleian, is summarised in *Calendar of Clarendon State Papers Preserved in the Bodleian*, II, 67–8, no. 349.
5 1673 folio, p. 198.
6 David F. Gladish, *Sir William Davenant's Gondibert* (1971), p. ix.
7 Cf. essays on 'The Royal Society' and 'Science', Pepys *Companion*, X, 361–8, 381–90.
8 *Essays of John Dryden*, ed. W. P. Ker (2 vols., 1900), I, 11.
9 Gibbs, p. li, n. 4.
10 Folio, pp. 28–30; Gibbs, pp. lvi–lvii; Gladish, Appendix i, 269–71.
11 Gladish prints *Certain Verses* . . . in full, Appendix ii, 272–86; see also Nethercot, pp. 244–5. The laureates Davenant and Dryden are both thought to be satirised by Buckingham as the character 'Bayes' in *The Rehearsal* (1671).
12 See Hotson, p. 164, n. 27; and, for a later ballad 'How Daphne Pays his Debts', pp. 141–6.
13 Ker, *ed. cit.*, I, 151.
14 Gibbs, pp. 182–98, 431–5; as he explains, there are two manuscript versions of *Disquisition*, one attributing it to Rochester. See also his pp. li–liv for a discussion of the two poems.
15 Quoted by Gibbs, p. 408. See also his pp. 131, 408 for Davenant's unfinished poem (1654) 'Upon the Marriage of the Lady Jane Cavendish [Margaret's daughter] with Mr. Cheney'.
16 For a fuller account of these and other reactions, see Gibbs, 'Critical Comments, Seventeenth to Nineteenth Centuries', pp. lv–lxv.
17 *CSPD 1650*, p. 167.
18 *CJ VI*, pp. 434, 436, 437; *CSPD 1650*, p. 229; Harbage, pp. 113–14; Nethercot, pp. 267–8.
19 *CSPD 1654*, 107, 75.ii.

J

20 *HMC 31*, p. 389.
21 Gibbs, pp. 153–5, 419–20; 177–9, 429–30; and xxxii for a commendatory poem addressed in 1652 to Henry Carey, Earl of Monmouth.
22 For the relevant documents in PRO, *CSPD 1654*, 106–8, 75.i–iii; Nethercot, p. 284.
23 *CSPD 1651–2*, p. 432; *CSPD 1651*, p. 251.
24 Quoted in full by Harbage, p. 117.
25 Hotson, pp. 138–9; and for the documents in full, his Appendix, pp. 356–63, Davenant *v.* Crosse, Mary Davenant's Bill of Complaint, 13 November 1684, and pp.364–76, Answers of Thomas and Paul Crosse, 14 February 1684/5.
26 *CSPD 1654*, pp. 224, 439; Harbage, pp. 118–19; Nethercot, p. 294.
27 MS parish register, GL 6673/4.
28 P. 295.
29 Hotson, p. 139; Nethercot, p. 296; Harbage, p. 120; College of Arms Davenant pedigree; Harl. Soc., X, *Westminster Abbey registers*, ed. J. L. Chester, p. 168.

CHAPTER EIGHT

1 See Hotson, Ch. I, 'Players and Parliament', *passim*.
2 *Miscellania*, quoted by Hotson, pp. 54 and 79, n. 201.
3 Hotson, pp. 55 and 79, n. 207.
4 *Ibid.*, pp. 55 and 79, n. 202.
5 *Ibid.*, pp. 56–8.
6 See Gibbs, pp. 152–3, 418.
7 SP18/128/no. 108, summarised in *CSPD 1655–6*, p. 396; Secretary Nicholas notes at the end: 'Junij 1656 / Sr Wm Dauenantes Opera'.
8 Hotson, pp. 121–2, 141–9, and *A Transcript of the Stationers' Registers 1640–1708*, ed. Eyre & Rivington (1913), II, 38. The title-page gives the date of first publication as 1657, but a contemporary hand has altered this on a copy at BL, E.1648(2) (microfilm) to 22 November 1656; see Nethercot, p. 307 and n. 30, and Harbage, 291–2 who suggests that there were several issues.
9 See *Dramatic Works*, III, 193–230 and folio, Part I, 341–59.
10 It is difficult to determine the placing of 'the Musick'. The official observer clearly states that they sat 'aboue', and Professor Orrell has kindly suggested to me that possibly Davenant had already adapted Rutland House to the pseudo-theatrical form he was to require for *The Siege of Rhodes*, and had contructed a music gallery above, with louvred doors in front of it. The observer's phrase 'Loouer hole' is puzzling, but I think he is probably employing 'hole' in a usage then current (see *OED*) meaning 'a secret place'.
11 See Gibbs, pp. xxxii–xxxiii, lxxxiii, 146–9, 415–17, and for the music, 303–16.
12 *New Grove*, IV, 526, for Coleman; 710–11, for Cooke; and VIII, 762, for Hudson.

13 Evelyn, *Diary* entry for 28 November 1654; Pepys, *Diary*, II, 142.

14 *Diary*, VI, 283; *New Grove*, IV, 526, for Ned Coleman.

15 Gibbs, pp. 243–4, 455.

16 *Ibid.*, pp. 244, 455 and 47, 373.

17 *Diary* entry for 7 February, V, 40.

18 See Hotson, p. 151; Nethercot, pp. 307–8; Harbage, p. 123; and *S.R. 1640–1708*, II, 157, entry for 7 December 1657.

19 See Gibbs, p. 439, for sources; also Nethercot, p. 314; Harbage, pp. 244–5; and *New Grove* entry on Davenant, V, 259.

20 For the address 'To the Reader', *Dramatic Works*, III, 233–5.

21 See Richard Luckett's essay on 'Music', Pepys *Companion*, X, 258–82.

22 Gibbs, pp. 158, 421.

23 For Locke see *New Grove*, XI, 107–17; and Luckett, Pepys *Companion*, X, 261.

24 Pepys, *Diary*, I, 63, n. 1, states positively that he was Purcell's father, but *New Grove*, XV, 457–8, and others are more cautious.

25 II, 81.

26 See Hotson, pp. 151–2; Harbage, p. 124; Nethercot, p. 309.

27 Gibbs, pp. 156–62, 421.

28 The Davenant entry in *New Grove* surprisingly suggests that 'political events probably prevented its performance' in 1656.

29 Gibbs, pp. 245–50, 455–7, for the songs.

30 Most recently in the Davenant and Flecknoe entries in *The Oxford Companion to English Literature*, 5th ed., ed. Margaret Drabble (1985).

31 See Hotson, pp. 144–5 and 165, n. 62; Harbage, pp. 125–6; Nethercot, pp. 321–2.

32 Hotson, p. 156; Harbage, pp. 139–40; Nethercot, p. 323; Gibbs, pp. xxxiii–xxxiv; *S.R. 1640–1708*, II, 157.

33 *S.R.*, II, 208 and 211.

34 For Hotson on the size of the two stages, p. 157, and for Orrell's answer, p. 74.

35 For the whole subject, see John Orrell, *The Theatres of Inigo Jones and John Webb* (1985), Introduction, Ch. III, 'The Cockpit in Drury Lane', *passim* and conclusions, pp. 187–8, also H. M. Colvin's review of the book, *TLS*, 3 May 1985; see also W. G. Keith, 'The Designs for the First Movable Scenery on the English Public Stage', *The Burlington Magazine* XXV (1914), 29–33, 85–98; and MS Lansdowne 1171, BL, and John Harris, Stephen Orgel and Roy Strong, *The King's Arcadia: Inigo Jones and the Stuart Court* (1973) for Strong's notes, p. 208, on nos. 401–3.

36 See *Dramatic Works*, IV, 1–13, 76–94; for the songs, Gibbs, pp. 250–6, 457–60; and for sources, Hotson, p. 157, Gibbs, p. 458.

37 The 'cloud borders' were suspended from a wooden grid called a roof, see Orrell, pp. xiii, 60 and facing plate 9.

38 Cf. M. C. Bradbrook, *The Rise of the Common Player* (1962), in particular Ch. IV, and for Tarlton, p. 164, also the jig (there is a 'Jigg' in the Fourth Entry of Davenant's *Drake*).

39 See Hotson, p. 158; Nethercot, p. 328; *N. & Q.*, 4th series, ix, 49–50, gives all fourteen verses.

40 See Nethercot, p. 328 and n. 68.

41 Herbert, p. 122. In writing of *Peru* as having two parts, he obviously

confused it with *Rhodes* – cf. Nethercot, p. 326.

42 See *Dramatic Works*, IV, 49–76; *Drake* is described on the titlepage of the 1659 ed. as 'The First Part', but no second part is known. For the songs, Gibbs, pp. 460–2, 256–60.

43 See Gibbs, p. 460, and Nethercot, p. 333.

44 *Diary* entry for 28 June 1660, I, 187; n. 1 suggests that Pepys had been to *Rhodes* or *Peru*, but the quotations indicate that it was *Drake*.

45 *S.R. 1640–1708*, II, 225.

46 See entry on Davenant, Pepys *Companion*, X, 86.

47 See Hotson, pp. 160–3; Nethercot, pp. 329–32; and for the 'Panegyrick', Gibbs, pp. 81–2, 391–2. For the lease of the tennis court, Hotson, p. 124, and for the pass to France, *CSPD 1659–60*, p. 571.

48 Dryden's Essay *Of Heroic Plays*, prefixed to *The Conquest of Granada* (1672), ed. cit., I, 149–51.

CHAPTER NINE

1 See Peter Holland's essay on 'Theatre', Pepys *Companion*, X, 431–45.

2 Bradbrook, *The Rise of the Common Player*, p. 282.

3 See Orrell, Ch. 11, 'The theatre at Christ Church, Oxford', pp. 24–38, and plate 2.

4 Schoenbaum, *Shakespeare's Lives*, p. 105.

5 MS register, WCL.

6 *William Shakespeare*, II, Appendix C, 238–302 *passim*, and see I, 573–4.

7 Nethercot, p. 244. It used to be thought that a portrait of 1638 by Van Dyck at Windsor represented Thomas Killigrew and Davenant's old friend Thomas Carew, but it is now believed that his companion is Crofts – Killigrew seems to be in mourning for his wife Cecilia who had just died; see Oliver Millar, *The Tudor, Stuart and Early Georgian Pictures in the Royal Collection* (2 vols., 1963), I, 101, no. 156.

8 *Diary*, 24 May 1660, I, 157.

9 Hotson, pp. 209–10; Nethercot, p. 364; Harbage, pp. 143–4.

10 Gibbs, pp. 82–90, 392–4.

11 The report, Downes, p. 17, is accepted by Holland, Pepys *Companion*, X, 433; but see Hotson, pp. 197–8 and 239, nn. 3–6; and *Roscius Anglicanus*, ed. Montague Summers (1929), pp. 149–50. Downes's rather ambiguous passage seems to be saying that Monck was then on the way from Scotland to London, and that Rhodes got a licence 'from the then Governing State', whatever that may mean.

12 *Diary*, I, 224 and nn. 3, 4.

13 Hotson, pp. 213–14.

14 Pp. 100–14.

15 See Hotson, Ch. IV, 'George Jolly and the Nursery', 167–96, and V, 'The Duke's Company, 1660–1682', 197–241, *passim*. Hotson's statement, p. 171, that Jolly was 'the first English producer to use the modern stage', is disputed by Jerzy Limon, *Gentlemen of a Company: English Players in*

Central and Eastern Europe 1590–1660 (1985), p. 31. He notes that in the period 1637–45 an English company under Robert Archer played at the Royal Theatre in Warsaw, built by Italian architects in 1637 and equipped with the necessary machines for complex opera productions, and suggests that they modernised their own staging techniques to conform with Italian advances.

16 Quoted by Hotson, p. 400.

17 SP29/8/no. 1; quoted in full by Hotson, pp. 199–200.

18 *Ibid.,* p. 200.

19 Full text in Herbert, pp. 87–8.

20 Allardyce Nicoll, *A History of English Drama 1660–1900*: I, *Restoration Drama 1660–1700* (fourth ed., 1952), 293; Jocelyn Powell, *Restoration Theatre Production* (1984), p. 8.

21 Orrell, p. 168.

22 Hotson, pp. 177–8.

23 Hotson, p. 217, and Nethercot, pp. 359–60, for the patent; Gibbs, pp. 90–103, 394–7 for the poem.

24 See LCC/GLC *Survey of London 35* (1970), Ch. I, 1–8: 'The Killigrew and Davenant Patents'.

25 Hotson, pp. 205–6.

26 Herbert, p. 93.

27 *Diary,* I, 264 and nn. 2, 3; 278 and n. 1; 267 and n. 2.

28 *Ibid.,* I, 283.

29 *Ibid., Companion,* X, 434–8.

30 Edmond Malone, *The Plays and Poems of William Shakespeare* (10 vols., 1790), I Part II, *Historical Account of the English Stage,* pp. 266–7; Pepys *Companion,* X, 438–9; Nicoll, pp. 352–3; Hotson, p. 206.

31 Nethercot, p. 367; Harbage, p. 144; and Hotson, pp. 208–9, who quotes the *Prologue* in full.

32 *Diary,* I, 297 and n. 4; 298 and n. 1.

33 *Ibid.,* I, 297 and nn. 2, 3.

34 *Ibid.,* I, 299–300 and n. 1; 303 and n. 3; 309 and n. 2; 309–10 and n. 1; 325 and n. 1.

35 On 6 May 1662 Herbert obtained a writ against Betterton, to sue him for wrongfully acting new and revived plays between 5 November 1660 and the above date, see Hotson, p. 212; the first date appears as '15 November' 1660 in Herbert, p. 109, but Hotson p. 239, n. 27, explains that this is a mistake. I am sure that the first date is taken because it was that of the establishment of the Duke's Company, and not as marking the start of performances.

36 Nicoll, pp. 303, 352–3; Pepys *Companion,* X, 439.

37 *Diary,* II, 5 and n. 2.

38 *Ibid.,* II, 6; 7 and n. 4; 8 and n. 2; 18 and nn. 5, 6; 25.

39 *Ibid.,* II, 25, and nn. 3, 4.

40 Harben, pp. 515, 580.

41 *Diary,* II, 27 and n. 3; 31; 34 and n. 3; 35 and n. 6; 37 and n. 3.

42 *Ibid.,* II, 41 and ns. 3, 4.

43 *Ibid.,* II, 47 and n. 2; 4 November, 207 and n. 5.

44 *Ibid.,* II, 48 and n. 2; 52; 54 and n. 2; 54 and n. 4.

45 *Ibid.,* II, 56 and n. 3; 59; 60; 62 and n. 1.

46 Jolly probably used all the older houses at various times, see Nicoll, p. 309.
47 *Diary*, II, 58 and nn. 1–4.
48 *Ibid.*, II, 64 and n. 1; 65 and n. 1.
49 *Ibid.*, II, 66 and n. 3.
50 Downes, p. 18, and Summers's ed., pp. 176–7; Harben, p. 31.
51 *Diary*, II, 80 and n. 3.
52 *Ibid.*, II, 89 and n. 1; 100 and n. 4; 106; 115; 116–17 and n. 1; 125 and n. 1; 127.
53 Pepys *Companion*, X, essay on 'Plays', 337–42 *passim.*
54 Full text in Herbert, pp. 96–100; see also Hotson, p. 207; Nethercot, pp. 351–2; Harbage, p. 146; Malone, pp. 250–5; Nicoll, p. 300 and n. 2.
55 C6/250/28, full texts in Hotson, pp. 356–76.
56 Hotson, pp. 120–7 *passim.*
57 Orrell, pp. 168–9 and 208, nn. 3, 4.
58 See pp. 139–40.
59 Hotson, pp. 220–2; 240, nn. 56–65; 373 and 401–3; also Nicoll, p. 301. Codicils 1 and 4 of William Ashburnham's Will, PCC 34 Bath, Prob.11/362/34 (1680), PRO, refer to the theatre and to Sir William's son Thomas.
60 Hotson, pp. 243 and 278, n. 1.
61 See overall Hotson's Chs. V and VI on the Duke's and King's Companies, pp. 197–280; Nethercot's Ch. XVIII on the Duke's Playhouse, pp. 337–67; and Harbage's Ch. VI on 'Players Restored', pp. 139–70.
62 Charles Gildon, *The Life of Mr Thomas Betterton . . .* (1710), pp. 11 – 174 *passim.*
63 Printed with Summers's ed. of Downes, pp. 55–9.
64 Gildon, p. 174.
65 Original will of Matthew Betterton, in which he is described as a gentleman, Book *Todd*, f. 211 (1663), WCL; will of Flowerdew, same book, ff. 48–48v (1637); Thomas Betterton baptised at St Margaret's, and Flowerdew buried 15 September 1637, *Memorials*, pp. 148, 581.
66 For Holden, see H. R. Plomer, *Dictionary of Booksellers and Printers 1641–1667* (1907), p. 100; Holden's will, PCC 121 Bowyer, Prob.11/222/121 (1652), PRO; and see *DNB*. Downes, ed. Summers, pp. 175–6, is wrong.
67 For Rhodes, see Downes, p. 17; R. B. McKerrow, *Dictionary of Printers and Booksellers 1557–1640* (1910), p. 227; Hotson, pp. 99–100; *DNB*; Gildon, p. 5. On 2 January 1663/4 Rhodes secured a licence for a touring company, Hotson, p. 216. There may well have been two John Rhodeses: G. E. Bentley, *The Jacobean and Caroline Stage*, II (1941), 544–6, assembles the evidence.
68 Downes's ordering, facsimile p. 20, is usually misunderstood.
69 GL MS 6419/7.
70 See the will of Robert Davenant's widow Jane, PCC 34 Drax, Prob.11/372/34 (1683), PRO: she names the family of eight, and also 'Dr James Molins Chirurgion in Salisbury Court in London' (father-in-law of Sir William's eldest son Charles Davenant).
71 See Aubrey for Butler, and *Brief Lives*, ed. Oliver Lawson Dick (1960), p. ciii, for de Laune.
72 See Mary Edmond, 'The Chandos Portrait: a suggested painter', *The Burlington Magazine* CXXIV (1982), 146–9.

CHAPTER TEN

1   Pepys, *Diary,* II, 130 and nn. 1, 2 and 131, n. 2; Downes, pp. 34, 20.
2   *Dramatic Works,* III, 231–365, gives the 1663 text with footnotes indicating where it differs from that of 1656.
3   Luckett on Davenant, Pepys *Companion,* X, 86; *New Grove* on Davenant, V, 259, states that at the Restoration he soon produced *The Siege of Rhodes* in expanded form, as 'a spoken play' (not distinguishing between Parts I and II).
4   *Dramatic Works,* III, 299, 288; *Diary,* III, 36 and n. 2.
5   *Dramatic Works,* III, 266, 275–6, 288 (where the Chorus line is wrongly printed as ' 'Tis the God of Love, 'tis the love of God . . .'; *Diary,* V, 34.
6   *Dramatic Works,* III, 353–4. In Evelyn's *Diary* is an entry saying that he saw Part III (he obviously meant II) on 9 January 1662, performed 'in *Recitativa* Musique', but this is now considered to be a later addition to the text, and to be mistaken, see Pepys *Companion,* X, entry on Davenant, 86.
7   1673 folio, II, 28–9; *Dramatic Works,* III, 303–4.
8   1673 folio, II, 66; *Dramatic Works,* III, 365; *Diary,* II, 132 and nn. 2, 3.
9   *Diary,* II, 130–1; Downes, pp. 21, 34.
10 P. 35.
11 *Diary,* II, 214; III, 32 and nn. 5, 6; on Hester Davenport's age, an astrological figure in BL MS Sloane 1684, f. 6, for 'Roxalana Anglica', gives her birth-date as 2 March 1640/1, while another MS, in the Bodleian, makes her a year younger, see John H. Wilson, *All the King's Ladies* (1958), pp. 137–9; see also Philip H. Highfill, jr., Kalman A. Burnim and Edward A. Langhans, *A Biographical Dictionary of Actors, Actresses, Musicians, Dancers, Managers & other Stage Personnel in London, 1660–1800* (1973), IV, 194–5. For a long account of the bogus marriage, *Dramatic Works,* III, 249–54.
12 *Diary,* III, 86; 295–6 and n. 3; VII, 190–1.
13 *Ibid.,* IV, 2; for the burial, MS register, WCL.
14 Nicoll, p. 346; *Diary,* VIII, 225 and n. 3; Gibbs, pp. 204–5, 438–9.
15 See *Diary,* V, 278, n. 4.
16 *Ibid.,* V, 278; VI, 247–8; VII, 235; IX, 396; for the *Bezan,* II, 177, n. 4; for the girls, *Companion,* X, 244, 195.
17 *Ibid.,* VIII, 24–5; VI, 283–4 and nn. 1, 2.
18 *Ibid.,* VI, 320 and n. 4; *Dramatic Works,* III, 350; plate facing *Diary,* VI, 320 for the song-setting.
19 *Ibid.,* VIII, 58–60 and nn..
20 For the verse, Hotson, p. 246; Dryden, *Of Heroic Plays, ed. cit.,* I, 149; for *The Rehearsal* (published 1672), ed. Edward Arber (1868), 136 for the *Epilogue,* and see also 93, 113, 121–2, and Davenant, *Dramatic Works,* III, footnotes, 261, 269, 289.
21 Quoted by Hotson, pp. 223–4; *Dramatic Works,* III, 246–7.
22 *Diary,* II, 155.
23 Downes, p. 21; *Diary,* VIII, 170–1 and n. 1, and 172; Nicoll, p. 346.
24 *Diary,* IX, 419; Downes, ed. Summers, pp. 177–8.
25 Downes, p. 21; *Diary,* II, 161 and nn. 2, 3.
26 *Diary,* 28 May 1663, IV, 162, and 31 August 1668, IX, 296.
27 See *The New Shakespeare,* ed. John Dover Wilson (1964) p. lxxiii, and

Chambers, II, 268.

28 See Downes, ed. Summers, pp. 172–3; Wilson, pp. 117–20; Highfill, II, 96–9.

29 I, II, 107.

30 See, for example, *DNB*; Malone, I, II, 108–10; Nicoll, pp. 70–1; Downes, ed. Summers, pp. 93–5; Pepys, *Diary,* II, 5, n. 2; Nethercot, p. 354 and n. 44; Wilson, pp. 3–8; *Dramatic Works,* I, lxvii–viii; Bentley, II, 487–90.

31 *HMC 5*, p. 158.

32 For Underhill's baptism, GL MS 6667/2; Hart, in her register of Merchant Taylors' School, II, gives his birth-date, and says he was admitted in 1644/5, the son of Nicholas, 'clothworker' of Cow Lane, West Smithfield. Nicholas, and his father John of Chichester, Sussex, were in fact freemen of the Drapers' Company and musicians: see *Roll of the Drapers' Company,* ed. Percival Boyd (1934), 188, and J. H. Morrison, *op. cit.,* p. 209.

33 'Satyr' on Underhill, Summers, p. 56; and see pp. 151–2.

34 For Highfill on Sir William Davenant, IV, 170–87.

35 *Diary,* V, 320; *New Shakespeare* ed. of the play, p. lxxii.

36 Quoted in *New Shakespeare* ed., p. lxxiv.

37 *Diary,* II, 177; IV, 6; 20 January 1669, IX, 421 and n. 2: Downes, p. 23.

38 P. 21.

39 *Diary,* II, 221 and n. 2, and 227.

40 Downes, p. 25; Pepys, *Diary,* II, 234, and nn. 3, 4; Pepys saw the play again on 5 August 1668 – after Davenant's death, and with the original title restored – but then thought it 'silly', IX, 272.

41 See Hotson, pp. 243–5; Pepys *Companion,* X, 434–6; Nicoll, pp. 296–7.

42 Harl. Soc., XXVI, 290 for the licence; references to St Giles are taken from the MS registers which are still at the church; for Kynaston, Highfill, IX, 79–85.

43 See Pepys, *Diary,* II, 223 and n. 2; Hotson, pp. 246–7; Herbert's list, pp. 116–18 (the date for *The Surprisal* should be 25 April, as copied by Malone from the original MS, not 23 April).

44 In 1673 folio, II, 272–329; *Dramatic Works,* V, 109–211.

45 Gibbs, pp. 260–1, 462; Nethercot, p. 387.

46 *Diary,* III, 32 and n. 5; IV, 56 and n. 2; V, 78–9 and nn. 1, 3; VII, 102.

47 P. 26.

48 Pepys, *Diary,* III, 39 and nn. 3, 4; Downes, p. 22, and see Summers ed., pp. 179–80.

49 Orrell, pp. 4, 64–5; Pepys, *Diary,* II, 165 and n. 1.

50 Hotson, p. 212.

51 *Diary,* III, 57 and nn.

52 He and a party went to another revival of the piece – 'a pretty harmless old play' – at the Duke's on 10 September 1668, a few months after Davenant's death, *ibid.,* IX, 304. During this month Pepys refers three times to a musical setting for Davenant's song 'The Lark now leaves his watry Nest' – probably the one by John Wilson for soprano, as given by Gibbs, pp. 322–4 – which pleased the diarist mightily: he took the words and notes from Mrs Knepp on the 4th, composed a bass part on the 9th, and taught Mercer the song in a quarter of an hour on the 10th, see IX, 299 and n. 3, 303 and n. 2 and 304.

53 *Ibid.,* III, 90.

54 P. 25.

55 For the licence, Harl. Soc., XXIII, 78; MS register at WCL.

56 *Diary*, III, 208–9; when the Pepyses saw *Malfi* again, on 25 November 1668, the diarist – who was then uneasy 'for fear of my wife's seeing me look about' – described it as 'a sorry play', IX, 375.

57 Downes, p. 23; Pepys, *Diary*, III, 229–30; Gibbs, pp. 205, 439–40, for the *Epilogue*.

58 *Diary*, III, 294; IV, 1–2.

59 Nicoll, p. 346; Pepys intended to see it again at the theatre on the following 24 October, VIII, 499–500, but went away when he learned that Betterton was ill and that Smith was playing his part: he was assured that Smith was as good if not better, but refused to believe it.

60 Highfill on Thomas Betterton, II, 73–96; for Mary Saunderson, Highfill, II, 96–9; Wilson, pp. 117–20; Gildon, p. 7.

61 For *Ignoramus*, Hotson, pp. 214–15 and Nicoll, p. 302, n. 3; Pepys, *Diary*, III, 273 and n. 1 for *Cid*.

62 *Diary*, IV, 8 and n. 2. There was a command performance at Court on 3 December 1666 (Nicoll, p. 346).

63 Downes, pp. 22–3; Nicoll, pp. 219, 38. When Pepys saw *The Adventures* again on 17 January 1663, IV, 16, he did not enjoy it so much, but only because he was 'troubled' with family business affairs. He saw it at the Hall Theatre at Court on 15 February 1669, IX, 450, but was so far from the stage that he could not hear well.

64 Pepys, *Diary*, IV, 32 and n. 1, notes that the performance took place, 'it being a Revelling time with them'. For the *Prologue*, see Gibbs, pp. 203–4, 438; he accepts a suggestion by Nethercot, p. 379, that the play was given before Clarendon during the Christmas celebrations at the Middle Temple, but I think the occasion must have been the one at the Inner Temple in February 1663.

65 For the marriage licence, Harl. Soc., XXIII, 81; for the St Pancras registers, Harl. Soc., XLIV, XLV; wills of William and Mary 'Derrack', PCC 263 Nabbs, Prob.11/302/263 (1660) and 154 May, Prob.11/305/154 (1661), PRO; for William 'Derrick' in the aliens' returns, Hug. Soc., X.3.30, 72, 105. The will of Enoch's mother indicates that he was in trade, and perhaps the clothing trade.

66 Islington MS register at GLRO.

67 It has always been supposed that Anne Bracegirdle was born in the 1660s, but it is now established, see Jean Haynes, *TLS* letter, 2 May 1986, that she was baptised at Northampton on 15 November 1671, making her age at death in 1748 about seventy-seven, not eighty-five as stated on her stone in the Abbey cloister. It is clear that she cannot have spoken the epilogues to two productions by the Duke's Company in the summer of 1676, for which see Highfill, II, 270.

CHAPTER ELEVEN

1 *Diary*, III, 93 and n. 4.
2 Hotson, pp. 179–86, 405–7; Highfill, VIII, 217–18; *CSPD 1663–4*, pp. 214, 539.
3 *Works*, 1673 folio, II, 71; Pepys, *Diary*, V, 132–3.
4 On Killigrew, *DNB*; Highfill, IX, 7–17; Pepys, *Diary*, III, 243–4; Downes, pp. 20, 3. On the Theatre Royal, Pepys *Companion*, X, 434–6; Orrell, p. 169; and see maps and plans at end of Highfill, vol. IV.
5 *Diary*, V, 165–6, and IX, 182.
6 *Ibid.*, IV, 126, 128 and nn. 1–3; for the placing of Davenant's music room, *ibid.*, VIII, 521, and IX, 552–3.
7 For the command performance, *ibid.*, II, 80 and n. 3. King Charles later commissioned a triple portrait of Lacy from Michael Wright, see Downes, ed. Summers, p. 73 and Highfill, IX, 98–104 (99 for a reproduction); the portrait of the actor, in 'three several postures or habits', is listed by Vertue, *Notebooks IV*, 92, and described in detail, V, 51.
8 *Diary*, V, 232 and n. 5; IX, 411, 438, 523 and n. 1; Downes, ed. Summers, pp. 75–6.
9 Bird was baptised at St Leonard Shoreditch on 7 December 1608, GL MS 7493, son of William Bird alias Bourne who was buried there on 22 January 1623/4, MS 7499/1. For the will, Commissary Court of London, GL MS 9171/31, II, 242v–243v; and see Bentley, II, 377–80 and Highfill, II, 133–5.
10 *Diary*, IV, 239; Highfill on Harris, VII, 123–32.
11 Under the terms of Davenant's patent, for which see Hotson, pp. 217–18, no actor ejected from or deserting one company was to be received by the other, without the consent of his original manager; for a more general ruling, see Nicoll, p. 360. Harris's demands, *Diary*, IV, 239.
12 *Ibid.*, IV, 347.
13 *Ibid.*, IV, 292.
14 1673 folio, II, 67–119; *Dramatic Works*, IV, 1–104; not mentioned by Downes.
15 See Gibbs on 'The Poems', pp. xxxviii–lv. Davenant's use of the term 'mock-heroic' is some fifty years earlier than the one given as first by *OED* (by Addison in 1711–12), and *OED* gives no entry for 'mock-burlesquers'. Davenant also used 'burlesque' (as a noun or adjective in the literary or dramatic sense) earlier than the examples cited in the dictionary – for example, in the title of his vacation poem, almost certainly written in 1635, and first published in 1656. He had shown his interest in mock-heroic and burlesque forms even earlier, in the poem 'Jeffereidos', written in 1630.
16 Gibbs, pp. 262, 462.
17 *The Rehearsal, ed. cit.*, pp. 65, 67, 89.
18 Downes, p. 26; Nicoll, p. 38, suggests November 1663.
19 After the destruction by fire of Shakespeare's Globe during the performance on 29 June 1613, the only recorded date for a pre-Restoration staging is 29 July 1628, at the second Globe, when the piece was commissioned (within a month of his assassination) by the first Duke of Buckingham, see Chambers, II, 343–4, 347.
20 *Diary*, IV, 411, and entry on 20 February 1667, VIII, 73; Downes, p. 24;

Nethercot, p. 395–7. For the Greenhill portraits, see the Ashmolean catalogue, no. 134, pp. 81–2.

21 Pepys, *Diary*, IV, 431; V, 2 and n. 4, 28–9 and n. 1; IX, 403–4; *The Rehearsal*, p. 111.

22 Pepys, *Diary*, V, 77; Downes, ed. Summers, p. 160.

23 For the original *Prologue* and *Epilogue* of *The Unfortunate Lovers*, see Gibbs, pp. 140–2, 413; as well as being in the eds. of 1643 and 1649, they are in the play in the 1673 folio, II, 120–65; the amended Restoration versions are in folio, I, 299–300. *OED*, citing the lines on 'termers' in the *Epilogue*, dates them 1668, but both *Prologue* and *Epilogue* appear in the 1643 and 1649 editions of the play. The dictionary defines the termer (a word commonly in use *c*. 1550–1675) as one who resorted to London in term, either for business at a court of law, or for amusements, intrigues or dishonest practices: Davenant uses it in the first sense in *The Playhouse*, when the Poet tells the Player: 'Your busie Termers come to Theatres, / As to their Lawyers-Chambers, not for mirth, / But, prudently, to hear advice.'

24 Pepys, *Diary*, V, 124 and n. 2; IV, 163 and n. 4, and 177 and n. 2. The play has been attributed to a Mr John Holden (perhaps a relative of Davenant's actress Mrs Holden); and Downes, p. 26, attributes to him *The Ghosts*, which Pepys saw at the Duke's ('a very simple play') on 17 April 1665, see VI, 83.

25 Downes, pp. 24–5; Pepys *Companion*, X, 342; *Diary*, VI, 4 and n. 2; VII, 347 and nn. 1–4; and IX, 178. There were further command performances, at the theatre, on 9 April and 28 December 1667; the apparent warrant entry stating that *Mustapha*, as well as *Love in a Tub*, was done at Court on 29 October 1666, must be a mistake; for the warrants, Nicoll, pp. 346–7.

26 *Diary*, V, 215 and n. 1; Downes, p. 26. The company gave a command performance at Court on 26 November 1666, Nicoll, p. 346.

27 Pepys, *Diary*, V, 240 and nn. 2, 3, and V, 245; Downes, pp. 27–8. The play owes nothing to Shakespeare. For the command performance, Pepys, *Diary*, VII, 423–4 and Nicoll, p. 346.

28 For Boyle, Pepys *Companion*, X, 41; *DNB*; *Complete Peerage*, IV, 263 and X, 175–8. For the poem, and its dating, folio *Works*, I, 275–86; Gibbs, pp. 107–22 and 397–9; *S.R. 1640–1708*, II, 157.

29 For the play, *Dramatic Works*, V, 213–93; for Pepys's comment, V, 267; for 'Under the Willow shades . . .', Gibbs, pp. 264 and 463, and for a setting, pp. 337–8; for Celania's songs, Gibbs, pp. 265–7, 463–4.

30 Pp. 23–4.

31 Pepys, *Diary*, VIII, 91, and 101 and nn. 3, 5; Nicoll, p. 346; Downes, p. 27.

32 Pepys, *Diary*, VIII, 375 and n. 2; Nicoll, pp. 346–7; and for Howard's piece, Nicoll, p. 414, and Nethercot, p. 390. Pepys saw Howard's play on 20 September.

33 Pepys, *Diary*, 11 January 1668, IX, 19 and n. 3; 14th, IX, 24 and n. 2; 31 May, IX, 219; and see 21 January 1669, IX, 422 and 15 February, IX, 450.

34 *Ibid.*, V, 230 and n. 3; when the two men met at Lord Brouncker's house 'to hear some Italian Musique' on 12 February 1667, the manager had to tell the diarist that he was 'defeated in what he intended in Moore Fields', *ibid.*, VIII, 54–6.

35 Cf. Highfill on Davenant, IV, 170–87; Nethercot, p. 391; *New Shakespeare*, 1960 ed., p. lxx; *New Grove* on Matthew Locke.

36 Herbert, pp. 136–8. His record of fees paid – £2 for new productions and
£1 for revivals – occupies three printed pages of transcription, and the last
section, consisting of twelve entries in all, has, towards the end, consecutive
references to what are obviously three of Davenant's shows: 'Reviv'd Play.
Makbethe' (£1); 'Henry 8 Reviv'd play' (£1); and 'House to be let' (£2).
This group is headed by an item with the date 'Nouember. 3. 1663' – the
only date in the whole three pages, which together cover the period 1663–4;
it has been taken, I am sure wrongly, to refer to succeeding entries as well.
On the strength of the list, of which of course he saw the original MS, now
lost, Malone cautiously dated *Macbeth* to '1663 or 4'.

37 *Roscius*, p. 33. *Dramatic Works*, V, 295–394. Downes's description lies
within his survey of Dorset Garden activities, and states explicitly that
although the text used (not published in the 1660s) was Davenant's, the
production – including the costumes, scenery and 'flyings' – was entirely
new; he adds as a footnote that the play itself had been '*Acted*' at Lincoln's
Inn Fields. See Blaydes and Bordinat, items 177–91, for a comprehensive
list of editions. They, in common with many others, speak of the 'Davenant
version' of *Macbeth* as being performed from the 1660s until 1744, without
mentioning Shadwell.

38 Pepys's visits, 5 November 1664, V, 314 and n. 3; 28 December 1666, VII,
423 and n. 1; 7 January 1667, VIII, 7; 19 April, VIII, 171; 16 October, VIII,
482; 6 November, VIII, 521; 12 August 1668, IX, 278; 21 December, IX,
398 – when the Pepyses sat just under the King and Court, and the diarist
was pleased that the King and Duke smiled at him, and that his wife looked
as pretty as anyone, but 'vexed' that the King and Moll Davis, who was in a
box above, exchanged glances; and 15 January 1669, IX, 416, when Pepys
had time to see only the last two acts.

39 See Richard Luckett on 'Music', Pepys *Companion*, X, 258–82; Nicoll, pp.
363–5, 379–80.

40 *New Grove* on Locke, XI, 107–17; on Shakespeare, XVII, 214–18; on
Davenant, V, 259, and his 'profound influence on the development of
English opera'; and on Robert Johnson (ii), IX, 681–2. Gibbs, pp. lxxvii,
262–4 and 462–3, for the new songs in II.iv. Chambers, I, 472, *New
Shakespeare*, p. lxx, and Gibbs, p. lxxvii, for stage directions in the Shake-
speare First Folio for songs borrowed from Middleton's *The Witch* (III.v
and IV.i). See also *New Penguin*, ed. G. K. Hunter (1967), Introduction, pp.
32–4 (mainly on Davenant's adaptation, and pp. 44–5, 172–3, on
Middleton and the songs); for Middleton, and the Hecate passages, *New
Arden*, ed Kenneth Muir, University paperback with new Introduction and
additional notes (1984), *Introduction*, pp. xxxii–xxxiv, and 190 (at
IV.i.61), also 108–9.

41 Pepys visited Cheynell's dancing-school on 24 September 1660, *Diary*, I,
253; for his appointment to the Duke's company in 1664 – which supports
the argument that Davenant's *Macbeth* was put on in that year – Pepys,
Companion, X, 56; and see Downes, ed. Summers, p. 210. For Priest, *New
Grove*, XV, 226.

42 Downes, p. 34; and see *New Shakespeare*, pp. lxx–lxxiv, and Highfill on
Mary Betterton, II, 96–9.

43 Nicoll, pp. 37, 134, 401, 407, 428; *Dramatic Works*, V, 302; *New Shakespeare*, p. lxxiv; Nethercot, pp. 394–5.

44 Downes, pp. 25–6; Pepys, *Diary*, VI, 73 and nn. 1, 2; VIII, 5, and 421. A command performance was given at the theatre on 22 October 1667, Nicoll, p. 346.

45 Pepys, *Diary*, VI, 85 and n. 3; Orrell, pp. 1–3, 112 and Ch. 10, 'The Hall Theatre at Whitehall'; Nicoll, p. 305.

46 Pepys, *Diary*, VI, 120 and n. 1; Christopher Morris on 'The Plague', Pepys *Companion*, X, 328–37; also 437; Hotson, p. 249; Nicoll, p. 299 and n. 3.

47 Pepys, *Diary*, VII, 76 and nn. 4, 5 and 77 and n. 2.

48 Downes, pp. 26, 31, 33; Nicoll, p. 434. A version of *Julius Caesar* published in 1719 and attributed to the late laureates Davenant and Dryden was no doubt cashing in on their reputations: there is no evidence that they were in any way responsible, see Nicoll, p. 402; Nethercot, p. 385; Harbage, pp. 253, 293–4. Summers prints Tate's *Lear* in his *Shakespeare Adaptations* (1922).

49 Pepys *Companion*, X, 437; *Diary*, VII, 347 and 399; Nicoll, p. 321 and n. 2; Orrell, p. 1; *CSPD 1666–7*, pp. 232, 299; Hotson, p. 250.

50 Pepys, *Diary*, VIII, 44–5; 122–3 and n. 2; 137 and n. 4; 348; Nicoll, p. 346.

51 *Athenae Oxonienses*, III, 309.

52 Downes, p. 28; Downes, ed. Summers, pp. 152–4, 194–5; Nicoll, pp. 68, 404. In the S.R. entry dated 24 June 1668, the play is attributed to Lord Newcastle, who, as Downes says, gave Dryden 'a bare Translation' of the work on which it is based (Molière's comedy *L'Etourdi*). Dryden's name does not appear on any title-page until 1691.

53 *Diary*, VIII, 386; 387 and n. 1; 390; 392; 455; 481 and n. 2; IX, 2; 174; and 209.

54 *Ibid.*, VIII, 421–2 – and, for *Tu Quoque*, VIII, 435 and n. 1: he liked it better on the 16th, VIII, 440, and there was a command performance at the theatre on 16 December, Nicoll, p. 347.

55 *Ibid.*, IV, 4–5; 163; 182; VI, 9; VII, 341; VIII, 463–4 and nn.; and 575.

56 *Ibid.*, VIII, 482; 499; 521.

57 For Dryden's *Preface*, the 1670 quarto, and *Dramatic Works*, V, 413–15. Herringman contributed to the confusion by reprinting Dryden's *Preface* from the 1670 quarto, and the *Prologue* and *Epilogue* for the 1667 Davenant production, in the 1674 (Shadwell) quarto – particularly curious because (as Summers notes, *Adaptations*, p. xliii) a *Prologue* and *Epilogue* written by Shadwell himself for his version exist, BL MS Egerton 2623. Summers reprints the 1670 edition, claiming that this is the first reprint since 1701, but see Blaydes and Bordinat, p. 53, items 155, 156, for a limited edition published in Cleveland (1911).

58 Pepys, *Diary*, VIII, 521–2; 527; 576; IX, 12; 48; 179; 195; and 422. For Banister, *Dramatic Works*, p. 398; Luckett, 'Music', Pepys *Companion*, X, 265; *New Grove* on John Banister (i), II, 117. There were command performances of *The Tempest* at the theatre on 14 and 26 November 1667, and 14 March and 13 April 1668, Nicoll, p. 347.

59 Pelham Humfrey (1647–74) composed a setting for 'Where the bee sucks', and music for masques in Acts II and V, for Shadwell's version at the end of his life, see *New Grove*, VIII, 776–80; see also Banister and Locke entries. For *The Tempest*, Downes, pp. 33 and 34–5; Harbage, pp. 260–3; Nicoll, pp. 133 and n. 1, 134, 404, 407, 430; Powell, Chs. III and IV; Summers, *Adaptations*, prints Duffett's *Mock-Tempest* from the 1675 quarto. For

Shadwell and Davenant on Shakespeare, Chambers, II, 253–4.
60 Nicoll, pp. 307, 347; Pepys, *Diary*, IX, 53–4; Downes, pp. 28–9.
61 Pepys, *Diary*, IX, 62 and n. 3; 85–6 and nn. 3–5.
62 Downes, p. 30; Nicoll, p. 347; Harbage, p. 256; *Dramatic Works*, V, 1–107; 1673 folio, II, 329–83; for the song 'in Recitativo and in Parts' – 'The Bread is all bak'd' – and the *Epilogue*, Gibbs, pp. 268–71, 464–5; Pepys, *Diary*, IX, 133–4 and nn.; 189; command performance, Nicoll, p. 347.
63 *Diary*, IX, 148; 155–6.
64 *Ibid.*, IX, 158; Aubrey, *Brief Life*; Aubrey letter to Wood dated 19 May 1668, see *Brief Lives*, ed. Andrew Clark (2 vols., 1898), I, 209, footnote; Downes, p. 30. For elegies on Davenant, Gibbs, p. xxxvii, n. 5; Hotson, pp. 224–6.

CHAPTER TWELVE

1 Pepys, *Diary*, IX, 157, and 183 and n. 2; Downes, p. 29.
2 *Diary*, VIII, 421–2.
3 On production expenses, cf. a Chancery suit in the 1660s which shows that a single scene commissioned by the Theatre Royal took the painter, Isaac Fuller, six weeks' hard work and was valued at £335 10s, see Hotson, pp. 250–3; Nicoll, pp. 41–2 and n. 1, 322. In a petition to the King in 1676, *CSPD 1676–7*, p. 192 Lady Davenant estimated her late husband's wartime losses at some £13,000.
4 Pepys learned of Cowley's death from Herringman, who by this time was one of his principal booksellers, see *Diary*, VIII, 380 and n. 3; Cowley's will, PCC 104 Carr, Prob.11/324/104, PRO; for theatre sharers, including Hervey, in 1674, Hotson, p. 231.
5 Highfill, IV, 168–9, argues that the Nicholas Davenant involved was Sir William's son, then only a few years old, but this seems most improbable. For the theatre, Hotson, pp. 228–38, and plate facing p. 234; for maps and plans, Highfill, end of vol. IV, and for the exterior, II, 480; Downes, p. 31; for Gibbons, Vertue, *Notebooks I*, p. 125.
6 Nicoll, pp. 322–3; Pepys *Companion*, X, 437–8; for Jolly, see Hotson, pp. 184–94; Pepys, *Diary*, IX, 531 and n. 3; Nicoll, pp. 312–13. A long undated complaint by Jolly, written between April 1673 and February 1677 – which must be read with some scepticism – seems to indicate that he regarded past difficulties as the fault of Killigrew rather than Davenant.
7 *S.R.* II, 380; for handover to Charles Davenant, Hotson, p. 236. For the injury to Cademan, Downes, p. 31; Nicoll, pp. 367–8; and Highfill on Harris, VII, 123–32. It may have happened during a command performance at the theatre on 3 or 9 August, for which see Nicoll, p. 348.
8 For Medbourne, Downes, ed. Summers, pp. 169–70; Nicoll, pp. 258–9, 302; and for his brief nuncupative will, Archdeaconry Court of London, GL MS 9051/10, pp. 758–9. For burial of Wintershall, Harl. Soc., XXX, 84.

9 MS register at WCL; for career, Nicoll, p. 69; Downes, ed. Summers, pp. 73, 147–8; *DNB;* Bentley, II, 495–6.

10 Hart's will, PCC 105 Drax, Prob.11/374/105, PRO; for career, Hotson, p. 281; Downes, ed. Summers, pp. 71–2; Nicoll, p. 67; *DNB;* Bentley, II, 463–4; Highfill, VII, 147–53. Earlier theories that he was related to Shakespeare are now largely discredited.

11 For Mohun, Nicoll, p. 67; *DNB;* Downes, ed. Summers, p. 72; Highfill, X, 271–6; Anne Mohun's will, registered copy, PCC 8 Herne, Prob.11/463/8, original will, with a codicil in her own hand, PCC Prob.10/1347; Henry Mohun's will, registered copy PCC 54 Dogg, Prob.11/469/54 (1703), original, Prob.10/1361, all PRO. For Elizabeth Boutell *née* Ridley, see Highfill on 'Mrs Barnaby Bowtell', II, 260–1. Her husband may have been related to the player Henry Boutell, for whom see Highfill, II, 247.

12 For Shatterel, Commissary Court of London admon., 3 November 1684, GL MS 9168/24, f. 160, relict Anne: he is entered as 'Shortered' and 'Sherteredd'. For career, Downes, ed. Summers, pp. 76–7. He had served as quartermaster to a troop of horse in Prince Rupert's regiment during the civil war. For Cartwright, will PC 46 Foot, Prob.11/387/46, PRO; he was the son of an Elizabethan actor of the same name, see Highfill, III, 89–93.

13 Chambers, II, 252–4, and plate facing p. 252, and Schoenbaum, *William Shakespeare: A Documentary Life,* p. 205, item 166, for Aubrey's first lot of scribbled notes. For King's Head Yard, *LCC Survey of London,* VIII (1922), 14; the Yard is numbered 68 on Chassereau's map of the parish of St Leonard Shoreditch (1745), see Plate I. Lacy was evidently a good informant on players generally: he also told Aubrey about Clun's appearance – Ben Jonson 'had one eie lower than t'other, and bigger, like Clun the Player', see *Brief Lives,* ed. Lawson Dick, p. 178.

14 For the burials of Mr and Mrs Beeston, GL MS 7499/2; for Alice's first husband, and the son Sackville, Hotson, pp. 102, 104; for William's will, Archdeaconry Court of London, GL MS 9052/23, and for Alice's, PCC 125 Lloyd, Prob.11/384/125, PRO; for William's career, Highfill, I, 414–19; Bentley on Christopher and William, II, 363–74; for Sheppey, see Hotson, pp. 254, 261, 264–5, 266, 273, 282; and for his dispute with the orange-woman Mrs Meggs ('Orange Moll', Nell Gwyn's first employer), Hotson, pp. 291–3.

15 Shadwell's will, PCC 231 Fane, Prob.11/412/321, PRO; Leigh was buried in the middle aisle of St Bride Fleet Street on Christmas Day 1692, GL MS 6540/2; for him, Downes, ed. Summers, pp. 214–15, and for his wife, pp. 203–4; Nicoll, p. 73; Highfill, IX, 223–8. Pepys, *Diary,* VIII, 503, for Nell's upbringing; for Moll's parentage, Downes, ed. Summers, pp. 173–4; Pepys, *Diary,* IX, 24 and n. 2; and *Complete Peerage,* II, 150–1. For the warrant prohibiting the entry of outsiders into the tiring-rooms at the Duke's, *CSPD 1664–5,* p. 218; for gallants bribing staff, Nicoll, p. 13 – and see his p. 360 for a general order (1663) forbidding people forcing their way into both theatres during performances 'with evill Language and Blows', and without paying.

16 For direction of the playhouse, Hotson, p. 286; for killing another actor, Pepys, *Diary,* VII, 369 and n. 3; Smith's burial, GL MS 6419/11; will, PCC 149 Bond, Prob.11/433/149, PRO – not proved until 1705, presumably when his son came of age; for the baptism of Charlotte Davenant at St

Bride's on 8 February 1684/5, GL MS 6540/2.

17 Will, PCC 209 Bond, Prob.11/434/209, PRO; see also Nicoll, p. 68; Hotson, p. 290; Downes, ed. Summers, pp. 152–4. He had a connexion with Cornhill, see will and registers of St Michael Cornhill, Harl. Soc., VII, but is unlikely to have been the James Nokes who according to *DNB* kept a 'Nicknackatory or toy-shop' there.

18 Hotson, pp. 304–5; Downes, p. 35; Nicoll, p. 69; *DNB*; and Highfill entries on Anne Bracegirdle, II, 269–81, and Mountfort, X, 354–9. For the marriage licence, *London Marriage Licences 1521–1869*, ed Joseph Chester (1887), p. 950.

19 For the attack on Ralph Davenant, Narcissus Luttrell, *A Brief Historical Relation of State Affairs from September 1678 to April 1714* (1857), IV, 382; will, PCC 247 Lort, Prob.11/448/247, PRO; for the burials of Ralph, and of William (on 17 January 1707/8) in the old vault of St Bride's, the burial-place of this branch of the family, GL MS 6540/3. Both brothers are named in their mother Jane Davenant's will, PCC 34 Drax, Prob.11/372/34 (1683), PRO.

20 See *DNB*; Nicoll, pp. 65, 69; will, PCC 162 Pott, Prob.11/452/162, PRO.

21 See Hotson, pp. 281–310 *passim*; Highfill, II, 88–9, on Betterton.

22 See in particular *Diary*, VIII, 28–9; IX, 12–13; 178; 218–19; 138; 139; 277; 265 and n. 1; 292–3 and n. 1; and Mary Edmond, 'Limners and Picturemakers', Walpole Soc. XLVII (1980), 106–7 and 'Samuel Cooper, Yorkshireman – and Recusant?', *The Burlington Magazine* CXXVII (1985), 83–5.

23 For marriage licence, Harl. Soc., XLVII, 22; burials, Harl. Soc., XXXVI, 125 and 193. Harris's will, PCC 183 Ash, Prob.11/478/183, PRO; for career, Highfill, VII, 123–32; Nicoll, p. 67; Downes, ed. Summers, pp. 164–5.

24 For the Bettertons' burials, Harl. Soc., X, 268 and 274; for Betterton's 'pictures', Vertue, *Notebooks I*, p. 52; for his benefit, Highfill on Bracegirdle, II, 269–81, and Barry, I, 313–25, and Gildon on Betterton, p. xii; Highfill on the Bettertons, II, 73–99. Mrs Betterton's will, PCC 65 Barnes, Prob.11/526/65, PRO, Anne Bracegirdle, who had been brought up by the Bettertons, died on 12 September 1748 and was buried near them on the 18th, Harl. Soc., X, 375–6. There have been attempts to make a mystery, or a scandal, out of the fact that Downes, p. 25, refers to Mary Saunderson as 'Mrs Betterton' when writing about *The Cutter of Coleman Street*, performed in December 1661 – a year before her marriage – but that seems flimsy evidence on which to base the argument; and on the previous page, Downes was writing of her when she *was* Mrs Betterton and playing in *Love in a Tub* in 1664.

25 See Highfill, IX, 79–85; Downes, ed. Summers, pp. 78–9; for Kynaston's burial, Harl. Soc., XXXVI, 226.

26 Will, PCC 239 Leeds, Prob.11/536/239, PRO.

27 For first marriage and daughter, GL MS 6540/1, and for second marriage, Harl. Soc., XIII, 116; hearth-tax list, E179/147/627, 3v, PRO, and for second daughter, Harl. Soc., XXIX, 77; for 1695, *London Inhabitants Within the Walls 1695*, ed. D. V. Glass (1966). The year of Underhill's death is usually given as 1709, but he played his original role of Trincalo in *The Tempest* in 1710, see Downes, ed. Summers, pp. 151–2. There are two

entries reading 'Caue Underhill from Carter Lane' in the burial register of St Andrew Holborn, GL MS 6673/7, on 14 October 1709 and 26 May 1713: the player's must be the second. For career, *DNB*; Nicoll, pp. 68–9; Bentley, II, pp. 609–10.

28 See Highfill, IV, 222–6. On 4 December 1686 Paisible, described as a gentleman of about thirty, secured a licence to marry Mrs Mary Davis, about twenty-five, both of St James Westminster, the marriage to take place at that church (it is not entered in the MS register at WCL). When Paisible made his will in January 1720/1, he described himself as a musician of the parish of St Martin-in-the-Fields, will (proved 1722) Prob.11/585/124, PRO; for his career, *New Grove*, XIV, 96–7.

29 Their nuncupative wills, inventories and bonds are in CRO, Oxford: both mention their brother Nicholas and niece Mary Swift, Sir William's daughter; his son Charles, then at Balliol, and daughter Mary sign Elizabeth's bond.

30 Marriage licence, Harl. Soc., XXIV, 43; Robert's will PCC 86 Bunce, Prob.11/345/86 (1674), Jane's PCC 34 Drax, Prob.11/372/34 (1683), PRO.

31 Dr Sherborne's will (where he is described as Vicar of Lugwardine) in National Library of Wales, Aberystwyth; see also C. J. Robinson, *A History of the Mansions and Manors of Herefordshire* (1873), pp. 224–30, and C. D. Sherborn, *A History of the Family of Sherborn* (1901), and typed *addenda* in BL (1918).

32 For Nicholas living with the Sherbornes, Chancery suit C8/101/70, PRO; for London in 1662, *Calendar of Treasury Books 1660–67*, p. 436.

33 See Jonathan Swift, *Correspondence,* ed. F. Elrington Ball (6 vols., 1910–14), I, 9, n. 2; 59 and n. 1; 362 and n. 1; 367–8; 369–73 and notes, also Nethercot, pp. 345, 406. In 1667, the Rev. Thomas Swift senior, Davenant's son-in-law, was staying at the London house in Aldersgate Street of the Bishop of London, Dr Henchman, who had married a niece of Dr Davenant the Bishop of Salisbury. In the 1690s Jonathan Swift visited his cousin Thomas (then at Balliol) and aunt Mary *née* Davenant at Oxford.

34 See *DNB*, and for his theatre activities, Hotson, pp. 227–8, 271, 273, 277, 285, 296–7, 306 and Highfill, IV, 164–6; for dates of death and burial, Mawson and Matcham Davenant pedigrees and GL MS 6540/3.

35 For the Molins/Florio marriage, Frances A. Yates, *John Florio* (1968), p. 257 and BL MS Harleian 6140, p. 79. For Pepys on Edward Molins, *Diary,* IV, 340, 345 and VIII, 41; Molins entry in *Companion*, X, 246; the will of Dr Robert Davenant's widow Jane supplies the information that he lived in Salisbury Court; wills, and registers of St Andrew Holborn and St Bride Fleet Street at GL, for Molins dates – often given inaccurately in *DNB* entries. James Molins's will, PCC 40 Foot, Prob.11/386/40, PRO. Charles Davenant's projected marriage to a daughter of Sir Lionel Walden, for which see Hotson, p. 236, and *CSPD 1677–8*, 615–16, and *CSPD 1678*, p. 371, did not take place.

36 See *Alumni Oxonienses,* where William is said to have been sixteen when he went up to Magdalen Hall in August 1673. *DNB* calls him Sir William's 'fourth' son, but he is described as 'second' on admission to Gray's Inn on 12 February 1675/6, and in his mother's petition to the King in the same

year – in which she unsuccessfully seeks a fellowship at All Souls for him, calling him a youth of 'very pregnant hopes in learning'.

37 Described as 'third' son in mother's will; and see Hotson, pp. 220, and 284–93 *passim*; Nicoll, pp. 332–3; Nethercot, p. 414; Highfill, IV, 162–4.

38 For death of Thomas, 'Celibis', PCC Prob.6/74, 98v, PRO, 25 May 1698 – letters of admin. granted to his brothers Charles, George and Richard (probably indicating that Nicholas was dead).

39 See *Musgrave's Obituaries*; Matcham and Mawson pedigrees and GL MS 6540/1 for marriage; MS register at WCL for burial of 'Colonel Richard D'Avenant'; will, Consistory Court of London, Register 3, 137v–138, GLRO. The death of 'Colonel Richard Davenant' is noticed among those of prominent people dying in 1745 in *The Gentleman's Magazine*, p. 332.

40 MS register at WCL for burial; will, PCC 81 Smith, Prob.11/514/81, PRO; Matcham and Mawson pedigrees. Matcham describes his father-in-law John Ford as an alderman of London, but there is no such man in A. B. Beaven, *The Aldermen of the City of London* (2 vols., 1913).

41 GL MS 6540/2 for burial; will, Commissary Court of London (not Consistory Court as stated by Nethercot, p. 449), GL MS 9171/43, 164–5. One of the witnesses is Thomas Cross.

SELECT SOURCES

Acheson, Arthur, *Mistress Davenant*, London, New York and Chicago 1913.
—— *Shakespeare's Sonnet Story 1592–1598*, London 1922.
Aldermen's *Repertories*, MS., CLRO.
Aubrey, John, *Brief Lives*, among Aubrey MSS., Bodleian Library, Oxford.
—— ed. Andrew Clark, 2 vols., Oxford 1898.
—— ed. O. Lawson Dick, London 1949.
—— *Wiltshire Topographical Collections 1659–70*: ed. J. E. Jackson, London 1874.
Autograph Letters and Historical Documents, Catalogue of, 2nd series, III(D), ed. Alfred Morrison, 1896 (for Davenant's letter to Lord Conway, August 1640).
Bailey, J. E., *The Life of Thomas Fuller D.D. with Notices of his Books, his Kinsmen and his Friends*, London and Manchester 1874 (includes a Davenant pedigree).
Bald, R. C., *John Donne: A Life*, Oxford 1970.
Barton, Anne, *Ben Jonson, dramatist*, Cambridge 1984.
Beaven, A. B., *The Aldermen of the City of London*, 2 vols., London 1913.
Bentley, G. E., *The Jacobean and Caroline Stage*, II, Oxford 1941.
Blaydes, Sophia B. and Philip Bordinat, *Sir William Davenant: An Annotated Bibliography, 1629–1985*, New York 1986.
Blezzard, Judy, contemporary musical settings of Davenant songs: *see* Gibbs, A. M., Appendix B.
Bradbrook, M. C., *The Rise of the Common Player*, Cambridge 1962.
—— *John Webster, Citizen and Dramatist*, London 1980.
Bridge House accounts, MS, accounts of the Bridgemasters, City of London, CLRO.
Buckingham, George Villiers, 2nd Duke of, *The Rehearsal*, ed. Edward Arber, London 1868.
Burke, A. M., *Memorials of St Margaret's Church Westminster*, London 1914.
Butler, Martin, *Theatre and Crisis: 1632–1642*, Cambridge 1984.
Cecil Papers, MS, Hatfield House (for petition from Davenant's uncle Thomas Sheppard).
Chamberlain, John, letter to Dudley Carleton about Frances Duchess of Richmond, among State Papers, PRO.
Chambers, E. K., *The Elizabethan Stage*, 4 vols., Oxford, 1923.
—— *William Shakespeare: A Study of Facts and Problems*, 2 vols., Oxford 1930.
Chancery, Court of, MS records, PRO.
Charlton, John, *The Banqueting House Whitehall*, London 1964.
Clarendon, Lord, *see* Hyde, Edward.
Clarke, Sir William, *The Clarke Papers*, Camden Soc., New Series, ed. C. H. Firth, 4 vols., London 1891–1901 (vol. II for Nicholas Davenant).
Clayton, Thomas, *see* Suckling, Sir John.
College of Arms, Davenant pedigree in MS *Visitation of Essex 1614*, and *see* Mawson, Richard, for another, 1725.

Common Council, Court of, City of London, MS *Journals,* CLRO.

Commons, House of, *Journals,* vols. II, III, IV and VI.

Customs accounts, Port of London, from 1565, MS, E190 series, PRO.

Davenant, Sir William, *Works,* 1673, folio.

—— *Dramatic Works,* ed. James Maidment and W. H. Logan, 5 vols., Edinburgh 1872–4.

—— *Sir William Davenant's Gondibert,* ed. David F. Gladish, Oxford 1971.

—— *The Shorter Poems, and Songs from the Plays and Masques,* ed. A. M. Gibbs, Oxford 1972.

—— letter to Lord Conway, 1640: see *Autograph Letters.*

—— MS letter to Prince Rupert, 1644: PRO.

—— MS letter to Sir Richard Browne at Paris, 1646: Bodleian Library, Oxford.

—— MS draft for the Attorney General of the Davenant/Killigrew stage monopoly warrant, 1660: PRO.

For a comprehensive list of publication dates of all Davenant's works, see Blaydes and Bordinat.

Downes, John, *Roscius Anglicanus, or, an Historical Review of the Stage from 1660 to 1706,* 1708: facsimile ed., Joseph Knight, London 1886, and ed. Montague Summers, London 1929.

Drapers' Company, Roll of, ed. Percival Boyd, Croydon 1934.

Dryden, John, *Essays of,* ed. W. P. Ker, 2 vols., Oxford 1900.

Early Voyages and Travels to Russia and Persia, ed. E. D. Morgan and C. H. Coote, Hakluyt Soc. LXXII–LXXIII, London 1886.

Edmond, Mary, 'In Search of John Webster', *TLS,* 24 December 1976.

—— 'Limners and Picturemakers', Walpole Soc. XLVII, 1980.

—— 'The Chandos portrait: a suggested painter', *The Burlington Magazine* CXXIV, 1982.

Essex MS records, various, ERO, Chelmsford.

Exchequer MS records, various, PRO.

Feil, J. P., 'Davenant Exonerated', *MLR* July 1963.

Flecknoe, Richard, *Ariadne,* London 1654.

Ford, John, *The Dramatic Works of,* ed. W. Gifford with additions by A. Dyce, 3 vols., London 1895.

—— *The Broken Heart,* ed. Brian Morris, London 1965.

Forman, Simon, MS casebooks among Ashmole MSS, Bodleian Library, Oxford.

Gentleman's Magazine 1745, for Richard Davenant.

Gibbs, A. M. (ed.), *Sir William Davenant; The Shorter Poems, and Songs from the Plays and Masques,* Oxford 1972.

Gildon, Charles, *The Life of Mr Thomas Betterton,* London 1710.

Gladish, David F. (ed.), *Sir William Davenant's Gondibert,* Oxford 1971.

Grove Dictionary of Music and Musicians, The New, ed. Stanley Sadie, 20 vols., London 1980.

Hakluyt, Richard, *Voyages,* Everyman, London, 1962 reprint of 1907 ed.

Harbage, Alfred, *Sir William Davenant, Poet Venturer 1606–1668,* University of Pennsylvania Press, Philadelphia 1935.

Harben, H. A., *A Dictionary of London,* London 1918.

Harleian Soc., publications of, for parish registers, Visitations, marriage licences.

Harris, John, Stephen Orgel and Roy Strong, *The King's Arcadia: Inigo Jones and the Stuart Court,* London, Arts Council, 1973.

Henrietta Maria, Letters of Queen, ed. Mary A. E. Green, London 1857.

Herbert, Sir Henry, Master of the Revels, *Dramatic Records of, 1623–1673,* ed. J. Q. Adams, Yale University Press, New Haven, Conn., 1917.

Herefordshire, Royal Commission on Historical Monuments of, III, 1934 (for Pembridge).

Highfill, Philip H., jr., Kalman A. Burnim and Edward A. Langhans, *A Biographical Dictionary of Actors, Actresses, Musicians, Dancers, Managers & other Stage Personnel in London, 1660–1800,* University of Southern Illinois Press, Carbondale and Edwardsville, 1973–

Holland, Peter, essay on 'Theatre' for *Companion,* vol. X of Pepys *Diary,* ed. Latham and Matthews.

Holman, William, eighteenth-century MSS on Hundred of Hinckford, including material on Sible Hedingham and the Davenant family: at ERO, Chelmsford.

Hotson, Leslie, *The Commonwealth and Restoration Stage,* Harvard University Press, Cambridge, Mass., 1928.

Hyde, Edward, Earl of Clarendon, *The History of the Rebellion and Civil Wars in England,* 7 vols., Oxford 1849.

—— *State Papers Collected by Edward, Earl of Clarendon,* 3 vols., Oxford 1767–86.

—— *Calendar of the Clarendon State Papers Preserved in the Bodleian Library,* 5 vols., Oxford 1869–1970.

Inns of Court, printed admission lists.

Keith, W. G., 'The Designs for the First Movable Scenery on the English Public Stage', *The Burlington Magazine* XXV, 1914.

LCC/GLC *Survey of London,* vol. VIII, 1922, for the parish of St Leonard Shoreditch; and XXXV, 1970, on The Theatre Royal Drury Lane and The Royal Opera House Covent Garden (for 'The Killigrew and Davenant Patents').

Leeds, E. T., *see* Oxford, printed records.

Limon, Jerzy, *Gentlemen of a Company: English Players in Central and Eastern Europe 1590 – 1660,* Cambridge, 1985.

Lindley, David, *The Court Masque,* Manchester 1984.

London Inhabitants within the Walls 1695, ed. D. V. Glass, London 1966.

Lord Chamberlains' Books, MS, *see* Royal Household.

Lords, House of, *Journals,* vol. IV.

Luckett, Richard, essays on 'Music' and 'Plays', Pepys *Companion,* vol. X of Latham-Matthews ed.

Luttrell, Narcissus, *A Brief Historical Relation . . . 1678–1714,* Oxford ed. 1857.

Machyn, Henry, *The Diary of Henry Machyn 1550–1563,* ed. J. G. Nichols, Camden Soc., London 1848.

Maidment and Logan, *see* Sir William Davenant.

Malone, Edmond, *The Plays and Poems of William Shakespeare,* 10 vols., 1790: I, Part II, *Historical Account of the English Stage.*

Matcham, George, section on Hundred of Frustfield, including Davenant pedigree, in Sir Richard Colt Hoare's *The History of Modern Wiltshire,* 6 vols., London 1822–1844.

Mawson, Richard, Portcullis Pursuivant, Davenant MS pedigree at College of

Arms, 1725.

McKerrow, R. B., *Dictionary of Printers and Booksellers 1557–1640,* London 1910.

Merchant Taylors, Company of:
MS records at Hall, microfilm at GL:
Apprentice Binding Books from 1583;
Lists of Freemen from 1530;
Court Minute Books from 1562;
Liber Probationis Scholae Scissorum from 1607 (at Hall).
Printed records:
  Clode, C. M.: *Memorials of the Guild of Merchant Taylors,* London 1875; and *The Early History of the Guild of Merchant Taylors,* 2 vols., London 1888.
  Hart, E. P.: *Merchant Taylors' School Register 1561–1934,* 2 vols., London 1936.

Millar, Oliver, *The Tudor, Stuart and Early Georgian Pictures in the Royal Collection,* 2 vols., London 1963.

—— *Van Dyck in England,* catalogue for NPG exhibition 1982–3, London.

Ministers' and Receivers' Accounts, MS, *see* Royal Household.

Miscellanea Genealogica et Heraldica, 2nd Series, II, for Gore family.

Morgan and Coote, *see* Early Voyages.

Morrison, J. H., *The Underhills of Warwickshire,* Cambridge 1932.

Nethercot, A. H., *Sir William D'Avenant, Poet Laureate and Playwright-Manager,* University of Chicago Press, Chicago, 1938.

New College *Leasebooks, see* Oxford, MS records.

Nicoll, Allardyce, *A History of English Drama 1660–1900:* I, *Restoration Drama 1660–1700,* 4th ed. revised, Cambridge 1952.

Nixon, Anthony, *Oxfords Triumph,* Oxford 1605.

Orgel, Stephen and Roy Strong, *Inigo Jones: The Theatre of the Stuart Court,* 2 vols., London and Berkeley, Cal. 1973.

Orrell, John, *The Theatres of Inigo Jones and John Webb,* Cambridge 1985.

Oxford, City and University of:
MS records:
  New College *Leasebooks:* in college muniment room;
  Oxford City Council Books I and II (1520–92 and 1591–1628); *Oxford City Audit Book* (1592–1682); and *Oxford City Draft Council Minutes* (1615–34), all at Town Hall.
Parochial records: at CRO
Oxford subsidy rolls: E179 series, PRO.
Printed records:
  Alumni Oxonienses 1500–1714, ed. Andrew Clark, 4 vols., 1891–2.
  Fasnacht, Ruth: *A History of the City of Oxford,* OHS, 1954.
  Hutton, W. H.: 'Shakespeare and Oxford', in *Catalogue of Bodleian Shakespeare exhibition* 1916.
  Leeds, E. T.: 'Note on the Crown Tavern at Oxford' in Bodleian 1916 cat.; 'The Cross Inn and the Tavern at Oxford', Appendix to Acheson's *Shakespeare's Sonnet Story,* 1922; 'A Second Elizabethan Mural Painting in No. 3, Cornmarket Street, Oxford', *Oxoniensia I,* 1936.
  Pantin, W. A.: article, plans, photographs and appendices on the Golden Cross inn and the wine-tavern in Cornmarket, with an article on the

wall-paintings by E. Clive Rouse, *Oxoniensia XX, 1955.*

Register of the University of Oxford 1571–1622, ed. Andrew Clark, 2 vols., 1885.

Rouse, E. Clive: *see* Pantin above.

Salter, H. E.: *Surveys and Tokens,* OHS, 1923; *Oxford City Properties,* OHS, 1926; *Oxford City Council Acts 1583–1626,* OHS, 1928; anf *Survey of Oxford I,* ed. Pantin, OHS, 1960.

Wood, Anthony: *Athenae Oxonienses 1500–1690,* 2 vols., London 1691–2, and ed. of P. Bliss, 4 vols., London 1813–20; *Life and Times of, 1623–95,* ed. Andrew Clark, 5 vols., OHS, 1891–5; and *Survey of the Antiquities of the City of Oxford 1661–6,* ed. Clark, 3 vols., OHS, 1889–99.

Pantin and Rouse, *see* Oxford, printed records.

Parochial records, MS, at ERO, Chelmsford; in London at GL, GLRO, WCL; at CRO, Oxford; at East Suffolk RO, Ipswich and West Suffolk RO, Bury St Edmunds; and at York, Borthwick Institute. The registers of St Giles-in-the-Fields are retained at the church.

Parry, Graham, *The Golden Age Restor'd: The culture of the Stuart Court, 1603–42,* Manchester 1981.

Pepys, Samuel, *Diary,* ed. Robert Latham and William Matthews, 11 vols., London 1970–83.

Plomer, H. R., *Dictionary of Booksellers and Printers 1641–1667,* London 1907.

Port of London, *see* Customs accounts.

Powell, Jocelyn, *Restoration Theatre Production,* London 1984.

Requests, Court of, MS records, PRO.

Reynolds, Roland, *The History of the Davenant Foundation Grammar School,* Abingdon 1966.

Robinson, C. J., *A History of the Mansions and Manors of Herefordshire,* London and Hereford 1873.

Rogers, Malcolm, 'The Meaning of Van Dyck's Portrait of Sir John Suckling', *The Burlington Magazine CXX,* 1978.

Royal Household, MS series at PRO including *Certificates of Residence, Lord Chamberlains' Books* and *Warrants, Ministers' and Receivers' Accounts* (for Queen Anne's Household) and *Wardrobe Accounts.*

Salter, H. E., *see* Oxford, printed records.

Schoenbaum, S., *Shakespeare's Lives,* Oxford 1970.

—— *William Shakespeare: A Documentary Life,* Oxford 1975.

Shaw, W. A., *The Knights of England,* 2 vols., London 1906.

Sherborn, C. D., *A History of the Family of Sherborn,* London 1901 and typed addenda by the author at BL, 1918.

Stationers' Registers, 1640–1708, A Transcript of, ed. G. E. B. Eyre and C. R. Rivington, 3 vols., London, 1913–14.

Stow, John, *Survey of London,* ed. C. L. Kingsford, 2 vols., Oxford 1908.

Strong, Roy, *see* Harris, John *and* Orgel, Stephen.

Subsidy rolls, MS, for London and Oxford, E179 series, PRO.

Suckling, Sir John, *Works of, in Prose and Verse,* ed. A. H. Thompson, London 1910.

—— *Works of, I: The Non-Dramatic Works,* ed. Thomas Clayton, 2 vols., Oxford 1971.

Summers, Montague, *Shakespeare Adaptations,* London 1922.

—— ed., Downes's *Roscius Anglicanus,* London 1929.

Swift, Jonathan, *Correspondence,* ed. F. Elrington Ball, 6 vols., London 1910–14: vol. I for Davenants.

Testamentary records, MS, at ERO, Chelmsford; in London' at GL, GLRO, PRO, WCL; at East Suffolk RO, Ipswich and West Suffolk RO, Bury St Edmunds; at York, Borthwick Institute; and in National Library of Wales, Aberystwyth.

Vertue, George, *Notebooks,* transcribed in Walpole Soc. vols.

Vintners, Company of, MS records including *Account Books I* and *II* (1522–82 and 1582–1617) and *Book of Apprentice Bindings and Freedom Admissions I (1428–1602),* all at GL.

Wardrobe accounts, MS, *see* Royal Household.

Wedgwood, C. V., *The King's Peace 1637–1641,* London 1955.

—— *The King's War 1641–1647,* London 1958.

Willan, T. S., *The Muscovy Merchants of 1555,* 1953; *The Early History of the Russia Company 1553–1603,* 1956; and *Studies in Elizabethan Foreign Trade,* 1959, all pub. Manchester.

Wilson, J. H., *All the King's Ladies,* Chicago 1958.

Wine Act of 1553, HLRO.

Withie, John, Davenant pedigree up to 1667, MS Harl. 1398, BL.

Wood, Anthony, *see* Oxford, printed records.

Works, Office of the, MS accounts, E351 series, PRO (for the 'Masking Room' at Whitehall).

Yates, Frances A., *John Florio,* New York 1968.

Yorkshire, Visitations of, 1584–5 and 1612, ed. Joseph Foster 1875.

INDEX

WD stands for Davenant, LIF for his Lincoln's Inn Fields theatre and DG for Dorset Garden; TK for Thomas Killigrew, TR for Theatre Royal and DL for Drury Lane; WS for Shakespeare

◦➣ₒ⊂➣◦|